Existential Waltz

by

Drew M. Valla

PublishAmerica
Baltimore

First printing

ISBN: 1-4241-2837-4
PUBLISHED BY PUBLISHAMERICA, LLLP
www.publishamerica.com
Baltimore

Printed in the United States of America

War produces no winners.
You become a killer or you're killed.
Maybe it's time that we stopped.
Peace.

Acknowledgments

I would like to thank Kathleen Valla, Katherine Parlato, Laura Angelle, and Kieran Valla for helping me edit the book. Your encouragement and suggestions were always helpful. I would also like to thank the people who read the first book and enjoyed it. Your feedback gave me the motivation to continue the saga of Matt Kronchek.

Chapter 1

No one I've ever known was buried on a nice day. Three weeks before, I had just turned twenty-one, and I was sick of standing around an open grave—always a cool, open pit rife with the malodor of deep dirt; the moldy smell intensified by the damp gloomy weather. Sub-strata grave dirt that normally wouldn't have seen the light of day, with the reek of the cold, wet clay always a sure bet to awaken my own existential fears. I never go back after the burial. If there's anything after this life, it sure isn't six feet under the ground.

My father died three years ago, with my grandparents following in quick succession, five in all, and I never visited the cemetery. That is, except to bury someone else. It was hard to accept that life ended that way, but I couldn't fathom any other explanation that made sense. It was so disheartening to finish it in a neutral hole in the ground, forever cut off from the pleasures of being alive.

Life also produces misery, and maybe some people found the concept of the grave a comforting hideaway from their tortuous existence. Not me, no way, no how. As cynical as I had become, being alive meant that my cup was still half full. I just couldn't see the advantage of being stuck in a wooden box six feet below the surface of the planet.

The coldest rain I had ever felt for late August drenched the graveyard. The slow, steady downpour framed the scene; a penetrating wetness that combined with the funeral ceremony to produce the deepest of chills—

thermal and existential. A gray sky served as a reminder of the purpose of the event. The dull patter of the precipitation muted the sobs of the mourners, diluting the tears falling from their cheeks, but doing nothing to ease their sorrow.

For once, instead of having the sensation of being in a hangman's noose, the tie around my neck felt comforting against the dampness. The monkey suit ensemble only came out of the closet if someone died, or occasionally for a wedding. I had never been a dress-up kind of guy or a dedicated mourner, so I couldn't wait for the funeral to end.

It had been a painfully long service at the church, a High Mass I guess they called it in the Catholic religion. Out of traditional rules of respect, I was forced to enter a place of worship for the first time in three years and spend an hour going through the motions of religious mourning. We had moved on to the cemetery in a formal vehicular procession, and now I waited for the priest to finish it up. The pasty white padre droned on and on—ashes to ashes, dust to dust. What a comforting thought for the future. Maybe that's why I never cleaned my room. As a child I would examine the dust under my bed and wonder if the little balls of fuzz had been a person once, or at least a part of their existence.

The scene before me became progressively twisted to my way of thinking. The twenty-one gun salute split the relative solitude of the cemetery, piercing the dark, rainy atmosphere like cracks of thunder. Most people flinched as the loud retort of the rifles increased the level of agitation among the next of kin, especially since the guest of honor had died in a war. In your mind's eye, with each discharge of the rifles, it was easy to envision someone dropping on the battlefield, their dying body gushing blood over the dirt that they were about to become in the near future.

After the soldiers finished firing their weapons, they folded the flag in a precise manner. Did you ever watch them? The entire flag exercise appeared quite complicated: with horizontal folds, a diagonal fold, and then some rolling before it was presented solemnly to the family, which intensified the grief another notch. Thanks for your son; here's a flag in return. Not quite an even trade in my mind.

The service ended and we stepped forward to put our flowers on Paulie's casket. Twenty-year- old Paulie Kovak, the nervous, ever hesitant follower of others from our old neighborhood—killed in Vietnam, August 9, 1969. He was not old enough to drink, too young to vote, but ripe as hell for dying. As Country Joe would say; Paulie was the first one on our block to be brought home in a box, and a very small box indeed if they hadn't used a casket. One of my life-long friends had been blown to bits by a little Vietnamese kid strapped with grenades. The little kid had given Paulie a hug, and they both left this life in one big, bloody blast.

I heard from the old friend network that the kid was only six or so, apparently giving up his young life to help drive us out of his country, or maybe he didn't have a clue either. I wondered sadly if the little boy had a funeral of his own in Vietnam, and if they had collected his body parts in a bag, and if his mother had cried like Paulie's. Two mothers sacrificed their sons for God and country, different countries, but soon nobody would give a shit or remember. I guess God didn't choose sides. Two lives snuffed before they had barely begun, and dead for reasons that escaped me totally.

My name is Matt Kronchek, and I had begged my friend Paulie not to enlist. I remembered what Detective Lipscomb taught me about war when I was thirteen, and I told Paulie that it wasn't our fight in Vietnam. It was their country, their civil war, and we didn't belong there. I wanted him to go to Canada, but I knew that it would never happen. He wasn't pleased with my opinion. Paulie had always been a traditional, follow-the-rules type of guy. We were good friends since I could remember, but diametrically opposite in our approach to life. He called me an un-American hippie who didn't care about his country. In some ways perhaps he was right. I gave up the argument to preserve the remnants of a long friendship, but my attitude had been heading in a different direction for a long time.

I went off to college in New Haven, but Paulie had never taken much of a liking to school. Not that I was a stellar scholar myself, but a matriculating student wasn't eligible for the draft, so for once school became an earnest pursuit. It's funny what a little threat of death will do for your motivation.

Paulie and I grew up together in the town of Bellington, Ct., and our other good friend, Mike Rotillo, enlisted in the Marines right out of high school. Mike drew the long straw, ending up in Germany walking up and down the Berlin Wall while trading stares with the East Germans on the other side.

No such good fortune came Paulie's way. He was always the kid who grabbed the short end of the stick and stepped in the solitary piece of dog shit on the baseball field. He enlisted in the Army to train as an electrician, but within six months he was a combat medic with his final destination being Vietnam. See the world, be what the Army tells you you're going to be, like it or not. Your ass was theirs for four years. Now his entire body belonged to the ground.

Paulie wrote to me quite often in the beginning, but then his letters became infrequent. As a matter of fact, I hadn't received a message from him in at least two months. In his last letter, the words were tinged with a hard edge; overlaid with an alien tone that I didn't recognize from the old days. I don't think he appreciated my stance on the war, and I guess I couldn't blame him since he was stuck in the thick of the killing ground called Vietnam. We had been living in two different worlds, with neither one of us having a clue as to the feelings or experiences of the other.

It wasn't my war. I had no intention of killing anyone or being killed, but now it had come back to leave its mark on all of us, and had brought me home to Bellington for the day. I didn't drive up from New Haven much except to play in the summer basketball league. Basketball was still a common bond with my old friends in Bellington, with politics left behind at the opening tap. Occasionally a player on another team would make a disparaging comment about my hair, but that was easily silenced with a blocked shot or a well-placed elbow.

After my friend, Nellie Cabrera, died back in eighth grade, I never fit into Bellington society. That horrifying experience had transformed me into a cautious, cynical teenager during high school. My views had become jaded, and my attitude toward hypocrisy in our government; especially concerning the war, had pushed my behavior to a point just short of civil disobedience. As the war escalated, I felt a crushing pressure on my brain brought on by mourning for dead friends and the fear that I could be next in line. I had seen death in a friend at a young age and wanted no part of it just yet, but here it was again.

When death touches you, it burrows into your skull and sits in your mind somewhere, sending out steady currents of existential fear, painfully reminding you of your mortality. I made it through high school fairly well by being the class comedian and playing basketball, but there were dark secrets hidden in my mind, and I never let anyone get too close to me.

Bellington desperately fought change even as it was being rammed down its throat. The factories were rapidly bleeding jobs to the Midwest and the South, and the town's economy was beginning to hit the shit heap. Racial diversity was still not welcomed, but as apartments began to empty from the loss of jobs and an aging population, minorities began to move in to take advantage of the cheap rents.

The town took a pro-war and anti-long hair stance, which made me stand out unfavorably in the funeral crowd. Being six-two with wavy brown hair down to my shoulders didn't blend me in with the Bellington faithful very well. I must have represented a walking billboard against the war and our government, and felt uncomfortable in the town that had raised me. I hated coming home, and I think everyone hated having me there, but it was Paulie's funeral and they were doing their Christian best to be outwardly polite. Their eyes told a different story, however, and so did mine.

Thankfully, my mother was sick that day and wasn't able make to the service. A running parcel of shit from her mouth would have made the experience even more unbearable. Throw my flower, walk away with my head down and then say a few nice words to Paulie's Neo-Nazi parents in private. They would act grateful, I would be respectful, and then we would all make believe that this was necessary for truth, justice, and the American way. It would have been the wisest and most deferential path, but that's not what I felt in my heart, and unfortunately my emotions still ruled my brain.

Powerful waves of guilt flowed through me when I realized that I wasn't so much as sad, as that I felt lucky that it wasn't me in the casket. I had become cold; hardened by life and afraid to let most of my emotions free. My anger, however, always flowed hot and fast.

As the line moved forward to place the flowers on the casket, I thought back to all the fun we shared as kids, and how we fantasized about our bright futures. Paulie's dream was to play baseball for the Red Sox, and I figured my destination would be the NBA. Never in my nastiest thoughts did I imagine a scenario such as this. Hell, when we were juniors in high school, we had barely heard of Vietnam, except as a tough question on a geography test. None of us saw it coming, and when it did, we all scrambled in different directions.

Tears pooled in my eyes, but wouldn't come out, and hadn't in eight years. The anger imbedded deep within me surged in rebellion to what I perceived as a sham, and the fury overpowered my sense of discretion. As I placed my flower on his polished cherry coffin, I guess I said, "What a waste, what a goddamn waste," a little too loud. Paulie's father's patriotic anger snapped through his grief as he lunged at me with rage-induced agility, but I jumped back just enough as the priest held him at bay with his authority from God and two bony arms. Paulie's massive Uncle Rocco told me to leave immediately or he would beat the hell out of me, and the seven soldiers in full dress uniform appeared more than willing to join in with the butts of their rifles.

One of my most regrettable and embarrassing moments, but I had meant what I said. I wouldn't take it back and wouldn't apologize. It was a waste, and I hated Bellington and America for sending my friend to die. We were supposed to have the good life denied our parents and grandparents, but it wasn't turning out that way. The politicos in Washington saw the Communist bogeyman around every corner, and Vietnam was to be the place where we stopped the dominoes from falling. They had pissed Paulie's life away, trying hard to make us believe that it was a noble pursuit. Maybe they were just full of shit. I think the latter is more accurate.

The voices of the mourners could be heard in bits as I left the gravesite, but 'coward', 'hippie', 'asshole', and various combinations of the three pierced my eardrums. Screw them! I wanted to give them the finger, but I was done there. My red Mustang convertible was jammed between two fat Caddies, but I would be able to get it out with a little patience.

The path to the road took me through a small pine grove, and before

I reached the end of the trees adjacent to my car, a raspy voice called out in a low whisper from what seemed to be nowhere.

"Kronchek, Matt Kronchek. Hey! Don't turn around, but make like you're fixing your shoelaces. Bend down and keep looking at the road."

"Who the hell are you, and why should I do anything you say? I don't want any more trouble. I want to leave before that crowd catches up with me, so screw off."

"Get down and shut up! You never were able to do as you were told. Some things never change. And you thought I was a punk in eighth grade."

Out of the corner of my left eye, a short, emaciated man with a full beard, ripped jeans and a dirty army jacket, stood halfway behind the biggest tree. Even from ten feet away, the smell of fresh dope and stale booze wafted along in the rain-soaked breeze. The name on the jacket read 'Combs', but the Tommy Combs I had known many years ago didn't fit the body in front of me.

Tommy Combs served as the school bully throughout grade school, but he had attended a technical high school, so I hadn't seen him in years. We didn't run in the same social circles. Bones showed through his jacket where fat once stretched the seams of his clothing to the breaking point. He looked sickly, with his pasty complexion revealing an indoor lifestyle. I never remembered him as being so short. I must have fought Tommy a dozen times throughout grammar school, only winning the last time back in eighth grade when he had pushed me too far.

"Is that you, Tommy? I don't have any beef with you, unless you're still holding an eight-year grudge. What do you want?"

"Your brain is still caught in the past, Kronchek, isn't it? Do you really think anyone besides you gives a shit about 1961 any more? Bet you still can't get that dead nigger girlfriend out of your mind. Wake up and look around you, dipshit. It's a new world, and it's not getting any better. Do you see what they did to your little friend in the Army? He's taking the eternal dirt nap now. He ain't the first and ain't going to be the last coming out dead from that jungle paradise."

Tommy certainly hadn't lost his ability to piss me off. If he had wanted me to be prudent, he certainly chose a dumb way of going about it, since

I fully intended to smack his head against a tree for the racial slur concerning Nellie. The last time he used that word in front of me, the school nurse spent the morning picking tar out of his forehead.

"Tommy, I don't know why, but you are messing with me at the wrong time, and if you say anything else about Nellie, I'm going to bust you up. I just watched them bury Paulie, and I'm in no mood for any shit from you."

"Relax, Mister Justice League. I was just fooling with you for old time's sake. I couldn't help myself. I knew I could get a rise out of you. I'm actually here to do you a favor."

"What favor, Tommy? Spit it out, because that crowd is breaking up near the grave, so I'm not sticking around and letting them take out their grief on me."

"Pissed off a whole crowd of people again; at a funeral no less, huh, Kronchek? We sure do have a lot in common. Did you know that I was stationed with old Paulie in Vietnam?"

"You're full of shit, Tommy. Paulie never said anything about you being over there with him. He would have told me. You ought to lay off the dope for a while and take a bath."

"Didn't think so, smart ass, and I'll bet there's a lot of things he didn't tell you. Things were getting pretty hairy over there, even for me, and I don't mean from the Gooks. I shot myself in the leg with a NVR rifle and bought myself a ticket home. Hurt like hell, but they gave me a Purple Heart and a nice little disability pension. I'm a genuine war hero, Kronchek. I even have a certificate and a medal to prove it. Aren't you proud of me? I limp a little, but I'm alive, which is a step up from Paulie's situation."

The crowd moved closer to my position, and Tommy's cryptic ramblings were beginning to get on my nerves.

"That's all very interesting, Tom, but is there some point to your story? If you keep babbling, the only favor I'm going to get is a beating from Paulie's Uncle Rocco."

Tommy limped deeper into the brush as the mourners slowly moved our way.

"You're so fucking ungrateful, Kronchek. You never had any patience and you never listened to anyone. Always being the smart guy, thinking that you know everything, but you don't know shit this time."

"A goddamn telephone pole is a smart guy to you, but why should I be grateful when you haven't done anything but give me shit my whole life. Thanks for the cruise down misery lane, Tommy boy, but I need to roll. Bye, Bye."

I began to walk toward my car. Uncle Rocco had moved too close to my comfort zone.

"Wait, Kronchek. Listen, please. I'm taking a big chance talking to you. I could end up with Paulie in the dirt. The Viet Cong didn't kill him, Kronchek. I came here to tell you that. You need to understand what happened to Paulie."

"No, no they didn't, Tommy. He's dead because he was a follower. The government sent him to die a meaningless death, and in a few years no one will give a shit. There will be some new war, a new enemy, and Paulie's name will be on a piece of granite at City Hall, which no one will ever look at, or know who he is, if they do."

"Skip the moralizing, you bleeding heart fuck. I've been over there, and I know better than you do what a goddamn hellhole it is. It's easy for you college boys, but some of us weren't given a choice. Our own people killed him, Kronchek. They iced him because he knew too much and was ready to spit the truth all over Vietnam. If you remember, Paulie was always ready to crack over the smallest thing, but this time he stood his ground. That's why I bailed out of there and stay to myself."

I needed to get out of the cemetery, but the fear and uncharacteristic sincerity in Tommy's voice cemented me to the ground. I must have been a cat in a previous life because curiosity was my biggest temptation.

"What did he get involved in, and what's in it for you? Why would you take the chance and talk to me? What if I don't give a shit, and even if I did, what could I do about it? Vietnam is far away, and I don't intend to visit for any reason."

My jacket and pants were thoroughly soaked from the wet tree branches, and Tommy had disappeared completely into the misty woods. Only his smell remained behind.

"He saved my life, Kronchek. The little bastard kicked a grenade out of our tent one night. It was right under me, and besides, you always give a shit. You just can't help yourself. That's why I told you. I knew you might be good for something one day. I don't like owing people, especially dead ones. He didn't deserve what he got, and maybe you can set it straight. New Haven might be a good place to start. Be like the Hardy Boys, Kronchek. I remember what a great detective you were at the post office that day. You and Paulie did make the neighborhood proud. Look out for the Cobras. Be a mongoose, Kronchek. Ha, ha, that's a good one. I'm gone. My debt is paid. Do what you want with it, but don't try talking to me again. I'm even now, and nothing else is coming out of me. You have to figure out the rest for yourself."

"Wait! Even if I believe you, what the hell were you guys involved in that would cost him his life?"

The last words I heard from Tommy Combs as he melted into the mist didn't fit in with the Paulie I had known.

"What else these days, Kronchek? Drugs. Your straight little buddy got boxed into a nasty corner. Tough shit to swallow, isn't it?"

Tommy had given me a massive headache. He had always been such an asshole that it was hard for me to trust him. Drugs? Paulie involved with drugs at the level where his own men would have him killed? It was surprising to hear that he had been brave enough to save Tommy's life, but Paulie had always been dead set against drugs. He didn't even drink as far as I knew. Perhaps there was a lot I didn't know.

Even if it were true, what could I do about it, and why did he say New Haven was a good place to start? What the hell were the Cobras? What could that possibly have to do with Vietnam? I couldn't make the connection, but then again, Tommy had never made much sense, plus I'm sure that the weed hadn't helped his rationality any.

The rain had let up and it was time to go. I worked my car out of the tight spot, put the pedal to the floor, and ripped a shot out of the cemetery, all the while staring down that fat bastard Rocco as I drove past. I needed a nap before work or I wouldn't get through my shift without falling asleep on my feet.

Chapter 2

I arrived at my apartment in New Haven around noon, but no one was home. Most of them hadn't come back from summer break, and the people that occupied the other apartments in the three-story house were either asleep or at work. My roommate Leo and I shared a large bedroom on the second floor that faced the street, and our room was not a pretty sight. He had gone back to his hometown to work for the summer, and the place hadn't been cleaned for three months.

My dirty clothes were heaped everywhere and a thick layer of dust coated the furniture and floor. Empty beer cans and half-filled soda bottles were strewn about the room in random groups, with the crumbs from various foods crunching under my feet as I entered the bedroom. It needed to be fumigated before he returned or we would start the year with one of our patented arguments. Not that it ever got serious. After rooming together for three years, we bickered like an old married couple.

Leo stood a head shorter than I did and a foot wider at the shoulders, but we shared a common passion for basketball and a cynical, irreverent lifestyle. Leo was my perfect complement on the basketball court, a tolerable roommate, and a loyal friend. We both knew what the other person would do before they did it, on the court and on the streets. He would return the next day, and I couldn't wait to hit the courts in the city. Basketball was a therapeutic diversion for me, and I needed to get this thing about Paulie's death out of my mind. The filthy bedroom would have to wait, since there was only an hour for a nap before work.

I snapped on the old black and white TV in the living room, playing with the rabbit ears until the local station came in passably clear. Flopping down on the musty couch with a soda and a packet of stale crackers, I hoped that the TV's drone would put me out. The midday news had just begun, with the lead story covering the increasing violence in the anti-war demonstrations at the nation's colleges. I hadn't noticed the escalation of the protests because I had been so busy working that summer, and our school started a week later than the other colleges. A live broadcast from New York showed policemen using shields and batons to push back the protesters.

In the next story, a couple of huge construction workers had beaten up a long-haired college student, much to the delight of their colleagues. The kid was defiant to the end, giving the workers the finger as they beat him unconscious. His face and shirt were covered with blood as the medics hoisted him onto a stretcher and into an ambulance. The War had been home for awhile, but I hadn't been paying attention. I wanted to head for the city and lay a pipe to those sadistic bastards, but then I would be just like them, not to mention that they would probably kill me. It was going to happen soon. You could feel it. People were going to start to die for protesting the war.

Frightened, angry, and confused, I couldn't get the image of Paulie's splattered body out of my mind. I might find myself on one side of the police barricade, while my uncles or my neighbors could be on the other. The second civil war had hit America. Father against son, brother versus brother, old divided from young. There was a generation gap so wide that no one could reach across it at the moment. I turned off the television when they panned to Vietnam to show clips of body bags being loaded on a plane. That hit too close to the day's experience, and I wanted it to all go away for just a little while.

As soon as my head hit the pillow I knew there would be no sleep. The memory of Paulie's funeral would make it hard enough in the coming weeks, and Tommy had really stirred up my emotions. Tommy had been a nut job for years, and was obviously beaned out on drugs and booze, so it was difficult to take him seriously. Something had rung true in his words this time, though, and I couldn't get them out of my head. It couldn't hurt to look into it a little for Paulie's sake.

If the Viet Cong had killed him, then part of it would have been Paulie's choice, with the government being complicit for its own reasons. It would be a frightening alternative; however, if his own men were involved in his death. He had been my friend, and the guilt about our last words hung heavy on my soul, not to mention my asshole display at his funeral. In a selfish sense, I could see that there might be a story behind it. Maybe people needed to know how bad things had gotten in Vietnam, with Americans killing Americans for drugs or whatever Tommy was talking about. I began having delusions of grandeur about stopping the war with a big scandal disclosure and avenging Paulie's death in the bargain.

A nap wasn't going to happen, so I grabbed a quick shower, put on a starched white uniform and headed for my nurse's aide job at the Veteran's Hospital. The temperature had done a complete turnaround, as it only could in New England. The wind now blew in from the south, and it was twenty degrees warmer than it had been at the funeral. The stationary cold air of the morning clashed with a warm front pushing up from the southern waters of the Atlantic. Mean, black thunderheads began to consolidate over Long Island Sound as I drove into West Haven toward the hospital.

Thunderstorms could mean a bad shift in the orthopedic ward where I was usually assigned. Patients who had been wounded or dismembered by mortar rounds didn't find thunder very comforting; especially Robert, a black draftee who lost an arm and a leg in Vietnam when a shell scored a direct hit on his bunker. The doctors kept telling him that he was lucky to be alive, but Robert told me a dozen times that he wished that the Vietnamese had finished the job. He said that he felt like half a man, and that a half of a black man didn't stand a chance in America.

As I walked from the car, the rain soaked my shirt. The storm began to reach its full fury just as I started to make the rounds of my assigned patients. Checking the assignment list, it appeared as if I had gotten a good draw for the shift. Mrs. Finch, the head nurse, had given me a section of the large ward located at the end of the floor. It housed about twenty patients, most of them around my age and wounded in Vietnam.

Constructed in the thirties, the hospital had some private and semi-private rooms, but each floor always contained a large ward holding from ten to twenty patients. Fifteen-foot ceilings were illuminated with hanging globe lights, continually dull from hard-to-reach dust. Wide floor-to-ceiling windows provided much-needed light, but not on a day like this. The setup afforded no privacy, except for the curtains around each bed. They blocked visual encroachment, but not the sounds of pain, bodily functions, and family arguments. Everyone pretty much knew everyone else's business. The well-intentioned design of large windows in the massive ward had met its match with the depressed psychic energy of twenty sick and crippled men. The atmosphere in the big ward gave off an aura of gloominess as you walked through the door, no matter how sunny the day.

Mrs. Finch could be pretty cool at times, although she would put your nuts in a vise if she didn't think you had taken care of your patients properly. On Fridays, she normally assigned me to the younger patients and turned her head as we played penny ante poker after visiting hours. We were breaking the rules, but she understood the importance of interrupting the constant routine of pain and rehabilitation.

The storm was right on us, and the lightning crackled outside the south window, illuminating the otherwise sooty sky. Thunder rocked the building with one rolling jolt after another, rattling the windows and blinking the overhead lights. Robert leaped out of a morphine-induced nap in total terror caused by the atmospheric attack. Day had turned into night from the black thunderheads rolling off the Sound with increasing intensity. New England weather could change in an instant, and this storm was a prime example of the fickleness of our weather.

"Incoming, incoming! Down! Everybody down!" Robert screamed as he attempted to get out of bed with half a body.

I reached the bed just in time, preventing him from spilling over the side and splattering on the gray tile floor. Robert's sweat-drenched body shook with terror, his glazed eyes indicating that he had returned to the jungle in a waking nightmare.

"Robert! Stay in bed. You're in the hospital. You're safe. Be cool, you're having a nightmare. It's a pretty bad storm, but it will be over soon."

I took a glancing shot off the side of my head before I leaned my weight into him, keeping him safely on the mattress. A couple of ambulatory patients gave me a hand, and we were able to settle him down as his mind cleaned out the remnants of the nightmare. The sweat continued to stream down his bare torso, even as his eyes began to clear.

"Kron! Jesus, Kron, I thought I was still in Nam. In my dream, I'm a whole person again, and then they came as they always do. The sky lit up as the VC began lobbing mortars into our camp, one after the other, with no break. Every time I get whole in my dreams, the VC come into my sleep and blow my arm and leg away. Sometimes I wish that I wouldn't wake up at all, so I could remain in one piece or die. I would like to be able to change the nightmare just once, Kron."

I had been designated Kron by one of the black players at the downtown basketball courts, and the nickname found its way into the hospital by way of the city grapevine. Muslim names hadn't come into complete vogue yet, and the black guys were always Robert or James or Richard. They never used Bob or Bobby, Jim or Dick. The shortened versions seemed to be names of white designation. Once I got to know them better, they figured it was time to stop saying "the white boy is on your team," or point to me and say, "you've got him," when we were playing basketball. Kron was my ticket for limited acceptance to their world.

The storm kicked down as quickly as it had rode in, so once everyone settled down, I took their vital signs, cleaned a few bedpans and dressed the perpetually draining gunshot wounds that had shattered bone and muscle with devastating results. One of my patients had been in the hospital for two years while they unsuccessfully tried to repair his splintered and infected femur. The bullets used in Vietnam were meant to maim, spreading as they hit flesh and bone, with the end result being massive tissue damage. A wounded man occupies several other soldiers, a dead man none. The Viet Cong realized early on that Americans would rescue their wounded even while an ambush was in progress. They could wound one soldier, and then attempt to kill the other three that tried to save him.

My medical responsibilities kept me cranking until dinner as we passed out the trays and helped feed the quadriplegics. They saddened me the most since they had zero hope of recovery. Spinal cords did not regenerate. They would die in the hospital or a nursing home, never again interacting with the outside world. Most of them wanted to die, but they weren't physically capable of committing suicide. Some of them begged me to kill them, and it was easy to understand why.

Dinner usually meant dirty bedding from food, liquid spillage, or incontinence, so it was another hour before we were able to begin the card game.

Five of us played that night near Robert's bed, since he was the least mobile. The occupational therapist had fixed him up with a cardholder to use when we played draw poker. The small ante and limited bets made it difficult to lose or win more than a few dollars a night.

I brought in a radio to liven up the ward, setting it low to the local soul station as we sat down to play. After an hour, I was the big winner with a dollar fifty in my pile.

John, basically a boy of eighteen who had lost his foot on a land mine, said, "Hey, Kron, you like black music or do you feel sorry for us crippled niggers."

"I feel sorry for the way you play cards, but I'm into this stuff. I've been listening to soul since I was twelve. Maybe you should fold that poor-ass hand and listen to the song."

Robert took up the slack after John tossed in his cards.

"Since you was twelve? How you ever hear soul in that white bread town where you grew up? What is it Bell-ing-ton? Not many brothers there, Kron. I went there once with my sister, and those I-talians and Pollocks scared me back home."

"True enough, during the day it was all Beach Boys, Beatles, and the Four Seasons, with a little Sinatra mixed in for the Wops, but after six, WKBW from Buffalo cranked up their signal. That's where I heard my first soul music, and I've been hooked ever since."

Little Anthony and the Imperials were on, so I stood up making a sad attempt to imitate their choreographed dance moves. My spastic movements really got them going as they clapped their hands and laughed their asses off.

John said, "Oh, you got soul, Kron, but it ain't talking to your feet. You dance like a white boy. Oh, that's right, you are a white boy, but you haven't figured it out yet. Your Mamma never told you? Did they hide all the mirrors in your house, so you'd think that you were black?"

They all cracked up again, slapping their legs and pointing at my gyrating body. I did one more spin before I laid my flush on the table, taking the biggest pot of the night while quieting my critics who were now cleaned out. I went to the auxiliary kitchen and grabbed five sodas as we took a break to bullshit.

Samuel, a sharecropper's son from Alabama had lost his left hand and his right eye when he hit a trip-wire bomb in the jungle. He compensated for his lack of education with natural intelligence and keen perception. Taking a long draw on his soda, he locked his good eye on mine before he spoke.

"Whatcha gonna do next year, Kron? I heard that even if you stay in school the government is gonna have a lottery, and you could get your ass drafted."

"I ain't getting drafted, Samuel, or if I do, I'm not going in. I'm not going over there. Look what happened to you guys? You all know how I feel about the war. I went to my friend's funeral today. He got killed in Nam, and it was a waste."

Robert took my side. "Sorry to hear that. It's a bad place, Kron, real bad. Everybody and everything is fucked up over there. Don't go. Run to Canada if you have to. Look at me. I'll never be right again, and I didn't even know why I was there. I had no beef with those people. Little kids and women were dying in the crossfire, with friends getting blown to more pieces than me."

A few tears fought their way out of his eyes, and it became apparent that the conversation had taken a bad turn. I knew little about Vietnam except that I wasn't going, and that American soldiers were dying in increasing numbers. The thought did occur to me; however, that these patients might know something about the shit that Tommy had been babbling about.

"Listen, I'm sorry for what happened to all of you, and I don't mean any disrespect. You know that, but maybe you can help me out with something. At my friend Paulie's funeral today, someone told me that Paulie had been involved with drugs. You guys know anything about drugs in Nam?"

A few started laughing, the remainder looking at me incredulously as if I was putting them on, but they could see by my face that I didn't have a clue.

Samuel slapped his knee and knocked his stump against my head for effect.

"Drugs! Are you shitting us, Kron? Where you been living, in a cave somewhere or are you going to retard college? Vietnam is drug heaven, baby. Every soldier ends up wasted one time or another, or all the time if he's lucky. Reality sucks over there. You could get anything you wanted real cheap: LSD, weed, smack. Oh man, they had some sweet smack in Saigon. Made life a little easier in that Gook hell, that's for sure. They'll be a lotta boys bringing back a habit to the neighborhood. I might have one myself if I wasn't stuck in this shit hole hospital."

"Wait a minute. Stop yelling for a second. I know that soldiers use drugs. It's not like we don't have it at school, but this is serious shit, not just some guys getting high to escape reality. The guy claimed that Paulie died because of his involvement with drugs."

Samuel nodded. "That's possible, Kron. I seen guys get so high that they got careless, and bang they were gone. Sometimes it was bad shit or they just took too much. I knew a guy that totally lost it on acid. Pulled the pin out of his grenade, let the handle go, set in his lap, and splat! It happens more than you think. Saw lotta guys OD. Saigon was loaded with addicts, fucking loaded."

"That's not what I meant. He said Paulie died because of drugs, not from doing drugs. He said that Americans killed Paulie. Why would anyone kill someone over drugs if they were so easy to get and so cheap to buy?"

Thomas hadn't spoken all night. He usually didn't say much, but he slid his chair next to mine, leaning his bulk into my shoulder. A large man with a hard edge, he didn't mince words when he finally had something to say. Thomas had never been the overly friendly type.

"Ever think maybe your buddy was dealing, white boy? Maybe he fucked over the wrong people, got greedy and paid the price. Some of those dudes over there were pretty nasty, and there was dirty things going on behind the scenes. Cheap drugs or not, there was still a lot of money to be made, and guys protected their turf by any means necessary. It might not be such a good idea for you to be asking these types of questions."

Thomas was crowding my personal space with his intensity, so I stood up to gain some distance from his threatening persona. Maybe I was being too direct, but I was on a roll.

"Yea, good point, Thomas, except that Paulie had always been a total follower and a basic teetotaler. He may have been somebody's lackey, but he would go two miles out of his way to avoid trouble. Believe me, I know because we hung around together since we were four, and he always disappeared at the first sign of trouble."

Thomas pressed his point. "People change fast over in Nam. The guy that gets off the plane in Saigon is not the same one that returns home. Maybe your friend changed and you didn't know it. Some families think maybe the Army sent home the wrong guy, or that they put something in his brain."

"Maybe. That's possible, I suppose. I hadn't written to Paulie for a couple of months, and I guess that a lot could happen in a short time, especially in a war. I don't know, but it just doesn't fit."

Shrugging their shoulders with indifference, they headed back to their beds to deal with their own problems. The lights went out one by one, signaling that the patients were settling down for the night. Robert needed my assistance using the urinal and getting ready for bed. After he was dressed and washed, I stayed with him for a moment. The nurse would be in later with his morphine shot. He had a difficult time getting to sleep unless someone sat near his bed and talked to him as he waited for the narcotic to dull the pain and ease the ever-present fear locked in his mind.

"Robert, I know you've had enough misery in your life, but there is one more thing I'd like to know. I didn't want to say anything in front of the other guys. The person who gave me the information at the cemetery; he was afraid. He believes, or at least he wants me to believe, that he's in danger from the same people that killed Paulie. Maybe it's all bullshit because the dummy has been an asshole his whole life, but he did give me a name. He said to look for the Cobras, and that New Haven would be a good place to start. You ever hear of anything like that in New Haven? I just want to find out if this is total crap, or if there's something to the whole thing that might matter."

The look on Robert's face said it all. He recognized the name that I had just spoken.

"Kron, you don't want to go down that road. Leave it alone! Your friend is dead, and that isn't going to change, no matter what you find out."

"Who are they, Robert, a gang in New Haven? What could they have to do with Paulie's death over there?"

"Don't you understand good advice, Kron? I knew them only by reputation. Supposedly, they provided a lot of services to the troops in the Saigon area—booze, prostitutes out in the bush, and especially drugs. One rumor had it that they were shipping high grade smack back to the States. I don't know if it was true, and I don't want to know. I've had my share of problems and more. I don't get the New Haven connection. It doesn't fit in with anything I know, and I'm from here."

"I'm sorry, Robert, but this has been bugging me all day. I've been this way my whole life. If there's a mystery or something doesn't fit, I feel compelled to look into it. Plus, Paulie was my friend, and I feel guilty because I had a beef with him about going in the Army. Our last words to each other were angry words, and that's a horrible way to leave things."

"Your friend should have listened to you, Kron. The only thing you should feel guilty about is not arguing more. He might be alive today, but what's done is done, so why not let it go. Vietnam is out of your reach unless you have a death wish. Why don't you enlist and continue your investigation in the jungle?

"Of course it would be a little smarter if you start with that buddy of yours from the cemetery. He's the one who stirred up all this shit, and to me it smells like death."

"That might not be a bad idea, Robert. I don't want to get you involved, so forget we had this conversation. He told me not to contact him, but I'll cruise up to Bellington after work tonight and talk to him. I'm not letting him lay a guilt trip on me and walk away, even if I have to beat it out of him. Thanks for your help, Robert. I'll see you next week. I owe you one."

"You owe me nothing, Kron, except to never mention this again. You understand? Hey, take your radio and learn how to dance."

I understood, but dancing was the farthest thing from my mind. I had to see Tommy that night or I wouldn't get any sleep. I didn't know if I cared, or if it mattered, but it didn't fit, and if it didn't fit, then it would bother me until it did.

Chapter 3

The club in Saigon was nothing more than a large hole in the wall wedged between tightly packed colonial-era buildings. A few GI's stood at the tiny bar drinking watered-down booze as they tried to hook up with one of the girls that turned tricks in the dump. There were some gorgeous bar girls in Saigon, but not at that place. The area was for soldiers who had spent or lost most of their pay, and if you did have any money by the end of the night, it was fair game for the muggers when you left.

A skinny soldier, his face still full of adolescent acne, drawled loudly with a strong southern accent, made thicker by his drunkenness. He attempted to negotiate terms with a woman who had seen better days, but the language barrier led to several misunderstandings, and the bouncer soon had him on his ass and out on the street. The road outside rattled with every imaginable wheeled vehicle: bicycles, rickshaws, motorcycles, cars, and jeeps. Downtown Saigon was a very busy place.

At a small table in the darkest corner of a very dim room sat two American soldiers with a bottle of whiskey set between them. They preferred this particular bar because it didn't attract many Americans, especially officers. It was a dangerous place to hang around, but one of the men at the table had nothing to worry about. Sgt. Ronald Williams, a twenty-five-year-old black man with a bear-sized head, filled up half the space around the table. At six-four and two-seventy, he had played two years of college football before flunking out and winning himself a tour in Vietnam.

A wiry thin, sallow Caucasian with hollow cheeks, Cpl. Charles 'Whitey' Volkman stood six feet tall, but appeared almost tiny next to the big man. It wasn't just the difference in size that created the illusion; it had as much to do with the aggressive posture and attitude of Williams, whose countenance did not welcome close examination by anyone.

Speaking in hushed tones, Volkman's voice cracked as he leaned across the table. "So, you'll be heading home for good next week and getting your ass out of this hellhole forever. I wish I were in your boots instead of having to pull three more months. I guess we'll wrap it up and pay everyone off before the end of the week. Right?"

Williams shook his head like a big black bear shaking off a swarm of honeybees, back and forth slowly, with the authority and confidence of an absolute leader.

"Wrong! You're not closing anything down just because I'm leaving. I made sure that you'll be promoted to my position, so why should we stop? You have to take over. You know the whole operation as well as anyone. You're going to be Sgt. Volkman by the end of the week."

Volkman's hands shook as he replied, "The Wops put out the word a month ago that they were going to shut down any side operations, but you kept it going anyway. They'll waste us when we get back home if we don't end it now. They were close to figuring out how we were cutting into their action. Plus, you blew up that scared little medic, and there's still one more asshole back home that might talk."

Williams reached across the table, locking Volkman's thumb in his massive hand, applying just enough pressure to create excruciating pain without breaking it. Volkman's face twisted into a freakish mask of agony.

"I don't take orders from them, and I don't take suggestions from you. My people aren't slaves anymore. We've been helping them ship the smack out to the States, taking all the risks and what did we get? Shit! Fucking peanuts, until I came up with this idea to cut ourselves a share!"

"Williams, stop! You're breaking my thumb! Those are bad people we're dealing with. I've had enough. It's not worth the risk crossing the Mob."

"Bad people? Who the fuck do you think we are, Whitey? The good guys? We deal drugs to soldiers, iced the medic, and wasted the little gook kid in the bargain. We did, Charley. You did. We've done things that would make your folks back home sick. We smuggle drugs and kill people who get in our way. You're in this just as deep as I am. If I go down, you go down. Paulie did what he was told in the beginning, but the nervous little bastard always ran scared. Nervous people make me nervous."

"I wish I never saw his body after the explosion. Did you have to kill him like that?"

That's why we, we, Whitey, not just me, used the gook kid to kill Paulie. Make it look like it was combat-related. HQ didn't even question it, even though they've been nosing around our guys for months. I heard that Captain Robertson, the main investigator, is on his way home with food poisoning or something parasitic. What a shame for him, and lucky for us that we have a few guys in the kitchen. Everything's cleaned up here, and pretty soon the operation will be back on line in the States."

Williams eased up on Volkman's thumb, leaving the other man with tears of pain quietly rolling down his cheeks and on to the dusty table, where they formed little moon craters as they landed on the wood. Volkman belted down a shot of the watered-down whiskey, massaging his thumb as he slowly lifted his gaze from the table.

"They'll kill us for sure if they think we're still skimming and shipping the stuff back to the States, Ronald. They only believed that we were dealing here in Nam, and it should stay that way. Those Wops don't think twice about wasting people like us, especially a black guy. It's business for them, big business, and killing is simply part of the overhead."

Ronald's anger began to boil over. "I'm not doing their dirty work for the scraps that they throw us. We're grabbing a part for ourselves. We do all the work and take all the risks. I'm not going back home to some shit job that pays $2.50 an hour. I'm sick of watching my Mamma beat her life down working ten hours a day just to scratch by, especially with my sister starting college this year. How am I going to help them out? Flipping burgers and saying 'yes sir' to every white shithead that I hate."

"I never thought of you as a family guy, Ronald, but that sister of yours is pretty hot. I saw her picture the other day."

"Don't ever talk about my sister like that, Volkman, or I'll break your thumb clean off and shove it up your ass!"

"Easy, Ronald. I didn't mean nothing by it, but who's going to handle things back home?"

"When I get back to the States, I'm taking over that end of our operation. I've got a guy lined up that works on the base. I intend to continue our business on the street with my own men. There's a new supply source here, but you'll ship the shit out to me the way we planned. When you leave, Hill will take your place. Hopefully, this fucking war will go on forever, but I've heard rumors that the protests are really starting to heat up back home. I'm not afraid of the Wops. I've got men lined up back home and we'll have firepower of our own soon enough with the money we're making. It's time for the black people to take over their own neighborhoods."

"Even if you get away with all of this, how are you going to get rid of the junk? They'd be on to you in a second. The Wops still rule the drug trade; even in the ghetto. You can talk tough here, but when you get home it'll be different."

Williams was clearly losing his patience, but he needed Volkman to continue the operation on the Vietnam end. There was no one else with the experience.

Williams continued his explanation with reluctant forbearance.

"About a month ago, I met a brother from New York whose cousin controls a good part of the smack trade in Harlem and the black neighborhoods in Queens. They're tired of being dependent on the Wops for their supply, taking their degrading shit, and paying ridiculous prices. He promised me that his cousin would buy everything I could get, no questions asked. They're ready to take control, but they need a supplier that's not in bed with the Wops.

"Plus, I'm going to move a lot of it in New Haven through my old contacts. I plan on taking over my hometown. Remember that slick Italian guy who shipped out last month? He's providing the money and cleaning up our messes along the way. I've got it all worked out. You stay with me and you'll get rich. You screw with me; you'll end up talking to that other white boy in hell."

Volkman knew that he was caught between two deadly forces, trapped there by his own ambition and greed. There would be no easy way out, just like there was no easy way out of Vietnam. All you did in both cases was survive, even if you had to go through the motions like the living dead. He understood that there would be a lot of pieces for everyone to pick up after this shit war was over, but he did intend to live.

"Okay, okay. I'm with you so far, Williams, but what about Combs, the one who shot himself in the leg to get out? What if he decides to rat? I never did like that sloppy, annoying bastard, but I had to admit he was crazy enough to be useful at times."

Ronald smiled. "I wasn't worried about him when he left because I figured that he was just scared, but he was spotted talking to some friend of Paulie's at the funeral, a guy from his old neighborhood. Our man at the funeral said he saw Tommy on the edge of the woods trying to talk to this character as he was leaving. It was probably just old time bullshit. I doubt if he said anything or that anyone would believe him, but I'm having it checked out."

"Jesus, Williams, we can't go around killing everyone, especially in the States. Over here, no one suspected that we rigged that little kid up with the grenades. Those suicide attacks happen around here, so at least it's accepted as possible, but back home they'll look into a death, especially if you kill two more. Everything is running out of control. It's not worth it."

"Fucking relax! Who said anything about killing him? Jesus, I thought you were the right guy to take over. I guess I was wrong. Maybe I'll suggest to the Captain that you go back with your unit instead of stepping into my job. Where are they? Oh yeah, your squad is running night missions along the Ho Chi Minh trail. It's shitty, dangerous work even in the daytime, but if that's what you want instead of a chance to make big money, I'll be glad to give you my highest recommendation. Didn't we just black bag a couple of your old buddies to the States the other day?"

Williams had made his point, leaving Volkman with nowhere to go.

"Stop! I can't go back out there in the bush. I won't last a day, but we can't keep killing people without blowing everything. We have to be smarter this time, because if we get caught, everything might be exposed. I might go to jail for the drugs, but I know we're all going to hell for killing Paulie."

"It's a war, Volkman. Nobody goes to hell for what they do in war. If they do, then hell's going to have a long waiting line after this mess is done. I have no intention of wasting anyone else unless they talk or run scared. Drink up. Let's get out of this dump and find some real women."

Volkman finished his drink, rising from the table to follow Williams, sick with the feeling of being carried in the rapids of a raging river. He had lost control of the situation and had no choice but to go where the current of this intense man took him.

Chapter 4

My shift ended at ten, and I reached Tommy's house an hour later. I had given serious consideration to giving it up, but Tommy and Robert had poked at my curiosity. It sounded pretty stupid, like something out of a movie, with gangs called Cobras and drug lords, but parts of it were real. Paulie being dead was real, even though it seemed like a bad dream. It never took much for me to take up a cause, so who knew what my motivation happened to be. Maybe it was just an attention-getting scheme of Tommy's, but it couldn't hurt to check it out.

I didn't know how to feel about the whole thing. If Tommy had been telling the truth, I wasn't sure which way to go. Should I care how Paulie died? In my mind, whatever the method, it was the War that had killed him, a war that I hated with a burning passion, but if he was involved with the drug trade, then he had placed himself in a different kind of danger. I realized that I was prejudging Paulie's motives even though I hadn't known much about his life since high school. Maybe he died bravely or perhaps he had been a drug dealer, but Tommy made me feel responsible for discovering the truth. Vietnam had divided family and friends, and as I approached the end of college, I knew that the war would come looking for me, and panic had begun to set in.

It wasn't supposed to happen this way. All during our lives, adults had told us that the big war was over, and that we would get the college education that many of them were denied. A better life with easier and more rewarding jobs was in our future, or so we were led to believe. We expected to receive our diplomas, enter the work force and raise our own families, but now they were sending us to die in a place that most of us had never heard of, and for reasons that made no sense. I thought that all wars were senseless in the end, but Vietnam made the least sense of all. I was, as always, afraid of dying, and now my end could have a name, Vietnam.

The increasingly visible conflict caused recurring nightmares that snapped me upright in the middle of the night, leaving my body shaking and my shirt drenched in sweat. In every scenario, I would be lying face down in a muddy rice paddy amidst other floating bodies as the survivors of my unit retreated in terror. The Viet Cong would arrive minutes later, probing our bodies with their bayonets for signs of life. The sharp blades produced no pain because none of us were alive. I was unable to picture my life beyond that image. Vietnam blocked any perception of the future.

Memories of Paulie as a little kid flowed through my mind as the car cruised toward Bellington. A slide show of our lives flashed in my mind: sliding down our hill on a snow day off from school, chasing the ice cream truck in the summer, and Paulie hitting the home run our senior year that won the league championship. The foundation of my past provided me with some of the motivation that I required to check this story out. Perhaps I had a need to believe that it was someone else who had killed Paulie, someone I could blame personally, and something solid that I could lay my hands on. The War and the government stood too large for me, light years away from my reality and control, with many conflicting issues that had begun to tear my world apart. A portion of my childhood had died with Paulie, times that he and I had shared alone, times that now would only be remembered by me.

Tommy lived a few blocks over from my mother's house on the same dead-end street as the Samelas. The Samelas were a semi-psychotic, violent family, and they were our worst nightmares as children. The four Samela brothers, older than us and mean as badgers, had terrorized us until we reached high school. I felt a little uncomfortable being on their street, but most of them had moved away, and besides, I was big enough to handle myself if any of them were still around.

Tommy's sister had inherited their mom's house when their mother died of lung cancer three years ago, and she let Tommy live there rent-free because he had become a basket case with no income except for his disability check. Even in the dark, it was apparent that Tommy didn't believe in home maintenance. The street in general had started a slow decline as the older people died off, but Tom's house raced ahead of the others for rat hole of the year. The tiny lawn was more like an overgrown weed field, and it seemed that every broken appliance had been dumped into the front and side yards. Fred Sanford would have been proud of Tommy's landscaping.

A dull light from within framed a yellowed shade that covered a solitary window on the back porch. Peeling white paint speckled the deck of the collapsing porch like a coat of freshly fallen snow. Through the shadows, the old wooden garage in back tilted precariously to one side, appearing as if it could go over at any time.

I walked around to the back door to see if Tommy was at home. The night turned a shade darker away from the streetlights. My knee smashed against an old sink that had camouflaged itself in the tall brush, causing me to curse loudly as I threw the sink about ten feet into the woods. As I bent down to rub the stinging pain from my leg, I wondered what the hell I was doing there. Goddamn Tommy was still giving me pain after all these years.

Apparently, my yelp and flood of profanities had roused someone from inside the house because the screen door slammed and heavy footsteps pounded down the porch steps. Tommy must have heard me, running out to see what the ruckus was about.

"Tommy, it's just me, Kronchek."

No answer from the rapidly moving figure, so I limped to the porch where the kitchen light threw a beam into the backyard, revealing nothing except more trash and two junk cars that had been in the same spot since we were kids. Brush rustled in the woods behind the house and I hoped that Tommy hadn't spooked and ran up the steep, heavily wooded hill in back. I wasn't about to chase him in the dark through a forest of brush and protruding ledge. I pushed aside the tattered screen while knocking on the window of the partially opened backdoor.

"Tom. Are you in there? Who just ran out of your house? It's me, Matt

Kronchek. You told me not to talk to you again, but you can't just lay shit like that on someone and walk away. I want to settle this right now. Can I come in or what? Tom! Come on, asshole, answer."

Sticking my head inside the door, I listened for sounds of habitation. Nothing, only a refrigerator's hum and the buzzing of a florescent light above a counter loaded with crusted dishes and empty frozen dinner boxes. The dishes were spotted with cigarette butts that had been ground into the porcelain, stuck to the glaze from gooey food and tobacco tar.

I moved in to the middle of the room where the stench of rotten food and soggy cigarettes ripped into my nostrils. Flies were everywhere, and Tommy had about ten of those sticky yellow strips hanging from the smoked-stained ceiling. Coated with rotting fly corpses, they rocked slowly in the breeze that flowed in from the open door, casting strobe-like macabre shadows on the walls. A pink plastic fly swatter with the words, "Courtesy of the Bellington Oil Company", contained the bodies of a dozen more crushed flies.

"Tommy, are you home or what? It's late and I don't have time for this hide-and-seek bullshit. If you don't come out now, I'll just come back tomorrow."

Inky blackness bathed the other rooms, and I didn't appreciate the fact that I couldn't see more than a foot beyond the kitchen. My nerves began to jump as the fine hairs on my arms and neck rose in alarm. Who knew what shit the weirdo had gotten into, considering the story he told me? It would be best to make tracks, returning when I could see. As I turned to leave, a faint light under the bathroom door just off the kitchen caught my eye.

"Yo, Tommy, are you in the can? Come on, answer me or I'm splitting right now."

The door creaked open just a crack from the breeze, and at that moment I should have walked away. I really had no desire to find Tommy asleep on the crapper or in the tub. I used the word should an awful lot, which meant that I didn't leave, as I should have. Leaving; however, wouldn't serve the purpose of the visit, which had been to talk to him and settle this issue in my mind, so I took a courage-inducing deep breath and pushed the door open just enough to get my head through. Dressed only in his underwear, Tommy's ashen body lay sprawled on the moldy tile floor.

"Jesus Christ, Tommy! Wake up and put on some clothes, you stupid ass."

I kicked his gaunt, but flaccid body, producing no response; not even a groan. I kicked him harder, somewhat enjoying it, and still nothing but residual shaking of atrophied muscle matter and loose skin. Upon closer examination, I saw a needle sticking from Tommy's left arm, and on the floor was a small bag of white powder that had partially spilled on the ground. The dumb bastard must have been shooting up heroin. He wasn't moving and didn't appear to be breathing.

I didn't want to touch his creepy body, but I felt for a pulse on his clammy neck, hoping that he had only passed out. Not one beat. I tried again, but couldn't feel anything. Tommy appeared to be dead. What an asshole! He tells me about Paulie's supposed murder and then blows himself away with drugs, leaving me to find his disgusting body. This was bad, real bad for me. If I called the cops, they would splatter my name all over the papers and people would think that Tommy and I were drug buddies. My mother would die from the embarrassment, not to mention the potential prison term and the reputation of having been Tommy's last friend on earth.

It wouldn't bother me morally to leave him there until his sister came around to find him. She was always miserable like her brother, and I might have paid to see the look on her face when she opened the bathroom door. I came to Bellington to find some answers, but Tommy had left me with a true dead end, and I was pissed.

Luckily, my car was parked down the street near a patch of woods, and I doubted if anyone would recognize me in the dark. I wanted to find out more information about Paulie, but now it would go to the grave with Tommy. I had wished him dead many times when we fought as kids, but the one time that I wanted him alive, he took the final trip to the other side.

Screw it! There was nothing I could do, and it had been one long, disheartening day. I rubbed down anything that I had touched with my handkerchief and started out the door when it hit me. If Tommy was dead, then who ran out of the house when I arrived? I had become careless. Someone else had been in the house moments before me. I wasn't a coroner, but his body was warm when had I felt for a pulse, meaning that he hadn't been dead long.

Why couldn't I just leave? It had always been this way for me. When things didn't add up, it would itch at me until I found the solution. I went back into the bathroom, scanning the scene carefully, my skin crawling with existential fear. I looked over my shoulder every two seconds in case the missing person returned.

There was no heroin paraphernalia; no matches, a cooking spoon or used needles, but the oddest thing came to me from the past. The needle dangled from Tommy's left arm, but I remembered from all our fights that Tommy was left-handed. He should have used the needle with his left hand, shooting into his right arm unless he had made too many tracks in his right. But that was the clincher. Tommy had no track marks at all. Not on his arms, hands, between his toes-nothing!

Now things really didn't add up. Tommy didn't appear to have been an addict, at least to mainline heroin, and the first time he shoots up, he dies with the needle still in his arm. A pretty lethal dose for his maiden smack voyage, but not impossible. I had a strong feeling; however, that this was not self-inflicted. Boxes of empty beer bottles were piled in every corner, and a hash pipe lay on the bathroom sink, but nothing else.

It appeared as if someone had helped Tommy along to hell, so it wouldn't be too smart to stick around any longer to look for more evidence. The puke came up my throat as the reality of Tommy's corpse hit me in the gut, but I forced it back down as I turned away to ease the nausea. No wonder he had been so frightened at the cemetery. He had been next in line, and maybe because someone had seen him speaking to me.

A bit of a tattoo showed on his upper arm, so I checked him out one more time as I fought to control the gag reflex. Using my foot to lift his flaccid tricep, two intertwined cobras came into view. What had started as innuendoes and bits of vague information had begun to gel into a pattern, and now a dead body. Not a dead body from Vietnam, but a corpse right here in Bellington.

Whoever the Cobras were, they meant to silence anyone who got in their way. Right then, I knew that I had crossed their path. I should have called an ambulance in case I was mistaken about him being dead, but I wanted out of there. I left quickly, but with caution, hoping that whoever had iced Tommy hadn't recognized me or was waiting outside. If they had seen me, I might get to lie in the wooden box at the next funeral. Apparently, some of what Tommy told me had been the truth. There was little doubt in my mind at that point, and now I would need to have answers about Paulie and the war, even though panic had settled deep within my psyche.

A bigger issue began to stand out in my mind. It appeared that Americans were killing Americans for money, drug money in the middle of a war where they were supposed to be watching out for each other. A dirty war had just gotten dirtier in my plane of awareness. I took a circuitous route back to New Haven, making many unnecessary turns while checking my mirror for signs of pursuit. It appeared as if no one had followed me, but it still wasn't comforting. They probably knew who I was and where I lived, considering that I had yelled out my name to the fleeing figure at Tommy's. I hadn't been this frightened since eighth grade.

Chapter 5

Fortunately, I didn't have to work all weekend, so I remained in my room and didn't contact anyone. Every half-hour I would peer out the blinds to see if the house was being watched. The streets had been empty most of the day, with nothing out of place or strange cars parked near the curb. The door to the apartment remained locked with a chair jammed against the handle. The phone rang several times and stayed unanswered.

Late Sunday morning, the phone rang and rang, and I felt compelled to answer it because it was right on schedule. My mother's weekly call couldn't be ignored, and it occurred to me that if anyone had found Tommy's body, my mother would know about it before the newspapers. I also realized that I hadn't called my, on again, off again girlfriend, Karen, for three days, but it was my mom as expected.

"Hi, Mom, what's up? Sorry I didn't get to the phone right away, but I've been kinda sick."

"You don't sound sick to me unless you've been drinking. You have a hangover, don't you?"

"I haven't been drinking. I told you that I was sick, and besides there's no one here to drink with anyway. Hardly anyone's back to school."

She ignored my explanation as she moved on to the next topic.

"You won't believe what's happened right in our neighborhood."

I knew what she was going to say, so I presented a bit of sarcastic disinterest.

"What, Ma? Did the Johnson's dog poop on our lawn again? The excitement never stops in Bellington."

"No, mister wise mouth. Your old classmate, Tommy Combs, died yesterday from drugs. Right in his bathroom, two blocks over. From heroin, that's what Mrs. Duggan told me, and she said that his sister found him on the bathroom floor Saturday morning, dead and stiff in his underwear. Heroin, right here in Bellington, probably being brought in by all these strangers moving in to town."

"No kidding? Thanks for the vivid description. Poor Tommy, although I must say he was most deserving of his fate. God does work in mysterious ways as they say."

"How can you talk that way about an old friend of yours? You have no respect for the dead or the living for that matter! And stop mocking God or he'll have a place ready for you in hell, if he doesn't already."

"Ma, God doesn't run hell, the devil does, and that turd wasn't a friend. Don't you remember all the times that he beat me up, and then you would send me back out for more?"

"Don't be so mean toward a dead person. You've gotten mean since you went to college. Anyway, the reason I'm calling is to tell you that his funeral will be tomorrow morning. They're not having a wake. I was surprised that they were able to arrange the funeral so quickly."

"Yea, so what? What does that have to do with anything? I'm not going. Why would I?"

I emphasized my opinion with a firm voice because the last place I wanted to be seen was at Tommy's funeral. Whoever punched his time card for the last time might be watching the cemetery to see if I was still poking around asking about Paulie. Someone must have seen Tommy talking to me at Paulie's funeral and decided to silence his mouth forever. Every move I made might be significant in their eyes, a signal to them that I might know too much. They may have known that Tommy spoke to me, but they may not have known the content. Maybe if I stayed out of their business, they would go away.

My mother continued her pitch. "Look, mister, I heard what you said at the cemetery. The whole town knows it by now, and I'm ashamed to go anywhere. Paulie's mother called me after the funeral, and for an hour I had to hear what a disrespectful, rude person you are, and most likely a communist. We didn't bring you up to act that way. I'm glad your father isn't alive to see this. I want you to go to Tommy's funeral and show some respect."

"What's the big deal, Ma? Tell the truth. You didn't even like Tommy or his family. You always said they were raggies and lived like pigs. What do you care if I show up or not, and what does it have to do with the Kovak's? I said what I felt at the funeral, and I can't take it back now."

She began to cry, and I knew that I was quickly losing ground. I couldn't tell her that she might be placing me in danger. She would call the cops and I didn't want them involved. The less my name was associated with Tommy's, the better. The crying terminated as her anger and guilt trip power play took over.

"I never ask you for anything (that made no sense because she must have used that line a thousand times), and you embarrassed the whole family at Paulie's funeral. (I must have embarrassed the family at least a million times over the years.) Mrs. Kovak asked me for a favor, and I want you to do it, for me." (For me, the all-time guilt clincher of parents everywhere.)

"I'll apologize to Paulie's family even though I won't mean it, but I'm not going to that ass's funeral. Listen, I'm getting some paper ready to write the Kovak's an apology."

"Don't play games with me, Matt, and watch your language. You remember Paulie's girlfriend, Debbie. Well, she wants to go to Tommy's funeral, but doesn't want to go alone, so I said that you would bring her. It would help set things right with the Kovak's if you did this little favor for Debbie. They loved that girl, and now she will never be a part of their family."

"Jesus, Ma! Why did you tell her that? This is no little favor. Debbie Blair and I have never gotten along, so why would she want to go with me? As a matter of fact, I don't think she even knew Tommy, so why is she so hot on going to his funeral?"

"When I called her, Debbie told me that she would be very happy if you would escort her, being that you were Paulie's oldest and closest friend. She wants to go because Paulie and Tommy were in the same unit in Vietnam. You must have known that, and besides, the girl is totally devastated from Paulie's death. Paulie's mother said that she hardly eats or sleeps."

I guess everyone had known about the Army connection, except for me. I realized then that I had grown even further away from Paulie and Bellington. Every time I came home, it felt as if I was stepping eight years into the past. I kept changing, while Bellington stood still in time.

This waking nightmare wasn't going to end as my mother dug her heels in hard. Besides, as usual, my mind had already recognized a possible opportunity in the situation. Debbie might know something about this Vietnam deal. Debbie and Paulie had been like conjoined twins, so he must have confided something to her about his fears and activities. I didn't like the idea of being seen at the funeral, but this new possibility of acquired knowledge had gotten me pumped up again. My paranoia was being overridden by my curiosity, putting me back on the scent.

"Fine. I'll take her if it will make everyone happy, but I don't want to ever hear anything about this crap again. As far as I'm concerned, this squares me up with everyone, you included."

"Good. Pick her up at eight tomorrow morning and bring her to the funeral home. Don't be late, and start writing that apology letter. I told Mrs. Kovak to expect it in a few days."

"Yea, yea, don't worry, but this is it." I tried to sound in control, but knew that I had lost.

Sunday night offered me little rest. Every sound in the old house made me jump up with a baseball bat ready to swing; my head swirling with complicated scenarios of plots and murder. I slept an hour before the alarm clock jolted me out of a nightmare about Vietnam. I dreamed that I was lost in the jungle, wandering and calling for Paulie. No one answered, but eyes glowed in the dense underbrush as they followed my movements. This time; however, I didn't have the sense of them being enemy soldiers, but something more frightening and hideous, with a smell of betrayal hanging thick in the air. As I stared into the trees, American soldiers came into focus, their faces distorted by greed and violence, with drug-glazed eyes and rifles at the ready. They called for me to join them in their jungle hell. My own countrymen frightened me the most in a foreign land. I awoke with my shirt drenched, feeling as if I hadn't slept at all. I would be tired and cranky, while looking over my shoulder the entire day. I needed to get out of Bellington quickly so I would have time for a nap before work.

The persistent alarm clock ended up splattered on the wall, with sharp pieces of plastic shrapnel strewn everywhere, cutting my feet as I dragged my enervated carcass to the shower. I stopped bitching to myself, realizing that there was no choice but to finish the job in front of me. *You should have been careful what you wished for Debbie, because here I come. Bellington's much-reviled native son returning once more to bury the dead.* I hoped to hell that it would be a closed casket. The private viewing the other night had been enough.

Debbie Blair lived in a brick cape on the newer end of Paulie's street, up the hill near edge of the woods where the entrance to the old granite quarries used to be. A group of homes built after the industrial boom years, they were mostly one-story houses with larger yards, attached garages with a patio on the side, or a gazebo in the backyard. High-end shit for Bellington, especially in our neighborhood.

Debbie had moved into town at the beginning of high school, having come from Hartford when her father decided that he wanted his kids to grow up in a smaller town with less crime. It seemed that she had harbored a crush on Paulie since the day that she arrived. A plain, but color-coordinated dresser with a hairdo from the forties, she was attractive in an old fashioned, Ingrid Bergman kind of way. Always fastidiously organized and neat throughout high school, Debbie carried a perfectly maintained binder with five divisions and several labeled pockets. Her diction was perfect, her manners precise, and she was always on time.

Debbie appeared to have been created as the perfect complement for Paulie. She knew exactly what she wanted and spared no effort to reach her goals. Where he was hesitant, she would charge forward and take control. He was timid and retiring, she was bold and opinionated, and that's exactly what Paulie desired from someone in his life.

Debbie had slowly and methodically commanded Paulie's attention by the middle of their sophomore year. After one date, which she painstakingly engineered, they were attached at the hip until he entered the Army. She had plotted the course of their lives down to the smallest detail, but even Debbie Blair had gotten blind-sided by Vietnam. Hadn't we all.

College wasn't a chapter in Debbie's book, which I could never understand since she was a straight A student. After a few years of working in Bellington, they were going to get married, have 2.5 children, live in a raised ranch, etc. Paulie started working for Debbie's father in the electrical business after high school, where Debbie kept the books and ran the office. It would have been his business someday if he had survived to kiss his future father-in-law's butt.

When good old Uncle Sam needed more bodies for the war, they began drafting anything that could walk and wasn't attending keg parties in college. Paulie knew then that he was screwed, but it was too late. He figured that if he enlisted, he could choose his area of expertise and hopefully avoid combat. I suppose that in Army lingo, signing up to be an electrician means you are trained to be a medic. I guess they are close from a military point of view. You know the rest.

I cruised up my street, and sure enough, there was my mother sitting in the window making certain that I would keep my promise. I leaned on the horn, waving wildly as she attempted to hide her interfering face behind the curtain. Normally, I wouldn't mind helping someone out, but Debbie blamed Mike and me for every bit of trouble that Paulie had gotten nailed for in high school.

I'm sure Debbie found me irritating, considering that my life consisted of disorganization, constant movement, and the ensuing trouble that comes with such traits. My world was her bizarro world, diametrically opposite, distorted, and misguided from her point of view. When Mike and I broke into the school gym to play basketball one Sunday morning, Paulie had tagged along to share in the excitement. Debbie wouldn't talk to us for a month when Paulie was suspended from school for a few days. He got himself stuck in the cellar window of the gym during our escape.

Debbie and I were just so different; it was as if we stood back to back on a circle facing 360 degrees in opposite directions. Strange analogy I suppose, since that would eventually bring us around to the same point, and here we were heading to Tommy's funeral together. Not quite the common ground that I would have ever imagined us treading together.

I squealed my Mustang into Debbie's driveway thirty minutes late, slamming on my brakes and leaning on the horn. There would be no going into the house and listening to shit from Debbie's mother. She had never forgiven me for borrowing her car when we were fifteen, even though Mike and I paid for the damage.

Mr. Blair, probably harangued by his wife, opened the front door, signaling to me in rather violent sign language to lay off the horn. I waved to him in my most preppie manner, prompting him to brush me off in disgust as he walked back into the house. Debbie emerged from the garage, slowly shuffling to the car. Exuding perfection even in mourning attire, she wore a solemn black dress with the hem resting slightly above her knee. A veil covered her face, and her hair was tucked under a pillbox hat. The funeral-appropriate apparel brought me to the realization that I had worn my khakis and a wrinkled blue shirt with no tie. Even in death, I guess Tommy wasn't going to get a tie out of me. Being so pissed about being forced to attend the funeral, I had forgotten what the occasion called for in the manner of dress.

Debbie reached the car and stood near the door, so I figured that she had lost her nerve, which was fine by me. It took me a moment to realize that she was waiting for me to open the door for her. Apparently hoping for a gentleman, she was barking up the wrong tree. I didn't get out, but reached across the console and pushed the door open, knocking empty beer bottles from the seat and onto her driveway. I brushed stubbornly imbedded petrified potato chip crumbs from the fabric in a desperate attempt at a last second clean up.

"Hey, Debbie, hop in or we'll be late. Wouldn't want to miss the show."

Trained eyes examined the seat, and being ever prepared as usual, she placed a clean towel on the cushion and another over the back, while ignoring my sarcastic humor.

"Hello, Matt. Thank you for taking me, although I'm sure you did everything you could to get out of it. I saw you at Paulie's funeral, but I didn't get a chance to speak to you."

"Yea, sorry about that. Everybody's pretty pissed at me, and I should have kept quiet. I kind of had to leave in a rush because of Uncle Rocco. He was dying for a chance to beat the hell out of me."

"He wasn't the only one, but you were right for once, Matt. It was a horrible waste, and I miss him so much."

Debbie started bawling with her head buried in my shoulder just as we pulled into the funeral home parking lot. I mean, I couldn't blame her. It was understandable since her boyfriend had been buried only three days ago, but it made me uncomfortable. This wasn't part of the bargain.

"Debbie, Debbie, please stop. I miss him too, and I didn't mean to screw up his funeral, but I was so angry."

"Why are you apologizing for saying what half the people were really thinking deep in their hearts? Do you think any one of them would have wanted that coffin to contain their child or their boyfriend? Whatever the reason, or cause if you want, why did Paulie have to die so young? We never had a chance to start our life together, and for what? You said it perfectly and concisely, "what a waste." A little boy blew him up, Matt, *a little boy*!"

I pulled my Mustang around a couple of beat up cars with temporary plates resting in their back windows. The Combs' fleet of vehicles, no doubt. We parked in a far corner where Debbie could put herself back together. Her head remained on my shoulder for what seemed like an hour; the tears forming a damp circle on my sleeve.

"You're asking the wrong guy, Debbie. I don't know why anybody has to die, let alone someone as young as Paulie or that Vietnamese kid. It isn't right no matter what the politics. He wouldn't even kill caterpillars when we were kids. I told him not to go in, Debbie. I told him. Vietnam is our fucking nightmare and we can't seem to wake up."

My voice began to crack, with tears pooling beneath my eyelids as I fought to hold them back. As weird as this was getting, I didn't want this girl to see me cry.

"Don't you understand, of all people, that he went in because he was Paulie—mostly just because he was Paulie? It's easy for you, Matt. Paulie explained you to me before he left. He said Matt would never go, but he had to because of who he was and who he had always been. Canada or prison weren't even a brief option in his mind. His parents would have disowned him, and he would never defy them. I can't deny that I believed he was doing the right thing by serving his country.

"You see, Matt; we all helped him along his path to Vietnam. First his parents made all his decisions for him, then you and Mike, and finally me. I knew what he was all about when I began dating him, and wanted to protect and direct him, but he didn't have us in Vietnam, and the Army wasn't too concerned about his health. It's not one of their strong points."

Shocked, but not left speechless, I tried to calm her down.

"It might appear easy for me because I don't think things through. I react like an animal would to danger. My actions have always come easier than Paulie's, but the consequences aren't always fun. I've paid the price many times for my impulsive actions. He wanted to join in on all the action, but he hated the consequences, so generally he gave things some thought before he jumped in. I guess to him, not going to Vietnam carried a greater price than resisting, but I don't think he figured in the death part."

Debbie lifted her cheek from my shoulder, exposing a face composed of swollen eyes and a runny nose. Diluted mascara formed streaks of black rivulets that ran down her cheeks. Lipstick smudged across her upper lip and chin made her look like the saddest clown on earth. My blue, red, black, and damp shirt sleeve stuck to my arm from the tears and makeup. There was nothing else to say. It was too late anyway.

Debbie re-did her face with her usual efficiency, and as we were about to go inside to pay our respects, we noticed the three-car junkyard funeral procession heading out of the lot. A mournful looking fellow of about eighty instructed us to get in line. They were heading directly to the cemetery, with no church services being held for Tom. Good for him. At least the bastard knew how to have a funeral.

As we crawled down Elm and cut over to Main, the irony of the situation hit me, releasing a nervous laugh. First a chuckle, then a full-blown belly laugh that echoed around the car.

Debbie moved against the passenger door, fearfully believing that I had lost my mind.

"Please stop that horrible noise, Matt. You're scaring me. What could you possibly find funny about this situation?"

"I'm sorry, Debbie. This just shows how screwed up our existence is, and how your life sneaks around and comes up behind you to say boo."

"Matt, what are you talking about? Watch the road! You almost slammed into that car."

I stopped laughing. The poor girl had been through hell and didn't need any more confusion in the form of my twisted sense of humor.

"I'm sorry, but a week ago if someone had told me that I'd be going to Tommy Combs' funeral with you, it would have been ludicrous. Three years ago, you swore that you would never get in a car with me again. Once after Tommy and his sister beat me up, I told him that I wouldn't be caught dead at his funeral and that I would dance on his grave. Do you see the irony in all this?"

"Matt, you need to see someone. You're getting weirder all the time. Pay attention, they're turning into the cemetery."

"Debbie, are you sure you want to go? I really don't want to get out of the car. His sister hates me, and I don't need another cemetery freak-out scene."

"You promised, Matt, and besides, everyone saw us pulling in behind them. It will be embarrassing if we leave now. Here, let me fix your shirt."

Okay, spooky time. Debbie had begun to manage my life with that small gesture, trying to make me presentable for the occasion as she brushed out the wrinkles on my sleeve. She held my arm steady with one small, but firm hand, as she miraculously removed the stains with her handkerchief and a dab of saliva. I must admit, it felt good to have a little direction and attention, but I knew her potential and it frightened me. Of course, any perception of control would send me in the opposite direction, and I was prepared to flee in an instant.

"All right, let's get it over with. I can't believe I'm doing this."

I checked out the area, making sure that no one had followed me. We cut through a small quad of mausoleums to reach Tommy's grave, which was located in the shabbiest part of the cemetery, near the edge of a steep bank with scrubby woods. The paranoia had been sublimated during my interaction with Debbie, but instinct took over as I scanned the cemetery for observers. Nothing, not even workers were in my line of sight. Watching all those James Bond movies five times each proved to be useful.

Tommy lay in a plain pine box, and mercifully for me, it was closed. I would have expected nothing more. They had always been poor, and hopefully someone had helped with the funeral expenses. Not that it mattered to me. Who cared what a coffin looked like once it was sunk into the ground?

A pastor from an unknown denomination had already started the mumbo jumbo burial chant. The hired gun mumbled in a low, rapid, staccato voice, leaving no doubt that he intended to get it done quickly and collect his fee. Tommy's sister, her husband, and their four kids sat in the front row of chairs. A couple of Tom's uncles wearing cheap suits with crooked ties, and whose rap sheets read like the who's who of petty crime in Bellington, leaned on the backs of the chairs. I could smell the booze mixed with cheap cologne from ten feet away.

"Ashes to ashes, dust to dust", droned the bald pastor. *Here we go again,* I thought, as I was reminded of my dirty apartment that should have been cleaned two weeks ago. I lifted my head and noticed that the weather was beautiful. Somebody finally got buried on a nice day—the unpredictable Tommy Combs. Amazing grace!

They must have scraped up some last minute soldiers from the local National Guard, and Debbie cried as they fired their rifles, with the salvo forcefully re-awakening suppressed memories of Paulie's funeral. Tommy wouldn't be an official statistic of Vietnam, but I knew that he was. The guns were loud enough to hurt my ears, and I wondered how it felt to get shot. I watched them fold the flag and tried once again to figure it out, but it was beyond me. I would never be Army material. There were a few people on the fringe that I didn't know, but one of them, a man with dark sunglasses, seemed very familiar. He exchanged a few quiet words with Tommy's sister, handed her an envelope, and then went through the trees to the opposite end of the cemetery.

"Debbie, do you know the guy who just gave his condolences to Tommy's sister?"

"That's strange because I was thinking that I've seen him before, just a little while ago."

"Where, Debbie? Do you remember where you saw him? I need to know!"

I had her by the arm, and the few remaining people at the grave looked our way when I raised my voice.

"Stop, Matt! Please don't cause a scene again. Why is it so important?"

"I don't know. Maybe it's not, but it could be. Ask Tommy's sister his name."

"Aren't you coming over with me to say you're sorry?"

"No, because I'm not, and I'm not taking the chance of Susan flipping out on me. I've had enough of this shit for one week. Please ask her, Debbie. It might be important."

Debbie traded hugs with Tommy's sister, with only a few words spoken between them. Never looking back, Debbie and I headed back to the car.

"You know, Matt, you should try cutting people a little slack. You always have to be such a hard ass. She asked who you were and I told her. She said that she would have never recognized you from the neighborhood because of your long hair and how much you've grown."

"Oh no! Why did you do that? Now there's going to be trouble. That girl hates me and Tommy's uncles might decide to have a little grief relief at my expense."

"Can't you shut up for once? Susan's not a girl anymore. She's a woman with children of her own. She thanked you for coming and said that Tommy always liked you, and that it would have meant a lot to him that you showed up."

"Oh bullshit! All we ever did was fight. He hated me with a passion because I wouldn't back down."

"No, Matt, his sister said that's why he respected you. He told her that most kids weren't worth picking on because they wouldn't fight back, and that made it boring for him. I guess Tommy needed attention that he never got at home, and you always gave it to him. You're not so good at reading people as you think, are you, Matt?"

Her words stunned and stung me. A new level of awareness had just been pushed through my wall of past prejudices. At times I acted worse than the bigots that I looked down upon.

"Wow, I had no idea. That's weird. They're such a strange family. They seem to thrive on conflict. It's like a form of affection or bond with them. Did you ask her about the guy with the sunglasses? I know I've seen him around."

As we reached the car, Debbie gasped before she could answer. My left front tire had been slashed to shreds, and the Mustang's side mirror lay in the gutter. The cemetery contained nothing but gravestones, with a living soul nowhere in sight. I understood the message immediately and wanted to go back to my locked room in New Haven to huddle in my bed. It was a warning, and I knew what the next move would be if I didn't back off. The people responsible for Tommy's death must have interpreted my attendance at the funeral as continued meddling.

"Matt, who would do this, especially in a graveyard? I don't see anyone around. What's going on?"

I didn't answer her. Passing information to Debbie would only frighten her and probably put her in the same position as me, if she wasn't already by association. They frightened me before, but now they had pissed me off. They, whoever they were, had been watching and following me. They knew me, where I lived, and probably where my mother lived. This wasn't just about me anymore. A lot of people could be in danger: my family, Karen, my roommates, and even Debbie.

The situation had been brought to a personal level by messing with my car, but they didn't understand my personality, or maybe they did and were playing me. I had been ready to give it up, but pushing me into a corner could change my mind. I understood where it was none of my affair, but I preferred to make my own decisions. In some ways I was an easy target. Push me and I pushed back.

"You know who did this, don't you? I've never seen you look this way before. You're frightened, aren't you?"

I ignored her question, answering with one as I began to change the tire in the rising heat.

"Who was that guy, Debbie? Was he at Paulie's funeral on Saturday?"

"Tommy's sister said that he had been in the same unit as Paulie and

Tommy in Vietnam. She didn't know his name, and he didn't offer it. Susan is a little freaked out because he gave her a sympathy card with three hundred dollars inside. Paulie's mother told me that she received an anonymous card with hundreds of dollars in it. Tell me what's going on. That's a lot of money for a sympathy card. Does he have anything to do with what happened to your car?"

"Nothing, nothing's going on. He just looked familiar that's all. He probably collected the money from all the guys in their unit. Forget it. Hop in and I'll take you home. Must have been some kids looking for excitement that did my car, or maybe Uncle Rocco spotted me around town and decided to even the score."

"You always were such a crummy liar. Paulie was afraid of something besides the war, Matt. He didn't say it, but I could tell, and he sent home a lot more money than he made as a Sergeant. When I questioned him, he told me that he made it playing cards."

"He was a lousy card player, Debbie. That's all I know. He never bluffed and his face always showed a good hand."

"You know more than that, Matt. I know now why you agreed to take me to the funeral today. You wanted to see if I knew something about Tommy and Paulie, but I think you know more than I do."

"You don't know anything right now, Debbie, and if you look at my car you can guess that it would be better to keep it that way."

Debbie didn't say a word on the way home, and I was comfortable with that, since I didn't want to answer any more questions. We pulled into her driveway, sitting there for a long minute.

"Do you want to come in and have a beer? My parents aren't home, and you need to wash off some of that grease and dirt."

Leaning over to wipe my face, she kept her body pressed to mine. I didn't like how good it felt. Her breasts brushed my arm, lingering there for a long, erotic moment. I didn't pull away, which made me wonder where my head was at, but this was getting too weird.

"Thanks, Debbie, but I have to get to work. I'll see ya sometime, okay."

"I'm holding you to that promise, Matt, and another thing…"

"Yea what, Deb?'

"If you find out something bad about Paulie, I don't want to know. I want to keep my memories as they are, and being killed in the war was bad enough."

"The bad has already happened, Debbie, and we can't do a thing to change it, but the why—now that's another issue. Why do we have to fight this war?"

"Does it really matter why? Do you think that we'll ever find a reason that makes sense to the average person? He's away from me forever until I die. Why doesn't change a thing for me or for Paulie."

"It has to matter, Deb, or else what's the use, and the why is just something that I always need to know. The why might be important for the next guy, and who knows what guy will be next. It might be me. I gotta go."

She cried as she left the car, and I bit my lip while watching her walk off with her head down; her posture exhibiting a defeat by life that I had never seen in her until that day. I was scared, but when I felt threatened I had to fight back or I would self-destruct. I had never been the running away type of person. I needed to find out who was following me and why. The man with the sunglasses was obviously the eyes and ears of whoever was behind this, or maybe he was the main man.

I changed my mind out of guilt and went back to drink a beer with Debbie. She would be lonely for a long time until she could find someone else that needed help managing his life. Before I left, Debbie handed me a picture of Paulie with his unit in Vietnam, kissing me long and hard, her beer-moistened tongue trying to find its way into my mouth. It could have gone farther, but I didn't let it. I was way beyond Debbie's management skills, and the timing was definitely wrong. The bodies were starting to pile up, and I didn't want mine to be next. The picture stayed in the envelope as I drove back to New Haven. *Let it lie*, my inner voice said, but maybe there wouldn't be a choice.

Chapter 6

As I arrived at my apartment, there wasn't a spot to park, so I pulled the car around the corner to an empty lot. The street contained numerous houses that rented to college students, and many of them had returned to school that morning. The flurry of activity raised my spirits until I remembered that I had to work later that afternoon. Some of the neighbors were in the process of moving in, others were drinking beer on their stoops, and a few guys were tossing a football on the street. I exchanged greetings with some old friends; met a couple of new freshmen, bullshitted for awhile, and then headed in to get ready for work.

"Kronchek! My boy is home! Time for some hoop, baby. Let's go. You and I are heading to the park right now, so get your basketball shit on. Move it, dickhead!"

Leo had returned to school full of his typical fury, his loud voice making my nervous body jump two feet back. A five-foot-eight, one hundred and seventy-pound block of psychotic energy that would never take no for an answer to one of his proposals. He kept his blond hair short, and as roommates, there was no better example of Mutt and Jeff in New Haven. We met on the first day of college at a freshman picnic, becoming instant friends. He was one of the few people that could draw me from the barriers that I had erected around myself.

Leo was generous, fiercely loyal, gregarious and totally rash. I never understood how he survived during the summer, because at school, I had to think for the two of us. Incredibly, I served as the brains and the voice of reason in our partnership. He reminded me a little of my old friend Mike, but where Mike would plan his trouble; Leo would just stumble in to it and need to be rescued or fight his way out.

"Leo, you're back. Hey, I'm sorry about the room, but I've been busy and—"

"And you're a slob, Kronchek. End of story, pig. Come on, hurry up. I've been waiting for two hours. Schultz said you went to a funeral. I thought they buried Paulie the other day."

"This was a different one, Leo. Remember that bully Tommy Combs I told you about, the one who hassled me unmercifully when I was a kid? He iced himself on smack a couple of days ago, and my mother forced me to take Paulie's girlfriend to the funeral. I never knew it, but Tommy and Paulie were in Vietnam together."

"I thought you hated that Combs kid, Kronchek. What were doing with Paulie's girlfriend at his funeral? Getting your rocks off? What's that lipstick stain on your shirt?"

"Look, pervert, it's a long story and I'm sorry to disappoint your sick imagination, but there was no romance involved. The girl was crying, and her makeup smeared on my shirt. I can't play ball today because I have to go work in an hour. I need some time to get ready. It's been a bad week, and I don't need any shit from the hospital."

"And you won't get any, Kronchek. You don't have to be in work until ten. The head nurse called and asked if you could sub in psychiatric for the third shift, and I told her no problem. I said that you would be a natural and would blend right in if you weren't wearing the white uniform. She didn't seem amused. She's a very serious woman with no sense of humor, real stuffy like she had a cork up her ass."

Oh shit! I had forgotten about being a floater for the weekend, which meant I could draw any floor. Working in psychiatric on third shift was brutal, not to mention that I had class first thing in the morning.

"Shit, Leo! Why did you do that? I don't want to work up there, especially at night. It's a full moon tonight, and the patients will be all cranked up. I won't be able to get any sleep before my class tomorrow. I don't mind sleeping in school, but not on the first day."

It was like talking to a statue or a totally deaf person.

"Hoop, Kronchek. We're playing ball down at Goffe Street. I've got some new moves to show the brothers. I've been working on them all summer, and I'm dying to try them out on some decent players. Everybody sucks in my hometown."

"Fine, Leo, but I have to get something to eat. I guess it's too late to change my shift at this point. Don't mess with my schedule again or I'll start dating your sister. Oh, that's right, she's already dating you. Sorry."

"Screw you, Kronchek. That wasn't a date. I just took her to her junior prom so she would have someone to go with. God, you're weird. Get ready, asshole, and leave my sister out of it."

Leo could be irrepressible when his mind was made up. It would have taken a call from the Governor to get me out of playing basketball that day. We enjoyed similar activities, but were complete opposites in our reactions to life. Leo loved to clown around and piss people off to the extreme. Again, he reminded me a little of Mike, except that Leo loved to fight. A good fistfight was not a serious issue to him. He barely lost a brutal battle to a guy twice his size at the playground last year, but still came up smiling, with blood running down his face and his nose off at a forty-five degree angle. Leo wanted to keep going, but the guy thought he was nuts and walked away shaking his head. Leo claimed victory, although his nose was broken and needed twenty-three stitches above his eye. He refused to go to the hospital until we finished the game.

With me, fighting was vicious and serious. Once the violence was aroused in me; I couldn't turn it off. Long ago, I learned the hard way to fight for my life, and I never took the time to make the distinction in a threatening situation. Leo told me that I possessed the mentality of a killer. I was one person that he would never prod into a physical fight, and I would never get physical with him because of my suppressed anger. If Leo made me angry, I would walk away. Leo was my best friend in college, and we watched each other's backs.

Leo drove us to the Goffe Street playground in his beat-up old Saab. The car had about one hundred and fifty thousand miles on it, but still purred like a kitten. My car had been moved to the front of the house so it would look as if I was home to prying eyes. Hopefully, if anyone were watching the house, the presence of my car would keep them occupied in surveillance.

Goffe Street Park was the gathering place for the best basketball players in New Haven, and most likely we would be the only two white players at the courts. The first time we had gone there as freshmen, no one would pick us to play, so we had to work hard to convince a few of the black guys to join our team. Respect took a long time to earn, and longer if you were white and unknown.

We played well, but lost frequently because our teammates were often the bottom of a very talented barrel. The local guys knew how to stack a team. A lightning quick player with a mediocre shot, Leo was an instinctual passer and knew just when to give me the ball. I could jump with most of them, and we began to win as we solidified our two-man game of cutting, screening and passing. Along the way, we absorbed some of the spectacular playground game, which supplemented our solid fundamentals.

Surprised that we possessed a decent level of ability, some of the regulars tried physical intimidation in the form of elbows, tripping, and pushing in order to test our commitment. We gave it back in equal measure, never losing our cool, excepting Leo's occasional fights. After three years, we had nicknames and limited acceptance-Leo was the Lion, and I had become Kron.

Arriving at the park during the high heat of the afternoon, only a dozen players were at the main court. The larger crowds trickled in after the sun went down, and the games would continue under the lights until sunrise the next day. The temperate, late-summer morning had given way to shimmering heat. A sea of black faces surrounded us, some gawking at our whiteness, but most just going about their business. People were having picnics, walking their dogs, sitting on porches, and loitering in front of the Red Dog Lounge, a seedy bar that sat diagonally across the street. As long as you were there for basketball, your race was not an issue.

Everyone was pretty cool, but we knew enough not to go near the Red Dog. The thugs pushing dope in front wouldn't have allowed us on the sidewalk. White people drove up to the Red Dog to buy their drugs, but stayed in their cars. Money went out the window, and a little bag went in, all in a matter of seconds. If you got some bad shit, you didn't go back to complain, and you didn't leave your car for any reason. We understood the rules, and following the rules was the price of admission. Our only purpose was to play basketball, so whatever went down across the street, was of no concern to us.

"Yo, look, it's the white boys coming down to get schooled again. You boys lost or something? The library is down the street."

"James, what the hell's happening? You better finish up your game so we can give a demonstration of some real ball to the people around here. You're putting everybody to sleep in the neighborhood with the air-ball shit that you're throwing up," I said while pointing to a snoring drunk on the bench.

"Bite it, Kron. That bum bastard could sleep through an atomic bomb he's so drunk. We're putting on a show, so wait your turn."

James laughed, slapping me five as he returned to the game. Leo and I watched them play while recruiting a team for the next game. When our turn finally came, we stayed on the court for at least an hour. Winners kept playing until they lost or quit, and we couldn't lose that afternoon. We had a young kid on our team who proved to be an unbelievable player and shooter for a fourteen-year-old. He later went on to play in the NBA, and that's no lie.

Two hours in the heat had wiped us out, so we sat down on the grass with James, drinking sodas that we bought from a local street vendor. We all went to the same college, but James had grown up in New Haven and commuted to school while living at home. He sat between Leo and me, and from above we must have looked like a reverse Oreo tucked into the mass of black bodies.

"I didn't come here to bullshit. I've been sitting on my ass all summer. They need another player. You going wait for me, Kronchek?"

"We're in your car, Leo. It's not like I have a choice, unless I want to walk home, and besides, you'd be afraid if I left you here alone."

James cracked a slight smile when Leo told me to screw myself as he forced his way into the game. It was fun to watch him from the sidelines; a rare opportunity for me. Leo loved basketball and competition, and he played hoop with an enthusiastic cockiness that fit well in the city. I laughed as he schooled a young kid who had never seen him play, falsely reading him as a slow white boy. Leo put his head down, bulled his way to the basket, and threw in a floater for two over a six-foot-five guy. He danced around the court like a baby ox, pointing at the other team as he put the ball in play again.

"You ready for school tomorrow, James? This is our last year, and it hit me the other day that I don't have a clue as what to do after graduation. It freaked me out that this might be it. Playtime will be over. I've kind of gotten comfortable with this college life."

"It could be over for me already, Kron. I might have to drop out and get a full-time job."

"Drop out! Are you crazy? They'll draft you before you get to your doorstep. Man, why would you want to do something like that? You only have a year to go for your degree. What's going on?"

"My girl, you know that girl that I'm with at school all the time? She might be pregnant and wants to have the baby if she is."

"I'm not sure that I've ever met her, but James, it won't make any difference. They'll never give you a chance to work. You'll be in Vietnam, and then what good will quitting school do for your baby?"

"Even if I get drafted, the Army pays you, and that takes care of your family. I'm not having my kid grow up without a daddy. I did, and it's not going to happen again in my house. I fucked up, but I'm not letting my kid pay for it. We're going to have to get married, Vietnam or no Vietnam."

"Your baby is going to have a dead daddy if you quit school. Think about it. Even if you survive, you might come back messed up. I see it every day at the VA hospital, and it ain't pretty. A lot of those guys aren't statistically dead, but they're mentally wasted, or so crippled that they will never work again or engage in life."

Social Problems 101 had left the classroom, entering my life with a slap of reality. James believed that he was doing the right thing, but it could get him killed or leave him a psychological basket case. I had nothing else to offer him. His problems were beyond the range of my experience. School was a refuge from Vietnam, a protective blanket that would soon be taken away. It was an unfair system, but I harbored no guilt because it was an unfair war perpetuated by our government. My enemies were Nixon and Kissinger, not Ho Chi Minh.

Leo's recklessness and overconfidence led his team to defeat, so he motioned for us to join him in the next game.

"Okay, Leo, one more, but then I have to get ready for work."

James hopped up to play, with basketball always providing a valuable distraction from our problems. Before we could join Leo; however, a verbal barrage erupted behind our backs.

"James, what the hell are you doing down here? Momma's been looking for you all day. Get your black ass home right now! Your little girlfriend has been at the house since noon telling Momma what you two have been up to, and you're here at the park playing games like a little kid. You messed up big time."

We turned toward the static, and the voice fit the face I knew so well from campus protests and meetings. Wanda Simpson, the campus civil rights activist, was apparently James' sister. I had never made the connection until that moment. James appeared to shrink by half in the face of her onslaught, even though he stood at least a foot taller than her. A huge Afro made up at least one third of her height, and it looked as if her hair would topple her over if she were to lean to one side. The entrenched inner city matriarchy gave Wanda an authority that would not be denied.

As Wanda ripped James a new asshole, it began to attract the attention of the bystanders on the court. They laughed at James and shouted insults to Wanda, so I kept my eyes to the ground to avoid being noticed, just as I remembered black people doing in Bellington. The screaming excited Leo, however, so he walked over to join in, not wanting to miss any action.

We played ball at Goffe Street for the competition and style of play, but it also provided me with a rough idea of how a black person might feel in a white school or white workplace. When I was at Goffe Street, I did my best not to stand out; being afraid that someone would question my right to be there because of my race.

Wanda, of course, noticed. "Whatcha doing with this white boy, James? Whatcha doing down here, honky Kronchek, buying drugs? You selling drugs, James? If you are, I'm going beat your black ass all the way home."

James didn't dare talk back. He knew better, but I didn't. Wanda and I had a long history of discord from school. The odd thing was that we basically shared the same values, but her aggressive approach to every minor problem ruined any chance for compromise with opposing points of view. We sat on several committees together at school and clashed over technique many times. I didn't like it, but I felt that change needed to be spoon-fed to bigots, making them believe that it was their idea to change a situation, but Wanda made people swallow issues whole or not at all. Her opinion was that if you were not for her cause, then you were against it. I did admire her energy and concern, but she made it difficult to be in the same room with her.

"Screw off, Wanda. I'm at a park with a basketball. What do you think I'm doing here? You want the right to go where you please, but white people are up to something if they come into your neighborhood. Talk about racism. Shit, James, I think your sister is in the black KKK. Did you leave your robe home, Wanda?"

Anger had pushed caution aside, forcing my eyes from the ground. My mind braced itself for a brutal verbal barrage. She possessed cuttingly cruel intelligence, so I intended to press my initial advantage, when suddenly a vision of bemused beauty standing behind Wanda struck me dumb.

When two members of the opposite sex are attracted to each other, there is one perfect moment, the first instance when nothing else has weight. I had become so jaded by my life, so suspicious of everyone and everything, but in that blink of infatuation, the world became perfect. When eyes meet eyes for the first time; there exists no history, and therefore no problems. Disagreements haven't been born, flaws not yet discovered, and the pain that is inherent in every relationship resides in an unfathomable distant future.

She had to be at least five foot ten, with long, black silky hair falling halfway down her gorgeous back. To me her figure looked perfect, with cut-off shorts revealing lean, shapely legs and a firm, proportional ass. But all that sexual beauty stood second to her smile. Perfect white teeth were surrounded by full lips and framed by luminescent black skin. I had always been attracted to dark-skinned women, but this girl was jet black, black as the night, and I felt whiter than white just like the line in the song, "Brother Louie." She was smiling at me, at me.

I felt like an idiot for screaming at Wanda, and suddenly there was this burning desire to be Wanda's friend. I had to meet this girl.

"Wanda, you haven't introduced me to your friend. It must have been an oversight on your part, because I'm sure you would never be that rude."

"Go home, Kronchek. This girl doesn't want to meet your white-trash ass. Take your little clown friend out of here when you go. James, get your ass moving home. Now! Mamma said right now!"

Wanda grabbed my vision by the arm, walking down the street while cursing my name, yelling back at James every ten feet, and for good measure she told Leo to fuck off as they crossed the street. He gave her the finger at the same time he drove to the basket. When the ball went in, he shook his ass in her direction, performing a weird victory dance of sorts, making him a hero to the guys on the court who wouldn't dare mess with Wanda on their own. Half the park was on their knees from laughter, and I couldn't help cracking a smile myself. Leo was just the relief I needed from all this death and war.

"Kron, I gotta go. I can't let Monica face Mamma and Wanda alone. I need time to sort this out."

"Shit, James, I'm sorry. I didn't know that was your girlfriend with Wanda. How come you never told me Wanda was your sister?"

"Wanda's just looking out for me, Kron. Ever since I can remember she kept me straight. If it wasn't for her I would never be in college, but I thought you knew that we were related. That wasn't Monica with my sister, but that girl's not for you."

The heat of my quick temper rose twenty degrees in a flash.

"Why not, James? Because I'm white?"

"Easy, Kron, of course not. I'm not that way. She's for nobody around here that wants to stay healthy. That was Angela Williams, Ronald Williams' little sister."

"She didn't look so little to me. How old is she? She's gorgeous, and who the hell is Ronald Williams and what's his goddamn problem?"

"Angela's eighteen, but still off limits to you and anyone else that wants to live. You remember Ronald Williams, the tackle on the football team when we were freshmen? You know the guy I'm talking about? Huge monster, strong and mean as hell."

"Yeah, I remember, but so what? What ever happened to him anyway, and what's the issue with guys dating his sister?"

"Ronald flunked out, got drafted, and ended up in Nam. He's the nastiest guy I've ever met, and there are some bad brothers in our neighborhood. He put out the word that if anyone even looked at his sister, he would make a jigsaw puzzle out of their ass. This is a hard neighborhood, but nobody is harder than big Ronald. Angela hasn't had a date in her life, not even a chaperoned one. Forget about it, Kron. Just trust me on this one. It's not worth it."

"Come on, she's a grown woman, and what could he do about it. He's ten thousand miles away. Besides, I only want to talk to her, maybe ask her out for dinner, you know. She's so hot, and her smile, James. What a smile!"

"You know, Kron, you've always been decent for a white guy, and who couldn't help but like Leo, but I've got enough problems of my own. Let it go. You're on bad ground with this one. She may look like a grown woman, but she's been treated like a little girl her whole life. Ronald's due home in few days. A guy from Nam told me that he's changed, and for the worse. I need to go. I'll probably see you at school, if I'm still in school."

Well, James took the magic out of that moment. I also had enough problems of my own, and another person looking to kill me wasn't something that I needed. The forbidden fruit angle; however, made her all the more appealing. Once someone told me not to do something, it was the one thing that I wanted to do.

"Yea, good luck, James, and don't quit school. Thanks for the advice."

"Don't thank me unless you take it, Kron. From what my sister says, you don't quit easily or listen well. Wanda appreciates a habit like that, but in this case it could make you dead. Don't fuck with that guy. No woman is worth having him on your ass."

James ran from the park in the direction of his sister's exit. I drank my soda while waiting for Leo to finish up his game. Basketball and Angela Williams had pushed the ghosts of Bellington away for a moment, but as Leo's car left the park, I checked the mirror to see if anyone was following. I had actually forgotten for a short time about the warning that I had received at the cemetery, and a lack of focus could prove to be deadly. No one was behind us, so I figured that maybe if I let the cause of Paulie's death drop, they might leave me alone. But could I let it go? I needed to for my health, but the itch of having to know began working its way beneath my common sense and fear. That itch might be the last thing I felt on earth if I didn't learn to ignore it.

Chapter 7

Ronald Williams walked down the steps of the plane, carefully surveying the tarmac for a familiar face. He hadn't set foot on American soil for a year, and it felt very good to be back. He had never appreciated his country before, but after Vietnam, the scene before him was like an asphalt version of heaven.

Other soldiers had relatives and girlfriends waiting to greet them with hugs and kisses, but Ronald hadn't told his family the exact time that he would arrive home. It had been purposeful. He would see his family in due time, but right now business occupied his mind.

As he watched the happy families, he wondered if they understood what had come home to them. They would find out soon enough that the person they had known before Vietnam wasn't the same one that had just gotten off the plane. Vietnam changed everyone, and very seldom in a way that made their family feel comfortable. In a few days they would wonder about the stranger living in their house. The children would hear frightening screams in the middle of the night. A wife would wake up to a husband drenched in sweat, shaking from deep-seated residual fear, or a reawakening malaria attack coursing throughout his body. You could take a man out of Vietnam, but it wasn't easy to take Vietnam out of the man.

He wanted to kiss the ground and thank God for being out of that hellhole, but he wasn't the overtly emotional type, and besides, the men unloading the body bags from the cargo-bay of another plane held his complete attention. One of those men was his contact, and Ronald wanted to connect up quickly. He would leave for New Haven when things were set up for business. This was the first test of his idea for smuggling drugs to the States, and it had to be perfect.

The base served as one of the main terminals for the casualties of Vietnam. From here, they would be shipped to their hometowns for burial, but not until selected ones were relieved of their precious cargo. Putting drugs in body bags had been thought of before, and maybe even attempted, but the government generally dismissed the idea as a wartime legend. Ronald's plan had become reality with this flight, and he had come home with the single-minded intention of taking control and expanding the business. He would set up his operation before he left for New Haven, explaining the process to his contact and starting the flow of drugs from Vietnam. They had used many methods of transporting the drugs, with some of it making it through, but too many packages were lost as the Feds caught on to all the little tricks.

Ronald checked in with the C.O., receiving permission to look around before he headed home. As he entered the morgue, the cold air of the embalming room provided a pleasant contrast to the heat wave that the Eastern Seaboard had been experiencing most of the summer. He finally spotted Henry Thompson, Ronald's main man on the base.

"Ronald! I don't believe that you're finally here. You must be one happy bastard to get out of that shit hole alive. I heard about the Wops getting close to your skimming operation, and that you had to play it cool. Did you get my message that the Feds were sniffing around the base last month."

"Yea, I got the word, Henry my man, but the shipment of stiffs that came in today will put us back in business. The Feds have nobody left to talk to, and don't have a clue as to which way to go next. They did a routine check of several bases, but they were just fishing. I've heard the theories and rumors about the body bags, but my sources tell me that the intelligence boys believe that it's just bullshit. When they reluctantly checked the leads, they never looked in the bags of the guys that had been blown apart. The word is that they don't believe the stories. My guy in

New Haven told me that the last potential leak bought it the other night. Did you hear about it?"

"Yea, the grapevine said that he checked out on some bad smack. The cops didn't even investigate it as a homicide, but I don't see how that gets the Wops off our backs."

"It changes everything because the two white boys were the only witnesses left. Everyone else is involved up to their ass, so they're not going to talk. We're up and running again, but with a more efficient method and a larger volume. We'll take it slow at first, but this time we're selling the stuff ourselves. There will be a lot more money in it for you, Henry."

"One dollar or a million doesn't help you when you're dead, Ronald. They must be thinking that someone will try again. The Mob wants all side operations cleaned up and shut down because small timers will get sloppy, and they don't want any more attention drawn to the drug problems coming out of Vietnam. From what you've told me, we're taking a big chance with all the players involved. If you're right about the CIA being in bed with the Mob in Nam, then we could get it from both ends. Those guys usually don't spook that easily, but the word is that if anyone crosses them, it won't be pretty."

"If they want to spook, let 'em. The way I see it, the FBI has no idea what the CIA is doing in Nam. Same government, but they don't share intelligence. If the story ever got out, the press would have a field day, giving the protesters more ammunition against the War. The FBI has caught a whiff of something going on that they aren't privy to, and they're pissed off royally. The last thing the FBI needs is some public relations nightmare that would add to the protesters' cause. It just goes to prove how fucked up this war is. Do you know how many of our guys are hooked on smack in Nam courtesy of the CIA? There are thousands, Henry, thousands in Saigon alone.

"All this came to me by accident. I was drinking with this jumper pilot one night in a Saigon dive. I hooked him up with a couple of girls and some cheap booze. He gets really loaded and starts a drunken confessional like I'm his priest or minister. The guy goes into detail about all kinds of weird stuff concerning his missions. Information that could get you killed, but I saw money in it. Tells me that he works for The Agency deliverying guns to the warlords in the Golden Triangle, mostly in Burma. The warlords keep the Commies out of their area using our weapons, and then pay for the guns with heroin. The CIA dumps some of it in Nam, and the Mafia smuggles the balance to the States with most of it landing in the ghettos to fuck up black people. Can you believe that shit? The CIA is dealing drugs, and the FBI is trying to stop it with no idea of how it's getting here. One agency is spending coin to bring it in, and the other is wasting money and manpower to keep it out.

"After that night, the pilot and I went out a few more times. He was impressed with my knowledge of the Saigon area and certain access that I had. He hooked me up with a side job unloading the planes, moving the product around Saigon and getting the excess ready for the States. It was risky, but I started to skim off the top. Being somebody's fall guy for peanuts was a role I never played well. My guys were moving a decent volume in the city, but I could see a bigger potential back home where it was worth far more. We started to send it home in packages with returning soldiers, sometimes mailing it from Hong Kong when guys went on leave. Our operation was pretty tight, but other people tried copying us and got careless, which meant more packages started to get checked. As you know, the flow trickled down, and the investigations drew attention to our business from our Italian friends.

"We had to shut down for awhile to save our asses. Things had hit a low point about the time I started working in the morgue, but that's when I got the idea to ship it home in the body bags. I remembered that you worked on this base stateside, and were always a guy that appreciated making good money. The dope that we sold for peanuts in Vietnam became a fortune in the States, and now we're able to ship a lot more volume. Nobody checks the dead, not even the narc dogs."

"Look, Ronald, I don't want to stop making money, but the Wops found out that the Italian kid started moving the stuff into the States on his own. I heard that they would have killed him if he hadn't been the nephew of some big Capo out of New York. We have to stop because they only give one warning, if any at all. Are you sure your Italian buddy didn't blow the whistle on us the first time?"

"Stop dealing! Bullshit! I've got my Mamma and my little brothers to take care of. Plus, my sister Angela is starting college tomorrow. What do you think, Henry? You think I can help them by flipping burgers for shit pay? I never did any work in school because I was the big star. The coaches kissed my ass and even did my term papers so I could pass. I never knew shit except playing football, but my football days are over. If people want to get fucked up on drugs, what do I care? I just want a piece of the action. Why shouldn't we get our share? They're going to get high whether we supply the stuff or not."

"Christ, I know what you mean, Ronald, but those people don't fuck around. They kill people who don't do as they say, and I'll ask you again. Do you trust the Wop kid?"

"I don't trust anyone, Henry, not even you, but he was nailed by his uncle because he tried to move the stuff in his hometown. Somebody ratted on him and his uncle cracked down. They don't even know about us—that's what a stand-up guy he is. He covered our asses completely. Told his uncle he was sorry and that he would give it up, so the old man let him off the hook for one time, and one time only."

"So why would he start again? He must understand that even his uncle will waste him if he gets nailed. He can't be too bright."

Ronald thought about it for a moment before answering.

"That's the thing, Henry. He's an ambitious, intelligent bastard, and doesn't intend to work his way up the ladder. The risk seems to mean nothing to him. It's like he's been in the crime business his whole life. I hate to admit it, but I'm more afraid than he is. Nothing seems to worry him. I don't think he's ever considered having a real job."

"So if he's not afraid, Ronald, why does he need us? We're just a couple of niggers to share his profit."

"Smack doesn't sell in white neighborhoods as he found out the hard way, and he sticks out like Frosty the Snowman in the ghetto. It would get back to his uncle again in a minute. I need you to unload the drugs from the bodies, and he needs me to move the junk for him on the streets. If he puts a few layers between himself and the drugs, then it's harder to tie the business to him."

There was an angle that Henry couldn't quite figure out.

"So what does he contribute for his share? We're taking the risks from the Feds and the Mob, while he's collecting the cash and hiding behind our asses."

"Well, Henry, it seems like he's already taken care of that little problem up in Bellington, and where do think all the start-up cash is coming from? It takes money to build a network, money that we don't have yet. Also, he's going to keep the Italians off our backs this time."

"Keep them off of our backs? He can't even keep them off his ass!" Henry said in amazement.

"Look, Henry, the guy is really slick. We'll have enough cheap product to start up other guys in business; small neighborhood routes run by desperate junkies. When the Mob gets suspicious, we set one of them up to get nailed. The Wops will think that they closed things down, but then it will begin again. These suckers will create a maze that will protect us from the long arms of the Mob."

Henry rubbed his eyes, taking a deep breath before responding. "I'm in, Ronald. I became awful fond of that extra money, so no burger flipping for me either. What do you want me to do?"

Ronald smiled. Money moved everything: fear, shame, pride, and loyalty.

"You pick one guy that you can trust and that will follow orders. We'll explain things to him together; make him understand the consequences and the rewards before I leave. If he even thinks of talking or skimming, I'll kill him. He will believe that when I'm done, and I know that you understand me completely. The dope will be in the body bags that are marked *closed casket.* Those are the bodies that have been blown to hell. Since you are the presiding officer here in the morgue, you can make sure that the marked bags are to be processed in your section and by your guy. If any gets by you, they won't be opened again anyway, but I don't like losing product."

"How are we going to get the drugs off the base, Ronald? Security is pretty lax, but they do check things occasionally."

"You know that food truck that services this end of the base for break?"

"Yeah, the food is stale and the coffee tastes like piss."

"Well, the food won't be getting any better because we bought the business through a third party. When you go out for break, you'll drop the bags in the trash chute. I might even be the driver at times. They'll never check garbage, and besides, security is light on this end of the base. The Army isn't too worried about anyone stealing dead bodies."

Henry was truly impressed. "Brilliant, Ronald. I have to admit it's a good plan, but whose idea was it?"

"I came up with the body bag idea, but everything else was from the Wop. Do you see what I mean about him? Show me a guy that wants to make some real cash, and then we're up and running again."

The two men walked out of the morgue to look for a greedy man. It didn't take them very long at all.

Chapter 8

After we returned home from the park, Leo went to a bar with some of our friends for a pre-school celebration, but I couldn't go with them. There were a few hours left before work, with enough time for a shower and maybe a short nap. The humidity and physical activity had drenched my clothes, with my sweat-saturated T-shirt clinging to my back and chest. My muscles, having been retrained for work in the hospital, ached from two hours of basketball. I wallowed in a long, cool shower in a vain attempt to stop the perspiration that continued its unabated flow from my armpits and neck.

After drying off and grabbing some shorts, I flipped on the fan over my bed and attempted to lie down for a moment in order to sort things out in my head. I stared at a poster above my bed that showed soldiers from both sides of a conflict facing each other without their rifles. The poster read, "*Old men start wars and young men die in them. War will end when young men throw down their weapons and refuse to fight.*" Any war was horrible enough, but senseless, avoidable conflicts that robbed young people of their future were inexplicable to me. I was sinking into deep-rooted depression.

The slow hum of the worn-out fan created an electrical mantra, the exhaustion controlling my usually hyper body, rendering it motionless and allowing my mind to settle into a semi-meditative state. My libido jumped at this opportunity as it attempted to encourage my mind to work out a strategy for meeting Angela Williams. Her physical beauty and apparent innocence had captivated me that afternoon. Being a jaded cynic, I found myself surprisingly drawn to her light.

The human libido is definitely the least rational fellow of Freud's psyche theory. It completely blocked out James' warning, and didn't even take into consideration the almost impossible hurdles of a racially mixed relationship, especially one between a white man and a black woman. There were black men at school with white girlfriends, but I had never seen the opposite. Not to mention that I was already involved with another female, plus the interaction with Debbie that morning.

My libido recognized, but ignored the warning from James that should have produced fear and the logic of being cautious. It took advantage of my state of mind; leaving Freud's other friends to deal with life-threatening issues, and countering rational behavior by flashing flawless images of Angela through my mind's eye. We were holding hands in one scenario with my arm around her as we walked in the park. Soon we were kissing on a bench, but without warning, a freeze frame of Tommy Combs' corpse in his bathroom popped into my head.

Mr. Libido vacated the premises without saying goodbye, driven out by my deepest fears, abandoning my now limp and sublimated passion. Paulie startled me from behind and grabbed my arm, forcing me to Tommy's bathroom window. He pointed down, sending an intense chill coursing up my spine, numbing my brain and immobilizing my body, leaving me with no choice but to look. As I peered out the window, which had suddenly become a cement bridge, I could see railroad tracks below me in the dark. It was 1961 again, and Nellie Cabrera's body lay splattered on the rails, her form outlined by the wooden cross ties and worn metal tracks.

I had relived that tragedy in my dreams and in my mind a thousand times, but this time she lifted her broken body from the tracks, rising up to the window with her shattered, bloodied face. "Help me, Matt. Please help me."

Someone jerked me away from my distant past, but it wasn't to spare me from the horror. Paulie had me by the shirt, his body shredded by shrapnel, a gaping hole where his stomach should have been, and a single solitary tear that ran down his one remaining eye. Half a mouth pleaded to me. "Help me, Matt. Please help me. I want to come home. Please bring me home."

As I wrenched free from the tattered Paulie, Tommy grasped me by the leg as he sat on the toilet seat with a needle dangling from his arm. "Help me, Kronchek, you fuck. You wouldn't listen. You never listened to anyone. You're useless to all of us."

They all chanted "help me" in unison as someone pounded on Tommy's bathroom door. "Open up, open up, Kronchek. We know you're in there. Open the door!"

Bang, bang, bang, the pounding increased until my eyes opened to my bedroom. I must have fallen asleep, but it had seemed so real. *Bang, bang.* "Open up!"

Someone was knocking on the apartment door, which I had locked as a precaution, and as I went to check the noise, my body dripped sweat. My hair and shorts were completely soaked, and I had the chills on a ninety-degree day. I couldn't stop shaking.

"Is that you, Leo? Don't you ever remember your key? Leo! Who's out there? If you're screwing around, it's not funny. You woke me up."

"Mr. Kronchek, would you please open the door. We need to speak to you."

An effective method of frightening me and gaining my attention was to call me mister. All my life, mister meant that I had trouble on my plate.

"Who is it and what do you want?"

"FBI, Mr. Kronchek. We need to ask you a couple of questions. It will only take a few minutes."

"Yea, right, the FBI. Pretty goddamn funny, Leo, but tell your friends nice try. I'm dead tired and you have to mess with me. The first day back at school and you're already wearing on my ass. Go away. I have to get ready for work. You're a big asshole."

"It's not a prank, Mr. Kronchek. We can come back later with a warrant if you won't let us in."

The voices on the other side of the door sounded serious and official, possessing the guttural timbre of older, mature men. A hint of anger and impatience imbedded in their last sentence made me realize that it was definitely not one of Leo's jokes. If it was a prank, it was much too sophisticated for Leo.

I opened the door a crack, leaving the chain hooked and keeping my weight against the wood.

"Okay, I'll bite. Let me see some ID."

The door opening framed two wallets with FBI cards, the photographs appearing to match the faces of the men outside. It definitely wasn't something Leo had thought up, but who could they be? They might be fakes, but if they had wanted to hurt me, they could have busted through the door or waited until I left for work to nail me. I flipped the chain, cautiously letting them in with curiosity outvoting paranoia.

As the men moved deliberately through the opening, they efficiently surveyed the room taking in every detail as they covered each other's back. They had a routine and went about it in a professional manner. Wearing neatly pressed dark blue suits with the jackets unbuttoned, it was meant for me to notice the holster straps and gun handles. Their highly polished black shoes glowed like radioactive ebony in the dusty, unkempt apartment. One of them put his sunglasses back on, and it became evident that he would be the bad cop, if necessary. Both seemed incapable of smiling, and their expressionless demeanors made it difficult to read anything from their faces, which was the whole point of their training, I suppose. Their positions were such that I couldn't watch both of them at the same time.

This was not a good situation for me. I had problems with authority in general, and my stance toward the FBI at that time was at a high level of disdain. As a kid, I had admired the FBI, but lately the agents were serving as Director J. Edgar Hoover's personal domestic spy agency; prying into every aspect of American life. They maintained files on movie stars, government officials, and college students. Anybody who was anybody had a file, and even anybody who was nobody could have a file. To me, they represented the indigenous arm of the Vietnam War machine, and now they were standing in my living room.

"Are you Matthew Kronchek from Bellington, Connecticut, and is anyone else present in the apartment?"

"I think you already know who I am, and no, there isn't anyone else home at the moment, but I expect people to return soon if you would like to wait."

The Fed with the sunglasses re-chained the door, creating a strong feeling of insecurity. A good move by them because it grated on my already tender nervous system. I felt trapped and threatened, which started to activate a fast-twitch muscle response. My body's systems had become connected to a hair trigger, conditioned by past experience and heightened by recent problems.

"I'll ask you once more, are you Matthew Kronchek from Bellington, Connecticut?"

The man with the shades enunciated his query with an irritated firmness, which did nothing but piss me off. Still rattled from my dream, it was disconcerting having these clowns in my face. It was another kind of nightmare. The FBI represented the government, with the government representing the War, and the War had taken Paulie. They were in my apartment, giving me an attitude and invading my sole private space, while irritating me with robotic questions that they already had the answers to. They frightened me, but I was also angry, and sometimes I had trouble separating the two.

"Yea, I'm Matt Kronchek. What's going on? Did I commit some federal crime? Spit it out because I'm going to be late for work, and unlock the door if you don't mind. I don't like strangers screwing with my door."

Mr. Shades took an aggressive step in my direction, but the other guy held him in check with a gesture. That would be Mr. Good Cop.

"Easy, Agent Lloyd, the kid's a little nervous. His attitude is understandable and predictable according to his file here."

"I'm not nervous, Agent what's-your-name. I don't appreciate being rousted when I'm late for work, and then locked in my apartment by a couple of junior G-men. That's a pretty thick file you've got there. I haven't lived long enough to merit such a voluminous write up. What's the deal? You guys been going through my underwear drawer? I guess you already know that Ho Chi Minh is my first cousin. I confess. I'm a Commie."

"Agent Francis to you, and why do you have to be such a hard guy, Matt? Maybe your little college friends find you amusing, but we don't.

We need you to answer a few questions, and then maybe we can help you out a little in the bargain. Latching the door is for your own protection. Why did you have it locked?"

"You don't know me well enough to call me Matt, and why would I need your help or your protection? Whether I lock the door is my own business. If you haven't noticed, this isn't exactly Beverly Hills. I didn't do anything wrong, and besides, I have to get dressed. As I said, I'm late for work, and for once in my life I think I prefer Mr. Kronchek."

Agent Lloyd put his hand on my chest, impeding my exit from the room. I slapped it away, and he pinned me up against the wall by my shirt. My knee drove into his groin in a pure reaction of self-defense, dropping him fast and hard to the floor clutching his balls. I regretted kneeing him, knowing that I was screwed, but it was a reflex action. I had fought for my life once, and learned then that the margin for survival can be a nanosecond of hesitation. I turned to leave, hoping against any rational thought that they would back off, but stopped dead when a metal cylinder pressed firmly against my head. It had been seven years, but I knew what it was—a gun. I froze in place. They were serious about whatever they had come to question me about, and I was beginning to get an idea of what the topic would be.

"Sit down, Kronchek, before somebody gets hurt, specifically you!"

Agent Francis screamed in my face as he spun my shoulder into a chair, holding me in place with his forearm. He was a nice guy no longer and very strong.

He put the gun away, eased up the pressure on my chest and tapped the folder, a slight smile crossing his lips for an instant as he watched Lloyd massaging his nuts. He seemed to be enjoying Lloyd's misery just a bit, but was still all business.

"It's all in here, Kronchek. We should have expected your reaction. Every page from high school on: can't handle authority, disregards the rules, lack of respect for teachers, coaches, police, etc. Says here you were a good basketball player, but were kicked off the team for pushing the coach and flooding the gym with profanities.

"Big shit. That doesn't make me a criminal, and that coach was an asshole, a hypocrite who was cheating on his wife by screwing the English teacher on a weekly basis; all the while preaching to us about morals and commitment. Everyone on the team hated him, but they were afraid of his bullshit. He always pushed us around, but one day I pushed back and he couldn't handle it. If you checked, and I'm sure you did, you'll see that he was fired soon after that, and I was back on the team the next year when we went to the State Tournament. As your partner found out, I don't like to be pushed. Why don't you secret agents screw off and find some spies to hassle? I don't think basketball dropouts are high on the most wanted list."

I think Agent Lloyd would have enjoyed shooting me at that point, but he was still preoccupied with his aching testicles. It was amusing in retrospect, although at the time I was terrified of his reaction when he recovered. I was so focused on Lloyd that I wasn't prepared for their next revelation. Agent Francis turned a few more pages in the file.

"You're such a tough guy, Kronchek. Why don't you cut the rest of us imperfect beings a little slack? Did you feel so tough when you found that girl's body on the tracks back in '61? Probably was nothing to a hard guy like you."

I went ballistic, jumping to my feet right through the pressure of his arm.

"Don't go there! I was thirteen years old, and she was my friend! If you want trouble with me, you just pushed the right button! Get the fuck out of my house unless you have a warrant! Nobody discusses that with me, especially you!"

Agent Lloyd straightened up, signaling that he had recovered from my knee, and I noticed that he was about my height, but thirty pounds heavier and solid as a tree. I had gotten in a very lucky shot, but I wouldn't catch him off-guard again. His sneering smile as he circled around the chair told me that I could be in for a beating, but I figured that physical pain wasn't their forte. I sat down before he reached me, realizing that they weren't going away until they got what they came for.

Lloyd's voice oozed confidence and contempt as he took my file from Francis.

"You're a punk, Kronchek, and not too bright. We don't need a warrant to bring you in. You invited us in the house and then assaulted a federal agent. That's jail time right there, plus we have your signature on a least a dozen anti-government petitions. We could haul you in and hold you for suspicion of anarchy against the government."

"Those are anti-war petitions, Einstein. I'm not trying to overthrow the government. I just want the war to end, and you put your hands on me first."

He kept his cool through my insults as the smile lengthened. "Anti-war is anti-government, you unpatriotic hippie, and there are no witnesses for your version. I have Agent Francis. Do you want to go to jail and be some murderer's bitch?"

They had me, or at the very least they could make things extremely difficult. There were rumors that they could hold you for a long time if they wanted to make you miserable.

"What do you want from me? What could I possibly know that would interest you two or the government?"

Agent Francis resumed the questioning. "No more games and insults or we question you down at the office. You won't be going to work or school for a long time, and you'll need a good lawyer to get you out. We know that you were friends with Paulie Kovak, and that you attended his funeral on Saturday where you were observed speaking to Thomas Combs, also recently deceased. There's an interesting pattern that seems to form around you."

It wasn't hard to see where he was going with it. They seemed to have the answers to their own questions, and had obviously been following me. Were they the people who snuffed Tommy? If they were, I was in deep trouble. Where the hell was Leo? Tommy did say that it was our people who killed Paulie. Since they had seen me at the cemetery, I was worried that they may have observed me leaving Tommy's house. I retained the cocky attitude to mask my rising fear.

"Gee, I'm sorry. I didn't know that it was a federal crime to attend a friend's funeral, and I didn't talk to—"

They slammed the chair into the wall, spilling me on to the floor. There was no longer a good cop in the room, and suddenly they were both in my face.

Agent Francis stood over me, screaming in my face. "We said no more bullshit, and you'd better drop the punk-ass attitude! We saw you talking to Combs, and if we did, then someone else could have and probably did. We figured that maybe your dumb-ass mind caught on when you found your car busted up after Combs' funeral. Do you have any idea who you're messing with?"

"Jesus, calm down! Do you people spy on everybody? How many times did I piss today? Is that in your file? How do I know that it wasn't you guys who smashed my car? Just say what you came here to say and leave me alone. I'm not messing with anyone." A bruise began to form on my elbow.

Agent Francis lifted me into the chair, while softening his tone. "Look, Kronchek, I'm going to level with you, but maybe I'm telling you something that you already know or are involved in. We didn't touch your car. Your buddy Paulie and Combs were in a unit among others that were under suspicion for drug trafficking in Vietnam. Our sources informed us that before he was killed, Kovak was about to give some information to an Army intelligence officer. Unfortunately, the officer is stateside with a belly full of parasites. Kovak's dead and we're getting cooperation from no one. The official version is that there is no serious drug problem or drug smuggling among the soldiers, and that it isn't within our jurisdiction since we are a domestic intelligence agency. The official version is bullshit. Heroin is flowing like raw sewage from Southeast Asia into our cities, but we can't identify the importation source. We know that the Mob is distributing it, but we don't understand their easy access.

"Your buddies knew something or were involved, and now they're dead. We want to know what Combs told you that day at the cemetery. You're already in danger, and the people you're screwing with can get to you in other ways like messing with your family, friends, or a girlfriend."

I didn't like them, probably for what they represented in my mind, but I had been here before when Nellie died. Trying to buck authority that couldn't be moved and fighting against a system so firmly entrenched was overwhelming. Whoever was behind all this would be way beyond my reach, so why not let the Feds handle it, or maybe they were it. I decided to tell them what I knew, except for finding Tommy dead and the money in the sympathy cards at the cemetery. I didn't want them to start bothering Paulie's family about a little cash, and I certainly didn't want any level of inquiry linking Tommy and I. I told them what Tommy had revealed to me at the cemetery, leaving out the Cobra part.

Agent Lloyd applied pressure to my arm. "Are you sure you're telling us everything, Kronchek? I hope that you're not involved with drug dealing because you'll be next in the ground. I don't like you. You're a sarcastic punk, but here's some free advice. Stay out of it, or get out of it because it's Mob related and they don't tolerate partners. Your buddies were probably just low-end lackeys, but we want the big boys. The Director has taken a personal interest in this case, so we're under a lot of pressure to deliver answers. And one more thing, wise guy, keep your mouth shut or we'll lock you down somewhere for a long time where you won't be able to talk to anyone. We'll be watching you."

"I'll keep quiet, trust me. I didn't ask for any of this. You're all sleeping in the same dirty bed and maybe even Paulie was crooked. Maybe you can rest in hell together. Now leave!"

Agent Francis headed down the stairs as Lloyd lingered behind to speak to me.

"Thanks for the help, Kronchek, and here something for the kick in the balls."

Before he left, his fist smashed into my solar plexus, sending me hard to the floor. My compressed lungs gasped in desperation for air. I could hear his footsteps on the stairs and the hall door slam shut. Leo came in twenty seconds later smelling like a brewery, just as I was pulling myself into a chair. Respiration began to return in gasping spurts.

"Hey, Kronchek, who were the suits that just left? Pretty serious looking guys, like insurance agents or Jehovah Witnesses. You smell like BO."

"FBI, Leo. Federal Agents, not insurance agents, and you smell like cheap beer mixed with BO."

"Yea, right. Pretty funny, dickhead. You're such an asshole. Can't you ever give a straight answer to a simple question without being a prick? You think I'm stupid or something?"

"Oh, I knew that I couldn't fool you, Leo. I've got to shower for work."

I straightened up painfully and headed for the bathroom.

"Okay, see you later. Who were they really, salesmen or something?"

"FBI, retard. I told you once already." I slammed the bathroom door and turned on the shower.

"You're such an asshole, Kronchek."

Chapter 9

The Feds had cranked me hard, but they had unwittingly relieved me of a burden. They now had part of my information and possessed the resources to finish the investigation. My visit to Tommy was presently unknown to them, and I intended to keep it that way. Vowing to myself to stay out of it, I was still concerned that whoever had been following me may have seen the agents enter my apartment. That could be a death sentence if you considered Tommy's fate. It would be seen as further meddling in their, whoever they were, affairs.

I decided not to ask any more questions concerning the Cobras or Paulie, but I knew that I would be looking over my shoulder for a long time. Maybe I needed to get out of town for a weekend to let things cool down. The dream had left me rattled. All those dead people seemed to expect something from me. I didn't feel competent enough to help the living, let alone the dead. Nellie, Paulie, and Tommy had all needed my help, but I was always one step behind.

I had to admit that even though the Feds had frightened me; they had tweaked my curiosity when they mentioned that the Director of the FBI had a personal interest in the case. J. Edgar Hoover, the founder of the FBI, was a paranoid of the highest degree. He wielded power by using private information as blackmail against people of all stations of life: Senators, Congressmen, entertainers, and some said even Presidents. He was obviously going to great lengths to complete and then silence the investigation.

Something bigger was behind it all, and that instinct kept a little motivation for the truth alive in the back of my mind. Drug trafficking was certainly a concern of the FBI's, but not to the point where the Director would get involved unless there would be a lot of adverse publicity. A factor was involved that I was obviously missing, but for now, it would have to wait. Every day life was calling, and I was late for work.

Making myself available for psychiatric ward duty wasn't too bright. Next to the terminal ward it was the worst draw in the hospital. Often dangerous and understaffed, a volatile situation could erupt without a moment's notice. Every time I worked there, a fight or two would break out, with restraints being necessary to restore order.

The psychiatric unit, a.k.a. the loony bin in staff parlance, was on the fifth and last floor of the hospital. Probably borrowing from the military's proclivity for specialization, the hospital was divided by conditions and diseases to a more specific degree than other medical facilities. There was a cancer ward, orthopedic ward, respiratory disease unit, coronary unit, and even a terminal ward, which as its name suggests, was the last stop in the hospital. No one was discharged from the terminal ward. They took the elevator to the cellar morgue, located two floors below ground level.

The bin appeared secure enough as you stepped off the elevator, but as always, looks were deceiving. The reception area, sans a receptionist, was separated from the bin proper by two thick, heavily padded doors. Each door contained a one square-foot double-plated safety glass window that was utilized for observation. What outsiders didn't realize; however, was that the keys were located on the inside of the ward attached to the belt of one of the staff members. No one could get in, but the patients could get out if they gained access to the keys. I hated having key ring responsibility for a shift. It was like having a giant bull's eye on my back for anyone who thought of escaping.

At times there would only be one nurse and two aides for as many as thirty patients. We weren't armed, so only three heartbeats separated the severely disturbed from the outside world. Escapes and injuries to staff members were quite common, and having knowledge of those statistics did nothing for my confidence as the head nurse buzzed me into the ward.

Shift changes provided a rare break in the hospital routine, not to mention the best escape opportunities, so patients tended to congregate near the door just before the end of a shift.

Some were fixated on the close proximity to the only means of escape, and Fred Collins always stood at the head of the line. Fred absolutely gave me the creeps, and I tried never to make direct eye contact with him. He had escaped a dozen times, seldom spoke to anyone but his therapist, and his suicide of choice was wrestling moving trains. Fred had been struck twice by locomotives and lived. His face, scarred from multiple plastic surgery, made Frankenstein look positively debonair. Fred had never been a suicide threat on the ward, but an escape liability at all times, since he only wanted to die by train. Fortunately for the staff, the railroad tracks didn't run through the fifth floor.

I squeezed my body through the second door while an aide held Fred at bay. His blank, emotionless stare gave me a chill as I hurried past him to the nurse's station, but once the door locked behind me, I was of no interest to him.

The ward contained a mixed bag of human psychoses, from the shell-shocked of WWII, to the drug addicts and the traumatically stressed from Vietnam, with everything in between. We couldn't have handled the ward without the help of the more stable patients. They buddied up on suicide watches and added some psychological balance to the therapy groups. Some of them were better adjusted than a lot of people that I knew on the outside.

Johnny, the day aide, handed me the keys with a sigh of relief. "Have fun tonight, Kronchek. Things are really on edge in here. Two therapists called in sick, and we've got five patients on suicide watch. I believe that's an all-time record. I'm gone."

Shit! I had volunteered for this mess or in this specific case, Leo had volunteered me. Never again would my name be on the floater list. The ward was a sad example of how the government treated its veterans. Most of the patients weren't getting better; they were just being maintained and kept from society's view. I would have to say that the staff was well qualified and dedicated to their jobs, and that they put in a heroic effort whenever I was on duty, but the resources and patient ratio made significant success difficult.

The young veterans from Vietnam saddened me the most. They were so screwed up, but kept hidden, so the public understood little about the war and its additional costs. They weren't listed among the casualties, but their lives were destroyed and the effects on their families will never be measured in official government statistics.

It wasn't just the drugs. I sat in on a few group therapy sessions, and the brutal combat that some of the men witnessed could have pushed anyone over the edge. The military did a poor job of preparing them for a return to society. The understandably paranoid became clinically paranoid fighting a war among a civilian population where the enemy could be standing right next to you while acting like your friend. Hesitation could lead to your demise, but survival instincts could put a little kid's death on your conscience for the rest of your life.

The next two people through the door eased my trepidation and lifted some of my despondency. Big Cliff Franklin was in charge that night, and the student nurse trailing behind him gave us an extra body for the shift.

And what a body! Karen Linkfield, a fourth year nursing student out of Bridgeport, dazzled me whenever she crossed my path. She had a petite, well-proportioned figure, scintillating blue eyes, and long brown hair that fell straight down to the center of her back when she was off duty. I would swear that even the catatonics came out of their internal world for a moment whenever she walked down the hall. We had gone out to eat several times during the summer, watched a few movies, and connected romantically in the back seat of my Mustang, but I hadn't spoken to her for three days, so I think she was more than a little pissed at me. Karen could communicate with her eyes very well, and as she passed by they were saying, "I'll be talking to you later, pal."

If I had been more focused, we may have been a steady couple. In a few months Karen would have a full-time job in the nursing field, while I had twenty bucks in the bank with no clue as to what the next year would bring. This week's paycheck was already spoken for in order to buy books for the coming semester. I actually couldn't figure out what she saw in me unless I was the ultimate project for women everywhere.

Cliff would be the head nurse on our shift and his presence lessened my anxiety. He was the rarest of the rare in 1969. Being a black male, plus an R.N., put him in a category of his own. Oh yeah, and his height. A former basketball player for UMass, Cliff was six-ten and possessed an advanced degree in psychiatric nursing. His intelligence, combined with his imposing size, made him adept at handling the most severe cases with firmness and compassion.

Cliff handed out our assignments, and Karen took off down the hall without saying a word to either of us. That would come later for me. Her job would be difficult enough that night since she was the only woman, and an attractive one at that, on the all-male ward. It made me doubly relieved that Cliff would be in charge that night. Cliff handed me only one folder.

"Matt, I need you on suicide watch tonight with Simon Rebrone. They brought him up last month, and he's so spooky that none of the patients want to go near him. He's sedated and lightly restrained with straps across his chest and legs. Go down and take over for Jim. I'll relieve you in a couple of hours after meds, so Karen can straighten out your ass during break."

I let out a nervous, false-bravado laugh. "So you noticed that, huh? I think she's pretty pissed, but I had two funerals this week. Also, Leo came back today and forced me to go to the courts. I wasn't even supposed to be on tonight, but the asshole told the head nurse that I would be available. I should have called her back, but my friend getting killed has messed me up."

"Leo did that? The guy is such a clown. Are you and that sawed-off human stump still trying to play ball at Goffe Street?"

"We went down today for two hours, and I'm sore as hell, but we could use you again before the snow flies. We kicked some serious ass the day you played with us. We stayed on the court for two hours. Everyone was ripped. They couldn't figure out where we found you."

"Yeah, it was so great that I couldn't walk for a week and had a headache for two days from the booze. It will be a while before my wife will let me out with you two fools again. It didn't help any that you got me drunk after the game and left me on my lawn at two in the morning. I woke up at dawn on the damp grass with my wife standing over me holding the baby."

"Sorry about that, Cliff, but that's one of Leo's favorite gags, plus you were too heavy to drag any further. I tried, but you're a pretty big load and I was shot myself. Leo never passes out from booze, so he enjoys leaving people in embarrassing situations. Once I woke up on the steps of a church on a Sunday morning, just as people were going to early mass. I got the little prick back for that one. I sent all his unpaid parking tickets to his mother, and he had his car taken away for a month. I better get going."

"Kronchek, I think you might be worse than Leo. You deserve each other. And, Kronchek…."

"Yea, Cliff."

"You ought to take a second look. That's a good woman and she seems to like your sorry ass, although I can't see why."

"I don't need a second look, Cliff, just a better brain. There's nothing wrong with my eyes when it comes to women. I'll make it up to her. It's been a bad week."

"You do that, Kronchek, but on your own time. We've got a tense night ahead. Now go."

I took up my position near Simon Rebrone's bed. The file listed him at twenty-eight, but he looked fifty. He carried nothing but parchment skin stretched out on a bony frame, with his wispy brown and white hair completely bald in random patches. The four or five teeth dangling in his gums were mostly black, with the brighter sections of the enamel stained yellow from nicotine. Heavy straps held him to the bed, and I wondered why the sedated skeleton needed to be watched. The only way he could get through his restraints would be if his bones snapped and cut through the fabric. I had all I could do to stay awake as Rebrone slept peacefully in a drug-induced stupor.

Cliff took over after dispensing early meds. There was time available for supper, so I brought my food to the common room where I could eat and watch my share of the patients. A game of Ping-Pong was in progress, and two of the dining tables were being used for poker. Fred Collins sat in the corner working on a jigsaw puzzle of a freight train traveling through a forest. Whoever donated that puzzle to the ward didn't have a clue concerning the nature of his choice of death. Fred could stare at pictures of trains for hours, so the puzzle commanded his full attention.

Karen had started her break before me, so I sat down next to her with an explanation already loaded into my mouth.

"Karen, I'm sorry that—"

"There's nothing to talk about, Matt. We're not going steady or anything, but why didn't you call me back today? That hurt my feelings. You didn't have to blow me off."

"Call you back? When did you call and who did you give the message to?"

"I called late this morning and Leo said that you were at a funeral. I told him that he must be mistaken because the funeral was on Saturday. He said that it was a funeral and that's all he knew. I thought he was lying, so I told him that he was a jerk. I asked him to give you the message that I called."

Leo was hopeless. He had forgotten about the call, or had committed a lie of omission so we could play basketball without the threat of interruption from Karen. By now, he wouldn't remember which lie it was anyway, but he was still going to hear about it.

"Leo never gave me the message, Karen, I swear. He does stuff like that all the time. Plus, if you pissed him off by calling him a name, he probably did it on purpose to get you back. He has the mentality of a six-year-old."

"He was lying about the funeral, wasn't he, Matt?"

"I wish he had been, but another old classmate from Bellington died on the weekend. Burned out on heroin. I didn't even like the guy. I fought with him constantly in grammar school, but my mother guilt-tripped me into taking Paulie's girlfriend to the funeral."

"So you were with another girl?"

"Yeah I was, but at a funeral that I didn't want to go to; plus she was Paulie's girlfriend and we never got along. I already told you that. I said some things at Paulie's funeral that didn't go over too well with his family, and I had to make it right by doing this favor."

"Paulie's dead, Matt. She's not his girlfriend anymore. You're so naïve. She's on the prowl for someone new, meaning you."

Karen stomped down the hall, leaving me alone at the table. The patients were having a good laugh at my expense, but at least it was defusing the tension on the ward. As I called after her in desperation, it felt as if my life was taking a constant beating from every angle. She did have a pretty good read on Debbie; however, but I wished that she would give me a little more credit concerning my self-control, although I have to admit there had been temptation.

I called after her. "What did I do? I went to a stinking funeral. It was so much fun and very romantic. Next time I'll be sure to ask you to go along to chaperone. Maybe that could be our next date, if someone would just die soon."

My sarcasm increased her angry stance, but she did stop to listen with a scowl on her face. I needed to salvage the situation or it would be over, and that's not what I wanted.

"We haven't gone out in a couple of weeks. How about going to the beach on Saturday? Just you and me in the sand, and then some dinner later at Jimmie's. We'll put the top down on the Mustang and cruise the shore."

If she accepted, I would have to find some money by Saturday, but it was a constant problem that I had become accustomed to dealing with. I suppose that I could do without a history book for a couple of weeks.

She stopped again with her face wearing a softer countenance.

"Just you and me, Matt, not that nasty Leo and one of his sluts, right? The last time we went to the beach, he made out with that girl all afternoon, and they were both slobbering drunk."

Leo irritated the hell out of Karen, and he deserved her fury this time for sure. Leo said that Karen was too serious, but I tried to explain to him that it was a matter of maturity, a foreign land that we had yet to visit, especially him.

"I promise, just you and me all day, and then dinner at night."

"Okay, Matt, but we're still going to talk about this funeral thing and that girl."

Karen went down the hall and relieved Cliff in Rebrone's room. She must have complained to Cliff about me because he came down the hall with a big sarcastic grin on his face.

As if my life wasn't screwed up enough, my talent for making it worse had been shifted into high gear. I had felt sorry for Debbie, telling her that I would try to see her on Saturday. Now I had two potential dates, with Angela on my mind for a third, and I didn't even know her. My dad always told me that if there was one thing worse than being without a woman, it was having more than one. Tommy Combs had been right about one thing—I never listened.

A piercing scream from down the hall snapped me out of my daze and jump-started my reflexes, which sent my lunch across the room, splattering against the far wall. I hit the floor running with a dozen aroused and curious inmates on my tail, while Fred remained engrossed in his puzzle, unaffected by the non-railroad commotion. Action begot action on the psych ward. The screams came from Simon Rebrone's room, and Cliff stood motionless as I flew through the door. Cliff stopped me dead with his arm, almost clothes-lining me because of his height.

"Don't move, Matt. He's got Karen. We have to stay calm."

I couldn't fathom this possibility, but Rebrone had wrapped a strap around Karen's neck, and he stood there grossly naked, his bones sticking out at every angle, unrestrained by the lack of muscle bulk and flesh. One incredibly skinny, but obviously powerful arm, held the strap taut, while the other pressed a pen against her jugular. Her red face gasped for a breath that was denied by a constricted windpipe. Rebrone's rope-like tendons bulged from his arm as he tightened his grip while ranting in a croaking, raspy voice. His eyes were focused only on Cliff as if his field of vision was only three feet wide.

"So you've come to silence me, Williams, all the way from Nam, but everyone's here to protect me this time. Paulie's next to you and Tommy's sitting in the corner. Look at him. He's so scared. Tommy was stupid, but he was smart enough to be afraid of you, Williams, and leave while there was still time."

What the hell was I hearing? Rebrone was looking straight at me when he said Paulie's name. When he mentioned Tommy, a quick shudder fired up the adrenaline factory. No one else was in the room, and linking the two names together couldn't be a coincidence. This couldn't be real, but the two entwined cobras tattooed on his scrawny shoulder made me consider the impossible. Rebrone had been in Vietnam with Paulie and Tommy!

Cliff continued to restrain me, not trusting my judgment, as Karen's body began to sag from a lack of oxygen. With a silent, pleading motion I begged Cliff to let me by, and he reluctantly allowed me to ease to the side, warning me with stone cold eyes to be careful as he struggled to keep the increasingly agitated inmates out of the room. I think he almost shit when I began talking.

"I'm here, Simon. Take it easy. I won't let him get you, but ease up on the girl. She's not in on it. It's me, Paulie, Paulie Kovak from Bellington."

Rebrone loosened his grip a bit as his eyes lit up in recognition and relief. Karen was still under his control, but at least she could breathe again as she gasped and choked for precious air. Using Paulie's last name and hometown added weight to my claim of being him. Cliff's training told him that he shouldn't allow an amateur to proceed, but he could see that I had made a connection with Rebrone, so he signaled for me to continue. He appeared totally confused by the interaction, since he knew that I had never met Rebrone before that night.

"Paulie Kovak, I knew that you would come through. You always helped me when I needed a fix or a couple of bucks. They think I see things that don't exist, but I knew you would be here. I knew it. Tommy's scared of Ronald. That's why he's crying in the corner just like he usually does when things get rough. You were always afraid, Paulie, but at least you tried to help people."

"That's Cliff in front of you, not Ronald, Simon. He's here to help us get out of this mess. Please let the girl go."

Bad move! The strap tightened in response to his paranoia.

"That's Ronald Williams! Don't tell me different! He's here to finish the job. He'll kill you next, Paulie. I heard him talking, but you didn't know it, so stop acting stupid like Tommy. I haven't led a good life, and I know that the devil is waiting for me, but I never wanted to go where Ronald took us. I used to think that Ronald was the devil, but he's something worse."

I moved further to the left side of Cliff, so Simon would have to turn his head in order to watch both of us. Every time he checked Cliff's position, I would edge a little closer. I desperately hoped that his depth perception was off, and wouldn't be able to recognize the slight changes in my position. It was important that he didn't perceive me as a threat. We didn't want to spook him into driving the pen into Karen's throat.

My emotions were tearing up inside as I thought back to Nellie's death and how helpless I had been. The responsibility for someone's life was like walking a tightrope or crossing a narrow log over a gorge. One slip and Karen would be dead, and it would be my fault.

Cliff understood now that he was perceived as the threat, so he remained motionless and left it in my hands. The sweat poured down my forehead, and my armpits were spreading water across my back and down my side. My legs began to shake, so I took a deep breath before I continued. Karen's mouth framed a silent, *Help me, Matt!* It was the nightmare all over again!

"Ease up, Simon. You and I and Tommy can take him, but you won't be able to help us if you're holding the girl. We can't do it by ourselves. He's too big. We need you."

"We can't do it at all, Paulie. You of all people should know how weak we are. He's the devil's master!"

Drool ran down his chin as the feral eyes appeared to open even wider, but at least he loosened up on the strap. The pen; however, pushed deeper into her skin. Karen impressed me with her bravery. Tears streamed down her cheeks, but she understood that movement would mean death. Her beautiful blue eyes closed tight in fear, but she opened them wide as she begged me to help her. All those dead people in my nightmare asked me for help, but it was too late for them. Karen was still alive, and I couldn't let her down.

"Let her go and help us, Simon. He can't win this time because now we know what he is. Let's get him now!"

Simon let loose with scream to boost his courage, stepping forward as he raised the pen to attack Cliff. He kept Karen tightly strapped, but made his mistake when he used her as a shield on Cliff's side. He wasn't worried about me, because to him, I was Paulie, and we were going to attack Cliff together.

I stayed low and drove my shoulder into his chest just like Coach Babcock had taught me in football, wedging my body between the pen and Karen, causing him to lose his grip on the strap as we hit the floor. Cliff quickly scooped her up, but now he and the other aide had bigger problems on their plate. Five of the more disturbed patients had become violently excited by the action, and had started ripping up the place, trying to force their way into the room while grabbing at the keys. A few of the others were attempting to bust open the medicine cabinet to get at the drugs.

If they gained possession of the keys, we would have a full-scale riot on our hands, and the rest of the hospital would be in danger. Where the hell were the police!

I could see Cliff throwing people right and left as he began to gain some control, but I couldn't help him. My biggest worry was the powerful bone bag under me. I had him by a hundred pounds, but could barely hold on to his arms. He tried to buck me off his chest, spitting rancid bile into my face and scratching my neck with hardened nails that hadn't been cut in months. Rebrone had gained superhuman strength from his hallucinogenic panic attack.

"Stop, Simon, it's me, Paulie. Remember? We got him, Simon, we finally got him."

He went completely limp in an eye blink, relieving the strain on my muscles. I took some of my weight off of him, which almost cost me my life. His eyes cleared as he scanned my face for recognition. I didn't see the pen that was still in his hand until it was too late.

"You're not Paulie, Paulie's dead."

He drove the pen into my left shoulder. If I hadn't reacted to his voice and dodged the blow, it would have struck my neck. I screamed from the intense pain, but survival instincts and latent anger forced me to ignore the burning agony. I punched him flush in the nose, figuring that a shot that hard would stop his clock. No way. He laughed maniacally as I hit him with two more clean blows. The second one snapped his head back to the floor, and blood erupted from his nostrils, putting him out cold. The gruesome laughter had mercifully ceased. I closed my eyes, pulling the pen out of my shoulder in one motion, causing another cry of torment as a bloodstain spread quickly through my white shirt.

A chaotic, surrealistic scene surrounded me as the police rushed into the ward to subdue the riot. Medics hauled Karen off in a stretcher as I viewed the scene through increasingly hazy vision. She had been so smart and brave in the face of a psychotic attack.

Sitting up, I leaned against the bed to ease the dizzying pain, the significance of the last few days roiling around in my head. Knowing the name of Paulie's potential killer had changed everything because now it was personal and concrete. As the scenery around me became increasingly blurry, I remembered what Rebrone said. "*I never wanted to go where Ronald took us.*" Where did Williams take them and what did it mean? It would be impossible to run away. I considered myself as having led a rather ordinary life, but bodies and violence had turned up everywhere I had been.

I understood now that it was my war, but in a different way. I might not go to Vietnam, but the fallout would find us all. If one hundred people are killed in a war, thousands more are affected back home. There would be no more running. I now believed that Paulie had not wanted to deal drugs, but had been intimidated by this Ronald Williams and forced to play along until they killed him.

I braced myself up, staring down at poor Simon Rebrone. His suddenly lucid eyes opened wide as he moved his bloody lips.

"He'll get you too. I don't know who the fuck you are, but Ronald will get you. You've made a date with the devil, and you can't run away from hell."

I don't know why, but I hit him flush on the jaw, putting him out again. All my fear, anger, and frustration were invested in that punch. It sounded as if he was predicting my future, and I didn't like the prognosis. I must have passed out from the pain and excitement because the next thing that I remembered was waking up in the emergency room, clearing my vision to Leo standing over me with his stupid grin in full bloom. The room spun as I tried to get up, and Leo's excitement made the scene even more chaotic with his hyper movements.

My shoulder hurt like hell, my head felt three times bigger, and my right hand was purple and puffy from punching Rebrone. After an hour of observation, they let me go home with Leo and a bottle of pain pills and antibiotics. On the way home, he pulled up to a bar without asking and dragged me inside. He said a drink would help me sleep and dull the pain. I asked about Karen, and he told me that she had gone home with her parents after being treated, so I wasn't about to bother them at that time of night. According to Leo, her only injuries were some nasty bruises on her arms and neck.

Leo was all worked up from my experience, but was sorely disappointed that he had missed the fight. He told everyone at the bar what had happened, and performed several animated fight moves to demonstrate how he would have handled the situation more efficiently. Two beers and a painkiller muddled my mind, but Ronald Williams seemed to be a name that I had heard recently. The source was on the edge of my consciousness, but the drugs and alcohol had me nodding off the barstool and finally on to the floor. Apparently, we were kicked out of the bar for me being inebriated, and the only thing that I remembered was Leo throwing me on the bed as he complained about me being such a lightweight drinker. I know that I told him to screw himself at least once before I passed out.

Chapter 10

A newspaper hit me in the face, startling me out of a rare, drug-induced, dreamless sleep. Shuffling footsteps and the rhythmic pounding of a basketball circled my bed as I struggled to focus my eyes.

"Hey, Kronchek, get up! It's four o'clock and we need to go to the courts. You're a celebrity now. The story of the skinny psycho whipping your ass is all over the papers, and your bitchy, little nurse girlfriend got some major print for her, and I quote, "stoic bravery." What does stoic mean? Too serious to be serious?"

Four o'clock! I had missed the entire first day of classes, and when I tried to move my stiff left shoulder pulsated with pain. My right hand wouldn't close into a fist. Nausea rumbled in my head, and my mouth felt like it was filled with cotton. As I fumbled for the pain pills, the safety cap proved to be a frustrating task for my swollen hand and muddled head. Instead of helping, Leo stared at me with a smirk of pleasure. He knew how to get me going, so I struck back.

"Asshole; bring me some water, and are you crazy? I can't even move, let alone play basketball. Why didn't you wake me up for school? And stop pounding that ball. It's like a hammer rapping the inside of my head every time the ball hits the floor."

He walked away laughing, returning ten minutes later with a bottle of cheap beer, ignoring my question about school and continuing to dribble the basketball without pause.

"I said water, ass wipe, water! Is that so difficult for you, or are you just a total dick? Why didn't you wake me up?"

I was injured, tired and pissed. Leo's smile faded as he appeared genuinely insulted and hurt. He brought his dribble to a lower, lighter patter.

"Easy, Kronchek, I just thought a little hair of the dog, yuh know, plus you wouldn't wake up. I tried three times. You should go easy on the booze when you're taking pain pills. In health class they said that it was dangerous to—"

"I don't have a hangover, Leo! I drank two beers, two beers that you bought for me, plus you flunked health anyway. My shoulder's on fire, and it was the pain medication that put me out last night."

I put a pain pill and an antibiotic in my mouth, washing them down with a sip of the watery, bitter beer, all the while giving Leo my most disgusted look. It was similar to being angry at a dog. Two minutes later and Leo wouldn't even remember what he had done wrong.

"Take the beer away, Leo, and thanks for picking me up last night. I'll get up in a minute or so, but I can't play ball today. Maybe in a couple of days my shoulder will be better. The doctors said that nothing major was damaged."

"Will you at least come down to the park with me, Kronchek. I don't like going there alone."

"Yea, yea, just let me read the paper and take a shower. The day's shot anyway. Go make me something to eat. Be my bitch."

My promise to go to the park distracted him for a moment, but he finished the beer as he went upstairs to annoy someone else, totally forgetting the food and ignoring my insult.

The riot article made page one, complete with a picture of Karen being carried out on a stretcher. Cliff and I were highlighted as having controlled the situation and saving Karen's life until the police arrived. Apparently Rebrone was double-jointed, and when Cliff left the room for a moment, he dislocated his shoulder, making it possible to slide out of his straps and grab Karen. There was going to be an inquiry as to why the earlier shift had not strapped his wrists as protocol demanded.

Unfortunately for my future health prospects, Simon Rebrone's name was now linked to mine by the article. The people behind Paulie's death might be concerned about my contact with Rebrone, not to mention the FBI, if they were able to make the connection.

Feelings of vulnerability washed over me, reminding me of 1961 when I had felt powerless to investigate Nellie's death. I was an adult now, but the players were still on a plane above me. They were murderers and drug dealers, along with government agents, and they would find me if I didn't find them first or at least discover the truth to use as leverage. I knew some of the players, but how they fit together was not clear at all. Vietnam reached out to me in a different manner, forcing me to pay attention and to read between the lines. I kept trying to walk away, but seemed to get in deeper with each incident. And Rebrone's hypnotic, cryptic words kept ringing in my head.

The headline below the hospital story read, "Four US Servicemen Killed Outside of Da Nang. Twenty Wounded in Mortar Attack. One Connecticut Man Among the Dead." In between those two lines were hundreds of other stories: a lost son, a dead husband, a father gone, a boyfriend crippled, missing limbs, eyesight blotted out forever, ten more addicted to heroin, and so on, and on and on into an uncertain future.

I don't believe in fate, but that non-existent concept always seemed to come around to bite me in the ass. I could ignore Ronald Williams, whoever he was, but I didn't think he was going to ignore me. The narcotics began to take effect, and I had just dozed off when Leo stormed into the room screaming and slamming the door.

"Kronchek! Let's go. You promised that you would go with me and it's getting late."

I dragged my ass out of bed, took a shower and watched Leo play basketball for an hour while I ate some chips. Having gotten his daily dose of basketball, Leo was satisfied to leave me alone.

We ate dinner together with relative maturity, and after Leo went upstairs I called Karen to see how she was making out. Her parents answered the phone, thanking me profusely for saving her life, but explained that Karen was asleep for the night. I would be golden with her parents forever. It would be smarter to call her the next day when we both felt better. I went straight to bed, locking Leo out of the room so I could make my eight o'clock class the next day. He could sleep in the living room, or go upstairs and argue with someone else.

The shoulder felt considerably better the next morning. The extra day's rest had helped. Luckily the pen had hit mostly empty space in the shoulder cavity, nicking a few tendons, and missing major blood vessels. Infection was the biggest danger, so the wound had to be kept open and cleaned regularly. I didn't want to miss my other classes, and needed to catch up with the professors from the classes that were missed the day before. Driving with one hand, I made it to class on time.

After two classes in a row, I walked to the cafeteria for some breakfast. The common sight of Leo arguing with three of our friends in the far corner of the dining hall brought back a semblance of normality.

The black students sat at one large table in a self-imposed segregation, and as I passed by their table, James and a few other players from the park started heckling me. It was good to see that James was still in school.

"Hey, hero, can we have your autograph? Are you going to move up in weight class the next time, Kron? Maybe you can take on a ninety pound waste case now that you're experienced." I guess everyone had read yesterday's paper.

"Give me a break. We had to be careful. He had a hostage."

"Yea and we read that he had a weapon. You better start arming yourself, Kron. Here, you want to borrow my pen?"

Shaking my head, I laughed with them. They were just having fun busting me, but you could tell that there was apprehension hiding behind James' smile. I wanted to ask what had happened with his girlfriend, but not in front of his friends. That's when I noticed Angela sitting alone at the end of the table. I couldn't remember her last name. She smiled at me and I smiled back, prompting James to grab my wrist firmly and say no, I told you no, with his eyes.

Heeding James' advice, I kept moving since racial tensions were high at the time, and I didn't need additional problems added to my long list. The black men at the table were friendly, but I wasn't welcome to sit there, certainly not with a black girl. Heading for Leo, I tried to remember her last name and why James had told me that she wasn't for me. It hadn't been a race issue, but the painkillers and the trauma of the fight at the hospital had tangled my neurons a bit. I didn't want to cheat on Karen, but the girl was intriguing, and a little talking wouldn't hurt anyone.

Watching Angela's table for an opening while eating breakfast, I listened to Leo argue with Schultz about whether Mantle or Mays would break Babe Ruth's career home run record. I told them that they were both wrong, and that it would be Hank Aaron because of his age and consistency. My opinion galvanized them for a moment as they agreed on the matter of my ignorance concerning baseball statistics. Their solidarity lasted for twenty seconds or so before they continued bickering, ignoring my presence completely.

All the black students left the dining hall except for Angela, and she was in the process of cleaning off her tray when I looked up. Scooping up a huge pile of books on the way out of the cafeteria, she headed out a side door. Leaving my tray on the table, two chairs hit the floor in my haste, and against James' advice, I decided to follow her outside to look for an opening to introduce myself. Tommy had been right—I never listened. I really liked Karen, and didn't want to hurt her, but I think it was just racial curiosity that drove my intentions. My relationships with black women had been limited, and were never romantic.

I stayed ten feet away, not having a clue as to how I would approach her, when I remembered an old trick Mike had taught me high school. A new spiral notebook was in my hand.

"Uh, excuse me, did you just drop this?" I held out my notebook.

I'm sure she had been hit on before, but never with such a lame attempt. It was apparent that she had been taught to be cautious with white people, and she also possessed an inherent shyness that forced her eyes to the ground. Angela's hesitation to my overtures exposed our differences. The paucity of my exposure to the black culture of New Haven that had surrounded my college for three years was now obvious. Beyond the basketball courts and soul music, my experience was circumscribed.

The sheer blackness of Angela became enhanced during the moment of silence that followed my weak attempt to introduce myself. Her skin glowed ebony, mine pink like a skinned rabbit. The full lips framing her mouth appeared to possess the capacity to engulf mine entirely in a kiss.

Her flat nose spread across her face, and my Roman beak could have served as a ski slope for a race of little people. If it is intended that you are to be attracted to the attributes of your own race, then I must have misunderstood the infatuation in my soul and the interest in her eyes when we first met at the park. Perhaps our physical differences heightened our societal-bred paranoia of mixed race relationships, with the fear born primarily from ignorance and lack of interaction with each other's race. As she finally met my eyes and flashed that penetrating smile, which I returned in my own cautious way, our sameness, our humanness, explained the inexplicable attraction and overwhelmed all else.

"No, that's not my mine."

Silence again. Now what to say. What a dummy! The first rule when you use a lame pickup line is to have a second one ready, no matter how ridiculous. My best bet was to look stupid and back out of it.

"Oh, sorry. I thought you dropped it."

I began to leave when Angela, shy Angela, saved my supposedly big, bold ass.

"Didn't I see you at the park the other day with James?"

"Yeah, we're friends from basketball, and you were with Wanda the other day, weren't you?"

"Yes, that's right. Wanda told me that you were on a committee together at school. Actually, I'm surprised to see you at all. I read the paper yesterday, and it said that you were injured at the hospital when a patient attacked a nurse. The story said that you helped save the woman's life."

"Well, it was more than me that saved her, and pure guts helped her save herself. The guy stuck a pen in my shoulder, but it feels better already. Hey, don't believe anything Wanda says about me. We don't get along very well."

"I won't, if that's what you want, but she told me that you were a pretty good guy."

"Wanda said that about me? Well, maybe you should listen to Wanda just this once."

Angela emitted a nervous laugh, shyly turning away. I wasn't quite sure what I wanted out of this. I was already semi-committed to Karen, but maybe the semi part and my curiosity is what made it feel acceptable to try.

Angela turned to leave and said, "I've got to get to class. I'll see you around; maybe at the park or in the café?"

"Yea, I go to the park to play basketball quite a bit, but where's your class?"

"At the gym."

"Mind if I walk with you? I have to go that way to get to my car."

"That would be nice, but I have to hurry or I'll be late."

The flow of the conversation had improved, and I couldn't even remember what I was supposed to be afraid of, although I now recalled that it had something to do with her brother.

"Great, but let's start over. I'm Matt Kronchek, and let me grab those books for you."

"Angela Williams, and that's a nice thought, but you seem to be having enough trouble. Come on, let's just walk."

My left arm was in a sling, the other filled with books, and my best move was to offer to carry her stuff. A brilliant pick-up artist I was not, especially when I was practically shaking with nervousness.

Williams was the name that Rebrone had been afraid of, and had screamed in total terror. It was a common name, but common or not, it made me a little nervous. I covered it up as we talked on the way to Angela's class. What the hell was the guy's first name that Rebrone had mentioned? The conversation along the way was superficial: what's your major, where do you live kind of stuff, but physical chemistry existed between us; you could feel it.

I thought of Karen and Debbie, and worried that maybe I had been playing with my chemistry set a little too much lately. It was weird because danger and tension increased my sex drive. I think survival instincts release hormones to produce a-you're-going-to-die soon, so you'd better procreate mode.

As we reached the gym, I took a leap of faith.

"How about having lunch with me after your class. I know this place downtown where we won't be hassled."

"I don't know, Matt. I'm supposed to take the bus with Wanda today, and I'm not allowed to go out with boys unless they meet my family, especially my brother. It's never happened because no one has ever asked him, but if Wanda came with us, I guess it might be okay."

"Why do we need Wanda? She would be the chaperone from hell."

"If she won't agree to come, I can't go, and you wouldn't want me to. This is the first time anyone has asked me out on a date. Everybody in my neighborhood is afraid of my brother Ronald, except for Wanda. If you want, come by after class, and I'll know by then if Wanda will be willing to cover for me."

"Sounds okay, Angela. Just tell Wanda to ease up a little today. I'll be back in an hour."

Her face radiated excitement, with that beautiful smile lighting up the entryway of the drab old gym, but I couldn't appreciate the moment. Ronald Williams—the same name that shook Rebrone's reality. Ronald Williams, a man described as worse than the devil. Paulie's killer? Angela's brother? Were they different men or the same person that had been in Vietnam? Was it just a coincidence of common names? I hoped the hell so, or I could be walking into the life of the man who wanted me dead. Now I remembered why James warned me. Sometimes I did listen, but then there was the remembering and following advice thing.

Chapter 11

The taxi dropped Ronald off in front of his mother's house, and the driver offered to help with the bags, but Ronald insisted on carrying them himself. There was precious cargo in two of the bags, which explained the double locks. He didn't want his mother accidentally opening them before he could deliver the goods to his distributors. Ronald slipped his pistol into the small travel bag, clipping the top together with a small padlock. Mamma didn't approve of guns either.

He threw the driver a ten-dollar tip, telling the man to make himself available when called. He surveyed the neighborhood as the taxi sped off. The well-compensated driver would come whenever Ronald beckoned—another perk of having extra cash. It made him feel important, like he was somebody meaningful, and he intended to be a bigger somebody very soon.

He had only been gone a year, but the deterioration of his street was noticeable at first glance. Groups of young black men were hanging around on the corners, sitting on porch steps, leaning against telephone poles, with some drinking from bottles in paper bags. The sour aroma of weed hung in the air, with trails of wispy smoke indicating where the stoners sat. Many of the small yards were strewn with miscellaneous junk, broken bottles and twisted bicycles. Cars that would never run again clogged driveways and sat in empty lots, most of them stripped of any parts that had cash value. It would be a fertile recruiting ground for the dealers he sought and the customers that he would exploit-unemployed, angry young men. A slight twinge of guilt became quickly suppressed by his understanding of the laws of survival in the ghetto. You were either the eater or the eaten. The choice seemed simple to Ronald. He had always been a hungry man.

His mother's yard had escaped the downward spiral of the neighborhood by the force of her hard work and pride. Her spotless property stood apart from the decay, with a fresh coat of paint covering the porch that ran the width of the house, no doubt accomplished by his two younger brothers under the stern eye of Mamma. She worked two jobs and still found time to run a household and raise four children. Ronald intended to make certain that she wouldn't have work again. This neighborhood was a bullshit life that would lead nowhere, except eventually down for all of them. She could paint the house, cut the grass, and work her ass off, but they would still be floating in the middle of a sewer at the end of the day. While she was away at work, her younger children would get caught up in the flow of the neighborhood, two more victims of the disenfranchisement of the black race.

As he climbed the porch steps, he sensed that he had drawn everyone's attention. The men on the streets kept their eyes averted when he turned to face them, and the slight parting of curtains in the neighbor's windows registered within the range of Ronald's peripheral vision. They feared him in this neighborhood because they knew his penchant for violence, and that's the way he preferred to keep it. They had not forgotten him, so part of his plan was already in motion. There didn't appear to be anyone around that would challenge his authority, and if there were, they wouldn't be around for long.

Pots and pans clanged in the kitchen as he entered the foyer. Roast beef cooking in the oven saturated the air along with the smell of freshly washed linens. There wasn't an iota of dust on the furniture, and the worn wooden floors shined with a new coat of wax. She had taken the afternoon off to prepare his favorite meal and put the house in pristine condition.

Ronald crept up behind her at the stove, covering her eyes with his hands. "Guess who?"

"Ronald, Ronald, you're finally here! You're safe at home. Every day I worried that you might be killed. Are you okay, baby? You look like you've lost weight."

She threw her long, skinny arms around Ronald, practically squeezing the air out of his lungs.

"I'm fine, Mamma, now that I'm out of that stinking mess. It's real bad over there, but I made it. I'm done with the Army forever."

The truth was that Ronald hadn't seen much combat in Vietnam, except at the beginning. If his Mamma knew that he had spent the war running guns and dealing dope, she would whip him right there in the kitchen. Knowledge of other things would kill her. He wouldn't fight back and would rather die before he would let her discover the real Ronald. It had been done for them, but she wouldn't buy that excuse. She was the only person he ever remembers being afraid of in his life. Maybe it was respect and gratitude that always held back his hand. People had told him that his Daddy was a good man; a hard working one, but fearsome when provoked. Ronald could only remember how whipped tired the man was every night and the large funeral after he was killed on the docks.

"This roast beef is for dinner, baby, but do you want some lunch? Come on, sit down at the table and tell me how you've been."

"No, Mamma, I ate already, but where's Angela and the boys?"

"The boys are still at school, and she's at college thanks to the money you sent home. Why don't you take the car and pick her up. She usually takes the bus or grabs a ride with Wanda, but you can surprise her. Let me check her schedule. Angela should be coming out of the gym at one, so if you hurry, you can catch her before she leaves."

"I think I'll do that because I have to drop off a couple of bags for a buddy of mine. I'm sick of lugging them around, and his house is on the way. I can't wait to see how she's changed."

"She's beautiful, Ronald, beautiful as a grown woman. Now that you're home, we need to start letting her get out in the world more. We can't hide her forever."

Ronald's visage darkened, but the depth of the shadow across his eyes was more intense than his mother had remembered. He had changed internally, with a hardness that his mother didn't recognize. She wasn't ignorant of his reputation on the streets, but there was always a part of him that would be her little boy, her first born, and for a long time, the man of the house. The little boy no longer existed within him, and it frightened her.

"Don't be talking about Angela's social life, Mamma. I don't want her knocked up by street scum, and not finish school. It's not open to discussion with me. I'll go pick her up."

Ronald borrowed his mother's keys, slowly backing the car out of the driveway; leaving his mother alone in the kitchen with a sense of dread that she couldn't shake.

Chapter 12

Infatuation and trepidation jostled for position in my reasoning center as I swung my Mustang into the parking lot. If it were the same Ronald Williams, then he would have two reasons to kill me. Incredibly, every event seemed to bring me closer to the people and a war that I had diligently tried to avoid. Fate, the fate that I didn't believe in, kept snapping at my heels, telling me to wake up and see the connections.

Angela and Wanda stepped outside as I pulled up to the gym door. I had the top down, and the mid-day sun pounded on my head, forcing little rivulets of sweat down my forehead and matting my long, curly hair. I quickly wiped them away in order to present a cool persona in the face of total panic. The heat wave showed no sign of letting up even though it was early September. I ran around and opened the passenger door, while throwing Angela's book bag on the back seat. I motioned for Wanda to hop in the back, and thankfully, for once, she glared in silence as she lugged her own books into the back seat.

The sweet sounds of Wanda's silence from the rear lasted only ten seconds, which was probably a record for her. Wanda apparently had a long list of ground rules and questions that she no doubt had formulated during the last ten minutes.

"I don't know what you're up to, Kronchek, but this ain't no date. I only agreed to come along because Angela begged me, and I don't give a shit about your sorry ass. We're having lunch, that's all, and it's on you. No holding hands, kissing, or hugging. You better get it, Kronchek, because if her brother finds out that you took Angela to lunch you're dead, and I ain't going to hell with you. He'll kill you once for being with his sister, and then again for being a white boy."

Well, that was subtle. Normally, I would have told Wanda where to go, but this date wouldn't be happening if she hadn't agreed to help. I couldn't resist sticking the needle in a little, however.

"Relax, Wanda, we're only having lunch, and again you exhibit the depths of your prejudice. Do you have a problem with my whiteness, or are you worried that people will think that it's us on the date?"

"Shut up, fool! I'm glad Angela is going out, but I think she could have had something better than your raggedy carcass for a first date, which isn't a date. I don't care if you're white, but her brother will, dummy."

Angela, who hadn't spoken a word, surprised me by cutting in to stop our bickering.

"Wanda, you promised me that you wouldn't argue, and Matt, please stop baiting Wanda. She's doing us both a favor. Okay?"

Wanda rode in silence after the intervention, so I decided to act like she wasn't in the car. I actually respected Wanda and her values, but we were too much alike to get along, and the chip on her shoulder was bigger than mine was. With the opening shit and aggravation out of the way, I needed to initiate a conversation with Angela or the date would be a bust before it began.

The only quantifiable emotion in the front seat seemed to be that we were both extremely nervous and tentative. It was similar to being on the first date of my life. I asked Angela to lunch, but had never given a ride to a black person in my car before, and I'm sure she had never ridden in a car with a white boy or a black boy for that matter, if you could believe James and Wanda. Considering the circumstances, she must have been doubly nervous, so I decided to break the ice as I drove down Dixwell Avenue heading into New Haven.

"So, I guess, is this the first time you've been in a white boy's car?"

Her nervousness faded as her perpetual smile evolved into laughter.

"Yes, actually it is, but that was a sad opening line. Of all the openers that I could have imagined, that one would have not been on the list. Am I the first black girl to ride in your car?"

"Yea, actually you are. I guess that was a pretty dumb start."

Wanda's derisive snort made me feel foolish, but Angela shot her an impatient, pleading look that sent her back to reading her Social Work textbook.

"Not really, Matt. You just said what was on your mind, and that's an honest start. So where are you from?"

"Up in Bellington, but I haven't lived there since high school. My dad died three years ago, and it seems to work out best if I live down here. My mom's a secretary and has plenty friends from her job. Besides, I make her nervous when I'm home. I gave her enough grief when I was growing up, so I think she deserves a break."

"We have one thing in common already. My father was killed unloading a ship at the docks when I was five. My twin brothers had just been born, and it was hard for awhile. My mom works two jobs, and my big brother Ronald sends money home from the Army."

"You mean your big brother Ronald as in the one who will pulverize me if he sees you in my car?"

"That's the one, but I thought you weren't afraid of anything. He isn't due home until tomorrow, and I'm not a little girl. I don't have to do what he tells me anymore. I'm going to have a talk with him when he gets home."

Could I hide the consternation in my voice? Guilt washed over me from various angles. Was I pursuing this girl because I found her attractive or was I now trying to get to Ronald Williams? I fervently hoped that he wasn't the same person that had killed Paulie, but everything matched up.

I also began to question my motivation for revenge. A few days ago I didn't have a lot of feelings left for Paulie, but Rebrone's description of the situation in Vietnam had made me rethink my pre-formed and long-standing prejudicial opinions about Paulie. I felt like a cold, hard person, and maybe that's what I had become deep inside from my experiences.

Perhaps my desire for retribution was parochial and moral, not emotional. They had killed an old friend from my neighborhood, and I was pissed at a society and a country that had let me down again. All the philosophy was a moot point, however, since Paulie's killers were probably stalking me, or were so far from my reach that it didn't matter.

I did care about this girl's safety, and didn't want to involve her in this mess.

"Your brother wouldn't hurt you, would he Angela?"

"No, my mother would disown him, and that would kill him. She's the one person that he respects. He loves his family, respects my mother, and hates everyone else. Let's just forget about my brother and have some fun."

I couldn't have agreed more.

"Let's go eat, I'm starving. This place is a little hippie joint, but the food's good and no one will give us a second look. We'll probably be the most conventional looking menage a trois in the place."

Wanda erupted. "Don't go saying that shit, Kronchek. I'm your babysitter, not a second date."

We all had a laugh at that one as the tension began to ease. Putting the subject of Ronald behind us, the convertible kept a cool breeze on our heads as we cruised down Dixwell. People were hanging around outside of the shops, and the vast Yale University complex could be seen just beyond the confluence of Dixwell and Whalley. The intersection was New Haven's little Times Square, with the Yale Co-op and the huge Cutler's Record Store dominating the left side of the street.

The black neighborhoods of Dixwell had given way to the melting pot of downtown New Haven. No one appeared out of place as we swung around the Green and pulled on to Chapel. Long-haired college students, racially mixed couples, Hasidic Jews, and construction workers all mingled without biting each other's heads off. I felt comfortable in New Haven and would often sit on the Green to watch humanity go about its business, oblivious to the differences of the people around them.

I located a spot to park, and we walked the two blocks to the restaurant. It was a home run for the first date. The food was decent, and no one stared, except when Wanda flew off on a social diatribe in a voice that was better suited for an outdoor rally. All the patrons had some aspect that was far left of conventional, so a contrasted definition of normality was in force.

"So, Angela, what do you want to be when you grow up?"

"I'm studying elementary education. I want to teach in the city. The kids are so far behind and they drop out in large numbers. Half the girls that I went to high school with already have babies. How about you, Matt?"

"I wish I had a clue, Angela, but I switched majors so many times that I'm not sure I have one. I started off in teaching, but now I'm taking a lot of science courses. Men might not have much choice because of the war. I know your brother went to Vietnam, but I won't go in the service. I don't believe in the war or any war for that matter. I'll have to go to Canada or jail if I get drafted."

"We didn't want my brother to go in the Army, but he flunked out of school and got drafted. My mother worried every night. I could hear her praying that he wouldn't get killed, and I guess it worked. We're a very religious family. What religion are you, Matt?"

"I was raised as a Catholic, but I don't go to church anymore. My mother's pretty religious, so she's not very happy with my choice."

That wasn't the best topic for me to expound on, and Angela's visible disappointment concerning my faith stunted the conversation. I needed to change the subject before I began a vicious denunciation of the Church. Wanda thoroughly enjoyed my discomfort, but at least she kept her mouth shut.

"What unit was your brother in while he was in Vietnam, Angela?"

"I have no idea, Matt. He never spoke about the war in any of his letters. He started off in a combat unit, but all I know is that he worked in a medical unit toward the end. Why?"

"Just curious. A few of my friends were in Vietnam. One was killed, and the other one died of some bad dope when he got back home. I went to two funerals this week."

"That's terrible. I'm so sorry. Oh my God! It's three o'clock, and I'm supposed to be home by now. My mother will have the police out looking for me."

I paid the check, and the conversation was kept light as she guided me through the back streets to her home. The shoulder was killing me, so I let her steer part of the way. Even though she was eighteen, she didn't have her license yet and had never driven a car, so it turned into a pretty hairy, but fun experience for Angela. As Wanda bitched and screamed about our driving, I offered to drop her off in front of a bar, but she didn't intend to leave us alone in the car.

"Matt, leave us at the bus stop, and we'll walk home from there. I don't want my mother to see us. She's not ready for this yet, and a white boy in a red convertible will be noticed. Don't get out to open the door. I'll grab my books. Thanks for lunch. Come on, Wanda."

I didn't argue since I understood the rules about impinging on foreign territory. She thanked me with her killer smile, touching my arm lightly, but there would be no kiss. It was the first date of her life and it would be dangerous for me anyway.

It hadn't gone as well as I would have liked, but wasn't a total disaster. I learned something that day about differences. The color thing turned out to be a minor problem, but the culture issue would be a much bigger hurdle. I had never thought about religion as being a barrier to a relationship, and maybe down the road it wouldn't be, but I had stepped into a different world that day. Another level of understanding had revealed my ignorance to me.

Wanda disappeared around the corner while Angela stayed behind for a moment to wave goodbye. As my car pulled from away the curb, I never saw the big Oldsmobile cutting me off until the last second. Quick reflexes stopped my car inches from disaster, sending a current of pain to my shoulder from the sudden stop. Four black men jumped out of the Olds, and one giant stood out above the rest. I heard Angela scream, "Ronald, no!" I knew instantly that someone had arrived home a day early.

I scrambled painfully over the door before they reached me, instinctively knowing that I would be a sitting duck in the blockaded convertible. Angela ran out into the street to head off her brother, and the commotion began to draw an instant crowd. The barbershop and bars emptied of men and boys that had been loitering on the street corner in a heat-wave stupor. The entire block had become animated by the activity. Free entertainment in the form of a beating was always standing room only.

"What were you doing in that white boy's car, Angela? Go home, now! I'll make sure that he understands not to come around here again, since you didn't make it clear to him, or maybe he didn't listen."

The crowd egged Ronald on. What had promised to be another boring day on the street suddenly gave hope of some action. They all knew Ronald's temperament, and they were urging him to beat the hell out of me. Better that Ronald had a white boy to beat on instead of them.

"Ronald, stop! We only had lunch and he gave me a ride home. That's all. Wanda was with us the whole time. Ask her! Let him go. He's a nice guy. We go to school together. It wasn't a date."

"There are no nice guys, Angela, and I don't see that bitch anywhere 'round here. Anybody see Wanda 'round here?"

Of course they had, but they weren't about to speak up and possibly interrupt the fun. That might focus Ronald's attention on one of them, which would be a bad turn of events from their point of view.

"Nobody's seen her, Angela. You're lying to me. Go home! He doesn't belong here, and you shouldn't have been in his white-ass car. You know that! Wait till Mamma finds out you've been lying to her. They all want the same thing, but he ain't getting it from you."

She held her ground, staying right in his face, distracting him for a moment, which gave me some measure of relief since she had said that he would never hurt her.

Ronald turned away from his sister, gently moving her aside with a sweep of his huge arm. He crowded me, getting up close and personal, invading my comfort zone to within inches of my face. He wasn't that much taller than I was, but he had me by ninety pounds or more, and his arms were as thick as my thighs. I felt more confident in a fight if I had more room to use my long arms and quick hands, but he was right on me. It wasn't the size issue; however, that pumped the adrenaline into my bloodstream and fired off the beginnings of a flight or fight reaction. The man had a countenance cut from granite, with no emotion or warmth evident in his eyes, mouth, or crevice of his skin. I was two inches away from the inanimate face of a very violent man, maybe a killer, if the connections were correct.

It reminded me of Antonio's expression at the railroad yard years ago, moments before he intended to waste me, but he wore a lamb's face compared to Ronald's. Angela's screams did nothing to change his posture, as he pinned me against the car with his bulk while his companions closed off any route of escape. Diplomacy might offer slight hope.

"Look man, I wasn't doing anything wrong. Like she said, we had lunch with Wanda, and then I dropped them off. Wanda went down that side street over there. I'm Matt Kronchek."

I offered my hand, which he ignored. At the mention of my name, a light of recognition had flickered in his eyes.

"Did I ask you anything, fuck head? I don't give warnings about my sister, so your white ass is going to get a beating no matter what story you want to tell. Where did you come from, and why the fuck are you with Angela?"

"We go to school together, and I asked them to lunch. I made certain that I said them. What's the crime in that? We just met for Christ's sake!"

He demonstrated his opinion of my supposed transgressions with his sister as he backed up a bit to throw a short left hook at my head without warning. Having learned a lot about survival in my short life, I anticipated the punch when I saw his left shoulder twitch before he let go. I bobbed down and away from the blow, which grazed my right ear. My dodging movements, combined with the force of his forearm hitting my head, bent my upper body into the back seat.

"Ronald, stop! His left shoulder is hurt. He can't defend himself," Angela screamed as she ran into the road.

Her voice caused him to redirect his attention to the street, giving me time to recover my reflexes. If he had made a solid connection, it would have been over already. The man was so powerful that my life could be in danger from one punch.

Momentarily dazed, I quickly reoriented myself out of a desire to survive, with my clearing eyes spotting Leo's billy bat on the back seat. It was a drilled out piece of rock maple, ten inches long, with lead poured in the middle for added weight. I wrapped my hand around the handle, securing the grip with the leather thong as I waited for his next move. Ronald turned away from Angela, reaching over the car and grabbing my shirt to drag me out for a more thorough beating. His overconfidence allowed me to bring the bat down hard on his clenched hand, scoring a direct hit on the knuckles.

Ronald buckled over, howling from the pain, and I kicked myself upright using the car and his massive chest for leverage, but my full effort only knocked him back a few feet. We faced each other in the street a yard apart, my eyes locked on his in defiance, with the ever-enlarging crowd stunned to silence. One of Ronald's boys held Angela back as she struggled and screamed for her brother to stop. Ronald's left hand had already begun to swell, and blood trickled from my ear where his punch had swept across it.

Anger filled Ronald's eyes, animating his mouth into a wicked sneer. "You little white bitch! I was just going to give you an educational beating, but I think you broke my hand. I'll make it painful and slow, so you'll understand where not to go in this city. Which shoulder was it, Angela, the left?"

Ronald shot a straight right at my injured shoulder, blasting through my defensive forearm, dropping me to the tar in agony. I rolled away from a short kick as I heard police sirens wail in the distance. I would need to buy some time, but my mouth was all I had left.

"That's right, Ronald, it's my left shoulder. The one that Simon Rebrone jammed a pen into at the VA hospital."

Ronald's foot hung back at the mention of Rebrone's name, so I pressed the issue to keep him occupied.

"You should have heard that boy ramble on about his unit in Nam, Ronald. You want to hear what he had to say? It was crazy, but pretty interesting stuff if you could make the connection. You see the connection, Ronald?"

The sirens drew closer, only a street away, but my babbling had bought enough time for that day. Ronald shouted orders to his men.

"Get Angela in the car, and let's get out of here. Too many people around."

Ronald stayed behind. He picked me off the ground and slammed me against my car, pinning the bat to my side.

"You think you're cute. I know who you are now, and you're a dead man unless you move to Alaska. I'm going to hurt you bad for messing with my sister, and then I'm going to make you beg me to kill you for interfering with my business."

He shoved me to the ground, running to his car and speeding away before the police arrived. The street emptied as quickly as it had filled, with not a witness in sight. Heat shimmered off the sticky tar, and it was hard to believe that there were so many people standing in the street a moment before. I told the cops that I had taken a wrong turn and gotten into a little beef with some of the downtown people. No, I didn't want to press charges, I said. I just wanted to go home. They had no problem with that, since charges would mean paperwork, so they sent me on my way, telling me to stay out of that part of the city.

It was an excruciating drive home, and I didn't know what I was going to do next. Ronald hadn't done any additional damage to my arm, but the punch had increased the pain. A part of me wanted to keep on driving to Florida and hide out for a year, but I had no money. Plus, I would be leaving other people behind that they could get to. Once again, I had gotten myself involved in some nasty business, but I hadn't gone looking for trouble. I gave some serious thought to calling those boys from the FBI, when I remembered the picture of Paulie's unit in Vietnam.

Parking in a crowded supermarket where there would be safety in numbers, I pulled out the picture. I found Paulie and Tommy in the front row, and there was no mistaking the man-mountain in the back. There was only one Ronald Williams in my life—Paulie's killer and Angela's brother. A white guy with dark hair and sunglasses in the second row caught my eye. There was a familiar look to him, and I realized that it was the man at the funerals. I knew him from somewhere, but the picture contained no names on the bottom or the back. Debbie might know something about the photograph. Perhaps she had a list of the men that were in Paulie's unit at the time of the photo.

I had confronted the supposed devil's master and lived, but I had a feeling that it didn't happen twice, and I didn't intend to give him a second chance.

Chapter 13

Ronald cherished his family above all else, and it hurt him that Angela wouldn't speak to him on the way home from the fight with the white boy. He wasn't worried that she would tell Mamma because she had been caught in a lie, but she understood that angry silence would be the worst punishment for him.

He had to admit that she had grown up to be a beautiful woman, and that was all the more reason to keep an eye on her. Whenever he wasn't in town, he would spread some money around to make sure that no one got near her, especially Kronchek. He wanted Angela to get married someday, but not until she had finished college and found a good job.

That Kronchek asshole had shaken him for a moment with his words. The surprise had spared the bastard a nastier beating, but a dimmer future from Ronald's perspective. His hand throbbed, but the mention of Rebrone's name had done the most damage. He couldn't kill Kronchek in the near future without arousing Angela's suspicions, but the Rebrone issue would have to be taken care of immediately. Ronald would put a call in to his partner to arrange the details. Angela's silence was torturing him, and she knew it.

"Angela, I'm sorry, but you know that I don't want you going out with anyone while I'm away, especially that white piece of shit. Look what he did to me."

"Matt is a nice guy, Ronald, and I'm old enough to pick my own dates.

Why won't you believe that Wanda was with us the whole time? Call her. I love you, Ronald, but you have to stop interfering in my life. You could have killed him, and for no reason. I want you to stay out of my business."

"Nice guy! Look what he did to my hand. I don't think that he grew up on a farm somewhere. You don't learn to fight like that in the country, or by being a nice guy. You don't even know him, Angela, and you rode in his car like a silly child. That's why I have to interfere. You bet your ass that I'm calling Wanda, and if you're lying, I'll go looking for Kronchek tonight and finish the job."

"Wanda knows him from the Interracial Council at school, and she said that he was annoying, but a good person. I wouldn't get into just anybody's car, and besides, you hit him first. What was he suppose to do, let you beat him to death?"

Even though he was angry and jealous over his sister's defense of the white boy, Ronald continued to draw information about Kronchek from Angela.

"Yea, but where's he from? He should have shit his pants when I went after him, but he held his ground. There's something weird about that guy."

"God, Ronald, he grew up in Bellington, and he's a student, not a gangster, which is more than I can say for the group that you were with today. What alley did you find them in? I think you're angry because someone finally stood up to you."

"He got lucky this time. Bellington? That white bread town up north? I bet his parents will be real proud when he brings you home for the first time. His mamma will be thrilled to see your black face. Stay away from him for his sake, Angela, if not yours."

When they arrived home, Angela jumped out of the car, slamming the door hard as she ran into the house.

"I hate you, Ronald! I wish you hadn't come home. If he gets hurt, then I'll know it was you, and I'll never talk to you again."

Her anger bit painfully into Ronald's fragile base of familial stability. He would smooth things over with Angela later, but right now he needed to talk to his partner about this Rebrone issue. Ronald wanted to kill Kronchek that night, but he would have to be patient and make it look like an accident. A drunk-driving crash or drug overdose would be perfect for a college student. He would hold his hand back until he discovered what Kronchek knew. If he knew too much or attempted to talk to the authorities, then Ronald would be left with no choice. As it went down; however, he would be right in front of Angela. When Kronchek checked out of this world, Ronald's alibi would be secure. He pulled over to a phone booth, fumbling in his pockets for a dime.

"Hey, it's me. We need to talk. Can you do West Rock in about an hour?"

"No problem, but come alone and bring the stuff. I don't want any of your boys to see me."

"Don't worry, I'll be alone. Wait till you see the quality of this smack."

"Hey, not on the phone." The line went dead, and Ronald knew that he had screwed up.

Ronald cruised around campus looking for Kronchek's car without success before heading up to West Rock Park. New Haven was flanked on the east and west by rock cliffs and woods that had been consolidated into two separate City parks. East Rock loomed over the other end of New Haven.

He parked the Oldsmobile on the lookout, left the engine on and gazed over the city, a city that he would be running soon, at least in the projects and alleyways. His men were already setting up a network of runners, dealers, and enforcers. The men that worked for him would become his first customers, and they would be motivated to addict others in order to support their own habits. Soon they would be pushing the Wops out of the black neighborhoods. His first purchases would be guns for his men.

The white addicts in Vietnam had given Ronald an idea for broadening the heroin market. The New Haven area was loaded with drug-curious, white college students. Ronald's goal was to give whitey a taste of his own medicine and make a fortune in the bargain. The Wops funneled most of the hard dope into the ghettos, and it had fucked up the black neighborhoods in terrible way. Ronald wanted to expand to the suburbs and share the addictive misery, while boosting his sales. A tap on the passenger side window interrupted his entrepreneurial daydreams. He surveyed the area for cops.

"Donato, hop in and we'll take a drive. We should stay on the move. How's it going? Wait until you take a taste of this shit."

"I was doing fine until I heard about the incident with Kronchek on Dixwell Avenue in full view of fifty people. What were you thinking, Ronald? Are you going to blow the whole deal because you're worried that some white boy has a bone for your sister? We have a lot at stake with this dope, and your sister is a big girl. That type of crap draws attention to you, and that's the one thing we don't need. Remember my Uncle Vito?"

"Look, Donato, we're business partners, but don't tell me what to do when it comes to my sister. It might be too late for me, but I'm not letting her fuck up her life because of some guy, especially a white one. He'll just break her heart when his mommy freaks out about him being with a nigger."

"You know, Ronald, this isn't much of a partnership if I have to do all the thinking. Number one, Kronchek isn't afraid of what people think. If he likes your sister, he won't dump her for any reason, and will probably like her more if someone tells him not to, especially his mother. Second, if he's hanging around with your sister, then we'll know where he is, won't we? He'll be easier to watch, but why don't you let me handle him, and you take care of the shipments like we agreed."

"I think that he knows too much already, but why would you want to get involved with him and blow your cover? How do you know all these little facts about him, Donato? What about Rebrone?"

"I checked it out, and Rebrone is so heavily sedated that he won't be a problem. Besides, he's being transferred to a facility for the criminally insane where they'll drug him harder and humor his ranting in a padded cell. Nobody listened to him before, and certainly no one will take him seriously now. It isn't worth the risk trying to kill him. He's as good as dead to society, and his testimony isn't worth shit."

"Well, what about Kronchek? I'm not using my sister as bait to keep that asshole away from us. I'll finish him off myself."

"Listen, Ronald, I grew up with him. We lived in the same neighborhood, and he's been stubborn since the day he was born. The more pressure you put on him, the more he'll fight back, just like he did today. His whole life has been one big crusade. Let me talk to him and make him understand that it will be better for everyone's health if he backs off. He's smart enough to realize that this is way over his head, but I need to make him believe that it was his idea."

"Go ahead and handle him, but you'd better tell him to stay away from my sister or I'll kill him."

"Don't become a liability over this, Ronald. We can't draw attention to ourselves, especially me. I'm dead if we get caught again. Drugs are a big business for my uncle, and he wouldn't hesitate to have me hit. I need to be totally invisible in this operation, but I'll take care of Kronchek because you're too emotionally involved. I'm having him watched, so there won't be any surprises. Let me see the stuff."

Ronald didn't appreciate the word liability because that's what Donato had called Paulie and Tommy, and now they were dead. The little guinea should be terrified of him, but Ronald saw no flicker of fear or doubt in his partner. At least Ronald loved his family, but Donato never mentioned loving anything except power and money. Ronald didn't even know if Donato had a family, except for his mob relatives. Ronald handed Donato a small bag of white powder.

"This is the best smack we've ever had. It's never been stepped on. Flown in fresh to Saigon, skimmed by our guys, and shipped in the body bags. I've got another load coming in tomorrow, and within a week it will be all over Harlem."

Donato put a finger in the bag, touching a small amount to his tongue.

"Wow! You weren't shitting about the purity. Let the boys in Harlem cut and distribute the stuff. It's a lot harder to get caught if you don't have to set up a lab and a distribution network. There are less people to crack and rat us out. We're staying wholesale."

"Let them cut it? Then we have to buy it back from them to deal in New Haven."

Donato had already figured out that Ronald was harboring delusions of becoming the big New Haven drug king.

"Don't be stupid. This way, we stay out of sight, and if my uncle catches on, I'll rat out a few of the local boys that you set up in business.

It's quicker, cleaner money that way, plus we stay in the background by sticking to the wholesale end. People who strut around the streets always get caught, and that can't happen."

"But what about the crew that I've already recruited? I was going to expand into the suburbs using some of the white guys that were with us in Nam."

"Ronald, are you out of your fucking mind! If you bring that shit into the white neighborhoods you won't last a week. My uncle's men will put one shot to the back of your skull, and you won't even hear them coming. They're not the least bit frightened of a guy like you. To them you're like a fly on shit."

"Why? It's all right for black people to be junkies, but not whites? What are you trying to tell me here, Donato?"

"You know, Ronald, I decided to become your partner because you came up with a great plan for shipping the drugs. It was fucking brilliant, and I said to myself, now here's a guy who's smarter than the rest. Even people who hear rumors about how we're shipping the stuff don't believe it. I heard the body bag idea mentioned at a party once, but everyone said it was just an urban legend and laughed it off, but you made it work.

"I thought you were a guy who knows what he wants and how to get it, just like me, but now I'm not so sure. You think with your emotions, not your brain."

Ronald didn't appreciate the insults from someone half his size. His eyes burned with anger as he leaned menacingly across the seat to within inches of Donato's face.

"I'm not smart because I want to expand our market to white people? I don't give a fuck about the blacks, and I certainly don't care about the whites. What's the problem? I don't like you talking to me that way."

If Ronald presented an intimidating figure, Donato didn't let it show. He hadn't gotten this far by scaring easily, but violence had never been his forte. He may have pushed the big man a bit too hard this time, and would need to cool him off for awhile.

"Take it easy and let me explain how the goddamn system works here in America. Most people in the States have no idea what's going on with drugs in Vietnam. The FBI doesn't even know that the CIA supplies heroin to the Mob. You know that, and I know it, but our mighty FBI is totally fucking confused. Actually, they don't give a shit because it's flowing primarily into the ghetto. That's the deal the Mob has with the CIA. As long as it stays in the ghetto, the Agency will look the other way. If white people start getting hooked, especially white kids, then their sweet deal is off because it will draw heavy attention from the FBI. The Mob doesn't need any more scrutiny from the Feds, and the CIA would have some explaining to do. Not to mention the fact that there's plenty of money to be made the way things are. The old Capos were very reluctant to go into the drug business, so it's a real bad idea to spread it beyond the cities."

"Come on, Donato, even a bastard like me has a hard time believing a story like that. I think that you're just a nigger-hating bunch of guineas that want to exploit black people, and you're starting piss me off. I had big plans for this expansion, and I don't want to give it up."

"Yeah, I'll be straight with you. I never liked niggers, and I don't really like you, but that's got nothing to do with business. Understand one thing and you'll get rich. Business is business: simply that and with nothing more to read into it. I'll tell you one more time, and it better sink in. If the smack starts hitting white America, the CIA will lean on the Mob, and the Mob will find out who caused the pressure. And if my people don't get us, then the FBI will be all over the 'newly discovered' drug problem, and business will suck. It won't suck for us; however, because we'll be dead. That's the way it will be forever, Ronald. You can do business, or you can do time if you live. Are you with me on this, or do I have to cut you loose?"

Ronald sensed that the tone of his partner's voice contained more than a threat. Donato's frankness and total lack of fear made Ronald insecure. Maybe things would have to be Donato's way for now, but not forever. If the blacks couldn't run their own neighborhoods, then how could they take charge of anything? He'd take care of this little bastard in due time, but for now he would play the game because there were too many loose ends.

"I'm with you. I'll allow the New Haven guys to set up in their own areas, and we'll collect a percentage of their take if they want to stay in business. The local dealers will never see you, but you have to keep an eye on things when I go out of town to pick up the smack. What about Kronchek?"

"I told you that I would take care of it. If necessary, I'll pay him a little visit to explain the facts of life, but I have a feeling that he will eventually come looking for me once he figures it out. He's cocky, but he won't risk his family or friends, and he'll understand that I have a hundred ways to get to him."

"*And one big way to control you, Ronald. Your sister.*" Donato said to himself.

"I gotta go, Ronald. Call me when the next load comes in, and I'll send someone around to bring it to New York."

"Okay, see ya later."

Ronald thought as he pulled away, "*Oh yea, I'll call you after I take some for myself, and soon my dope will be shoved right up your Italian ass.*" He wondered if Donato had a sister, and how it would feel to make her an addict. Ronald would take her out, screw her and then shoot her up with smack, so Donato could see how Ronald felt when he caught his sister with that white asshole. Yeah, that would be sweet ghetto justice.

Chapter 14

I needed to talk to Debbie after my confrontation with Ronald Williams, but my body was too beat up to drive all the way to Bellington. It would be best to walk away, but I didn't think that Ronald and his boys were going to let it go now that I had confronted him with my information. They could have me marked for elimination, and it appeared that someone had been following me all along, but I had no clue as to who they were. Even though I was living it, the last few days seemed to be a ridiculous way to live. I had been rousted by the FBI, stabbed with a pen, and almost beaten to death by a giant.

As much as I hated the idea, eventually I would have to go to the FBI if I wanted to live, but first I needed to find out the identity of the soldier with the sunglasses. Also, it was important to me to understand why all this was happening. I was no stranger to drugs. To heroin yes, but was there so much money involved that it would warrant the dead bodies and threats? I also had a hard time believing that Paulie had been dealing heroin. A decision required more information, so Leo would have to drive me to Bellington at night. My car would remain in New Haven in full view of anyone that might be watching, and the plan was for Leo to pick me up on the next street where we could leave unnoticed.

Leo loved a road trip and anything to do with mystery and adventure. Once he understood that it might be dangerous, he became uncontrollably excited. Leo had been a good find as a roommate. He was intensely loyal and would fight for me at the drop of a hat. Fighting had always been more of a hobby for him, an enjoyable pursuit that helped drain some of his excess reserves of energy and latent anger. He would be an asset if things got rough. I told him only about the altercation with Ronald Williams, and that some people related to the incident were after me. He didn't care to know more, he just wanted to get going.

"Kronchek, hurry up in the shower. I've got all the weapons together: a baseball bat, a couple of knives, and some rocks. You think your friend Debbie can fix me up with someone when we get there?"

"Relax, Leo. If you had seen the size of Williams today, you wouldn't be so anxious to get going. I'm lucky to be standing here. We'll need more than what you're collecting if he catches up with us. Our best bet is to make sure that no one follows us. These are nasty people, and we're not going to Bellington to relieve your horny impulses."

"I know that you hit on your dead buddy's girlfriend the other day, even though you denied it. I figured you wanted me to take you up for more action, and that maybe she had a friend that would be desperate for some Leo love. It's the least you could do for someone who's risking his life."

"Leo, I didn't hit on her the other day, and you're worse than me when it comes to listening, or you only hear things the way you want to hear them. I already explained to you that I had an obligation to return the picture, and that I intend to discourage any further ideas about a relationship. I'm through with this multiple woman scenario forever. You need to watch my back in case Ronald Williams catches up to me because I'm too banged up to do this alone. Let's go. I'm ready, so please shut the hell up and get your mind out of your pants."

Leo left about two minutes ahead of me, giving me time to make a visible presence by locking my car in the driveway and carrying my books inside. I went upstairs, turning on the light in my room before leaving stealthily by the back door. I crawled through the bushes and over a small stream to the next street where Leo had parked his car.

We took a circuitous route to reach the main road so we could determine if anyone was on our tail. It took us about twenty minutes longer than normal to reach Bellington, but paranoia and existential concerns made the extra time worthwhile. I didn't like putting Leo in danger, but this couldn't be done alone. If I obtained the right answers, the information could be delivered to the FBI, but were they capable or motivated to protect my family and friends? Would they bother with my welfare once they obtained the information? Ronald Williams was probably a killer, perhaps a multiple murderer who could get to me by harming my family or anyone that was close to me, including Karen.

This would be much simpler if I knew for sure that Paulie had done nothing wrong, and that Williams had killed him. I could be vengeful towards Williams or turn him in, but the FBI had a hidden agenda that I couldn't decipher at the moment. There were too many missing pieces.

I felt as if I needed to be in three places at once, but perhaps I had been pursuing the wrong strategy. After tonight, I would be visible and accessible, but on my guard, so they wouldn't go looking for me at my mother or Karen's house. At least I knew that Angela would be safe from her brother. Through all the anger and cruelty in his eyes, a deep commitment to his sister sat firmly in the center of his focus. Tenderness and familial duty seemed incongruous in such a murderous soul, but brotherly concern had flared out at me when he threatened my life.

We decided to drive by Debbie's a few times to make certain that she wasn't under surveillance. As we cruised by the newly painted house with its well-manicured lawn, her parents' car was missing from the garage, but a green Volkswagen Beetle sat in the driveway. I told Leo to go by my mother's to check for strange cars. Her street seemed clear so we pulled around the corner to talk things over.

"Someone is at Debbie's house, Leo, but I don't recognize the car."

"Kronchek, you're usually the rational one, but are you retarded? Do you really think that Ronald Williams can fit in, or would be caught dead in a Beetle? There's more to this than you're saying, Kronchek. I'll go look in the window and see who it is. If it's Ronald Williams, you can have my car."

"I don't want this piece of junk, but it doesn't have to be Williams for it to be dangerous. You're right. There might be other people involved. I'll give you the whole story on the way home, but let me check out the house. If I get caught, at least they'll recognize me, but if someone spots your ugly face at the window, the townspeople will be out with torches and pitchforks. Pick me up in front in about ten minutes."

"Pitchforks and torches? Hey, I saw that in a Frankenstein movie. Are you saying that I look like a monster? Ungrateful asshole!"

I jumped out of the car, ignoring his offended ranting, while cutting through the backyards that abutted Debbie's property. Heavier, cooler, fall air had begun to filter into the Northeast, with the clouds that had formed from the collision of two weather fronts blocking the stars. A heavy mist limited visibility to a few feet, but I knew every inch of the terrain from years of taking shortcuts through the neighborhood. I could do this route with a bag over my head, if necessary.

I hopped Debbie's fence, which had been put up years ago in a futile attempt to stop us from using their yard as a pathway to the park. Quietly pushing the bushes aside, I moved cautiously toward the kitchen window. It had been left open as a relief from the heat of the day, and through the screen came moaning sounds from the darkened portion of the house. A streetlight shining through the front window framed two figures thrashing about on a couch. Debbie had a guy over and they were about to do the dirty deed in her living room!

I hated to spoil their fun, but my life was at stake, so I ran around the front and found Leo parked across the street.

"Leo, give me the picture. She's in there making out with some guy on the couch. I'm going to have to break it up, and this little tryst of hers should take me off the hook for Saturday."

Leo became animated, more like a cartoon character than human, and as I tried to leave the car, he held on to my shirt in desperation.

"Don't interfere with somebody's love making, Kronchek. That just isn't right. You're not a nice person."

"Okay, I'll wait a few minutes before I knock, but I don't want to hang around too long. We need to keep moving."

"Good idea. Let's go around back and watch. You said she had a great body."

"Are you a weirdo, Leo? I'm not watching, plus if any of the neighbors see us, the cops will be here before you stop drooling. You're really sick or just desperate."

"Geez, Kronchek, calm down. You ask me to risk my life, and then you deny me a little fun. I'll wait here if that's what you want, but I thought this was going to be an adventure, not a nap in my car."

"What a sacrifice you're making, Leo, but maybe you can go home next weekend and watch your sister through the keyhole in the bathroom."

Most people would have been insulted and angry at such a comment, but not Leo. He actually gave the suggestion some thought.

"Nah, that won't work anymore. I think my sister has caught on, because she hangs a towel on the doorknob all the time. Next summer I might drill a hole from my room into the bathroom when no one's home."

I think he was playing me, but with Leo you couldn't be certain. Shaking my head in disgust, I grabbed the photograph of Paulie's unit. Leo waited outside the car to stand watch. Just as I reached the door, a person emerged from the house, and I couldn't believe my eyes. It was my old friend, actually more like Paulie's friend, Billy Mancini. The little weasel had been plunking Debbie. This reunion thing was getting old.

Initially stunned by my unfathomable presence, Billy finally managed to stammer a greeting. He didn't look so good. Even in the semi-dark, I noticed his sunken eyes with dark circles, and a rail thin body that used to be stocky. His right hand shook as he raised it in greeting, and he must have sniffled three times before he stammered.

"Hey, Ma—Matt. Wha'—wha'—what are you doing here? I haven't seen you in years."

"I'm bringing back a picture that I borrowed from Debbie. I missed you at the funeral, Billy. You look sick. What's up?"

"My asthma has been acting up with the ragweed out and all. We were away on vacation, so I just heard about Paulie. I came over to see how Debbie was holding up. I hate those gooks for killing Paulie. We should nuke the whole country. Make it a big parking lot."

"That's real original, but if you hate them so much, why aren't you in the Army? They're looking for volunteers. A guy with your principles and passion could be a real killing machine. The war would be over in a week."

"Well, I'm still in school like you, and then I'll have a deferment because of my asthma. That's why."

"Yeah, but I don't hate the Vietnamese, and I don't want to go to war. Why don't you enlist, then you could kill lots of them. They say it's a lot more fun if you shoot them yourself, but of course the problem is that they shoot back, and then you would piss yourself."

"You're even more of jerk since you went to college, and I heard from my mom what you said at Paulie's funeral. I told you that I can't go in because I'm sick. Fuck off, Matt, you hippie freak!"

"That's damn fucking impolite of you, Billy, when I'm trying to carry on an intellectual conversation. I just think that people should be willing to fight for what they say they believe in. Excuse me for having principles, you gutless little punk. I never remember you having asthma."

He sensed the rising anger in my voice so he turned and walked away, deciding that he wanted no part of me. I cringed as I spotted Leo crossing the street. Billy and Leo had met a few years ago at a party in Bellington, and the experience led them to harbor a mutual distaste for each other. Leo overheard the interchange and couldn't resist playing with the opportunity.

"Hey, Billy boy. It's me, Leo. How's it hanging? Getting any lately, uhh like in the last few minutes or so. You are the man, Billy. Wham, bam, Billy's the man."

"Fuck you too, cretin."

Debbie appeared at the front door in response to the commotion. Her hair and clothes looked perfect, with nothing out of place. The girl was simply amazing that way.

"Matt, what are you doing here and who's that on the sidewalk following Billy? Why is Billy shouting?"

I gave Leo the shut up signal with my finger, motioning for him to go back near the car. Debbie needed to preserve her dignity, and didn't need us giving her a hard time about screwing around with Billy.

"That's my roommate, Leo, and Billy got a little upset because I wouldn't buy his theory about being an arm chair war hero. I brought back your picture, but I need to ask you something. Can I come in for a minute?"

"Just for a minute, Matt, because my parents will be home soon, and you know how my mother feels about you. Your roommate's weird. Why is he chasing after Billy's car and jumping around?"

"Ignore him. He's a good friend, but he's crazy."

Gesturing emphatically for Leo to get back to the car, I pointed to my eyes, reminding him to do his job as a lookout.

Debbie appeared to be uncomfortable, like she couldn't wait for me to leave, which was quite a change from the other day. I wanted to exit that weird scene myself, but not until she looked at the photo.

"Debbie, do you know name of the soldier with the sunglasses? I think it's the same person that showed up at both funerals. I know him from somewhere, but I can't put my finger on it."

Tears of loss and guilt began to roll down her cheeks as she studied the young faces casually leaning on an artillery piece, smiling with their arms on each other's shoulders, some with their shirts off as if they didn't have a care in the world. Seeing Paulie's picture so soon after her little rendezvous with Billy probably represented cheating to her. In fact, I'm sure it did. She blotted her tears with the cleanest white handkerchief I had ever seen, and my mother could do laundry with the best of them.

"I don't recognize him, Matt, but I remembered today that in one of Paulie's letters he mentioned that another old friend from the neighborhood had been briefly assigned to his unit. Maybe that's him with the sunglasses, and that would explain why he looks familiar to you."

"Did Paulie ever mention his name?"

"I can't quite remember, but now that I think of it, I heard one of Tommy's uncles say, "Take it easy, Rich", but I wasn't sure who he was talking to. Does that help any?"

Oh yeah, that helped. I hadn't seen him since tenth grade, but add a few inches in height and thirty pounds, and you had Rich Donato. Rich had been a criminal since he was ten, mostly shoplifting and petty theft. It took him years to get nailed, but when we were sixteen, Rich did a stint at the reform school for stealing booze and selling it to minors. How he fit in with all this was not clear, but given his criminal proclivities and raw intelligence, I would guess that he was in bed with Ronald Williams, and that he was most likely the brains of the operation. It would explain why they were able to track me so easily and know so much about me. And maybe how Tommy had checked out while Ronald was still in Vietnam.

"No, Deb, the name's not familiar, but no big deal. About Saturday—"

"Oh yeah, Matt, I can't see you on Saturday. I have to go to my uncle's house in Massachusetts. Maybe we can get together some other time."

What a relief! I had one less problem to worry about. I thought about saying something to Debbie concerning the weasel-like tendencies of Billy, but I let it go. He would be her next project, and unbeknownst to him, she probably already had their lives planned. Poor Billy went home feeling lucky to get laid, but couldn't see that his leg was already in the trap. He would have to gnaw it off to get away from Debbie, but he never had the stones to be in control, so he was doomed.

"Yea, maybe another time. And Deb, about Paulie and that stuff in Vietnam."

"Yes, Matt."

"There was nothing bad going on except the war. I'm sure he was afraid and who wouldn't be. I guess he must have become a better card player, which would explain the money. People change, you know? He was a good guy. Mike and I did all the bad stuff, not Paulie."

"Thanks, Matt. You'd better go now before my parents get back."

It seemed that I couldn't leave soon enough to satisfy her this time.

"Take it easy, Deb. I'll see you around."

As I left the house, I heard the door open behind me.

"Matt."

"What?"

"People do change, but not Paulie. Thanks for being his friend and helping me out the other day."

"No problem, Deb. I have to do something right once in awhile."

I suppose she figured out that I had lied to her, but Debbie appeared to be content to leave it that way. She was not a person that could live with uncertainty and gray areas. To her, the Vietnam War had killed Paulie, and she would have to go on to someone new to survive. She was not a heartless person, but a practical one who understood that life goes on, and in reality, it most certainly always does.

When I reached the car, Leo was nowhere in sight, and the keys were in the ignition. I panicked and started the car, driving slowly down the road when suddenly I spotted him stumbling across the street. Leo had one eye covered as he hopped in the passenger seat. A blood soaked handkerchief was under his hand.

"What the hell happened? Why didn't you stay with the car? I can't get you to follow the simplest instructions. This isn't a basketball game. We could get killed if you don't listen to me."

Leo had never been skillful at hiding his mistakes. He appeared embarrassed, which normally took a lot for him.

"I went around back to peek in the window to see if you were fooling around with the chick, and I noticed this guy in the hedges watching the house. I chased him for about two blocks, until he cut into the woods behind your mother's house. I ran into a tree branch and it knocked the shit out of me. I think I need stitches. When I got up, he was gone. He got away clean. I was faster than him, but he ran and dodged like he knew every inch of the terrain."

We cruised around the neighborhood for a while, but the streets were deserted. Whoever had been watching was nowhere to be found. My guess, from Leo's description of the chase, was that Rich Donato or one of his boys had been on the scene. He grew up in the neighborhood and knew it as well as anyone. I figured the safest course of action would be to head back to New Haven and bring Leo to the emergency room to get stitched up. I knew more of the players now, but I needed to enlist some help and obtain protection for my family and friends. Would I have time, or would they get to me first?

Chapter 15

Wanda didn't intend to be late for the meeting of the interracial council. A punctual person, who demanded the same of others, made it essential that she arrive on time. If she were late, Matt would harass her unmercifully, obtaining a free pass in his opinion, to arrive late any time he pleased.

Wanda's family lived three streets over from Angela Williams. She had taken the younger girl under her guidance years ago, working hard to keep her out of trouble. Wanda and Ronald were the same age and had gone to high school together. Well-spoken and fastidiously dressed as a child, he impressed most adults that met him, but she remembered the suppressed anger that he always carried within him, even as a young boy. It seemed to have surfaced after his dad was killed on the docks, but he never talked about it, so the frustration festered all these years. There was a lot of talk at the time of how the blacks were given all the dangerous jobs on the docks, and Wanda was certain that Ronald had heard the stories and taken them to heart.

Boys that were two and three years older than Ronald had been frightened of him; frightened of his intensity and brute strength. In a football game or even at practice, he played as if it were a life or death situation. He brutalized his own teammates in practice to the degree that he had to be left out of certain drills. Life had always been a war for him, one that he had no intention of losing. His high school lost only one football game during his career, and Ronald busted up the locker room, beating the hell out of a teammate who had fumbled the ball.

The word in the neighborhood was that he had returned from the war even harder, with his anger set on a trip wire, and the news about his brawl with Matt had ripped through the streets. Some bookies were taking odds on the length of Matt's life. Wanda knew it was wrong to tell Angela to stay away from Matt, but it was the prudent thing to do. She wished that she hadn't left so quickly when Matt dropped her off on the corner. If she had stayed with Angela, perhaps she could have stopped the incident from occurring. She screwed up and now had to make things right by explaining to the impossibly stubborn Matt why he was messing with death, and how he should make himself invisible for awhile. She would do it tonight after the meeting.

Rumors flew around the neighborhood about drugs and easy cash, and she worried about James. He needed money for his girlfriend and the baby, and the ghetto grapevine reported that there would be plenty of tax-free money to be made on the streets in the coming weeks. Everything seemed to be going wrong for her family. She had one year of school left, but her mother needed surgery, and James had screwed up big time by getting his girlfriend pregnant. Wanda felt old beyond her years, with the constant responsibility for her family beginning to wear her down. Not that she let it show. Weakness had never been an option in her life.

From years of surviving on the street, she instinctively scanned the area for potential muggers, praying that her beat-up Ford would start on the first try. A stationary woman provided an easy target. It was amazing that only ten years ago, even the youngest children could play outside until past dark. Wanda had worked diligently to make things better for black people in white society by volunteering for various social agencies, but black society was imploding before her eyes. More broken families, high unemployment among black men, and rising crime were ripping up New Haven. If all that didn't get the young black man, then Vietnam or drugs did.

Wanda started the car, slowly pulling away from the curb while checking her rear view mirror. The huge face that filled the glass froze her for an instant, but she had always been a woman of action. Slamming on the brakes while screaming, she jammed the car into park and attempted to leave the vehicle, but her potential freedom might as well been a hundred miles away. One huge hand pulled on her hair, snapping her head back over the seat as the other clamped down over her mouth with a thumb applying pressure at the joint, painfully sealing her jaw shut. She feared rape, but when the deep voice behind the hands spoke, Wanda understood that she had bigger problems than sexual violation or robbery.

"Relax, Wanda. I'm not going to hurt you if you do what you're told. Pull the car slowly around the corner and park in the vacant lot where Reverend Hill's church used to be. I want to talk to you."

Wanda did as instructed, all the while looking for an opening to escape or fight back.

"I'm late for a meeting, Ronald, but why did you go scaring me like that? Are you too ashamed to come around to the house? Talk, because I've got to go."

She had never been afraid of Ronald like everyone else in the neighborhood, but could sense immediately that this was a different man that had come back from the war. They had dated through high school until he was recruited to play big time college football. His violent outbursts had never involved her, and next to his family, she was probably the only person he had ever treated with respect.

The college, in violation of every NCAA rule, had provided him with money and a no-work job. There were continual drunken parties filled with football groupies that Ronald couldn't resist. It wasn't so much the sex, as it was the power and a sense of control that he desperately craved. He was somebody when he played football, but that ended long ago.

Their relationship shattered within a few months, and they hadn't spoken in two years. He assumed that he could have his groupies on the side along with Wanda at home, but she told him that it couldn't be that way. It had hurt her deeply, and she hadn't been in a relationship since.

Ronald figured he was invincible, with a rich future in pro football, and that studying was for other people. Eventually, his horrendous grades couldn't be fixed as he increasingly drew attention to himself with his explosive temper. His off-field behavior made him a liability to the team, placing the football program directly in the bull's eye of a NCAA investigation. They cut him loose to cover their asses, and Ronald was drafted into the Army before he hit the sidewalk. He didn't last a semester by studying on his own in real classes. Wanda hadn't seen or heard from him since the day that he went in the service.

"What do you want, Ronald? I'm late for a meeting and I don't need shit from you right now. Let go of my hair!"

He slapped her hard across the top of the head.

"Shut your mouth, you black bitch. You think that your super-mamma attitude still holds power with me? I should wring your skinny-ass neck for telling my sister that the white asshole is a nice guy. You know I don't want her going out with anyone, let alone that punk, so why did you stick your interfering ass in my family's business?"

Wanda twisted out of his grip, slapping his face hard with a sharp crack that echoed around the car.

"Don't you ever hit me again, Ronald. Maybe the little whores that you went out with in college took that shit, but not me. If you touch me again, you'll have to kill me to get me off you, and you'd better finish it because I'll tell your mamma what you did to me. Besides, Angela told you the truth. I was with them the whole time. Nothing happened except some conversation. It was three people, three 'people' having some fun!"

Ronald pulled a gun from his belt, pointing it at Wanda's head.

"You still going talk big now, bitch? I ain't the same guy that left this shit hole, and I ain't living here much longer. I'll kill you if I have to. You stay away from my sister and don't give her any more advice. I don't want to hurt you, Wanda, but you're not leaving me a choice with your attitude. You never did know when to shut up, and this time it might cost you big time."

The gun frightened Wanda, but not enough to keep her quiet.

"So this is what you've become, Ronald. A man, or someone who thinks he's a man, a coward that slaps around women and carries a gun 'cause he's scared. Your Daddy would be real proud of you now, wouldn't he?"

Wanda knew Ronald's Achilles' heel. Her words enraged him to shaking as he pressed the barrel against her temple, his finger one little push from pulling the trigger.

"Don't be talking to me about my Daddy, bitch. Where is he now? Who's going to take care of everybody if I don't? He did the white man's dirty work, and now he's dead. Are you going to help my family, Wanda? Talk around the street is that you got big problems of your own. Don't worry, I'm going help James out with a little job so he can marry that little whore he knocked up. That ain't happening to my sister."

"Leave my brother out of your business. He has to finish school, and I don't want him near your drugs and scum friends. Keep your crooked money. We don't want it, and we don't need it. We'll make it on our own like we always have."

"Okay, Wanda, I'll tell you what. You tell that white asshole to stay away from my sister, and I'll leave James alone. That is, if he wants to be left alone. He was looking awful desperate for cash when I talked to him this afternoon over a bottle of Ripple."

"I'll tell Angela not to see Matt again, but you'd better back away from my family or I'll kill you."

"You are a funny bitch, Wanda. That's why I always liked you. I'm holding a gun to your head, and you're going to kill me. That's just too much."

Ronald readjusted his grip on Wanda's hair, giving her a hard, wet kiss on the mouth before leaving the car. She spit on his back as he left, then wiped her mouth with her shirt sleeve. Wanda waited until Ronald had gotten out of sight before she pulled the car away from the curb and broke down in tears.

Two weeks ago, she and James were on schedule to graduate from college at the end of the year, but James' girlfriend was pregnant, her Mamma needed surgery, and now Ronald had come home to pollute their lives. Wanda didn't give in easily, but she understood when she had been beaten. She dried her eyes and headed for the meeting, hoping that Ronald would keep his part of the bargain. Getting Matt Kronchek to back off was another problem altogether.

Chapter 16

Leo sat uncharacteristically quiet on the ride back from Bellington. His normal state was happy or angry, but a contemplative mood was new territory. It couldn't have much to do with the cut over his eye. He had been injured fighting many times, and the wound was minor compared to others that he had suffered. Maybe his pride had been damaged by his failure to catch the prowler. Leo did not like to fail in action situations.

"Okay, Leo, what's the problem? You haven't been this quiet since freshmen year when they had to wire your jaw shut, and that was a blessing for all of us."

"I'm pissed off, Kronchek, pissed off because you're not being straight with me about this deal. I'm not a genius, but secret missions in the night, and people spying on some Bellington townie chick in the bushes tell me that there's more to know about this fairy tale. The guy hiding wasn't there to watch the sex show, was he?"

"No, Leo, unlike you, he wasn't. I'm sorry, but I'm not used to confiding in people. It was something that happened to me as a kid, and I'm not going to discuss that issue ever, but I'll tell you the whole story concerning tonight. I put you in danger, and I don't mean beating up danger, but as in we could get killed danger. I shouldn't have gotten you involved, but I needed help. I was desperate. I'm sorry, and it was wrong for me to use you without telling you everything."

Leo's face brightened like the highest click on a three-way light bulb.

"You mean someone's trying to kill you, Kronchek? I knew it. I knew it from the day we met. I was sure that you would piss someone off and push them too far one day. Who is it? What did you do to them? Screw the hospital for now. My eye is fine. Let's go find them right now and kick some ass! And don't worry, I know all about why you don't talk about some things. It's because you feel responsible for the accident that killed that girl in Bellington."

I slammed on the brakes, pinning Leo against the door.

"Stop! Shut the fuck up for one second! How do you know anything about my life in Bellington? I never told you a thing about any dead girl. Where did you come up with this idea? I ought to open up the other side of your head for saying shit like that to me. Who told you about Bellington?"

"Christ, Kronchek, calm down! It was one those friends of yours, you know, the guys you're working with at the FBI. The ones who were at our house the day that I thought you were bullshitting me. Seemed like a nice guy. He bought me a couple of beers earlier today, while he explained to me how the whole operation is hush-hush, and that I could help them by giving reports and stuff. I would be like an assistant agent for them. This is cool shit now that I know it's true. Why do you think I came today without asking you many questions?"

"This is not cool shit, Leo, and those guys are not nice or my friends! They want you to spy on me, and they had no right telling you anything about my life. I wasn't responsible for the accident. I was thirteen when I found my friend Nellie dead on the railroad tracks on Halloween. It was horrible, and I'll never forget how she looked that night, but it had nothing to do with me, and I'm going to pay back those bastards for bringing it up. They think they have the right to pry into people's lives without retribution. I'll make them sorry for messing with my privacy. Goddamn Hoover and his secret agent lackeys. Lloyd told you about Nellie, didn't he?"

Leo had seen me angry many times, but never with such intensity. He didn't appear surprised or threatened by my behavior. Appearing impressed and enlightened, his eyes dilated to the max.

"Wow! Lloyd said you might react this way 'cause it really fucked you up back then. He told me I would have to help you out, and I'm here for you buddy."

"Are you ignorant? No, no, that's a dumb question because I know you are, but I can't believe he sucked you in like that and bought you off with a couple of beers. He was playing you, idiot, puffing up your ego so you'll tell them what I'm up to. What did you give them, Leo?"

"I didn't tell him anything because I didn't know anything. You don't tell me what you're up to, except to do this or help you with that! What's going on, Kronchek? Agent Lloyd said that it had something to do with Commie spies who were trying to steal military secrets from our government."

Oh God, this was unbelievable, even for Leo.

"Leo, I'm not going to get angry because I dragged you into this, but I want you to take a deep, hopefully, revelatory breath and clear your head. I'll tell you the whole story, and then you tell me where Communist spies fit into the scenario. Okay?"

I went through the entire chain of events starting with the cemetery, Tommy's body, and how Ronald Williams and maybe Rich Donato connected all the dots. I held nothing back. Leo possessed a linear mind, but he could recognize the truth and deal with it when it was presented to him in a logical sequence. I needed loyalty and trust right now, not an analytical genius. When I had finished; crazy, hyper, Leo looked positively awestruck.

"Kronchek, I thought you were going to disappoint me with the truth, but your story is even more exciting than the one that the Feds made up. It's like you've been leading this secret James Bond life on the side. I fully intend to get that Lloyd guy back for messing with me and treating me like his donkey. You're not going to tell them what we found out at Debbie's, are you? I wouldn't give them shit now."

"Do I have a choice, Leo? We're dealing with the Mob, the government, and a multiple murderer, plus why should we give a shit? What's done is done, and we can't fight them, either side. Does it matter? Paulie's dead, but he was in with some nasty people. I don't know what his role in the whole thing was, but he made his choice, and we have to make ours. I want out of this shit. I'm beaten up and tired. The last four days have been hell."

Leo shoved me away with an angry force that I had only seen him inflict on other people.

"Yea, you do have a choice, Kronchek. You're always going around preaching how the truth matters, and crusading for every fucking, tear-jerking cause on campus, but the FBI guys were right about something. You're my best friend, and you've helped me out of a lot of jams, but there's always a distance. There's something angry and vicious deep inside you, just like when you exploded on me a few minutes ago. The look in your eyes when you get pissed is homicidal with no controls. I think I might feel sorry for Ronald Williams if he pushes the wrong button on you.

"It's the same with women. Even though that bitch nurse Karen hates me, she's a great chick for you, but you keep her at arm's length. Why would anyone hesitate with her? Have you asked yourself that question, Kronchek, even once? And the black girl, she's beautiful, everyone at the park could see that, but are you interested because someone told you not to be, or you're not supposed to be, or maybe because you know that nothing will happen in the long run?"

"I'm sorry, Leo—"

"No! Sorry doesn't make it. That kid used to be your best friend. You grew up with him, but you wrote him off because he went to Vietnam. You don't believe in the war, so you stopped believing in him. Half of America says they hate the war, while the other half is lying. Paulie didn't grow up saying that he wanted to die in Southeast Asia somewhere. How could a guy like Paulie deal with Ronald Williams or the power of the American government? In your little idealistic world, you wanted Paulie to be brave and say no to the bad guys. I think he finally did, and was killed for it. And something tells me that he learned to say no from you. Don't you care how he died and why? That should be important to someone. This war has fucked with everyone's mind so badly that we don't know what matters anymore."

Holy shit! Out of mouths of morons. So much for my theory concerning Leo's linear mind. Words that stung with so much truth about who and what I had become made my face flush from being exposed to myself. He had stripped me clean. I pulled people in and then pushed them away. Leo had hit it on the button. All in one instant I began to doubt my motives for everything. I guess you can't live with someone for three years and not have that person figure out some of your shit. I was impressed with Leo's depth and knew that he was right. If I didn't pursue this, then I would be a hypocrite to the most important person in my life—me. I would be living a lie, and that's the one thing that I had never wanted to do.

"Listen, Leo. Stop flipping out for a minute and give me a chance to explain. I can't deny that you're right about me, but I've seen things and know things that make me the way I am. You have to trust me on that because I can't tell you everything I went through in Bellington, but I agree with you about Paulie's killers. There's something really rotten going on in Vietnam besides the war, and I think it's being brought over here. We'll need the FBI's help to bring these guys in, but let's find out all we can before they wade in, screw it up, and then hang us out to dry. We have to set up a trail that they can follow to Williams and Donato, with us nowhere in sight when it all goes down. Don't give anything important to those assholes again until we're ready. Tell them as far as you can see, nothing's going on, and that I haven't learned anything else or even seem to care."

"Okay, but what's the next step? If you think this Donato guy is involved, why don't we go after him, beat the truth out of him and take him in."

"He's too smart for that, Leo. We wouldn't get near him, and I'm sure that at some point he'll be expecting me. Let me think about it for a while. Drop me off at the school. I have a meeting, and I'm late. Make sure you hang out where there are plenty of people. Pick me up around ten. We'll figure out what to do next, although I think that they'll try to find us first. And thanks for the wake-up call, Leo. I needed to remember what's important."

"No problem, and I'm not as dumb as I act you know."

"Yea, well, nobody really could be, shithead."

"Screw you, Kronchek. Get out of the car. I'll pick you up later if I remember."

Our relationship had returned to our own brand of normality, but I didn't have a clue as to the immediate future. A good chess player can see twenty moves ahead, but I couldn't even see the next one. I jumped out of the car, running full tilt to make the meeting on time. Wanda would rag me unmercifully if I was late, and I didn't need her shit right then. I flew around a corner with my head down and slammed into someone entering the building from the opposite direction, splattering both of us to the ground along with a bunch of papers. The pain was reawakened in my shoulder, but apologizing profusely as I started to help her up, I realized that I had flattened Wanda Simpson. The bad day wasn't over yet.

Chapter 17

Debbie lied to Matt about the impending arrival of her parents, knowing that he would leave rather than deal with her mother. She regretted having sex with Billy, but her entire world had been turned around with Paulie's death, and she desperately needed someone to cling to. Matt had been under consideration, but Debbie understood that he would have been more than just a difficult project. Any attempt to change Matt would have met with intractable resistance on his part. Debbie appreciated a challenge, but didn't have the patience at this point for a near impossible project.

When Paulie had been assigned to Vietnam, Debbie treated it as a temporary detour in her master plan. She had never even considered the potentiality of him getting killed. If something wasn't in her plan, it couldn't happen in her mind, but Vietnam didn't play by Debbie's rules. There was no backup option in place that allowed for Paulie not coming home. Billy would help ease the pain for the moment, but she lacked the enthusiasm for him to make it permanent. Debbie was a control freak, but Billy was already too willing to follow her like a puppy dog now that he had a taste of sex. Debbie liked to shape her men over time, not buy them finished off the shelf. Turning off the kitchen light, she headed to her bedroom where she would cry herself to sleep as she had done for the past month since learning of Paulie's death.

In many ways she was sick of being a woman, at least the perfect woman she had prepared herself to be since she could remember. She understood that the world had changed for women, but she wanted no part of women's liberation. Debbie could cook, sew, and manage a household to the finest detail. She fully intended to utilize her skills, even though she didn't fit into the changing world. Women were the ones always left behind; abandoned by men dying in wars, car accidents, and later on with heart attacks and strokes. Even at her age, Debbie could see that marriageable men were a declining commodity. A guy like Billy might make it to the head of the pack simply by outliving his more desirable rivals. Debbie thought that evolution might be heading on a backward slide.

A knock at the back door broke her out of her reverie. The stove clock read ten-thirty. It was late and no one had visited by the back door since high school. Maybe it was Matt and that idiot friend of his returning to ask her more questions about that damn war and men with sunglasses. Debbie needed no more reminders of Paulie's absence, so she turned on the porch light with the intention of telling Matt to go away and leave her alone. His energy and cynical sense of humor had been refreshing at first, but she lacked the endurance to deal with Matt at this point.

The face in the window startled her, partly from the lack of immediate recognition; except for superfluous sunglasses that covered the man's eyes in the dark. It had to be the person from Paulie's photo, the same man who had attended the funerals with envelopes of cash. Rich what's his name, the person that Matt had been so curious about. Another Bellington boy here at her door, and why? He seemed to show up in all the same places as Matt, and the connection frightened Debbie, who had no intention of opening the door. She didn't know what was going on or how it was connected to Paulie, and she didn't want to know. Wasn't him being dead bad enough?

"Who is it? It's very late, and I was just getting ready for bed. You'll wake my father, and he'll be very angry."

"Debbie, it's Rich Donato, an old friend of Paulie's from the neighborhood. We were in Vietnam together for a short stint. I attended Paulie's funeral, but we never got a chance to talk with all the commotion at the end. I won't wake your parents because they aren't at home. Their car isn't in the garage. Can I come in for a minute? It's important."

Debbie swelled with a mixture of anger and grief, kept only in check by instinctive fear. How could she move on and suppress her sorrow when people kept dredging up the past and Paulie. She was astute enough to realize that something wasn't kosher about the situation. Matt asks questions about a guy with sunglasses, and then just like that, he appears at her door an hour later knowing that her parents weren't there. Had he been watching the house? Why couldn't they leave her alone? Hadn't she been through enough?

"Please come back tomorrow. I'm tired and don't feel well. I don't want to talk about Paulie or the War anymore. I'm sick of it and it hurts too much. I'm sorry."

"I think you'll want to hear what I have to say tonight, Debbie. It's about Paulie and Matt, but it's more than just stories. You might be in danger. Your parents could be in danger. Just give me a minute to explain. Please."

Debbie's reluctance to open the door was being overruled by her need for closure, plus he had frightened her with his words of warning concerning her parents. Scanning the yard to confirm that he was alone, she opened the door slowly, hoping that it wasn't a deadly mistake. She always laughed at horror movies when people put themselves in needlessly dangerous situations, but here she was doing the same thing. Curiosity was stronger than common sense.

"You can come in for a minute, but say what you have to say and please leave. I've had enough of Vietnam, funerals, and people asking me questions. I'm very tired."

"That's what I'm here to speak to you about—people asking questions. I'm sorry about Paulie. We grew up together, and I understand your pain. He was a great guy and a brave man, and everyone in our unit respected him. He was always helping people out, and once he even saved Tommy Combs' life."

Slick in his speech and movements, Rich moved with the ease of a very confident man. No trepidation or emotions were revealed when he spoke or moved about the room. Rich appeared to glide about the kitchen, taking everything in, but leaving nothing of himself behind. He kept the sunglasses on, making it impossible to read anything from his eyes, which usually are the most revealing aspect of a person's intent.

Even though he possessed a natural ability to put people at ease, Debbie could sense that it was a predatory ease that he was trying to sell, similar to the way that a rabbit froze before the fox prepared to devour it. The mesmerizing cadence of his voice began to lull her into a false sense of security, but the almost perfect presentation began to set off an alarm bell deep in her mind. She remained silent, preferring to let Rich carry the conversation, waiting to see how much of his intent he would reveal.

"I know that you've been under a lot of stress, and some of the information that I have will be shocking and upsetting, but I think you need to know for your own safety and peace of mind. Paulie was a hero, Debbie, and I don't mean a war hero."

Rich had gained her attention with his words of praise for Paulie. He excelled in the skill of reducing a person's natural defense mechanisms, using compliments with a steady and reassuring voice. The woman seemed wary, understandably so, considering the circumstances and whatever Kronchek had told her, but information concerning her dead boyfriend would be hard to ignore.

Debbie said nervously, "I don't understand what you mean. He died in the war."

"You couldn't have known the whole story because Paulie was under strict security. Perhaps I shouldn't be telling you this even now, but Paulie and I worked in military intelligence, and at the time of his death he had been working on a major drug smuggling ring in Vietnam that eventually led all the way to the States. All the way into New Haven and the colleges within it; like the college Matt Kronchek attends, if you get my drift."

"Wait a minute. Are you trying to tell me that Matt was involved in drug dealing and Paulie's death in some way? Why are you telling me this? How could that be possible? Matt has never been near Vietnam. You're talking crazy, and I'm becoming more upset. I can't stand any more of this crap. Please leave."

"And well you should be upset with Kronchek hanging around asking questions. I'll bet I'm right about that, aren't I? Asking questions about Paulie, Tommy Combs, and even me."

Rich was fishing, but he could see that Debbie had become interested in the bait, and that he had guessed correctly concerning Kronchek.

Debbie didn't trust Donato. Nobody that slick could be sincere, but he seemed to be correct about recent events concerning Matt.

"Well, he did ask me a lot of questions, but he told me tonight that nothing was wrong, and that Paulie hadn't done anything illegal. I could tell he was lying to me, but lying in a way to protect my feelings."

Donato stepped closer to Debbie before he spoke.

"I'm sure that he was lying to you, but not to protect you. He's trying to protect himself by seeing what you know. He wants you out of his way now that he has gotten all the information that he needed. Paulie's not the one who did anything wrong. We've been watching Kronchek for a long time and we know he's involved in the drug ring, but we're not sure of his role. If he's the same person I remember from years ago, he has a violent temper and certainly possesses the intelligence to be the leader. You went to school with him. Wasn't he always in trouble, like when he got kicked off the basketball team? He was booted for drugs, but they kept it quiet because his dad was sick. We also think Combs served as his connection to Vietnam, and we're pretty certain that Tommy was ready to talk to us before he was killed."

Debbie gave the matter some consideration.

"Paulie never told me once about Matt using drugs, and what do you mean killed. Tommy Combs overdosed on heroin, and who are the people you work for? What agency?"

"That's the official version of his death, but the people I work with see it differently. Tommy was a lot of things, but he wasn't a heroin addict. Neither he nor Matt used heroin, but they were dealing it. Someone did him in. Someone here in Bellington that didn't particularly care for him to begin with, and would have no problem snuffing him if he squealed. He and Matt hated each other back in the old days. Paulie must have told you that. You don't want to know the people that I work for because our agency is not on any official list."

Donato's voice had a hypnotic quality to its tone. The more he spoke and the way he tied events together by forming logical connections, the more it sounded like the truth. It made sense except for one thing. It was too pat, like something out of a spy novel, and the inferences about Matt's personality didn't connect.

"Suppose I believe everything that you've just said. How do you explain Paulie's death and its connection to Matt? How could Matt have any responsibility or opportunity for killing Paulie? Tommy was already home when Paulie was killed."

"Easy, Debbie. I'm talking to you off the record as a friend of Paulie's. We're not having this conversation because if we were, my superiors would assign me to Tierra del Fuego for the rest of my career. I'm taking a big chance coming here, but I felt that you deserved to be warned because Paulie was a good friend. Paulie died the way they said, saving his unit by giving up his life, but you need to stay away from Matt Kronchek. He may have arranged the method of Paulie's death through his contacts in Vietnam. We haven't been able to prove it, but we're close. Other guys in Paulie's unit were good buddies of Tommy Combs. He wouldn't be the first soldier killed by his own people in this war. This network has long arms that can get to anyone, and the big money involved makes all things possible. If he still believes that you know anything about the drugs, it could be deadly since he has easy access to you and your family."

Debbie's head swam with confusion. Donato had presented a concrete explanation of events where Matt had only offered cryptic statements. There was definitely a connection between the two men, but which version was the truth? Or were they both lies? She desperately required closure to begin a new life, but neither of the explanations would ever provide that. Just as she was ready to surrender to Donato's rendition, her instincts tingled from the inconsistencies between the story and what she understood about men. Debbie didn't possess a strong analytical mind, but she had spent a good deal of time studying people, especially men. Debbie owned a doctorate in male studies.

Matt Kronchek had been a thorn in her side during the entire courtship with Paulie. He could be rude, obnoxious, and irritating, but even through all that, he rang true to his basic traits. He was always interested in social problems and having fun, always having fun, not business and money, and drugs were a business that involved big money. Yes it was true that he disliked Tommy, but Paulie said that Matt had never swung first in a fight, even with Tommy. Matt was supposedly vicious once provoked, but he never started fights according to Paulie. Matt Kronchek was honest to the point of being a pain in the ass.

Her head finally cleared, with trained instincts telling her that Donato was lying, but he terrified her and she wanted no more of this in her life. The man contained a harsh coldness within him, uttering an almost lifeless tone when he spoke of Paulie and Matt. Whatever was going on, it would have to go on without her. If she confronted him with her feelings, she wasn't sure what his reaction would be. She decided to play him and gauge his reaction, hopefully encouraging him to go away.

"You've frightened me, Rich. If he comes here again, I'm going to call the police and tell them everything."

"No! Don't do that! It will mess up our investigation if the locals get involved. They'll just screw things up with their bumbling. This is top level security. We'll watch him, but if he contacts you again by phone, give me a call at this number. You'll be safe if you just do as we tell you."

He handed her a slip of paper.

"Thank you, but I need to get some sleep now. I'll definitely call you if I hear from him."

"Good girl. You don't know how important this is to your country. Take this envelope. It's hazardous duty pay from our agency that we couldn't give to Paulie on the books. My superiors told me to pass it on to you, and don't worry; we'll be watching Kronchek. He won't be able to hurt you."

"*And watching my house also, I'm sure*", Debbie thought as he turned to leave.

With that, he left by the back door and cut through her yard over to the next street where Debbie could hear the sound of a car pulling away. She locked both doors, turned off the lights and went to her room with the money. Inside the envelope were ten one hundred-dollar bills; the reward for her silence and supposed gullibility. She shuddered when she realized that the penalty for talking could be her life.

They would be watching to see if Matt showed up again, or if she went to talk to him, and it frightened her to think of what the truth might really be. After Donato's visit, a mousy guy like Billy Mancini began to look a lot better, but she decided to take a long vacation from Bellington. Debbie would convince her father to send her to Florida to visit her grandmother for a month or more so she could try to get over Paulie. She also wanted to get away from the impending confrontation between the two men. Maybe by the time she returned, the whole thing would be over. Knowing Matt and listening to Rich, Debbie thought of two trains heading toward each other at breakneck speed on the same track. She wanted to be a thousand miles away when they hit.

Chapter 18

After flattening Wanda in the doorway and being twenty minutes late, I expected her to take it further than the usual withering verbal assault. I figured she would try to kick my ass in front of the administration building, but as I apologized and picked up her papers, she didn't appear angry. An uneasy sensation of dread washed over me because you could normally provoke a firestorm from Wanda simply by making an unconscious facial gesture as she was speaking in a meeting, and my collision had gone way beyond that. I would have expected a reaction equal to my clumsy violation of her person. Nasty predictability I could handle, but something was definitely out of sync.

"Gee, I'm sorry, Wanda. I was running a little late and wasn't watching where I was going. Let me help you."

Tears ran down her cheeks, glistening off her black skin in the yellow light of the door lamp, raising concern that she was seriously injured. She remained on her knees, keeping her eyes to the ground, the tears spotting the tar walkway like heavy drops of rain.

"What's wrong, Wanda? Are you hurt? Can you get up, or do you want me to help you?"

The crying continued, so I dropped to one knee to check for injuries. I put my hand on her shoulder, which she surprisingly allowed. An uncomfortable silence filled the gaps between sobs. It seemed as if aliens had come down and switched the real Wanda Simpson.

"How come you're not in the meeting, Wanda? Is it over already? I knew that I wasn't on time, but it can't be that late. Are you okay?"

The nervous chattering finally found the nerve that my personality had rubbed raw over the course of four years; jolting Wanda back to equilibrium.

"There is no meeting, dumb ass. We were both late, so everyone went home. I checked the room and it's empty. I was leaving when your clumsy ass smashed into me. Help me up."

As I pulled her upright, emotional agony occupied the usually combative countenance that Wanda wore as an everyday mask.

"Geez, Wanda, you don't look so good. What's going on? Are you hurt or is something else happening?"

"Something else? You're unbelievable! In the course of two days, you get stabbed with a pen, fight with the nastiest bastard in New Haven, and you're asking me if anything's happening. Is this your everyday life, Kronchek, or are you just having a bad week? Answer me, because I'm getting blamed and threatened for Angela going out on that stupid non-date. I want to know what the hell you're all about, and why Ronald wants to snuff the life out of you. He's always been protective of his sister, but the way he referred to you was different. There's more to it than the date. Do you two have a history?"

"Oh, I guess you heard about our little confrontation this afternoon after I dropped you off."

"Heard about it! Are you incredibly brave or just plain stupid? You should be thinking about leaving town right now and staying away for good. He'll kill you. He'll kill you without a second thought because he has totally lost it."

"Yeah, I've heard that a few times already, but you're right about it being different with me. It doesn't have as much to do with his sister, as it does something else. Perhaps you can help me, Wanda, and maybe I can do something for you. Let's go grab a cup of coffee in the lounge."

"Are you deaf, Kronchek? I told you that he wants to kill you, and you say, "Yeah, I know", like it's one of the events on your calendar. If he sees me with you, he'll kill me or beat the hell out of me. He has a gun, and I saw nothing in his eyes that would cause me to think that he wouldn't use it. I shouldn't have let Angela go with you to New Haven. I had enough trouble before this week, and now James' girlfriend is pregnant, my Mamma's sick, and your dumb white ass has brought Ronald Williams back into my life."

She began sobbing, dropping her head on my shoulder. I had never seen Wanda so helpless and frightened. Our relationship had always been based on contentiousness, and my skills at comforting people were underdeveloped, but I remembered the last time that I had to hold someone in distress. I had been too young and lacked the depth to understand the gravity of her problems, and I never saw her alive again. The parallels didn't escape me. I needed to pay attention this time. Wanda's world was falling apart, and I was involved and perhaps liable. The excuse of youth was no longer valid, and I didn't want to be responsible for her death. I already carried around enough guilty baggage to last a lifetime.

"Go inside. I'll grab your stuff, and we'll go up to Professor's Cantone's office. He doesn't know it, but I've got a key, plus there are no windows in his office, so we'll be hidden from anyone's view. Cantone has a coffeepot and some of the best Brazilian brew I've ever had. He won't tell anyone where he gets it, so we have to steal a cup once in awhile. Come on. And don't ask me questions about the key. You don't want to know."

Wanda didn't object, so I pushed her along to the basement office of my favorite history professor and advisor. Cantone was a stereotypical, absentminded professor in his mid thirties: a forgetful, sloppy bachelor with no social skills, and a total neophyte in the area of romance. We were fairly certain that he had never gone out on a date. He allowed Leo to use his key two years ago, and we kept it overnight to make a copy, with no one the wiser. We used his office as a make-out room for our dates on several occasions when we couldn't get privacy at the house.

The running joke for the last year had been the typewritten notes that Leo occasionally left in Professor Cantone's desk drawer. They would often go like this: *Professor Cantone - I'm madly in love with you, but I'm much too shy to express my feelings in person. When you give your lectures in South American History, I can't take my eyes off your crotch. I fear that I may lose control someday and bring embarrassment to both of us. Love, X. - Your mystery girl. P.S. I don't wear any underwear.*

Leo would make certain that he chose a class with a large number of girls, and a section that one of us was presently enrolled in. Cantone couldn't concentrate for weeks after receiving one of Leo's notes, and he worked diligently at hiding his pants behind the podium. The usually animated Cantone stood stiffly behind the podium during his lectures, while scanning the class for the sans underpants phantom stalker. Unfortunately it was a joke that we couldn't share with anyone until after graduation, if we wanted to leave the school with a degree. Anyway, I digress. Back to Wanda.

"Are we going to get busted, Kronchek, because I can't take any more trouble? Someone in my family needs to graduate, and right now it doesn't look good for James."

"Trust me, I've been in here a dozen times after hours and no one checks this area. You can't even see a light under the door. It's an inner office with no windows. The custodians clean it in the late afternoon when people are still around, so they don't come back this way all night. Leo and I know this building better than our apartment. Relax, kick back, and have a cup of coffee."

She took a sip. "It is good, if I gave a shit about anything right now, but what's your motivation for bringing me here. If it's about going out with Angela again, forget it!"

"Let's leave that topic for later. There are more serious things to talk about. You seemed to know a lot about Ronald Williams, and I need your help."

"You need my help? Weren't you listening outside? I've got enough of my own shit going on. It's piled so high that I can't see the other side. I can't help you, I can't even help myself, but here's some advice, and it's simple. Stay away from Angela and Ronald. It would help everyone.

"The bastard's taking over the drug business in New Haven, polluting our neighborhood with his smack, and I'm worried that James will become involved with Ronald because he needs money. Ronald threatened me with that prospect, a promise to corrupt my brother if you don't stay away from his sister. I have to protect my family before I would even consider your clown ass. He's been home less than a day, but the streets are buzzing with drugs."

"Try Matt for a change, Wanda. Why not drop the tough ghetto bitch attitude for five minutes and let me explain how our problems relate."

"What did you call me, honky?"

"You see, that's what I mean. I don't call you nigger or black ass, but you think that you have a license to say whatever you want to me. I just described how you were acting, not what you are, and your attitude is pissing me off."

Wanda would never admit that she had been wrong, but her silence served as an apology for the moment. Her natural combative personality made normal discourse an arduous task. She listened carefully, however, as I explained my story from the beginning, giving her my take as to how everyone fit into the scenario. Wanda remained quiet and pensive for a moment after I had finished. Only for a moment.

"You know, Kronchek, black people can walk out their front door and find themselves in a bucket of shit for no reason, but a guy like you doesn't need to have trouble. From your story, it seems like you go looking for it. Things were getting bad enough in our neighborhood, but now Ronald will finish it off and turn it into one big sewer of drugs, hookers, and the crime that comes along with all of it in the bargain. I always believed that I could fight something like this, but it's too much. He'll mess up my brother and kill me if necessary. James is a smart boy, but he's desperate right now, and a wad of cash will carry more influence than I will. You can't fight people like Ronald, especially if you have family to watch out for. You can only try to stay out of his way."

"Shit, I suppose life has become a useless exercise. I never thought I'd see the day when the irrepressible Wanda Simpson would give up because of a threat from the neighborhood bully. All those great causes for racial equality and women's rights sound so sincere and noble, until an oversized punk returns home making you want run and hide. It took that idiot Leo to make me see myself, and I'm saying the same to you. It's all talk unless you're willing to back it up."

"You're an asshole, Kronchek. You don't understand what it feels like to live in that neighborhood your entire life. A person can't walk out on the street without looking over their shoulder. Rape, robbery, and drugs are in your face every day. Victims aren't anonymous names that you read about in the paper; they're the people next door or even you. You never feel safe.

"I guess you wouldn't know what it's like not to feel safe, Kronchek, would you? Must be nice to grow up in a quiet little town like Bellington, where everyone looks after you, making sure that you're secure and comfortable. Makes it easy for you to lecture people like me on social responsibility. And Ronald's not a punk or a bully, Kronchek; he's a killer. He's beyond anything that you've ever dealt with in your safe, white bread life."

"Normally, I would have to agree with you, Wanda, and I'll ignore the analogy to a bread variety for now, but you've got it all backwards. You can't walk away from a problem like Ronald because it is in your face every day, and you're wrong about me. Inside, I haven't felt safe since I was thirteen, when I discovered the dirty side of life. I learned back then that you can't run away from these people. You don't have to believe that, but it doesn't matter anyway. He's coming after me for what I know about his drug business and murder, so I have no choice, just like you. It's right outside my door, and I'm not going anywhere. If you help me, I'll do what I can to put Ronald away, but it won't stop the drugs for long. He's just filling a space, and if he goes, someone else will slide in."

"You are one strange white boy. I don't know what your game is, but something makes me want to believe you. How can I help you, Kronchek, if I decide to, and what can you possibly do to save my family or take Ronald off the streets? They'll eat you up in the streets, boy. You got lucky the first time. Talk fast, because I have no time for bullshit."

"I have no intention of taking him on in his territory. Give me some credit. You grew up with him, so you can tell me everything you know about his habits, weak spots, friends, and the drug network. Make a truce with him, be his friend again and get him to talk. If I go to the authorities, I need all the evidence that I can gather, because if he beats the rap, I die, and your family loses."

"What about Angela and my brother James? If you see her again, he'll hurt me, and I'm worried that my brother is already involved with Ronald's drugs."

"I'll stay away from Angela even though I think she's a great kid, but I realized yesterday that we're a million miles apart. It has nothing to do with color. She's too young and naïve, and very religious. I'm a jaded, cynical heathen, and there's no turning back for me. She is beautiful, and that did blind me, but it ain't going to happen. It may actually work in our favor if she believes that her brother is keeping us apart. She'll be angry with him, and it could be a distraction that could keep him off balance. As for James, let Leo and I check it out. Maybe it's nothing, but if he starts using or dealing, we'll let you know."

"It sounds like a fair deal, Kronchek, but what do you really want out of this, not to mention the fact that you're in over your head. You don't really appear to be the law enforcement type, so what do you care if more drugs get dumped on the niggers."

"You know, Wanda, I have to be honest with you. I'm not sure what it means to me. At the very least, I got caught up in it by accident and can't figure a good way out, but I'd like to think that there's more to it than that. I'm pretty sure Ronald killed an old friend of mine, a friend that I had grown away from, and I feel guilty for not understanding what he was all about. I thought he was weak or ignorant for going in the service, but after talking to his girlfriend and Leo, I realized that it's not so simple. I carried a prejudiced opinion of him all the way from childhood, and that's wrong. And if there's something I hate, it's ignorance, especially when I'm the ignorant one.

"Maybe it's all linked to this fucking war, and the way that it has affected everyone. It's sucking the life out of our generation, perhaps scarring us forever, and now it has turned us against ourselves, both here and in Vietnam."

"So what's the solution, Kronchek? I don't see how these things are related."

"I don't know the answers, but when Karen almost got killed the other night at the hospital, I realized that I couldn't ignore this War any longer, and this deal with Ronald is all part of the same issue. I really like her, but I've been afraid to make a commitment, and I almost lost her before I could tell her that. I thought I had learned to mind my own business years ago, but Leo woke me up tonight and showed me that some things have to matter, and that there are issues that need to be everybody's business."

"That clown? He's not awake enough during the day to be giving anybody advice on awareness."

"True enough for himself, but he knows me from all the shit we've been through in college. He nailed me dead on. He said that I was afraid to have feelings for people, and he gave me some interesting insights into my behavior.

"Paulie getting killed and Ronald bringing his hard dope into your neighborhood should piss someone off. Someone should care. That's what Leo said, and he was right. I knew Paulie, I know you and James, and I want Karen to be my steady girlfriend. None of you should have to be in danger, so it's personal with me now. And to tell you the truth, my instincts tell me that there's something bigger going on, and I want to find out what it is. The Feds are trying to hide something, something dirty that they don't want the public to know about. I can feel it."

"What do you mean bigger, and why don't you put the cops on Ronald right now if you have the evidence? Wouldn't that stop the whole thing, being that he's the big man?"

"But he's not. There's another guy that I grew up with in Bellington, and if he's anything like I remember, then I know that he's in charge, and putting Ronald away would only delay things for awhile. I want them all or it will never be safe. They'll come to me if I don't do anything. I know it."

"So what's next? Are you going to be okay? "

"Yea, I think so. I'm going to call Karen tonight and start straightening out my head with her, and we'll talk to James for you in the next couple of days. We do have a deal, right?"

"I want that bastard out of my neighborhood, and I'll do what's necessary, but if he finds out that we talked, my family is screwed. I'll tell you everything I know about him, and hopefully it will help."

"Right now, anything will help."

Chapter 19

Leo swung by to pick me up about ten minutes after we had left Cantone's office. His promptness shocked me, but I could see that the seriousness of the problem had sunk into his thick skull. We drove Wanda to her car, making certain that she wasn't followed. Leo drove around for awhile as we checked for anyone on our tail. We saw nothing, but an uneasy feeling stayed with me as we parked the car for the night in the old garage behind the house.

I called Karen when I returned home, firmed up our date for Saturday and spent an hour talking about our relationship and future plans, if I had a future. She knew nothing about the situation, and I intended to keep it that way for now, but from the tone of her voice, I could sense that my commitment-laced speech had made her a little nervous, being that it was so out of character for me.

Leo intended to fly into action that night, but I convinced him that it would be playing into their strength. We needed to lure these people on to our turf, into areas that we were familiar with, and near people that we knew. They were afraid of our knowledge, and we were frightened of their propensity for violence.

I had been thrust into a deadly situation for the second time in my brief life. The first time at thirteen, I was filled with passion to avenge my friend Nellie's death, but I had been a helpless kid. This time, even though I was older and stronger, I hadn't gone looking for trouble, but I seemed to be in the wrong place every step along the way, becoming involved initially only by happenstance. The formidable enemies facing me made it feel as if I had been transported back to 1961.

I had to admit it to myself at least. Leo was right. Up until that night, I had lacked passion and motivation for anything serious. The war could push my buttons at times, but I had chosen to ignore it rather than be proactive, until it came to find me a few weeks ago. I never imagined that Vietnam would have entered my life in this manner. I enjoyed a good prank and a game of basketball, but everything else had been held at a distance. The lingering scars from Bellington had dulled my emotions to the point where I wasn't sure what mattered anymore. Had Wanda's plight touched my feelings, or was it just anger over being threatened? Maybe I wanted pay back from Donato for the pride of the neighborhood. Perhaps it bothered me that he could become our most infamous representative.

For the immediate moment and practical considerations, my psychological health was not significant to the problem. This confrontation would go down, no matter what the reasons. There were people to protect and a promise to keep, so my mental health problems would have to wait.

Two relatively normal days passed. Leo and I went to class, played some ball around campus, studying just a bit and always treading carefully near each corner. James and Wanda were nowhere to be found at school. Late Friday night I called Wanda's house, but no one answered, fueling concern that something had gone wrong. We would go to look for James the next day, with the park being the logical starting point for a Saturday. The same car passed our house three times that day, and it had put me on edge.

"Leo, Schultz and Murdock went home for the weekend. Why don't we sleep in their room as a precaution, just in case someone comes looking for us tonight? It might buy us some time to defend ourselves."

"Good idea, Kronchek, but I'm way ahead of you. I've got all the doors bolted and braced, plus I set up some booby traps. I'll show you where they are so you don't set them off, but I don't think I'm going to sleep much. I'm too wired. I want some action tonight."

"Sleep, Leo, because I don't think they'll come tonight, and we'll hear them if they do. I'm beat and I want to be in better shape tomorrow. My shoulder is still killing me, and my eyelids are drooping from the pain medication. I'm going to bed. I don't want to face tomorrow wiped out."

The atmosphere in the apartment reminded me of a Cub Scout camp out, but we weren't making up any scary stories to tell around the campfire. There was no need. We were already living the nightmare. Flashlights, knives and baseball bats lay by our beds. I held a bat in my hand as I nodded off, with the hard ash handle giving me a small measure of security. Total exhaustion and narcotics made sleep come faster than I would have imagined.

Before this mess with Paulie and Tommy, I had already developed a problem with nightmares. I had accepted it as understandable considering what I had experienced back in Bellington. A good night's sleep without waking or dreaming had been a rare event for me.

The dream arrived quickly, pushing through my subconscious defenses and out a door with urgency spawned from the trauma of the previous two weeks. Fog formed the landscape in front of me, amorphous and damp, and there would be no going back. I pulled at the handle, but the door to the bedroom was bolted and unyielding as expected, so I walked resignedly through the heavy mist, expecting the ghosts of Paulie and Nellie, or maybe my dad to be waiting on the other side. I had become accustomed to this type of dream, or at times, a chilling nightmare.

The air cleared as I strode forward. A graveyard emerged ahead, with the landscape sending sharp, icy chills that shook my muscles with involuntary twitches. It was a burying ground that stretched beyond the limits of human vision on all sides. Thin, white marble slabs imbedded in the soil served as grave markers. They appeared infinite, set close together and lined up in perfect rows, all the same height, with no variation in thickness and color; a reminder of the uniformity and absoluteness of death, no matter whom we were. Many of them were obviously new, with freshly dug graves beneath them. The dew had coated the grass between the older, moss-covered stones, forming a cool, damp blanket for my bare feet. Of course, my first instinct was to turn and run, but in a nightmare your choices are limited. The rules dictate that you view its offerings without recourse, and if you protest, your legs take on the heft of stone, forcing you into being the perfect captive audience.

Slightly to my right, a large black man turned slowly to face me, with my heavy feet sinking into the soft ground, making escape an unreasonable alternative. Ronald Williams stood before me with a smile, not evil or threatening in its nuance, but rather a sad, knowing, parting of the lips, his mien indicating an irreversible story line. I didn't return the facial gesture, preferring to let the scene play out a bit longer. I wasn't really the smiling type. No immediate perception of anger emanated from Ronald as I would have expected, but his entire persona radiated a resignation to fate.

Ronald swept his arm in an arc, pointing to the stones within range of our vision. The dead from my past life and apparently his, were all present and recorded on the markers, with each stone indicating the dates of their existence. My dad, my grandparents, Nellie, Paulie, Hodges, and even Antonio were buried in a line. Apparently, Lipscomb was still alive because there was no stone with his name on it.

Ronald had been tending to the grave of his father at the time of my interruption. The stones held no information as to the character or accomplishments of the people below, only names and dates, as if there was nothing of consequence between birth and death.

Ronald spoke with an echoing boom, the resonance increased by the fog barrier, and if the soft soil had released my leaden feet from its trap, I would have jumped from gravity's grasp into a full sprint. Remaining in place, I shivered as he pointed out several nameless grave markers; the month and year of death chiseled into two of the pieces of marble: September—, 1969.

"Two people aren't going to make through this month, as you can see by the reservations on the stones. We're going to meet again soon, Kronchek, and there's no way out. You were lucky the other day, but it doesn't happen twice when people mess with me. Ask your friend Paulie when you get over to this side.

"It's a funny thing how I was born in Georgia, you in Connecticut, and our parents held us for the first time, most likely imagining nothing but good things for our future. Do you think in their wildest dreams that they could see us where we are now? I'm going to have to kill you and your friend, Kronchek. Your rooms are waiting. The story has been written, and I'm here to finish the ending."

Ronald began to dig in front of one of the partially marked stones, slowly and methodically without any emotion or exertion apparent in his movements.

"It doesn't have to be this way, Ronald."

I stalled for time in order to wake up from the dream. He hesitated, lifting his head to listen.

"You could stop it all now. I'm not out for revenge, but everywhere I turn this issue is in my face. You could end it by giving up the drug business and taking care of your family. One of those stones could be yours with the shit that you're into. You might be digging your own grave."

Ronald answered with a shake of his huge head.

"There's no going back. Don't you, of all people, understand that? Nellie will never return, or Paulie, or my dad—none of them. Besides, if I quit now, Rich would have me killed, and I would be digging my own grave for sure. We are what we are, Kronchek, and I'm going for the good life or nothing at all."

"What is the good life, Ronald? Money and power, or is it more than that? Don't other things matter, like your mother and sister?"

"They do matter, and that's why I'm doing this. They still have a chance to live right, if they have the money. You're either shit or the shitter, and I don't intend to be some turd working in a hamburger joint. I would rather be dead. Enough with the philosophy garbage. Time to join your friends."

Ronald pushed me hard to the ground, popping my feet from the soil. He stood over me shouting my name with reverberating repetition. "Kronchek, Kronchek, Kronchek." I reached out in desperation for a weapon, and my hand closed on the wooden handle of Ronald's shovel. I shook in terror from the imminent existential threat standing over me, and my entire body felt one with the soil, as if I was being sucked into the grave. I swung the shovel at Ronald's knees in a last ditch effort to save myself, with the accurate blow inducing a scream of pain from the big man. The force of his audible agony elevated me from the earth in a whirl of moist dirt and grass, instantly teleporting me back through the fog and on to my bed. As I opened my eyes, Leo lay on the floor clutching his shins and howling in pain. A baseball bat lay firmly in my right hand, with my knuckles white from the pressure of my grip.

"Jesus Christ, Kronchek! Are you fucking crazy? I think you broke my leg!"

I sat up quickly trying to authenticate the scene before me, making certain that it was not another part of the same dream. A thin line had separated reality and fantasy during the past two weeks.

"Oh shit, Leo, what the hell happened? I must have been dreaming, but it was so real. Ronald Williams was standing over me in a graveyard and he wanted to bury me alive, so I clocked him with a shovel."

The sun sat high in the sky as it streamed through the bedroom window, indicating a late morning hour. Apparently Leo's leg wasn't broken, because he hopped around the room cursing my name.

"Do I look like fucking Ronald Williams, asshole? Am I tall, black and six feet wide? It was me that you hit, and it wasn't a shovel. Put the goddamn bat down before you kill somebody. Dumb ass!"

"I'm sorry, Leo, but the dream freaked me out. He said that he was going to kill both of us, and he was starting to dig our graves when I came upon him. Are you okay? Why were you standing over my bed calling my name?"

"Because the pain pills that you keep taking like candy apparently wipe out your paranoia and desire to live. I've been trying to wake you for an hour. It's eleven o'clock. You promised Wanda that we would look for her brother, and today's the day. Plus, you have to go to work this afternoon. Remember, Mr. Mnemonic?"

"Oh yeah, but I thought that I was awake in the grave yard. The scene was too vivid to be a dream. Shit, I still feel tired. He said he was born in Georgia, and he mentioned Rich Donato. Ronald acted frightened of Donato. I think I was right about who's in charge. I'll grab a quick shower, and then we'll head for the park to look for James."

"Hurry up, dickhead, and trust me, you were sleeping right there the whole night and half the day. You haven't been anywhere except in painkiller heaven. It's a pretty sad day in history when you need me to wake you up. In fact, it might be a first. And all this shit that you think you understand and know came from your mind. It was a dream, Kronchek."

It was a first. I had spent three years getting Leo to class on time, making sure that he didn't miss work, and a thousand other situations in which he would have been screwed if I hadn't prodded him along. In a strange way, I think that the last few days had forced him up a step in maturity. For the first time since I had met him, he seemed focused on something other than his own comfort and enjoyment. The liability had become an asset at a critical moment.

Still, I worried about him and felt guilty for involving him in this mess. His rashness and odd habits often precluded fear, which could prove deadly in this type of circumstance. Fear produced panic in some, but it gave me a sense of perspective that helped me carefully gauge my actions. Anger was my weakness, dominating my rational self; putting me in situations that I would normally have the sense to stay out of. Lacking fundamental fear, Leo would often find himself in the middle of trouble before he realized it.

I jumped in the shower before we headed to the park. If we couldn't find James at the courts, it would be extremely difficult to track him down. There was no way I was going to poke around in a neighborhood where Ronald Williams held sway. Rumor had it that the drug trade had increased at the bar across from the park, so we would need to be cautious. The park wasn't really neutral territory, but there were always plenty of witnesses, and most issues were put aside out of deference to basketball. Leo pounded on the door for me to hurry, but the hot water felt good on my aching body. The dream had rattled me, intensifying the pull of destiny; perhaps signaling the impending confrontation. The first job; however, was to keep my promise to Wanda.

Chapter 20

Leo drove the Mustang to the park, since my shoulder was still stiff and sore. Even with the temperature hovering around seventy-five, you could smell fall in the air, and although the sun felt warm on my skin, the breeze blew in from the north, cooling everything that it touched. Once the sun went down, the temperature would drop rapidly.

Goffe Street seemed relatively quiet for a Saturday. A full court game was in progress, but there wasn't the usual crowd of people waiting to play. The sidewalk in front of the Red Dog; however, contained more than the normal traffic for afternoon hours. The clientele were noticeably different from the week before, with runners coming and going on foot with relative frequency. Bodies bumped, articles seemed to change hands, and mouths were pressed to ears as exchanges took place. The number of cars stopping to buy drugs appeared normal, but the increased volume on the sidewalk is what stood out. Wanda was right. The drug business had taken on a more local flavor in the matter of a few days.

I shouted out to one of the players on the court that I recognized from school.

"Hey, William, has James been by here today?"

William looked up at the sound of his name, but when he saw Leo and me, he turned his back and headed down the court. I asked several more times, but received no response. It was as if we didn't exist. They must have been ordered or threatened by someone not to talk to us, or had heard through the grapevine that it would be unhealthy to do so.

Leo immediately became pissed off and insulted. He started yelling, waving his hands and throwing an occasional finger at the court.

"Hey, assholes, are you all deaf, or do you suck so bad at hoop that you have to concentrate to dribble the ball. We said that we're looking for James, James Simpson. Is the question too difficult for you guys?"

Leo's ranting stopped the game. The two teams grouped together, consulting for a moment before moving aggressively in our direction. I pulled Leo away as he continued to shout insults, half dragging him toward our car at the far end of the park. Having made their point, the players went back to their game.

"Leo, this is what I'm talking about. Why did you go and aggravate those guys when you know that we have to keep a low profile? It was obvious that they were afraid to talk to us. Why couldn't you accept that fact and let it go? Do you want Williams or one of his men to hear the ruckus and come out of the bar?"

"They were being rude and wouldn't answer you, so I thought I'd shake them up a little."

"Shake them up? It was ten to two, and we're in their neighborhood. We could have gotten the shit beat out of us before we found James. I told you that we have to play this game in a time and place of our choosing. You have to control yourself or we're going to get killed. Think of it like a basketball game. You take the shots that are there, but if you have nothing, you keep probing, passing and driving until you create the opportunity that you want. Come on, we'll see if we can find James at school. I think he might have a late class. If we don't find him, I'll call Wanda and see if she knows where he's at."

We passed a park bench where an old wino sat with most of his earthly possessions stuffed into two shopping bags. He wore soiled woolen pants and a winter coat that reeked of stale wine. Heavily bundled up despite the heat of the day, he appeared to be homeless, so his outfit also served as his nightclothes.

A voice croaked out to us. "Hey boys, got a dolla' for some lunch?"

I began to look in my pockets for change, but Leo grabbed my hand.

Leo hated alcoholics with a passion borne from personal misery. His alcoholic dad had plunged their family into financial ruin and social oblivion. The booze eventually caused him to lose his job, so he spent his days in the tavern getting wasted while Leo's mom worked two jobs to keep the family afloat.

It all ended one afternoon when his dad, blind drunk and heading home, plowed into a school bus full of kids, killing three children. Before he could go to prison, he committed suicide by blowing his head off with a handgun. The family had to move out of town after the accident because Leo and his sister were treated like lepers at school, in town, and even in church.

The weird thing was that Leo drank heavily himself at times, more like binge drinker, but never quite seeing the potential danger or the connection to his father's problem. He believed that his father had been weak, that alcoholics lacked self-control, and that it could never happen to him. It was a subject that had only been broached once, because the second time I mentioned it while he was drunk, we had a wild fist fight. I had all I could do just to contain him. I could chastise Leo for any transgression or misjudgment, and he would accept it, but not his drinking or the fact that alcoholism is a disease.

"Kronchek, don't you give the drunk bastard a dime. You know that he's going to spend it on booze. What a stinking smell! He probably pissed and shit himself, and now he's sitting in it. Screw off, rum head!"

The cast of the wino's black skin was gray and dull even in the bright sunlight, and his rheumy eyes were buttressed underneath by puffy, wrinkled bags of loose skin. His hair had whitened before its time, and a swollen abdomen, indicative of progressive cirrhosis, bulged prominently under the multiple layers of clothing. The liver was protesting, but he was too far down the road to ruin to listen or care. He grabbed my arm, revealing a surprising strength imbedded in his bony arms.

"Hey, stretch, please give an old man a hand. Ya stubby friend ain't got no manners. Ya gimme a dolla', and I'll tells you what's ya wants to know. I hear ya talking to dos boys over der, but nobody but me gonna talk to you 'round here."

Leo flipped. "Shut the fuck up, you stinkpot lush, wino bastard. You don't know shit about our business. You're just trying to con the bleeding heart liberal hippie into buying you a drink. It ain't gonna work because I'm not going to let him."

"Leo! Stand over there and watch our backs in case those guys return. Maybe he knows something. Do you know James Simpson, sir?"

"Sure I does. He growed up on the same street where I used to live. I knows him. Ya a good boy, stretch, calling me sir. Ya mamma taught you respect, but ya fren, he been taught nutin but being pissy."

His baiting of Leo was working, but I froze Leo with my finger, stopping him in mid stride.

"Okay, so you know him. Is he around here or has he been around here today?"

"I'll tell ya, but first the dolla' or stumpy boy der gonna screw me outta my money once youse have the in-fo- mation. What's a matter, boy? Ya don't like dirty old niggers. Ya got the prejudice, stumpy boy?"

"No, asshole, I hate smelly, drunk bums like you, black or white. So fuck off. Come on, Kronchek. We're wasting our time with this lush."

The guy certainly knew how to push Leo's buttons, but Leo wasn't about to beat up an old black man in the park, although if this continued, I wasn't so sure. I fished around in my pockets and came up with seventy-five cents. Holding it out to him, he grabbed it from my hand with a quickness that startled me.

"I said a dolla', stretch. Ya a bit short. One mo' quarter."

Opening my barren wallet, I turned my pockets inside out to show him that I was broke.

"That's all I have. Now please tell me where James is at."

"I know where he's at, but I said a dolla'. I bet ole stumpy over der got a quarter. Just twenty-five cent mo'. Go on, ask old stumpy. He your fren', right? At least old stumpy der got one fren'."

Leo's eyes widened and his face flushed a crimson hue raised up to the surface from deep-seated childhood anger and bitterness, the color intensified from struggling to maintain control of his temper. He and I were about to have a confrontation over a quarter.

"Leo—"

"No, Kronchek, don't even ask me. He's not getting it. He's lying so he can buy a bottle of Ripple. The asshole knows that Ripple is eighty-nine cents plus tax. Let him go dry for a day, and then maybe he'll stop rotting his gut away. The DT's are a wonderful object lesson. Let's go, because if he calls me stumpy one more time, I will beat his ass right here and now."

What a ridiculous situation. I was caught between a drunken comedian and an irrational moron, all for a goddamn quarter. Life and death were the issues that we came to the park to resolve, but now we were entangled in a world of low finance. There was one more move to play on Leo before I gave it up, because if I wasn't smarter than those two, I wouldn't last long against Ronald and Rich.

"Sorry, mister, but he won't give it to me, so just keep the money and we'll be going."

"Whoa, Kronchek! What are you doing? Why are you letting him keep the money when he didn't give you any information? He doesn't know shit, and he'll spend your money on booze. He's been playing you for a donkey the whole time."

The hook had been set, and now the guilt trip line to reel him in.

"I'm not going to try to take it back with all those guys at the courts already pissed off. I've got bigger things to worry about than fighting with an old man. Let's go. I just hope that James is okay. I promised Wanda that I'd find him, but I guess it will have to wait."

Wearing a dejected look, I put my head down while slowly shuffling away.

"Fine, Kronchek, you asshole! Here's the quarter, but if he's lying, I'm coming back and taking every penny he has. I will rob his ass. You got me. If I pound him, it's your responsibility for laying the guilt trip on me. You think that I don't know how you're playing me. It's on your head."

Smiling away from Leo's eyes, I gave the quarter to the old man and waited for his part of the deal. He stalled and fumbled with the money, but the delay was mostly contrived to torture Leo. The man may have been an alcoholic, but he wasn't stupid or brain dead, and I was pretty sure that Leo wouldn't actually harm him. Pretty sure, but not positive.

"Da boy youse looking for is over der cross the street near the Red Dog, but I wouldn't be messing round der. Bad shit going round der now, especially for white boys who go where they don' 'posed to be."

"Forget it, Kronchek, you know we can't go to the Red Dog. He's probably not even in there. It will have to wait until we see him in school. I'm not into committing suicide."

"What's a matter wid old stumpy, stretch? He don sound so tough now. Ya scart stumpy? Ya scart of a few doped-up niggers?"

"If you call me stumpy one more time, I'll—"

"Leo, please leave the old man alone, and mister stop calling him names. I'll go over and check it out. I won't push it, but I'll just see if he's around or if anyone has seen him. If you hear any commotion, or if I'm not back in five minutes, call the cops."

"You have gotten dumber this week, haven't you, Kronchek? They'll beat the hell out of you for stepping on the sidewalk. You know the rules. What if Williams is there? I won't let you go. It's a stupid idea, even for me. You told me last night and ten minutes ago that the one thing we weren't going to do is mess around on his turf, and now your dumb ass is going right into it."

The wino seemed bemused by our dilemma, but being the ultimate park bench entrepreneur, he recognized an economic opportunity.

"For another fiddy cent, I'll tell ya a secret
bout the Red Dog."

The first bit of information had drained my meager resources, and asking Leo for more money would be out of the question, so I did what I had asked Leo not to do. I snapped and grabbed the man by his jacket. I had taken enough from the wino and Leo. This clown show had taken on the aura of the circus of the absurd.

"Tell me the secret now, and I'll bring you two dollars tomorrow if it's useful. If you don't, I'm taking my money back, and letting old stumpy here have a go at you."

I was genuinely angry and purposefully threatening, with my patience totally gone, but the old man only laughed.

"Ha, ha, now youse acting scart, stretch. Don worry, you okay, so dis one is free. Don' go in the fron' door. The dopers hang round back. Dat's where ya find da boy. I gotta go, boys. Der's a bottle of Ripple been sitting on the shelf waiting fo me to rescue it. Have fun over der. Ha, ha. White boys going to the Red Dog to look for one of Ronald's dopers. Looking 'stead running, dat's a good one. Ha, ha, gonna be some sirens soon. Ha, ha, ha, dumb white boys."

The old man's laughter continued until he shuffled out of sight down a side street.

Chapter 21

Leo and I stood alone at the edge of the park, with the cackling voice of the old man fading into the distance. His last words were not meant to be encouraging, but I understood his meaning and they were possibly prophetic. We agreed that it would be smarter to have the car running and accessible, so he went to get the Mustang while I circled around to the back of the bar. The plan was to find James and convince him to get in the car with us quickly, so we could take him home to Wanda. I promised Leo that if I didn't find James immediately, I would leave. He was right. We didn't need to be stupid.

I walked up two streets before cutting over to circle around to the back of the bar. Every street that surrounded the park and bar was a totally black neighborhood. I felt so obvious and exposed as I walked down the side street that led to the rear of the building. My presence produced stares of incredulity, but luckily no challenges before I reached my destination.

Cautiously turning the corner, eight or nine men were hanging around in the back of the building. I thought perhaps the old man had set me up for a beating, but there among the small group of junkies, as the old man predicted, sat James in a pitiful heap of drug-induced paralysis. His eyelids drooped, opening slowly for a moment, then shutting tight. When I spoke his name, James exhibited no signs of recognition. One man was shooting up, while it appeared as if the rest were anxiously waiting their turn from the same needle. They showed no awareness of my presence, or anything else around them, besides the dope.

"James, what the hell are you doing? You're all beaned out and drool is coming from your mouth. Are you crazy? You're a student, not a street freak. Get up and we'll take you home. Wanda's worried about you."

James made no attempt to move, nor exhibited any response to my voice, so I pulled him roughly to his feet, arousing the interest of one of the more lucid men in the group, who disappeared into the back of the bar. His departure meant trouble, and I hoped that it wasn't Ronald he was going to get.

Where the hell was Leo? The Mustang was nowhere in sight, and the sound of running footsteps and verbal commotion from inside the bar indicated that my time could be short. Five men rushed out the back door with Ronald Williams in the center of the mob, a head above the rest. I had taken a foolish chance, and for the second time in a week, found myself confronting Ronald in the wrong place. It felt like three times considering the nightmare. I hadn't chanced upon trouble this time. I had gone looking for it.

"Well, well, it's Kronchek, the boy who wants to fuck my sister. Isn't this sweet? A white boy hugging a junkie nigger, holding him up for a few more minutes before he hits the gutter where he belongs. That uppity bitch Wanda would be surprised to see her brother now, wouldn't she? She always thought that her family was better than mine, but look at him now, and she can't do a thing to help him."

"I'm not here for trouble, Ronald. This isn't about you and me. I promised Wanda that I would find James, and you promised her that you would leave him alone. If he goes home, we both keep our promises. Whatever beef you have with me can wait until another day."

"The noble white man coming to help the poor black slave. Is that who you think you are, Kronchek, a fucking savior of the black race? Wanda broke her part of the bargain by talking to you again, but I've got no hold on this boy. He's married to the smack now. That's the master he serves, so I kept my deal. He can go, but you and I will finish our business right here. Don't worry, it'll be quick this time. You won't get lucky again."

"He can't walk, and we have no business together. Wanda kept her agreement with you by telling me to stay away from Angela, and I will. Is there something else we need to discuss in front of your friends? Why don't we tell them how they'll eventually end up like James or what will happen to them if they don't follow your orders. I could have them ask Paulie, but he's dead."

"Shut up, Kronchek!"

Ronald didn't want to go down that road in front of his men, so he signaled for them to surround me. I remember thinking-*Now would be a good time, Leo. I need the help now before they beat the hell out of me and kill me. Now, Leo!*

As they closed in, I would need to drop James if I were to make what would be a futile attempt to defend myself. The ever-present existential fear within me screamed in terror. Just then, like in a James Bond movie, the squealing of tires and the harsh sound of metal on concrete scattered Ronald's men like frightened rats. The Mustang, with the top down, jumped the curb, scraping the bottom as it pulled alongside of me with an inch to spare. It had been such a beautiful car.

Before Ronald's men could recover, Leo vaulted over the side, running toward the front of the car with a gun in his hand. Where had that crazy bastard gotten a gun? It appeared to be real, but the bizarre image of Leo and the weapon had me momentarily mesmerized. He had no knowledge of firearms that I was aware of, and it terrified me that he might shoot someone by accident.

Leo panned the gun in a long, horizontal arc, his hands shaking with each pass as he screamed orders to Ronald's boys who backed up in harmony with Leo's lunges. The uproar instantly drew a huge crowd from the houses that surrounded the bar. I began to believe my life had become more like a movie, a fantasy that people wouldn't accept as realistic. Everything was happening in front of me, but I began to feel detached.

"Back off, mother fuckers! Back away from the car, or I'll blow a hole in your head. Who wants it first?"

Leo had watched too much television throughout his life, but his scripted lines, backed up with a real gun, produced the desired effect on the crowd, except for Ronald. He kept his eyes locked on me, but didn't retreat a step as he circled slowly toward my side of the car with a slight smirk on his lips. He obviously had faced a gun before, and appeared to be stimulated by the confrontation. As he waited patiently with confidence and authority, he studied his men to see who had the balls to handle the situation.

Leo was in charge for the moment, but Ronald watched for an opening with penetrating, experienced eyes. I held James upright, lost in amazement.

"Kronchek, throw James in the back seat and drive the car. Everybody just clear away and no one will get hurt. Hurry up, Kronchek!"

Flipping James upside down into the back seat, I ran around to the driver's door, which was the moment that Ronald had been waiting for. He rolled over the trunk with a quickness that belied his size, wrapping me in a bear hug before Leo could react. In retrospect, I had to admit that it was a brilliant, athletic move. Ronald's men were in the front of the car occupying Leo's attention, and Ronald was crushing the life out of me on the side. If Leo turned to help me, he would be overwhelmed in an instant. Besides, he might hit me if he tried to shoot Ronald, and knowing him, I hoped that he wouldn't try.

It may be a cliché or misperception that your whole life flashes before you in critical situations, but pertinent pieces of your experiences definitely do. As Ronald attempted to end my existence, I remembered the night that Antonio was about to shoot me at the railroad yard. I had always wondered what came after life, and as I did back then, I figured that I would finally get my answer. My body relaxed as prey often does when it knows that it has lost the battle to the predator. I couldn't move. The man was too big, and in close quarters his strength was overwhelming.

Leo, his confidence eroding, was close to total panic. His linear solutions usually didn't include a back-up plan. The crowd started to realize that the situation had tilted in their favor, and a few of the braver men edged closer to the gun.

"Christ, Kronchek! Fight back or we're both going to die. I don't want to go out like this. Come on, Kronchek, it's not like you to give up. Are you going to let that asshole win? What about your family, and what about Karen? Do you think he'll leave them alone?"

Ronald eased up a little, realizing that Leo had given him information that he could use to torment me with before he finished me off.

"Your buddy's right, Kronchek. I'm going to find your mother and kill her, and then I'm going to rape your girlfriend and let her live with it for the rest of her life. I'll explain to her that it was a going away present from you before I sent you to hell."

Even though Ronald had relaxed his grip, I still couldn't free my arms, and with my feet slightly suspended off the ground I possessed no leverage, which rendered any counter moves ineffectual. His words had enraged me, breaking me out of the resignation to certain death. By lifting me off the ground, he had lined up his face with the back of my head. I threw my head forward, and then back into his face with tremendous force, just as he began to increase the pressure to finish me off.

I remember four things from that moment: Ronald's dull grunt, an instant loss of his grip, blood gushing onto my hair, and nothing but stars of agony in my eyes as he dropped me to the ground on my back. Leo's scream "to get up and move" partially cleared my eyes, while survival instincts pushed my damaged body into motion.

"Get in and start the car! He's down. Hurry!" Leo said as he waved the gun at a crowd that had suddenly lost its nerve.

I crawled through stars and fog, opening the door and staring at the blurry instrument panel. Looking down at Ronald near the rear wheel, a murderous thought arose in my brain. He was out cold with blood flowing from his nose and a cut above his eye. Maybe this would be a good time to finish it. Tired of almost getting killed and constantly being afraid, I knew that he would come after my family as soon as he recovered. This was way over my head, and it had to stop. I couldn't watch out for everyone all of the time, and there was no concrete evidence to bring to the police. Leo jumped into the car, continuing to train the weapon on the stunned crowd. Once their leader had been put down, they had lost their nerve.

"Go, Kronchek, go, before one of these guys gets their guts back or Ronald wakes up."

"Give me the gun, Leo."

"No. You drive and I'll handle the gun. We need to get out of here quickly. Why do you want the gun?"

"I'm going to finish this right now while he's down. I can't take it anymore. Jesus Christ, Leo, we're college students, not the vice squad. He'll hurt people that I love, and I'm not letting that happen. Give me the gun!"

My head throbbed with bright light pain, and I could barely see.

"Are you nuts? You can't kill him here in front of all these witnesses, and besides, the gun isn't even loaded. Watch."

Leo pointed the gun at the crowd, pulling the trigger with a jerk. The powder burned my nose as a deafening blast completely shattered the bar's back window. The mob scattered in all directions, screaming as they ran for cover and closed their doors, but nobody could have been more stunned than me, except for Leo. Police sirens wailing in the distance made me forget about killing Ronald. I dropped the car into first, fishtailing down the street, barely seeing the road in front of me. My mind was working in high gear from fear and shock.

"Not loaded! You brought a gun to save me and you thought it wasn't loaded! Wipe the gun and throw it out when we get to some brush. Throw the bullets in a separate spot. If we get caught with that, we'll go to prison. Where did you get it?"

"It was the gun that my father used to kill himself. My mother buried it in the backyard, but I dug it up and cleaned it. I figured I might need it someday if I became like him. Now it's been put to good use twice."

Reluctantly following my instructions, Leo chucked the gun out in a patch of woods. We made our way back home unmolested by the law, circling the block twice before we parked the car in the old garage. Luckily no one was hanging around in the yard, or it would have been hard to explain the unconscious black man upside down across the back seat. With every inadvertent step along the way, the mess had gotten messier. As I stepped out of the car, the last thing I remembered was the earth spinning and the dirt floor of the garage racing toward my face.

Chapter 22

Four police cruisers and a paddy wagon roared to the rear of the Red Dog, with backup on the way. The scene contradicted all the reports and calls that had come into the station. The mob of angry men surrounding the bar and two white men in a red convertible with a gun were nowhere to be found. In fact, the streets were deserted, unusually deserted for a Saturday afternoon.

The reports were not totally false as evidenced by the solitary bloody black man lying unconscious in the street, and the blown out window with scattered masses of broken glass on the sidewalk and in the bar. An ambulance's shrill siren could be heard racing toward the scene from St. Raphael's Hospital. One officer attempted to rouse the man in the street, while another went through his pockets looking for identification.

As more patrol cars arrived, officers entered the bar and began assembling the few remaining patrons on the street for questioning. They knew nothing, except that two white boys attacked Ronald Williams as he left the Red Dog, while kidnapping another black man at gun point. Their story sounded ridiculous, but each was consistent in its content and simplicity.

They knocked on a dozen doors, but few people seemed to be home, and the ones that did come to the door knew nothing and had heard nothing. The police had a positive ID on the man from his wallet, but Ronald remained unconscious as they loaded him into the ambulance, which sped away to the emergency room. His breathing was shallow, his pulse down to forty, and his blood pressure had dropped to 85 over 50.

The officers asked a few more questions and then gave it up. This shit happened all the time, and it would eventually take care of itself in the form of revenge. One of the officers headed for the hospital to question Williams, if and when he regained consciousness. Although the investigation would be officially left open; it was closed for all practical purposes unless the victim was willing and able to talk.

Ronald finally came around in the emergency room with a dose of oxygen and smelling salts. The doctors originally feared that part of the broken nose may have entered the brain, but his semi-comatose state was apparently due to a severe concussion. His left eye was swollen shut, prompting concern of a possible detached retina. A call was put in for an opthamologist. They stabilized Ronald for the moment, patching his eye. He would need surgery to repair the nose, and perhaps the eye, but that would have to wait a few days. They brought him upstairs to a private room, where they restrained him with heavy straps in a hospital bed. Ronald had become quite agitated when they told him that he had to stay in the hospital. Even though his eyes were open, Ronald didn't respond to any of the officer's questions.

An officer was posted on the floor in case Ronald's awareness improved, and also to limit access to his room by anyone besides family. The cops weren't concerned about Ronald's injuries, but they were very interested in the four grand discovered in his pocket. Having the money wasn't a crime, but the amount seemed to give credence to the rumors coming off the street about a boom in heroin traffic. Nobody had that kind of money in their pocket unless they were involved in drugs or some other criminal activity.

Ronald hadn't moved or struggled in two hours, so the patrolman went down the back stairs to grab a smoke and look for the coffee machine. Nothing was happening right now, so why should he suffer, and besides, the guy was strapped to the bed. The officer had been nodding off, and he needed to piss again from all the liquid.

Rich Donato had been on his way to meet Ronald in New Haven when the call came over the police scanner that he kept on in his car at all times.

When he heard Ronald's name and the mention of two white boys that had escaped the scene, he pretty much figured out what had gone down. The only part that seemed stupid was the kidnapping of a black man.

Rich was a successful criminal because he understood what had to be done, and was willing to do it, or have someone do it for him. It was always business with him, never personal. When Tommy needed to be neutralized, Rich understood that it was a necessary part of the crime business. Now Ronald had become a liability because of his obsession with Kronchek, and this couldn't be allowed to continue.

The radio squawked excitedly when they found the large wad of cash on Ronald. They pretty much had him pegged as a drug dealer. If the police could make him talk, the whole operation would be blown, and the law would be the least of Rich's worries. His uncle always had a cop on his payroll, and the information would reach the old man before it hit the papers. His uncle was also a man who would do what was necessary for business, and what would be done, was Rich; family not withstanding.

Donato was on route to meet Ronald on the Green, but he banged a right on to Sherman Avenue, which took him directly to the hospital. He found a space near a rear exit and walked around to the main door. Privacy laws weren't in existence, so it only required a simple inquiry at the front desk to find out that Ronald had been moved up from the ER to Room 313. Except for family, visitors were not allowed, so Rich thanked the polite receptionist for her help, while inquiring as to the location of the rear exit.

Rich had no intention of leaving. Finding the back stairs, he walked up to the third floor where he spotted the cop sitting outside Ronald's room. Some men would have panicked or become frustrated, but not Rich. His patience and cool were legendary among those who had seen him work. He walked right past the cop into the waiting area, nodding a greeting in passing. From his seat in the lounge he watched Ronald's room, commiserating with another visitor concerning the health of their elderly uncles. Pulling out a newspaper, he lit a cigarette and waited.

When the cop headed down the back stairs for a break, Rich excused himself graciously, ducking into Ronald's room. He wouldn't have much time.

"Ronald, wake up," Rich whispered in the big man's ear.

Ronald's good eye fluttered a bit, so Rich shook his shoulder and whispered his name again.

"Ronald."

He pried Ronald's eyelid open, exposing a glazed eye. He was in bad shape, much worse than the police report had indicated.

"Why did you have to screw it up, Ronald? I told you that I would take care of Kronchek, and I will, but first I have to take care of you. You had two shots at Kronchek, and in this business you're lucky if you get a second chance, but you'll never get a third.

"There won't be a next time, Ronald. Not for you, and not for him, but you're leaving first. Kronchek is nothing more than a nosy guy who stumbled on to this by accident, but I don't think he knows what's going on. You do, though. If you talk to the cops my uncle will find out, and then I'm dead. I'm more important to me than you are, Ronald."

Determined to have the big man hear him out, Rich shook him hard, tugging at his hair, but there was no response. The rant was more for Rich's peace of mind than anything that he wanted Ronald to understand. Rich's hands trembled, which was a new sensation for him. He had never even been slightly nervous during a robbery, but killing someone up close was a different matter.

"This is where you disappoint me, Ronald. You had one great idea, and it made me believe that you were a smart guy, but one idea doesn't make a genius, I guess. The cops were blabbing away on the scanner. They found four thousand in cash in your pocket, plus the names some of your boys on the street."

Drool oozed from Ronald's mouth as his neck went slack. There was a disgusting smell of shit coming from under the covers, and a wet stain spreading from Ronald's crotch area. Ronald was dead. Rich had seen enough of it in Vietnam to know the signs, but he checked for a pulse, which predictably did not exist. That crazy bastard Kronchek had actually done in Ronald Williams in a fight. Kronchek was either really lucky or a person to be cautious of. Perhaps all of them had underestimated Kronchek, but at least the job was done. Rich was relieved that he didn't have to do it himself, but he needed to get out of there quickly without being caught in the room.

He put on the sunglasses, surveying the hallway as he headed for the back stairs where he nodded to the officer who was plodding up the stairs to return to duty. Even if they suspected murder, they would never be able to ID him. None of Ronald's local men knew his name, and Henry from the body depot on the base was on Rich's payroll, Rich having bought his loyalty a week ago. One problem was out of the way without any effort, and there was one to go.

If Kronchek hadn't figured out that Rich was involved, it would be simpler to let the whole thing die. Donato believed that even if Kronchek had connected the dots, what would he do with the information? With the FBI snooping around, there wasn't much room for error. They couldn't eliminate him without intensifying the investigation, plus it would be necessary to finish off his crazy friend to close all the doors. He decided to wait for Kronchek's next move. If Kronchek let it go, then Donato would go on with his business, but it was a doubtful course of events. Matt Kronchek never let anything go.

Chapter 23

Two hands were in the process of lifting me as I regained consciousness, dusty dirt coating my tongue like dry plaster, but the gritty particles were quickly washed away as I vomited in mid-air. The hands dropped me in revulsion, leaving my body propped up against the car in the semi-dark garage. I went down again as the bare rafters swirled before my eyes, causing me to retch anew as the raging headache within my skull begged to be released.

"Jesus, Kronchek! We need to get you to a hospital right away. I'll go get my car. You smell and there's blood all over your head."

I grabbed Leo's leg from my position on the bare floor.

"No, Leo, we can't go to the hospital! They might connect us up with the incident at the bar. Where's James?"

"He's still passed out in the car. I think he's alive, but he hasn't moved since we got home. What should I do, Kronchek? You look like you're going to die, and what if James overdosed? You know that I'm no good with medical shit, and the puke smell is making me sick."

Leo opened the side door, taking in a breath of air so he wouldn't vomit along with me. I could barely enunciate the words, but Leo needed instructions, and he was right—I required medical help, but it wasn't going to be at the hospital.

"Leo, I'm pretty sure that I have a concussion. I recognize the symptoms from health class. My head feels like somebody's pounding it with a hammer, and if I move it, the room spins. Go up to our room and find Wanda's number. Call her and tell her to come here and pick up James."

"Where in the room, Kronchek? The place is a total mess."

"I don't where I put it, Leo, but just go because he may need a doctor if he doesn't come around soon, and we can't bring him to the hospital. We need him out of here. He's just one more link to us and that gun, and we can't handle any more trouble."

"He needs a doctor? James is probably just sleeping like a contented heroin hog, and you're puking and passing out every thirty seconds. What about you, dumb ass?"

My arms were wrapped around Leo's lower legs to make certain that he wouldn't move. I needed time to finish my instructions, and didn't want him to leave with half of the necessary information. It was imperative to keep my eyes closed or I would continue to vomit. I did anyway from the pain pounding in my head, but my stomach was pretty much empty. Death might be a welcome relief from this misery.

"After you call Wanda, get in touch with Karen and tell her what's wrong with me, but don't tell her how it happened. Repeat what I told you about the concussion and then describe my symptoms. She'll know what to do. Now hurry! Oh, call the V.A. and say you're me. Tell them you have diarrhea and can't work tonight. They'll accept that excuse every time."

Leo was on the very edge of losing it. Having entangled him in some nasty business, it looked as if I would be out cold at any minute, leaving him to make all the decisions. Leo hated responsibility and it strained his concentration to follow all my instructions.

"Where are these numbers, Kronchek! Please think!"

I pressed my hands tight into my temples and eyes, trying hard to deaden the swirling pain. Suddenly the color yellow popped into my head.

"Wanda's number is on a small piece of yellow paper, and Karen's is written on the phone. She can give you the hospital number. Now go, please!"

I released Leo and curled into a fetal position, cradling my head in my hands, with my eyes closed tight against the pain. A persistent ringing in my ears refused to be blocked out. Medical treatment was called for, but if Leo went into a panic mode, nothing would get done. It was necessary that he remain calm in order to get the facts straight when he made the phone calls. Direction from me he understood and accepted.

Leo returned in five minutes, having enough sense to bring some water, a towel, and a fresh shirt. I sat up slowly, washing my face and torso and throwing the puke-laden shirt into the corner of the garage. I decided against trying to stand and refused to go into the house. As far as anyone else knew, we were working on my car in the garage.

"Kronchek, we should get you up to your room. Wanda will be here in about twenty minutes, but Karen told me it would be forty minutes before she could get here. She said that you need to lie down and take something for the headache. You were out for quite awhile."

"Leo, I'm not going inside until Karen gets here. I don't want to talk to anyone or answer questions. The other guys will think Karen and I are going to my room to make out, so it will appear normal. I'll clean myself up and then we'll have to wait. Go outside and look for Wanda's car. Make her park up the street and come through the neighbor's yard behind the bushes. If anyone sees a black person in this neighborhood, they'll call the cops before we can get her into the garage. Go!"

The collision with Ronald's skull had caused severe physical disorientation, but at least I could think straight, straighter than Leo anyway, which wasn't saying a hell of a lot. There could be heavy consequences if the police were able to tie us to the gun. It could mean serious prison time, and Leo seemed to grasp the seriousness of what he had done. In retrospect, I'm glad that he brought the gun, but if there had been someone sitting near the window that he blasted, we could have been up for murder, or at the very least, manslaughter.

Since the day of Paulie's funeral, it had been one continuous path of being in the wrong place at the wrong time. Was this to be the direction of my life? No matter which fork I chose, it always brought me to a place where I shouldn't be. Just like in Bellington eight years ago when I ran through the railroad yard and crashed into Antonio. What if I had taken the street? Where would I be now? I never considered myself a superstitious person, but I was starting to believe that all this was meant to be. Each incident had gotten more deadly, but this last one had been too close. I had become careless, putting us in a position that was beyond our ability, and it almost cost us our lives.

Battered and exhausted, my body had reached its limit, but one potential solution remained; however reckless it would seem to any rational mind. Find Donato and put an end to this mess. The FBI and the cops couldn't or would have no interest in protecting my family, so I would have to work out a deal with the crooked bastard. Once Ronald recovered, he would come after me or someone close to me with a vengeance. I would ask him to call off Ronald, and in return I would stop interfering in their business, even though most of what had happened was accidental. Rich could understand a deal like that, and I was positive that he was the man in charge. The side door of the garage opened, framing Wanda and Leo in the fading light.

"Jesus, Kronchek, you look like shit, and it smells in here. Where's my brother?"

"Thanks for the compliment, Wanda. Your brother is passed out in the car, but wait until it's totally dark to take him home, or even better, take him somewhere where Ronald can't find him. That way we don't have to explain anything to my friends inside. I don't need any more trouble. I can hear him snoring, so I think he'll be okay."

Slowly lifting my head, I tested my stability with each small rise to avoid another nausea wave, but the serious look on Wanda's face, combined with Leo's subdued demeanor, told me that I already had more trouble.

"Something's wrong, Wanda, and it's more than my head splitting apart and James being whacked out on heroin. Ronald's out and prowling the streets to kill us, isn't he?"

My question produced no reply, with no reassuring looks from the faces above me. Something was terribly wrong.

"What is it? What happened? Is Karen okay? My Mom? What? Tell me!"

Leo couldn't speak. I had never seen him so frightened. Wanda spoke in a hushed, hesitant voice.

"Matt, Ronald's dead. He died at St. Rhaphel's two hours ago. Angela went to visit him and found him dead in his hospital bed. The nurse told her that he would be okay in a few days, so Angela went in and tried to wake him, but he didn't respond and she couldn't see him breathing. When the doctor arrived, he pronounced Ronald dead. They could get you for manslaughter, or even murder, considering your fight with him the other day."

Leo said, "We're screwed either way, Kronchek. If the cops find out who we are, we're going to prison. If his men catch us first, we're going to die. We have to get out of town. Right now! What the hell did you get me into?"

My debilitated condition made it difficult to become hysterical, and the fact that Leo had lost it made it essential to remain calm. Any slight movement spun my head, with shards of pain cutting through my skull, poking at neurons and receptors, while sending the message that everything was not well in the brain of Kronchek. I kept telling myself that it was a good thing that I couldn't react physically because it would force me to think. Thinking, not just reacting, was what was needed at the moment. All my reactions of the past few days had produced the mess that lay in front of me.

"Dead? How can he be dead? I only hit him with my head, and he had me by a hundred pounds. Are you sure that someone's not feeding you false information so they can flush me out? Maybe he figures that if I believe he's dead, I'll let my guard down and come out into the open. I didn't want to kill him, I just wanted him to let me go."

Wanda stared down at me with a mixture of uneasiness, pity and concern.

"It's for real. I spoke to his mother. The police were at the house taking statements when I went over to console Angela. Everyone except the cops know that it was you and Leo on that street, but no one is talking right now."

"I never wanted to kill anyone, even him, but why hasn't anyone ratted me out? At least a dozen guys that know me from the park were in the crowd. I'll be glad to talk to the police. He attacked me first. I was only defending myself."

"And who will testify to that? Your main witness is Leo, the guy who fired the gun. He's your best friend and an accomplice in the eyes of the police. Also, the word is that you demanded the gun from Leo to shoot Ronald. The best scenario for you, Kronchek, is if someone did step forward with the truth, but I don't see it going down that way. The silence usually means that it's going to be handled privately, but nobody is saying by whom. That's not good news for you and Leo. I'm sorry that it turned out this way."

"Sorry? Why should you be sorry for us? It was an accident, and we'll prove it once we solve our more immediate problems."

God, I was sick of all the threats and fights. We went to the park to do Wanda a favor, and the biggest thug in New Haven jumps me with the intention of snuffing out my life. When I head butt him in self-defense, he dies, so now more people that want me dead or in prison have been added to the list. This had gotten too weird. I had become the villain, and from the beginning of this whole mess had done nothing wrong. Fucking war, fucking Tommy, and now fucking Ronald dying, with the whole affair sucking me into a vortex of shit! Leo prodded me with his foot.

"Get up, Kronchek. We have to hide out somewhere. I'm sure the cops won't spend much time on it, and maybe the others will go back to their drug business and forget about us. There are probably a lot of people that are happy to see him gone. Someone will just take his place and be happy to have it."

"I agree with you, Leo, but not in the way that you think. Wanda, do have any relatives outside of New Haven."

"Yea, my grandmother lives in Norwalk. I was born there. Why?"

"I think you should take James to her house for a few days. You'll be safe for the time being, and he'll be away from the drug dealers. He hasn't been using for very long, so I don't think it will be that difficult to chill down."

"How will a few days help? We have to come back and face the same situation, plus I don't have any money. I can't move out of New Haven permanently with my mother being sick and all."

"Leo, go upstairs and rob the keg fund. There's probably about eighty bucks in the jar. The guys aren't having the big party until next week, and by then we can pay it back. We'll give Wanda the money so she can get to Norwalk and buy some food. Wanda, it's just for a few days to let things cool down and cut a deal."

Leo shook his head. "Pay it back? You don't have a dime, Kronchek, but I have some money that Wanda can borrow. Those guys will kill us if we take their beer money."

Leo pulled out two twenties, and I don't who was more shocked, Wanda or me. My vision was still blurred, but I swear that I saw a bit of a connection between Wanda and Leo. Through all this shit, the most unlikely pair of people seemed to be looking at each other in a romantic light. I must have been hallucinating, but they say life-threatening situations can create reproductive urgency, and I believe that I was witness to the proof of that theory.

"Thanks, Leo, but I can't accept the money. I probably won't be able to pay you back, and like I said, what good are a few days?"

"Take the money, Wanda, before he changes his mind. His wallet doesn't open very often, so he must really want you to have it. A few days won't make a difference if we don't settle this, but it will keep you safe for the weekend."

Wanda screeched. "Settle what! You have more trouble than anyone. You should be the one hiding."

My head throbbed, but the waves of nausea were subsiding, and I was able to get to my feet without assistance. James began to stir, so I motioned for Leo to be on his guard in case James panicked upon awakening. The unfamiliar surroundings combined with the aftereffects of the drugs could make him freak.

"I have a plan. If Leo and I take off, we might be okay for awhile, but what about my mom and Karen. I'm positive that Donato has been in charge all along, and it won't end unless he gives the word. I think the main danger right now is that Donato might believe we know more than we do about his business, so I have to talk to him. Leo, you and I and Karen are going to Bellington tonight to stay with my mother. I'll tell her that we're visiting some old friends of mine for the weekend and going to breakfast Sunday morning. We'll all be in one place, making it easier to protect everyone. My mother loves it when I bring friends home, especially girls, so she won't be suspicious of my motives."

Leo appeared unconvinced of the plan's logic.

"Okay, genius boy, that buys us the weekend, but what about

Monday? Oh yeah, there are also the cops to think about. I bet your mom will be thrilled when they arrest us at her house."

"It isn't going to get that far. I'm pretty sure that Donato still lives in Bellington. I'm going to slip out and have a meeting with him while you watch over Karen and my mother. I'll try to cut a deal. We don't have anything on him that we can prove, but I need to convince him of that."

"Bad idea, Kronchek! I let you go alone today and we almost got killed. How do you know that he won't just make you disappear to protect his ass? Why would he leave you around as a potential loose end? Ronald was still in Nam when your boy Tommy got killed, so who do you think snuffed him? Dumb plan, dumb, dumb, dumb ass plan."

"I understand the risk, but I'm not Tommy. Someone would have tried already, if they absolutely thought I should be dead, but killing me is much more risky. He doesn't need the attention. I know him, Leo. Rich is a criminal, but violence was never his thing. His first and only interest has always been money and the influence it buys. It's all business to him, it always has been. Some kids used to rob for the thrill, but Rich always did it for the money. Ronald was angry and passionate, and would have killed me in a rage today, even if it ruined his business. Rich isn't like that. He'll make the best business decision, and that's what I have to sell him. We're going because we have no choice. If we could walk away, I would."

Just as Leo was about to continue the argument, Karen entered the garage. Her body gave a sudden start, making me realize that the garage was almost completely dark, with the last arc of the sun dropping below the horizon. Leo flipped on the one dull light, making things worse. I can only imagine how she felt at that moment. One moaning, semi-conscious black man sprawled in my car, a black woman with a two foot afro, her arch enemy Leo, and me with my hair caked with blood, not to mention the stench of vomit mixed with the sour, oil-soaked, earthen floor of the ancient garage.

"Matt! What the hell is going on? Look at your head! You need to go to the hospital. What happened to you?"

"Don't worry, most of this blood isn't mine. Karen, this is Wanda and that's her brother James waking up in the car. Wanda and James were just leaving to go on a trip. Leo, help Wanda with James. Karen, come on. Let's go up to my room. How would you like to meet my mom?"

Wanda gave me a long hug, while Karen looked on in quiet amazement. I realized at that moment what I loved about her. No matter how weird I got, she trusted me and looked past my wise guy exterior. A half dozen weird commands and comments had just been thrown around, but she held her ground while waiting patiently for an explanation.

Wanda was leaving the garage behind Leo and a semi-ambulatory James when she paused to speak.

"Thanks for everything, Kronchek, and I guess that I've been wrong about Leo."

"You be careful, Wanda, and take care of James. Tell him that we'll all be back on the courts in a few weeks."

"Basketball is the least of his worries, but I'll tell him."

"Hey, Wanda, just a minute. I need to ask you a question."

"What?"

"I know this sounds weird, but was Ronald born in Georgia?"

"Yea, they moved up here when he was a baby. How would you know that?"

"I don't know. I thought it came to me in a dream, but maybe I read it in the sports page while he was still playing football. I don't know now. It's weird. My reality and dreams have overlapped."

"You are a strange one, Kronchek. I'd better get going."

Karen waited until they had left before going off on me.

"Are you crazy, Matt? What is all this about? You're hurt. Look at you! You can hardly walk."

"Then help me, nurse. I'll tell you everything as we get ready. Did you bring any aspirin?"

She smoothed out my hair, gently probing the limits of the huge lump on my head.

"I brought aspirin, bandages, and some antibiotic ointment, but what's this about visiting your mother? This is all moving a little too fast."

"We're going on a little overnight trip, so you'll have to swing by your house to get some clothes. Karen, trust me. I need you and I'll explain everything on the way, but right now you have to help me in the shower or I might pass out."

Karen was on the verge of totally freaking out, and if it weren't for the presence of Wanda and James, she may have thought this was a scam of mine and Leo's to goof on her, or for me to get her in the shower. It was painfully obvious; however, that this was no joke, and that I desperately needed her help. Karen put her hat over my bloody head as we walked up to the deserted second floor, locking the door behind us. She told the guys downstairs that I had gotten drunk with Leo and needed to be put to bed, which drew a chorus of hoots from the perverts.

Leo decided to follow Wanda to make certain that she made it of town without being followed, and he watched her car while she went in to tell her mother where they were going. He wouldn't be back for awhile, so I explained everything to Karen. As I told the story, it surprised me that she believed it the first time around. I had lived it the past few days, but it seemed preposterous, even to me, as I laid it out. I omitted the part about my plans for meeting Donato in Bellington. Karen was frightened for me as it was, and she would have agreed with Leo, making it difficult to keep her out of the way.

She helped me to the shower, taking off my clothes and shoes, and I guess the threat of death that pumps testosterone into men, must trigger some hormone in women because we ended up in the shower together. I could almost get accustomed to this living on the edge of death thing.

Karen helped me dress, ordering me to lie on the bed. I stretched out; relaxing as she cleaned my head wound and rubbed my neck. Rolling over to watch her pack my clothes, the last thing I remembered was her cute little ass bending over the bureau. Apparently, I never heard Leo enter the apartment. Fatigue and injury had overcome my paranoia, putting me where I needed to be.

Chapter 24

It had taken me years after Nellie's death, but usually I was able figure out the difference between my nightmares and reality upon waking. They were regular and predictable, normally being perceivable as dreams, but no less disconcerting in the morning. The last two weeks had added a new set of parameters to my unconscious universe. My old reality, mixed with the intense experiences since Paulie's funeral, had blurred the line between substance and illusion. Were dreams any less real than our supposed reality? I began to think not.

The infinite graveyard of humanity lay before me once again; the chill from the mist and damp ground forcing a quick shiver from my torso. I stopped, taking a step back in revulsion as freshly dug earth squished through my toes. I was standing on Ronald's grave, and the date of his demise was now accurately chiseled into the stone. He actually had been digging his own grave during our last meeting, and maybe had been digging it for a long time, never realizing that it was his own. I felt a sense of sadness mixed with slight remorse over Ronald's passing, understanding the necessity of my self-preservation and his brutality, but he was what he was and knew no other way. I suppose it could have only turned out two ways, and the alternative would have been the end of me.

He came from my left, as good strategy dictated, knowing from the old days that it was my weaker hand. Rich had never been dumb. That was one thing you could say about him with certainty, and that innate intelligence is what caused him to be so dangerous. Funny thing was that back in the neighborhood, I believed that it was a potential weakness for him and would be his eventual downfall. Experience had taught me that no one was as smart as they thought they were, but I learned the hard way that certain people were never as dumb as I assumed.

"Feeling lucky today, Kronchek? I saw Ronald in action in Vietnam, and you should feel infinitely blessed. I observed you and Ronald from a distance the last time you visited this human dumping ground, and I must say that you did warn him. I have to give you that, Kronchek. You never throw the first punch, but that's a fatal mistake at the level you're playing on now. We're not kids anymore, and bullets don't give you an opportunity to punch back. The guy who strikes first usually wins."

"Lucky? Does a guy like you believe in luck? I always figured you for a calculating guy, Rich, leaving nothing to chance. You always had the odds figured on everything, whether it be a baseball game or a two-bit robbery."

"Well, I am a careful man, Kronchek, but there's always that small element of uncertainty in every situation. You taught me that with Ronald. What are the odds that someone like you would take him out? You've made me a true believer in the long shot, an underdog who triumphs over all odds, so I've become even more careful. He chose his fate and dug his grave, and now you're here to dig yours. There's one more reservation open next to Ronald. It's a great location, Kronchek, filled with irony; buried next to the guy that you're accused of killing."

"I'm not digging anything. If you want a hole, dig it yourself. Don't be so sure that it's my grave. It might be yours. Ronald thought that I would be next, but look at him now. If you kill me, it will look suspicious."

"Ronald was a fool, but I'm far from that, so I'm sure about you being next. You're going to have little car accident, Kronchek. Drunken college students crash and burn quite frequently, so no one will give it a second thought. Just you and your retarded friend roasting in your car. His grave reservation is way down there next to his wino father."

"I never figured you as being a killer back in the neighborhood, Donato. I mean, who would think of anyone that way when you're a kid? I saw you as a rip-off artist at the most, but I was wrong about you. This crime life fantasy is so important to you that you'll kill to keep it. That's sad and pitiful. You do understand that you will eventually get caught, right? You messed up once and went to reform school, and it will happen again, believe me. What made you turn to killing, Rich? You getting scared, scared of going back to jail?"

"I'm not afraid of anything. You're trying to piss me off, Kronchek, but it won't work. I don't make the same mistakes twice. Anyway, the sun is coming up here soon, and I've got to go. It burns your eyes in this place. I guess you can stand there or start digging. It's all the same to me. Do it now or do it later, but you'll be doing it for sure."

"I think that I'll wait, Rich, but thanks for the advice. The sun will warm up the graveyard."

"Not this sun, Kronchek. It shows the essence of your life and the ending. The clarity of it burns into your brain and your soul. It's not for the living, this place, if you haven't noticed. See you soon, old buddy."

Rich wove his way through the gravestones, gradually fading from sight as he entered a thick bank of fog in the west. He had purposefully exited opposite the path of the rising sun. The first white rays pierced the graveyard low and flat on the endless horizon of white marble.

I figured Rich couldn't stand the light at the graveyard because of the way that he had lived his life, but I was confident that I could handle it. I fixed my gaze directly to the east. As it seared the last of the mist from the dank ground, the white sun of the nether world ignited my eyes, shooting them back into my skull with the force of a blast furnace. My flaming sockets radiated intense heat, lighting up my pain center, causing unbearable agony in my head.

Was this the end of my story? Perhaps Rich had trapped me into waiting for the sun. He knew me too well. He understood that I would do the opposite of what he warned. We had already met and I had lost. A newsreel of my life ran by me; my human frailties exposed to the heat of that alien sun, burning me deep like an albino in the desert. The fire continued to spread within me, as voices called out my name. Who was it? God or Satan? Both, or the echo of my own voice in the nothingness? Was there a choice at the end? Somehow I didn't think so. Nothingness looked like a better alternative at the moment.

A heavy blow followed by a sharp pain in my ribs overrode the heat within my skull, bringing my environment into a hazy focus. I wasn't at the graveyard any longer, and the desk lamp from my room was set up a few inches from my face. Averting my gaze, I attempted to jump out of bed. Smooth, strong hands pushed me down, holding me prone and forcing my eyes in the direction of the light.

"Don't struggle, Kronchek, or I'll hit you again. Stay calm. It's Agents Lloyd and Francis, and this time we have a warrant, so we let ourselves in when you didn't answer the door."

"Turn off that light, assholes! You're blinding me! Leo! Karen!"

They turned the light to the wall, giving my eyes a much-needed reprieve. I sat up, while trying to rub the pain from my skull and the residual light from my field of vision. Dry-retching a few times before I could lift my head, I found their faces indistinct among the stars framing my view.

"How did you guys get in here, and where's Leo and Karen? You better not have busted my door or I'll—"

Lloyd laughed. "You'll what, Kronchek? Throw up on us. The door was unlocked, and there's note from your cretin roommate on the night stand."

A full sheet of paper leaned on my lamp. Leo must have forgotten to lock the door. *We couldn't wake you, so we went to get Karen's stuff. We'll be back soon. Leo.*

Grabbing the note, Lloyd said, "Going somewhere, Kronchek? Taking a little trip or maybe running away?"

These two secret agent men knew how to light the fire of my anger.

"What the hell do you guys want? Do you always have to play the little question and not getting an answer game? It's none of your business what I'm doing. Get to the point, although that doesn't seem to be one the talents of an FBI agent."

"Have to be a punk all the time, don't you? We're here to help you and you start getting vulgar on us."

"I told you everything the last time, Lloyd, and then you tried to get my roommate to spy on me, so I have no business with you two right now. You don't keep your word."

"Kronchek, Kronchek. You know what I did for a summer job during college?"

"No, I don't have a goddamn clue, Agent Lloyd, and I don't give a shit, but I imagine you're going to tell me anyway, so I might as well listen to your dumb-ass story."

Lloyd's hand came out of nowhere, slapping the back of my head with a jolting force that ripped my stiff neck from its rigid position. All the parts of my brain that had been starting to fall back into place were jarred loose. They had me back on the bed, helpless and in pain.

Lloyd screamed in my face from two inches away.

"If you swear at me again, Kronchek, I'm going to hit you hard and then even harder if you say it again. Now shut up and listen because we're all running out of time.

"I worked in a slaughter house for two summers, and the thing that amazed me was how the cows never knew what was coming. The cows getting killed or the ones that were next in line tried to warn them, mooing and crying, but they were just too stupid, stupid like you, Kronchek. You're too dumb or too cocky to see it coming, aren't you?"

I started to curse, but the thought of having my head rattled again caused me to consider my words more carefully. They had to be the most annoying people I had ever met. For some reason, the thought of these two agents in a TV sitcom made me crack up. The plot line would be about two federal agents who never said what they meant, but used riddles and analogies to question their suspects. The suspects would have to guess what they were being arrested for or questioned about; therefore, indicting themselves and making the agents look like geniuses. I laughed hysterically and couldn't stop, even though it was making me sick again.

Grabbing my shirt, Lloyd said, "You think this is funny? You and your simpleton friend are going up for manslaughter or murder, and you think that the whole thing is a joke. We don't make house calls for entertainment, so cut the laughing. I think that he's lost his mind or has taken too many drugs."

Agent Lloyd pulled his arm back to strike, but the threat of being whacked again brought me out of my fit. Plus, he mentioned something about manslaughter or murder. Now they had my attention. I played for time, hoping that Leo and Karen would see their car and stay away from the house.

"Manslaughter, murder? Why didn't you just say so? I'm relieved, but what the he…, uh, heck are you talking about? You two seem to have a fascination with me. Maybe we could hang out some time, but I told you everything the last time, so leave me and my friends alone."

Lloyd took up a defensive position directly above me. Agent Francis sat on the bed, and we stared unblinkingly across the short span, both attempting to size up the other. My life had become a total disaster, and I knew that it showed. I was crumbling on the inside, while physically battered on the outside. My cocky act didn't have much life left in it at that point. I expected Agent Francis to turn up the heat, but he surprised me.

"Look, Kronchek, let me lay it out for you, and then you can decide if you want to keep on playing the punk. We can help you, or we can become your worst nightmare. If you won't cooperate, then you're useless to us, and we'll hang you out to dry."

"Is it impossible for you two to get to the point? What do you want from me? I didn't do anything wrong. I'm a college student who stumbled upon some information. Even you must know that I'm not involved in this drug ring. I drink a little, smoke pot once in awhile, but that's it. I didn't ask for any of this, and that's the whole story. I don't even tell my mother what I just told you."

Francis nodded. "You're right. We know that you're not a dealer, but we had a man planted inside Ronald Williams' operation, and he witnessed the fight at the bar. You two clowns are lucky that you're still alive. The police are getting close to obtaining your names, and the gun turned up about an hour ago. We know the truth and have the power to make it go away if we get your cooperation. Or, we can turn your names over to the police and see where that goes. Your girlfriend can be charged as an accessory for helping you escape. We do have rights in this country, Kronchek, but it's that simple for us to take them away."

They appeared to have all the answers, except for something they thought I knew. This was no bluff on their part, and even I understood that they could pull rank and make it all disappear. Why were they so interested in this case? The last time they said that J. Edgar himself had a special interest in the situation, but I had a feeling that they wouldn't tell me why if I asked, and it could be that they didn't know everything. The FBI was pretty good at keeping their agents in the dark. I probed for some common ground.

"Suppose for a second we assume everything you say is true. You already knew about Ronald Williams, and now he's dead. Case closed, right? What else do you think I know? Tell me exactly what you want and maybe we'll have a deal; if I actually have anything."

Francis leaned in closer as he spoke. "You're in no position to deal, but let's make believe, since you want to be hypothetical, that you don't know what we're referring to. Here it is. Ronald Williams wasn't the top man, but we think you know that. The boss of this operation is a white guy, and by another strange coincidence we're fairly certain from what our man overheard that he's from Bellington. We were given that fact about an hour ago. You following me, Kronchek?"

"Yeah, I get it, but again what does that have to do with me? Bellington is full of white guys, and as a matter of fact we have a surplus of them right now."

Lloyd eagerly jumped in. "Cut the shit. We figure that you must know him, being that this whole deal revolves around your hometown and one of your best friends. We want his name so we can put a stop to this quietly. The Bureau is insisting on total secrecy. The bust won't even be in the paper, and your name will be left out of it. Everything will go away and you can go back to your draft-dodging college life until Uncle Sam pulls your lottery number. Williams never mentioned his partner's name to our man, and no one's ever seen him. We had to pull the agent from his cover after today's incident, thanks to you two."

I wasn't a rocket scientist, but the man didn't make a very good liar. I believed the basic story line, but the secrecy part didn't ring true. In an era where the government was increasingly looked upon as being a bunch of screw-ups, high profile busts were the favored method of finishing a case. These two wanted the whole mess to go away as much as did. There was a sense that they didn't even care about the drugs, but there was something deeper, more disgusting that could be embarrassing to the government, a revelation that would fire up the protests. Gaining some empowerment from that insight, I was able to meet Agent Francis' gaze straight on for the first time since they had rousted me out of bed.

"Before we take this any further, I want you two to explain in straight talk, like plain, direct English, where you see me fitting into this whole deal. You're holding something back, but you want me to be honest with you. Why would you want this to remain quiet? A public drug bust makes your agency look good, and trust me; right now you need it. Spying on college students and going through movie stars' trash can't be the glamorous career that you guys had in mind when you signed up to be G-men.

"I'm sure that it has also occurred to you that if I know this person's name, he probably knows who I am and is obviously a very dangerous person. The bodies are already piling up, and how could you protect my family or me, even if you wanted to? If I did know something, what guarantee do I have that everyone will be safe? Once I give you what you want, you'll just leave my friends and I hanging with no protection. And don't give me any shit about the witness protection program. I have no intention of starting a new life. I've barely started the one I was born with. You tell me the truth, explaining in detail what you'll do for me, and then maybe we can proceed."

Agent Francis gave my comments some thought before he spoke.

"I know you won't believe this, Kronchek, considering your cynical nature, but we don't know the reason for all the secrecy. Our orders are to break up the operation and turn over the main man to the Washington Bureau. The Director's instructions were to find out whom, not how or why. Apparently, the Bureau already has that information. You don't have to believe me, but that's the truth, and we're not any happier than you are. The only guarantee we can give you is that if you cooperate, you won't be charged with Ronald Williams' death. And you're right. As soon as we have what we want, we're gone."

Secrecy, especially the government kind, always aroused my interest, but they seemed to have my balls in a vise. I could give them Donato's name and walk away, but it wouldn't be that simple. First they would have to find him, and if they didn't put him away, I could be toast. It was easy to envision the two of them going to Donato and telling him that Matt

Kronchek said you were a drug dealer. They might be unable to prosecute him and then he would silence my ass forever. Even if Rich wasn't the killer, maybe someone above or below him was.

Perhaps I wasn't in such a bad position. The way out could be to play both ends against my middle. I didn't particularly like either side, so for the moment I didn't have any inhibitions about screwing over Rich or the FBI, especially if it bought a way out for Leo and me. I composed myself before throwing them my pitch.

"It looks as if you guys have me nailed in every direction, except for one problem. I was supposed to find out the identity of the white guy tonight, but if you hold me up, I'll never know. As a matter of fact, if this house is being watched, my informant probably ran scared. If you let me have this weekend to myself, I can give you his name by Monday, but you can't follow me or the deal is off."

"Ha! Nice try, Kronchek," said Lloyd. "You must think we're total idiots. You'll take off and by the time we track you down, the whole thing will be blown."

"I won't comment on the idiot thing because I don't need another slap, but take off? Where can I go? My mother's still around, and I'm five months away from finishing college. I'll be back because I have no choice. I'm not running because there's nowhere to go, plus I'm not a runner, Lloyd. Doesn't your folder tell you that?"

Agent Francis rubbed his left eye, while readjusting the part in his well-oiled hair. He appeared to be stuck in one long thought.

"You know, Kronchek, Agent Lloyd doesn't care for you all that much; actually he hates you, but there's something about you that makes me want to believe your line. I've been to war, the Korean War, and you have that same look of men that have been in battle. You're scarred, Kronchek, and underneath those scars, deep inside your mind; it's tender as hell, so you go to all lengths to protect it. Trust me, I know. I have a few myself. You have to keep the outside hard for self-preservation or you take the chance of exposing yourself to the pain. I buy your idea, but like I said, I've been around myself and I have to agree with Agent Lloyd concerning your return. We'll lose our jobs if we blow this one or it goes public."

"You guys want collateral? I don't have any. I'm leaving my car here. That's about the only thing I own, but think about it. If it was just about me, I wouldn't trust me either, but I'm not going to mess up Karen or Leo's life. Shit, she'll be a full RN by December. You have my word. I'll be back on Monday."

Lloyd sneered, and his tone spoke of his distaste for me."Your word isn't worth shit to us. Our careers are on the line, and we aren't taking a chance on someone like you. You have no understanding of how serious this is. You're a college student who lives in a fantasy world of partying and free-fucking chicks. Forget it. Let's bring him down to the police."

"My, my, you're a bitter man, Agent Lloyd, and you know nothing about me or what I've been through. I wasn't dropped into college from the sky. I've seen and known things that would make even you shiver. I have nothing else to offer you, but my word and my loyalty to my friends. Agent Francis, were you anywhere near Chosin?"

Lloyd grabbed my hair as he started to take out the cuffs.

"Chosin? What ching-chong crap are you babbling about? Let's go, screw-off. You're done."

Francis moved in between Lloyd and me, ordering him with his eyes to release the grip on my hair. He stared the younger man down with a mixture of disgust and anger, turning to me with a look of amazement on his face.

"He's talking about the battle at Chosin Reservoir in North Korea, Lloyd. I wasn't in it, but I had just started my tour in Korea when our men broke through enemy lines, finally escaping that frozen hellhole. We were part of the relief unit. I'll never forget the look on those faces. It scared the shit out of me. I wanted to go home, and I had just gotten there. How do you know about it, Kronchek? They don't teach anything about Korea in school as far as I know."

"Friend of mine, the cop in Bellington that helped me when I found Nellie dead got really messed up physically and psychologically at Chosin. Changed his whole life. Put it in the shitter for three years. It was a dirty war, but it looks like our latest one is much worse, and I've got a feeling that this is what the Director wants to keep quiet. He wants to sweep the dirt under some fall guy's ass. If you want, haul me down to the cops. Go ahead, Lloyd, but my final offer is still just my word, and if you follow me tonight, you will definitely screw it up for all of us. You have nothing without me, and bringing me to the cops won't make me talk."

It appeared as if the Korean War had also left some scars on Agent Francis' life. He struggled internally, but decided to make the same leap of faith that Lipscomb and I had taken together that day at my school. It seemed like another lifetime.

"Let him go, Lloyd. I think he's telling the truth. One of our skills is to read people, and his eyes are telling me that he's being straight with us. "

"Are you nuts, Francis? He won't come back and our asses will in a sling. I'm not losing my job by trusting the word of this hippie punk. If you do this, I'm putting in my report that it was your call."

Francis raised himself up to his full height, standing face to face with Lloyd. I had thought of him as the smaller man, but now that he was angry, he carried himself differently, towering above Lloyd mentally and physically.

"Put what you want into your report, Lloyd, and if we still have our jobs when this is over, you can find yourself a new partner. I could handle all your other idiotic shit, but when you're acting this stupid, I draw the line. In our work stupidity can get you killed, and I would rather be fired than dead. We have no choice but to trust him."

Lloyd backed away from the bed, putting some distance between himself and the ire of Agent Francis. Being who I was, I gave him a little smirk as he exited the room, which certainly made him my enemy for life.

"Thanks, Agent Francis, I'll—"

"You'll keep your word, Kronchek, or you'll wish that it was Lloyd after you instead of me. Monday at noon. Be here with a name, the right name, and no games. By the way, the New Haven Police ordered an autopsy on Williams. The doctor that treated him in the emergency room doesn't believe that he died from his injuries."

With that, they were gone, and I shivered from the cold air streaming in from an open window, or perhaps from my experience with them. The ominous emptiness of the apartment forced me to huddle in the corner of the bed to define my space. The house was freezing, but my clothes were completely drenched with the sweat and stink of fear. I threw them on the floor of the bathroom, washing my upper body until the skin turned a raw crimson. I hated to be afraid and wanted the fear removed permanently, leaving my body sanitized against further insecurity. The dizziness had returned, so I flopped down on the bed to wait for Leo and Karen. Time was running out, and so were my options.

Chapter 25

The drug money provided Donato with various luxuries, one of which was to keep three apartments, all of them under assumed names, except his flat in Bellington. He maintained one in New Haven and another in New York City. Landlords didn't ask many questions when they were paid in cash, six months in advance. Besides, he was a quiet tenant, entertaining very few guests, with only an occasional woman that always left before dawn. Rich didn't have relationships with women; he had sex. When that requirement was satisfied, he no longer had any need or desire for the woman to stay. Relationships or caring for someone could be an exploitable weakness, and Rich, if anything, was a careful man. Someday, when he was in full gear, he would find a trophy wife and have a couple of kids, while screwing whomever he wanted on the side.

That Saturday night, the piece of ass de jour whined incessantly about having to leave as she clumsily put her clothes on, stalling and fussing with the straps, hoping for a last minute reprieve; wishing for the never given permission to stay the night so she wouldn't have to go home and take care of her demanding kid. Her mother would baby sit until morning as she frequently did when her daughter didn't return home.

Donato let her go on for about thirty seconds, blocking out her bitching, making certain to finish his cigarette before he took action. This basically nameless slut was a first timer, so he gave her the full treatment to avoid any confusion in the future. They had gone to high school together, and she was already divorced at twenty-one with a two-year old at home. Wrinkle lines had begun to form around her mouth after a decade of smoking, with chronic exhaustion forming bags under her eyes years before their time. Alcohol-ridden nights combined with the daytime demands of a single parent told Rich that her best days were long behind her. He figured she must have peaked at around fifteen. He twirled her around by her hair, applying enough pressure to cause some pain in her neck.

"If you say one more word about staying, I'm going to slap your mouth shut! I only say things once, so you've been warned."

"But, Rich, you were so nice at the bar, and—"

She never saw it coming. The shock of the violence combined with the innate rejection made the emotional impact worse than the pain from the stinging blow. She had given him her only marketable asset, an attractiveness of dwindling value, but he had swatted her as if she were a filthy fly.

The efficient, painful slap, uninhibited by moral doubt or caring, made its point, but Rich preferred to punctuate his intentions. The tearful sobs had a short life as the next blow came in the form of a short punch to the solar plexus. Silence is what he demanded, and the message was delivered and understood. As she gasped for air, Donato kissed her on the forehead while showing her to the door, knowing that the slight gesture of affection would be enough to bring this poor, desperate woman back another time when he might be in need of some company.

"I'm sorry, Rich. I didn't mean to make you angry. You will call me, won't you?"

"Sure, baby, I'll call you sometime soon. Here, take this ten, and get yourself a cab. Make sure you give the whole thing to the driver. I'll call and have them send one right over. Wait outside, dry your eyes and fix your makeup. You look like shit."

Rich basically shoved her out the door as she thanked him profusely for the date, which had been a pick-up at the bar. He went back in to call a cab as promised. They had been to his house many times for the same purpose, so they knew the drill and that there would be a good tip involved. He turned off the lights, waiting for the sounds of the departing cab before he sat down to relax.

Flipping on the TV to watch the late news, he settled down to images of war protests filling the screen. College students across the country were protesting peacefully and sometimes violently in geometrically increasing numbers. The liberal news media had turned openly against the war, and were more than willing to give extra time to the demonstrations. Rich laughed when the camera panned over a scene of a cop smacking a long-haired male student with a baton. He dragged the struggling hippie to a paddy wagon while trying to push the cameraman away with his stick. Dumb fucking kids. Getting hurt over a cause with no profit involved was plain stupid.

Donato didn't have an opinion one way or the other about Vietnam. He was done over there and if the war meant more money for him, let it go on. He could see the increasing effectiveness of the protests as the message reached out beyond the colleges. The draft was starting to turn middle-class America against the war, and returning soldiers had even formed an anti-war organization: Vietnam Veterans Against the war. The soldiers were bringing back first person views and exposing the deteriorating situation in Vietnam.

The country hadn't been this divided since the Civil War, but this time it wasn't a geographical battle or a military debate over a system of slavery. Vietnam had split the country along age and culture lines, with children against parents, construction workers versus college students, and friends against friends. The turmoil provided a great atmosphere in which to sell drugs, especially to the disillusioned and disenfranchised people on the streets. The battle weary, disaffected soldiers added more misery to the emotional baggage left over from Vietnam as they came home to unemployment and public scorn. Drugs were a wonderful way to forget, and many of them were already hooked on chemical amnesia from Vietnam.

Donato made a difficult business decision that day. He decided to end the body bag smuggling operation. It was an interesting concept, but his sources told him that the Feds had gotten wind of their method and were taking the rumors seriously. The informant discovered that orders from high up were sent to the field agents to make the investigation a top priority. Ronald had obviously been skimming from Rich and he almost exposed them today because of his hate for Kronchek. Donato wasn't anxious to see who would get him first, his uncle or the Feds. Prison and death were two very bad options.

A smart guy knew when to cut his losses, and Rich considered himself a very bright man. He still had Ronald's heroin and the two shipments after that. He would sell two batches wholesale next weekend in New York through Ronald's contacts. Donato would then go to his uncle with the other batch and convince the old man that he had caught Ronald dealing in their New Haven territory. Ronald's death would give credence to Donato's claim that he had eliminated the black man in the approved manner. His uncle would reward him with a good position in the organization for icing Ronald and delivering the goods to the family. Rich would continue to run a soft drug operation out of Bellington through his lackeys-selling weed, speed, and other drugs that the mob had little interest in. He already had a front man for the operation, and although it wouldn't be big money, it would be enough to pay his bills. After tonight, none of the drugs would be on any property that could be traced to him.

It's not that Donato had lost his ambition, but he understood that he would have to move more methodically and carefully, especially with Kronchek still nosing around. The play for the top spot would be made when the time was right, buying influence silently with his secret heroin wealth, while cultivating potential allies. He would be a quiescent power until the opportunity for advancement presented itself.

He found it amusing that the media referred to the Mob or the Mafia as a family, since it was really all about business; a business where a son would kill his father to get ahead.

Everything fit into place except for one loose end: Kronchek. Donato found himself hemispherically split on the issue of his old classmate. A part of him relished the thought of a confrontation with the self-righteous bastard, but for the sake of business, it would be preferable if Kronchek would let it go. If Kronchek had found out that he was a drug dealer, it wasn't such a big thing. There were people close to Kronchek that could be threatened if he had a thought about talking. What really concerned

Rich is that Kronchek may have obtained information from Tommy or Paulie about their time in Vietnam together. Rich was the only one left alive, and he wanted the secrets to die with him. He hated even thinking about it because Vietnam picked away at something that he never believed that he possessed: a conscience.

Donato had been exposed to Kronchek's personality and behavior patterns for many years and it had always fascinated him to watch how emotional Kronchek became over social issues and matters of morality even as a child. The aspect that confused Donato was that he could see a pattern in Kronchek's behavior, but couldn't comprehend his motivations, and to control someone, you had to understand not just how, but why. If you didn't understand the why of it, predictability was not guaranteed and unanticipated reactions could produce defeat. There was something that he didn't get. Maybe that's what drew him to Kronchek. Rich was curious how someone could be constantly emotional about issues that didn't effect them directly, and still remain sane.

Donato, not acclimated to worrying, rubbed his aching eyes. He didn't want to spend another second thinking about the war, Ronald Williams, the protesters, the Feds, and especially Kronchek. He had just popped open a beer and settled down to watch Johnny Carson, when the phone rang in the kitchen.

The ring seldom brought good news, so it was a warning signal that shook the cautionary centers of Donato's brain. His men had orders never to call this late unless it was an emergency that they couldn't handle. He was very pissed off as he picked up the receiver.

"This better be fucking good or someone's ass will be on the line."

"Rich, it's Joe down at the pool hall. We were getting ready to close up when this guy comes in looking for you. We told him that we don't know where you are, but he's not buying it. Says he won't leave until he gets to see you. You want us to rough him up and fling him out the door?"

"Let me guess. His name is Matt Kronchek. Right?"

"How did you know that? Were you expecting him or something?"

"Oh, I was expecting him all right, but I didn't think that he would come so soon. Keep him there and tell him that I'll be right down. Clear everybody else out of the place. We're closing early tonight."

"Okay, Rich, but there's no one here anyway. Where do you want him to wait?"

"In the back, and lock the doors. You guys can wait in the pool room until I get there."

Rich hung up the phone, a slight smirk breaking over his lips. He saw it as a win-win situation. If Kronchek came to deal, it would be simple. If he came for revenge, then Rich would do what's necessary. He put a pistol in his belt, a knife in an ankle sheath, threw on his jacket and went out the door to put an end to all this uncertainty one way or the other.

Chapter 26

I must have dozed off again after the Feds left because I jumped up at the sound of the door opening, the creaky hinges hopefully announcing the return of Karen and Leo. Sitting up too quickly from the surprise, my head reminded me that my internal systems were still messed up from the bang on the head. The constant physical trauma and psychological disorientation of the past week made it difficult to discern what events had actually taken place. Even the FBI's visit of only a half-hour ago seemed unreal.

"Jesus, Kronchek, you still look awful. We have to get you to a hospital. This beef with your buddy in Bellington is going to have to wait."

"It can't wait, Leo, and you know it's not just a beef. Waiting has done nothing but get me deeper into this mess. We're going now."

Struggling to get out of bed, I fumbled for my clothes and the bottle of aspirin.

Leo said, "Look, we've been talking and we don't think this is good idea at all."

Karen and Leo stared at my shaking hands, the vibrating fingers dropping half the pills onto the floor before I got two in my hand. They stood in quiet solidarity against my stubborn resolve, which considering their past tumultuous relationship, seemed improbable.

"We were talking, Leo? You and Karen? I think you two have been discussing issues that aren't open to discussion? I don't believe this shit. You were supposed to keep certain facts to yourself."

Karen pushed Leo aside. "Shut up, Matt! Just shut up! This isn't just about what you want. What right do you have to keep me in the dark and lie to me? Leo, leave us alone for a minute. Please."

Leo sheepishly ambled out of the room, unwillingly to meet my gaze.

"You had to tell her, Leo, didn't you? You're a traitor and—"

"Matt! Leave him alone. You're going to apologize to him later because he's the furthest thing from a traitor that there is. You're lucky to have a friend like him. I don't have one person that I can depend on like Leo. He can be obnoxious and rude, but he's frightened and worried about you. You can't keep that big mouth closed for one second just to hear him out, but you're going to listen to me."

This was new territory. My anger was transformed into curious amusement, with the irony of an alliance between two incongruous people distracting me from my purpose for a moment. Normally, having two human beings besides your parents that care about you should give you a warm, fuzzy feeling, but right now it was a pain in my ass. Karen, however, appeared quite determined as she shut and locked the door behind Leo's perfidious ass.

"Matt, the other night on the phone you said that you wanted our relationship to change, and that we should make a serious commitment to each other. Do you still want that to happen?"

"Yea, of course I do, but what—"

"No but what's, Matt. You do or don't, and if you do, then cut the freaking bullshit and tell the truth about what's going on. I'm a nurse, not a detective. You're supposed to be a student, not a federal agent. Leo told me that you intend to confront the person who might be responsible for at least two murders. Is that what we're going to Bellington to do? Pick up your dead body when he's done with you? And what about that dead girl in Bellington when you were a kid? Leo told me everything. Who are you?"

I put my arms around Karen in an attempt to control her shaking and crying. She tried to pull away from my grasp, but I wouldn't let go. She ceased struggling while crying into my shoulder, but her stiff body told me that she was frightened of me, and would probably bolt if I released my grip.

I wanted to flip out on Leo for betraying my confidence, but as I stepped away from the situation, I could understand why he needed to talk to someone besides me about everything that had happened. Events had swirled so quickly that even I had lost perspective, and I knew the whole story from the beginning. It had been one weird week, even for me.

"Karen, please stop crying and listen for a minute. I'd like to make this go away, but from the minute Tommy Combs told me about Paulie, I've been sucked into an increasingly powerful vortex of misery that always seems to go back to Vietnam. Today was the only day that we purposefully put ourselves in danger, but even that happened because of a promise I had made to Wanda to help her brother."

"Why don't you just walk away, Matt? Leo said now that Ronald Williams is dead, that guy Rich will probably just ignore you if you stay out of his way."

"Leo didn't leave much out, did he? Just telling you Rich's name may have put you in more danger. Leo might be right, but I want to hear it from Rich's mouth. I can't take the chance that someone will look for revenge on you or my family. He's a criminal, but I've known him since we were kids, and if he gives me his word, he'll keep it."

"You're lying, Matt. Leo said that if you find out that Rich had something to do with Paulie's death, then you'll kill him. I thought it was ridiculous, but Leo said that when you snap you're a different person. He claims that it has something to do with that dead girl you found in Bellington."

Now I was really pissed. Leo 'Freud' had stepped way over the line. I jumped from the bed, unlocking and pulling the door open in one quick movement, spilling an eavesdropping Leo into the room.

"I'm sorry, Kronchek, but I thought you might listen to Karen and realize what a dumb shit you are."

"Now you sit down and listen. I'm trying to control myself because you two are my best friends, but we're wasting valuable time. You left the door unlocked when you went to Karen's house, and your FBI friends paid me another harsh visit."

I lifted my shirt showing them the welt on my ribs where Agent Lloyd had belted me. Leo bolted from the chair when he saw the bruise.

"Where did they go? FBI or not, they've gone too far. They lied to me and treated me like a clown, and now they're slapping you around. I'm going to find them and mess them up. I'm sorry about the door, Kronchek. I screwed up again."

I pushed Leo back in his seat, smiling at both of them as I paced the room.

"This reaction is coming from the guy who told you that I flip out like a murderous maniac, Karen, and you believed him. Check the look on his face. Now who's the killer? Don't worry about the door, Leo. They were going to find me one way or another, plus they had a warrant this time."

Karen missed the lame attempt at humor, appearing more frightened and confused than ever, so I put my arm around her while locking my eyes on Leo.

"We have no choice, Leo. The Feds found your gun and they had a guy planted in Ronald's operation. He witnessed the whole thing go down outside the bar. They knew every detail. We could go to prison for a long time on manslaughter or attempted murder if they decide to set us up. Just the gun could get you prison time. I know it seems unreal, but it did happen. You were there blasting away with the 'unloaded' gun."

"Real funny. So why haven't they busted us? Maybe they're just bluffing in order to scare you. They must want something."

"They want Rich, even though they don't know who he is, and they want him quickly, but with Ronald gone they think that I'm the only connection left who knows his name, and this time they're right. Their guy on the inside never found out who was running the show. They do know that there was someone higher up than Ronald and they want to take him quietly. I told them that if they gave me the weekend, I would give them his name in exchange for all the charges to disappear. I have until Monday, and then they're going to haul us in if I don't give them a name."

"I can't believe you're going to trust them, Kronchek. Even if you give them the name, they're going to nail us, or Donato will have us snuffed for squealing. This is stupid. It's lose, lose, for us. Working with cops has never been one of your strong points."

"Leo's right, Matt. It doesn't make sense, and you could be killed. I won't let you go."

Karen put me in a bear hug, which was kind of sweet since she only weighed about a hundred pounds.

"Give me some credit. I don't trust my own mother. It would never come down to that, but you had to be here to see their faces. I'm telling you that they just want to wrap it all up in plastic and have it go silently into the night. They said that it was very sensitive stuff and that Hoover has made the case a priority. There's a lot more to this thing than just drugs. I intend to find out what it is before I turn anybody in."

"How do you know that the Feds won't make us go away in the night without a squeak, Kronchek? I can't see the sense in getting curious about whatever shit those two weird G-Men are into."

"Well, Leo, I don't think either one of us has ever gone silently away from anything, and their secret, curious fact might give us a little insurance if the Feds go back on their word. That's why I have to go alone. If something happens to me, go straight to the newspaper. You both know everything that's happened, and there are too many coincidences to ignore. Good plan, right?"

Karen shook her head. "Dumb plan, Matt. Think about it. If they want to silence this case, how far do you think they'll let you go if you find out all the details? Right now, unless you're still lying, you really don't know what they want. You're not going if you still want to be with me."

"She's right, Kronchek. Usually you make sense, but you're not thinking this through. I'll help her keep you here if necessary."

"Leo, could you give me a minute alone with Karen again, and then we'll see where we're going."

"Okay, Kronchek, but don't try to go out the window because I've got all the car keys."

"Leo, go into the kitchen. We're on the second floor. I'm not going anywhere. Go, shut the door behind you, and keep your face out of the keyhole."

Leo walked out slowly, turning his head slightly to make sure that I wasn't going to bolt. I hadn't even thought of running until he mentioned the idea, but they didn't understand. I wasn't going anywhere without them because we had to stick together. My arm remained tightly around Karen as I formulated my thoughts. When I was ready, I picked up her chin with my free hand and locked my eyes onto hers.

"I can't figure what you see in me, but I'm glad that you see something, since you're the prettiest nurse at the hospital, not to mention the most compassionate. Every patient, aide, and doctor snaps their head around when you walk by, but you chose me. It certainly isn't for my looks, and believe it or not, I didn't fall in love with you for yours, although you are hot."

"Did you say love, Matt, or am I hearing things? I've never heard you use that word even when you want sex. A lot of guys play that word to death, but I didn't think it was even in your vocabulary."

"I said it, but it wasn't easy for me. You asked me two questions before, which I haven't answered. You wanted to know who I was, and about a dead girl in Bellington. That dead girl has a lot to do with who I am, and I've only talked to one person about that night, and he's been gone for eight years."

"I want to know about it, Matt. I want to know everything because I feel how tightly wrapped you are. The tension in your body is like a tiger ready to spring. You're always on your guard. Even in our most passionate moments, I can feel the wall around you. I want the wall to come down, or if that's not possible, I want to be on your side of the wall."

I took in a deep breath, slowly letting it out through my lips, struggling to gain enough composure to let my barriers down. I hadn't cried publicly since eighth grade, holding it back even at my father's funeral. I had never wanted to cry again, but as I began my story of Nellie, the tears began to ooze from my eyes; tears that hurt as they forced their way out, one by one, finally free from their eight-year prison. There were no choking sobs, just tears of release.

I started with my friendship and infatuation with Nellie, her horrible life situation, and the night that we'd kissed—the night she died. I told Karen how Lipscomb had discovered that Nellie was abused by her father, but I left out the train yard, Antonio's rape, and Father Joe's indiscretions. I wasn't ready to explain all that to anyone yet. The fact that her father raped her at nine years old was enough to stun Karen to near disbelief. The tears fell until my eyes were incapable of producing any more.

Karen's cheeks were streaked with thin rivulets of emotion and her spastic sobs told me that she understood and felt Nellie's pain.

"You see Karen, the night that Nellie killed herself, I was too immature to see it coming. Looking back now, I see that it was right in front of me, so obvious that she would want to commit suicide. I never would have imagined in my worst nightmares back then that anyone could do those things to a child, but I'm not a kid anymore and I know what people are capable of. I grew up with Rich Donato and watched him develop into a criminal.

"Bellington is where the story started, and it has to stop there before he comes after one of you. Running is not an option. It's not in my nature because that's who I am, and I am this way because of what happened back then. I wasn't capable of seeing Nellie's pain clearly, and I've been trying not to see Vietnam, but it's out there waiting for me, and it's real. All of it is real. There are dozens of young guys being killed over in Vietnam every day and many more wounded or crippled for life. It's like a movie on the evening news every night, but when you walk into the orthopedic ward at the V.A., it hits you hard in the gut. The people on television are dying for real and the guys in the hospital will never be right again. I will not run or turn my head from the obvious truth for one more minute."

"Matt, I fell for you the moment you walked onto the ward with that goofy uniform, messy hair and idiotic sense of humor. The patients trusted you right from the beginning. There was something special about you, something different from other guys. I've gone out with a lot of guys, but there was never the connection that I felt with you from the first minute you said something stupid to make me laugh. I don't want to lose you like you lost Nellie, just when we've found each other. He's a killer, Matt, and you're a student."

"I have to go, Karen. The Feds say I have to go, Rich expects me to come, and it won't stop until I do. You know when I realized that I was in love with you? It was in that split second when Rebrone was going to drive the pen in your throat. I thought that I would be too slow to save you, and I couldn't have lived with that again. I almost died inside from the fear before I reached you. Do you understand? You can't expect mercy from a person like Rich. You either forge a deal that he'll see as good business or you have to kill him, and I'm willing to do either at this point because I can't take the tension anymore."

"I don't understand completely, Matt, but I know that Paulie was your friend, and that you're the type of person that has to have things resolved. Please don't use the word kill anymore because you're making me believe Leo was telling the truth about you snapping into a killer. Leo, come back in here. We're going to Bellington with Matt."

Leo entered before Karen finished the sentence, accepting her decision without question, which indicated that he had been listening at the door again. I figured that Leo would give us an argument, but he was waiting for me to speak.

"Good story, huh rabbit ears? If you tell anybody what you heard or about my crying, I've got a lot stories to tell about you. So are you in or not? If you're afraid, you can stay here and wait to be arrested by your new friends."

"Screw you, Kronchek! I wasn't listening, and if you're determined to go, I'm going with you. Scared? Your pal Rich better be the one who's afraid. Let's go. Hey, Nellie's father must have been a real prick, a lot like this guy Rich."

"I thought you weren't listening, secret agent. Maybe you should tell Karen who your prom date was."

"Asshole! You promised never to tell anybody about me taking my sister to the prom."

"And I haven't. You just did. Come on; let's get a move on. I'll call my mother and tell her to make some food."

Leo shoved me on the bed, getting me in a playful headlock while Karen laughed in amazement over the instantaneous transformation from deadly serious to playful clowns. Hey, if I'm going down, I'd rather go down laughing. I called my mother who was thrilled to be meeting Karen even though it was late. We hopped in Leo's car and headed to Bellington to finish the story.

Chapter 27

The drive to Bellington was conducted in relative silence, broken only by the occasional insults between Leo and I. Karen fell asleep on my shoulder about halfway through the ride, and I followed her to dreamland minutes later. My first intention was to have Leo take all back roads to throw off the Feds, but I concluded that they wouldn't follow us. They didn't have to. They knew the story ended in Bellington, and most likely had men waiting near my house in violation of their deal with me. I didn't really care. They knew where I was staying, but they didn't know where I was going, and it wouldn't be hard to lose them in my hometown.

As we pulled off the highway into Bellington, I woke up on the exit ramp as 1961 came rushing back into my life. The shades of gray had become even fuzzier now, and the lines between the good guys and the bad guys were not so clear. The Vietnam War had made me hate my government, adding them to the list of institutions that I had learned not trust.

Boys, yes mostly boys, were dying in someone else's civil war. In the name of our global politics, the casualties increased as we tried to step up the carnage in order to keep the world safe from communism. It was all about body count to the military; a way to justify the effectiveness of our illegal occupation of Vietnam. The War was geopolitical strategy to McNamara, Kennedy, Johnson, and now Nixon and Kissinger, but the Vietnamese and young Americans were real people-not little tokens on a map. The FBI represented the government, and I was about to help them out by delivering a name to them.

On the other hand, Rich Donato was most likely a major drug dealer, and maybe in some way responsible for Paulie's death. There was also something important that the FBI wanted to keep quiet, and I had to know. I lied to Leo and Karen because I wanted revenge for Paulie, and believe it or not, Tommy. Tommy risked his life to do the right thing, and it turned out to be a deadly gamble. We had all played and fought on these streets, but back then the reasons never mattered much. Now it was different. I wished that Mike could be with me because although Leo was a good friend, Mike would understand the depth of my feelings. One of our guys had gone very bad, not just robbing-the-candy-store bad, and it was an insult to the integrity of the neighborhood and our upbringing.

At the train yard eight years ago, the sewage of Bellington was flushed cleaned by the roar of a locomotive, but not in time to help Nellie. I wasn't going to let that happen this time. Leo would keep Karen safe and I wouldn't let Donato's transgressions go unresolved and unexplained.

As we pulled into my mother's driveway, it wasn't hard to notice the car that didn't belong on my street. The Feds would be almost laughable if they didn't have so much power. Two men sitting in a big, black Buick on a side street in Bellington would normally have brought a call to the police within fifteen minutes or less. They were parked up the hill near an old barn, and if you lived there, you knew they didn't belong. Apparently, the local cops had been notified of the presence of the FBI because four different window curtains parted as we got out of our car. The neighbors didn't miss much on my street and they certainly hadn't missed the Buick. Let the boys sit there. It's exactly where I wanted them.

Although it was after nine o'clock, my mother had prepared a four-course meal, with enough food for eight people, or three people and Leo. All the food was wiped up, making my mother very happy, except that she worried about Karen being so thin.

"Let me fix more food for Karen. She hardly ate a thing, and look how skinny she is. You can get sick from being so skinny. Eat, eat some more."

"Ma, how could anyone eat enough? Leo just about took the food from my mouth."

"Leave Leo alone. You should be such a good eater as him. You're so damn picky. During the Depression we ate what was put in front of us or we went hungry."

"If Leo had been your brother, you would have all gone hungry. I think my mother wants to adopt you, Leo, instead of having a garbage disposal installed."

"Mrs. Kronchek, he's always picking on me. Make him go to his room. You've got a mean son there."

"Don't pay any attention to him, Leo. Here, have some more dessert. See, Matt, even Leo thinks you've gotten mean."

While my mother believed the whole argument was serious, Karen could barely control her laughter. She now understood that this bantering was the essence of my relationship with Leo. For a brief moment the reasons for coming to Bellington were submerged. We helped my mother clean up, and then we played some cards until she started nodding off at the table.

Her sexual paranoia and domineering manner provided me with a lucky break. My bedroom and the spare room were on the third floor, and I hadn't figured out how I would get by her to leave the house. She announced, however, that she and Karen would take the rooms upstairs, with the sole intention of making sure Karen and I didn't end up in the same bed. Leo would get my mom's room, and I would sleep on the couch, which would put us below her. If I was super quiet, I would be able to sneak out for a few hours to meet Rich.

Karen went upstairs with my mother to get the beds ready, the humor gone from her face with the realization that the hour of confrontation was near. I said goodnight, reassuring her with a secret hug behind my mother's back. As they went upstairs, I hoped that it wouldn't be the last time I saw them.

"What's wrong, Leo? You seem to have something on your mind, and if you do, say it now. I'm leaving as soon as I hear my mother snoring."

"What if she gets up to take a leak and doesn't see you on the couch? What am I going to tell her?"

"You'll be sleeping on the couch, and you're going to tell her that I kicked you out of the bed, which she'll believe since I'm so mean. We can lock the bedroom door from the outside and hide the key so she won't hassle or check on me. You bring those aspirins, Leo? My head is killing me and the painkillers are gone."

"Yea, I got them, but that's the other thing. I want to go with you. You're in no shape for this, so I want to be there if something goes down."

"Think, Leo. I appreciate you watching my back, but please reason it out. You're here to make sure nobody gets to Karen and my mother, plus I'm the only one who can deal with this guy. He won't want you there, and there's nothing to be in shape for. It's a negotiation, not a brawl, and if there's one thing that you're good at, it's starting a fight. If we go in fighting, we're going to lose."

"Okay, Kronchek, we'll do it your way, but if you get killed, we're not friends anymore. Can I have your girlfriend?"

"Sure, Leo, but she won't have you. You're just too good looking and charming. It would overwhelm her, especially now that she's seen you eat."

"That is the one true thing you've said all day. I am too handsome for most women."

"But not your sister."

"Rot in hell, Kronchek. I should have never told you about that prom. You are not to be trusted. Go. Your mother will wake up before you leave."

It took me a few calls before I could track down Rich's hangouts. Not many of my old friends were around anymore so I was forced to lower myself and call Billy Mancini. I doubted that the little weasel knew anything about Rich, plus he was probably still pissed at me for the other night at Debbie's, but he was my last hope. Surprisingly, he told me to check the pool hall on South Main, and didn't appear angry at all. Oh well, maybe other people didn't hold grudges for years like Leo and I did.

Leo began to take our makeshift weapons from his bag, but I waved him off.

"What? You're not going armed? Are you stupid or just suicidal? Stay on task here, Kronchek, or has that knock on your head removed your survival instincts? If he's a drug dealer, he'll be armed, and he probably wasted your boy Tommy."

"It won't matter, Leo. Rich is no dummy. His men won't let me near him without checking for weapons, and besides, I'm sure he has a gun, which will make all this stuff sort of useless. I gotta go. Billy said that Rich is usually at the pool hall. Lock the doors and be careful. I'm sneaking around the back through the woods so the Feds in front will keep watching the house."

"You're going on foot?"

"Yea, that way they'll never see me leave, plus my mother would hear the car start."

I eased the door shut behind me, keeping the tiny flashlight beam focused on the floor as I gingerly tiptoed down the creaky wooden stairs into the basement. The hoses were hung up for the winter, and hickory nuts were spread out to dry. Newspapers waiting to be recycled were stacked near the basement door, newsprint in one pile, and glossy magazines in another. That had been drilled into my head a dozen times by my mother, since I would mix them without a second thought to save time.

The edge of an envelope sticking out of the glossy pile was so out of place that I couldn't believe that it had escaped my mother's eye. Unwanted letters didn't belong with the glossy newsprint. The first three letters of Paulie's name showed in the return address area. What the hell was a letter from Paulie doing at my mother's house? He had always written to me at school. I pulled the unopened envelope out of the pile, deciding to read it when I gained some distance from the Feds. I wanted to open it so badly that my legs were actually shaking, but I couldn't risk them spotting the light in the basement. I flicked off the flashlight, quietly leaving by the back door.

I stopped behind the empty dog pen, my dogs gone soon after my dad, and remembered that it was last place I saw and spoke to Lipscomb. The dog pen made me feel like a kid again, with a gut-souring nostalgia for my dad, the dogs, and Lipscomb's perspective.

Lipscomb would tell me that it was stupid for going alone, but in the end he would also understand that it was the way it had to be for me. He would do no different, and hadn't that night at the tracks when he went after Antonio by himself. Fate had it that night that we ended up helping each other, two people in pain thrown together by accident, but tonight I would be on my own. I did have a choice, but I would not drag my friends any further into the mess that I always seemed to walk into. I slid flawlessly through the woods with my muscle memory of the terrain guiding me through the dark brush to the next street. I kept to the yards, crossing the main roads when they were empty of passing cars, making my way to find a safe place to read Paulie's last letter.

Back at the house, Leo rummaged through his bag for a toothbrush and realized that the stiletto and its sheath were missing. A thin, illegal five-inch blade of razor-sharp steel that he had purchased in the Bronx when he had gone to see a Yankee game last year. At the same moment he heard footsteps coming down from the third floor. Shit! There wasn't time to lock the bedroom, and he was a bumbling liar under pressure. The skillful interrogation of Mrs. Kronchek would have the truth out of him in a second.

"Leo, did Matt leave yet?"

"Jesus, Karen, you scared the piss right out of me! I thought you were Mrs. Kronchek, and I haven't even locked the bedroom yet. He left about five minutes ago. Why aren't you asleep or upstairs? If Mrs. Kronchek heard you move, she'll be down here in a minute thinking that you two are screwing on her couch."

"She's snoring so loud that a train ripping through her bedroom wouldn't wake her up. Leo, I can't sleep. I'm worried because I know that Matt was lying to us. He's going for revenge. When he lies, his nose gets red, and tonight it was shining like Rudolph on Christmas Eve."

"Oh shit! I can't find the stiletto and now you tell me this. He's such an asshole! That's why he said that he didn't want any of the weapons. I want go after him, but he insisted that I stay here and protect you guys. I don't know what to do."

Karen thought for a moment as she glanced out the side of the curtain.

"Do you know where he went?"

"Yea, he called some old friends, but the only one he talked to was that creep Billy Mancini, and I heard Matt repeat something about a pool hall down the south end of town. I still don't know what to do."

Just then, there was a light tap on the door, barely audible, and Leo ran over to look out the peephole. A short, dark-skinned soldier stood in the hallway. Leo almost freaked, but a smile crossed his face when he realized who it was. He opened the door quietly as Karen tried to stop him with a harsh whisper.

"Leo, don't open the door! Are you crazy?"

Karen stared in amazement as Leo shook hands and slapped the shoulder of a man who appeared to be his physical clone.

"Karen, say hello to Mike, Kronchek's other best friend."

"Hi Mike, I've heard a lot about you. Matt's not home right now."

"I figured the fool might be gone already, and that's why I'm here. I was hoping to catch him before he left, but I got held up. Come around back near the woods so we don't wake Mrs. Kronchek. I've got some people I want you to meet."

Chapter 28

The letter in my back pocket burned my ass with hot curiosity. I made it to downtown with another mile to reach the pool hall. The park in the center of town was fairly open, but a dense planting of shrubs on the south end had a few streetlights along the path. The shrubs would block my presence from the street and the light would allow me to read the letter. I couldn't afford to be rousted by a cop for hanging around the park at night, or hassled by a bum for money.

With my equilibrium still not right from the concussion, I fumbled to pull the letter out of my pocket. The postmark almost put me out on the ground. The letter, addressed to me at my mother's house, had been stamped two weeks after Paulie's death. Multiple chills ran streaks across my body, with the fine hairs on my neck and arms standing on alert. He must have written the letter just before he died, but the army either had lost it for awhile or somehow my normally impeccable mother had mixed it in with the glossy advertisements, throwing it all out in one batch. Clammy, shaking hands recklessly tore open the envelope, exposing several sheets of paper. It was more like a novelette than a letter. One sheet floated to the ground, almost getting away from me in the light wind. I stepped on it quickly, tilting it so the light would shine on the page.

August 9 1969

Dear Matt,

I know we ripped into each other the last time we wrote, but this isn't about you and I, or maybe it is. Listening to the news that we get from back home, it's easy to figure that we're not the only two friends who became divided because of this nightmare war. There's nothing here but death and misery, Matt. We're doing some good things for the people, but overall, our presence has ripped their lives apart. This is a divided country, but more and more of the people seem to be on the side of the Cong, just as more Americans want us out of the war.

We've become occupiers of Vietnam, not liberators, and some of the things I've seen our own people do have made me sick to my stomach. Don't get me wrong, it's a small amount of bad soldiers, and half of those have been dragged along by the circumstances. I lost someone that I was close to here and I finally understand how you felt when Nellie died. The sense of helplessness to prevent a horrible and needless death has left me an empty shell.

I have something to tell you, and I'm writing this letter because if I don't make it home, you're the only person that I can trust to do something. I never told you, but Tommy Combs, Rich Donato and I were all in the same unit for awhile. It was an unbelievable coincidence, and although I had never been close to those guys, I thought that having two people from home would ease the loneliness.

Things just got worse. As soon as Rich arrived, he hooked up with this crazy black guy, Ronald Williams, who had been running a small drug operation out of the base. It didn't stay small for long once Rich's highly motivated criminal mind was set to work, and I'm ashamed to admit that I profited from it. I don't know if it was greed or just the fear of saying no. I never actually dealt the drugs, but I was well rewarded for my silence and access to certain areas.

Anyone who got in the way found themselves in pretty bad shape and sometimes dead, although I could never prove who was responsible. Tommy freaked and wanted out after Rich fried Tommy's buddy's brain on some dope. Williams wanted to kill the guy, but Rich showed him a better way. The guy left Vietnam screaming on a stretcher, but bound tight with straps courtesy of Rich's drugs. Tommy didn't want to be next so he shot himself in the leg and was shipped home. He can confirm some of what I'm telling you, but he'll probably be too afraid.

Dope is everywhere here, and during a war it's hard for the Army to control these activities by their own people. It's enough just to worry about the Viet Cong and North Vietnamese who seem to be everywhere and then nowhere. We didn't attract much attention until Rich decided that he wanted to start shipping the dope home. His tour would be up soon and he didn't want to give up the business. Small amounts shipped home were risky, but not impossible, but Rich was talking about a lot of heroin.

As you know, I was attached to medical unit, pretty much keeping to myself. That is, until Williams came up with this idea to ship the stuff home in body bags. Rich tells him that it won't work and that stories of this type were considered war legends. There had been rumors for a long time about dead body smuggling, but the Feds or Military Intelligence never found anything, and if they had, I know it would have been kept quiet. That's why Williams said it would work. No one except for a few freaks back home believed it could or had been done. I got dragged into it because of my access to the body bags in the morgue. Donato volunteered me and I was afraid to say no.

It's amazing to watch Williams. He's very intelligent, but generally his constant rage overrules any rational thought. The man is massive and physically intimidating, and when he flips out, everyone runs except for Rich. Rich decided to listen to the full plan, finally agreeing to give it a test run, but only with bodies that had been blown to bits. They would be less likely to check those bags, and his guys at the other end would be able to cull out the closed coffin bags.

It worked very well, and the profits began flowing in, but I wanted out. You know how religious I am, so the idea of defiling a dead body just to make some money was out of the question for me. Even though I tried to convince them that I would keep my mouth shut, they said the only way out was in one of the body bags. As the profits rose, so did the brutality, and that's the main reason I'm writing this letter.

Last month, we went to a village to pick up a shipment, and it turned into the most gruesome scene that I had ever witnessed, even during some of the worst battles. This was no battle. Williams brought along three new guys for extra protection, since the village was in a hot zone for the Cong. The guys were loose cannons from various squads of the 11th Infantry, soldiers that had lost their sense of perspective about who was the enemy. They weren't wanted in their own units anymore, but they were the exact breed of guys that Williams could use. I had become very close to some of the people in the village, and felt safe there, despite the enemy's presence in the area.

Matt, I've seen some terrible things and helped deal drugs, but nothing could have prepared me for what happened that day. Williams was negotiating with the village leader for our drugs when a little girl of about ten started to run. One of Ronald's butchers panicked and blew her away, which provoked more chaos, with people running, men coming out of their huts, and people bending over to scoop up their personal possessions. Everyone flipped, including Rich and Tommy, and I'm ashamed to say, even me. We started shooting at anything that moved. One guy was screaming and firing his rifle in the air before Ronald took it away from him. Before it was over, ten villagers were dead, and twelve more were wounded. No one made it to the jungle. One woman and her two children had escaped injury. I raised my rifle and begged our men to stop, but it did no good. You have to believe me, Matt. It's important to me that you believe that I tried to stop them from killing the rest.

If it had ended there, a part of me could have understood the complexity of the situation, where the enemy is among the population. They rounded up the wounded along with the three survivors. Instead of looking at it as a tragic mistake, Ronald decided that they couldn't leave any witnesses. The cowboys from the 11th told him that this wasn't the first time something like this had happened, and that they were doing the right thing. I tried to stop them, but they slaughtered the wounded first, over the woman's begging and the wailing of her children.

I understood then the true capabilities of these men, and that some of the stories concerning atrocities had to be real. At that moment, I finally decided that I couldn't and wouldn't be the old Paulie any longer. As you always said, at some point you have to make your stand or someone will make it for you. I placed myself between the woman and her children and Ronald's rifle, telling him that there would be no more killing. He laughed and said that if I wanted to join them, then he would be happy to help me along. I lowered my rifle and charged at Williams, but I was like a rag doll to him.

Williams twisted my arm until my face was buried in the mud. Holding my face under until my lungs almost burst, the bastard picked me up by my hair and faced me toward the woman. He slapped me hard across the face, splattering mud all over the woman as he screamed for me to watch. They blew the woman and her baby away without hesitation, practically cutting them in half. In all the confusion, the older boy had escaped into the jungle, and the three hired thugs chased him into the bush.

As I cried in the mud, Williams kept kicking me in the ribs until Rich stopped him. I think Rich was afraid that Ronald was going to kill me in front of Tommy and the others, plus we heard shots deep in the bush. The three soldiers never came back, so Ronald dragged me into the jeep and we left before the Cong could kill us.

The boy escaped, but I was too weak to save the others. I've seen a lot of horror over here, but this was unimaginable. Tomorrow, I'm going to headquarters and tell the whole story: the drugs, the massacre, the names, including my name. Tommy won't talk and the other guy is headed home to a psych unit, so I'm the only one left.

I was able to avoid Williams for the last three weeks because they needed extra medics in an area that was taking heavy casualties, but when I returned to my unit, Tommy was gone. Rich warned me not to talk before he shipped out, but Williams promised to kill me once he had a chance. I told them that I was done with dealing, so he's just waiting for the opportunity. I'm staying close to other people to make it hard for him. A captain was sniffing around a couple months ago and had promised anyone a ticket home if they gave him what he wanted.

If I don't make it, Matt, give this letter to the FBI, Military Intelligence, or a newspaper if necessary. I have no one else that would believe me, and I know that you won't be afraid to expose the truth. I hope Debbie or my parents won't hate me for what I've done. I know what I have done is wrong, and I'll have to live or die with it, but I'm not sure they can. I don't think I'm going to make it, but I need to set things straight or I won't be able to look at myself in the mirror ever again. See ya, Hardy Boy, and stay out of the Army.

Paulie

I cried for the second time within a day, after a hiatus of eight years. I had always wanted Paulie to stand up and not be so afraid, and the one time that he did, he's killed for it. I felt some culpability for his death because I had bugged him to back up his beliefs with action since he was five. Poor Paulie was always trying to live up to my overworked sense of morality or Mike's recklessness. He should have just turned his head, finished his last month and gone home to Debbie. Let the drug dealers fight with each other and screw the war. It was beyond anyone's ability to change the reality, but Paulie felt responsibility for those Vietnamese villagers, and I was so proud of him that my tears turned to sobs.

If I had gotten this letter two weeks ago, all of my reluctance to pursue this matter would have melted away. I know that Rich wasn't present to kill Paulie, since he had already left Vietnam, but was he responsible in some way? If he were, then there would be no deal for me except him going down. Paulie's letter explained the FBI's motivation for secrecy. If this dirty operation using the dead bodies of American GI's to ship drugs were exposed to the public, a lot of fence sitters concerning the war would oppose staying there. My bet was that the agents didn't have a clue about the massacre. The agents believed that they were investigating a smuggling ring, but a story of a civilian massacre would push the drugs and even the body bags off the front page.

I let my buried rage push away the tears, as I dried my eyes and thought, *Well Paulie, for the first time since the Post Office debacle, we're partners in the justice business. This time; however, thanks to your guts, we're certain that we got the right guy. Nobody will be laughing at us this time. I'm going to finish it for both of us.*

Chapter 29

I ran from the park, making up the lost time by cutting through the back streets that led to the south end of town. Absorbed in the significance of Paulie's letter, I almost bumped into the street sign on the corner of South Main and Mason.

The pool hall's address was South Main Street, but the access door was on Mason. It sat on a litter-strewn lot that was just about as far to the edge of Bellington as one could go without crossing over into Ridgeville. When it was first built around fifty years ago, my great grandparents lived in the area, and my mom told me that it was a nice neighborhood to live in, but now it was the armpit of Bellington. Hard times had fallen on the workers as the factories moved West and South for cheaper labor and lower taxes.

Besides the pool hall, Mason Street had two or three unoccupied houses on the verge of condemnation, with the rest of the space being used for the landfill, dog pound, and rock processing plant. It was a street that was started with good intentions, never went far, and had stopped growing about forty years ago. The road was empty of traffic, and the howling dogs at the pound echoed their mournful song off the rock quarry walls and on down to the street where I picked my way carefully through the shadows. Most of the streetlights were busted, and along with the baying of the hounds, it set a scene reminiscent of a grade B horror movie.

It was the part of the movie where I usually thought, *Turn back dummy, anyone could see that there's a monster up ahead,* but I understood the determination or perhaps the rashness of a Van Helsing that night because I had a purpose that needed to be fulfilled. If you're afraid of Dracula, you shouldn't go looking for him. I can't deny that the alien turf gave me hesitation, along with the realization that I was in over my head, but Paulie's letter had opened up my locked box of caring and responsibility. I felt a new vitality in my mind that had been missing for eight years.

The pool hall occupied the second floor of a large three story building. The first floor had housed a small grocery store, which now had painted-over windows and a peeling, boarded-up door. The heavy lead paint hung off the door in wide strips, with the thick scent of mildewed wood leaving no reminder of better times. The partial third floor appeared to be a tiny apartment, and a dull, flickering light from a television set found its way around the edges of a yellowed shade.

The only indication of a business on the premises was a small florescent sign that crackled on and off, and was missing the l in pool and the H in Hall. Poo- -all was what you saw in the dark, and the ambiance fit the fragmented sign. A red arrow emitting a low hum pointed up the stairs. I stumbled over a beer bottle on the top landing, with my hand mashing soggy cigarette butts as I tried to break my fall.

The former apartment had been converted into a three- table billiards parlor, with a makeshift and presumably illegal bar set against the far wall. The place existed when I was growing up in Bellington, but never in my rashest moments had I considered frequenting the establishment. I looked up at two huge bikers in leather vests, with sleeveless shirts that exposed a mass of tattoos. They were playing pool, and the bigger of the two snapped up as I entered the room stumbling. His biceps were the size of hefty hams.

"Whadda want? We're closed for the night."

"Well, the sign is on and you guys are playing pool, so I figured you were open."

"You figured wrong. It's a private club after eleven, and you aren't a member. Take off."

"I'm here to see Rich Donato, not to play pool. I was told that I might find him here. Is he around?"

"No. You look like a college boy, although if you are, you can't be that smart coming down here this time of night. Whadda studying, Suicide 101? Ha, ha. What's your name, pussy?"

"Good guess on the college thing. We're not into the fifties retro punk look yet, but at least I'm not studying how to get fat and waste my life in a shit hole. If I were, you guys would be the instructors. It's Matt Kronchek, and smart or not, I'm looking for Donato. Where is he?"

"Fuck off, wise guy, or I'll jam this stick up your ass. He's not here."

"Call him and tell him Matt's here to see him. I wouldn't want to be you if you don't at least give him the message."

They came toward me with the pool cues gripped like baseball bats, forcing me to back up to the stairs. I had made an another mistake with my mouth. My hand was on Leo's stiletto, but it wasn't a good weapon unless they got close, and that wouldn't necessary with the sticks. These two weren't bright enough to process my subtle threats or they really weren't connected to Rich. Billy must have given me false information, knowing that I would probably get the hell beat out of me because of my attitude. Putting on a show of false bravado, I backed my way to the exit.

"Cool it. I'll leave, but you tell Rich that I'm looking for him. Understand?"

Suddenly lowering their sticks, they began to retreat. I thought about pressing my advantage since they appeared to be backing down. Their eyes; however, weren't looking at me, but at something behind me. I wouldn't have been more surprised if you put a board across my face. Billy Mancini stood over my right shoulder motioning for the thugs to back off. I didn't know whether to thank him or defend myself considering our beef the other night.

"Billy, what the hell are you doing here, and since when did you become an animal trainer?"

"You'd better shut up and stop baiting them, Kronchek. If they lose it, I won't be able or want to stop them. You wanted to see Rich? Joe, call Rich. See what he wants to do about this guy. Tell him that it's Matt Kronchek."

Billy's lines seemed scripted, but I was here to stay, so I let the game continue. Joe dialed the phone attempting to speak in muffled tones, but I could hear my name clearly and some instructions about me not leaving.

"I don't understand how he knew it, punk, but Rich guessed that it was you. Said for you to wait in the back room till he gets here. Don't touch nothing 'cause we're keeping an eye on you."

I shot Billy a disgusted look.

"I don't think it was much of a guess, Joey. I think a little stool pigeon brought him a message. Come on, Billy. You seem to know your way around here, although I must say it's a little rough for your taste. Let's go wait. We can talk about old times, like when you ratted Mike and I out to Lipscomb."

"You could be a little more grateful, Kronchek. If I didn't show up, they would have beaten you hard, and that's not what Rich wanted."

"Since when did you and Rich get so tight that you care what he wants, Billy? If remember right, you didn't think much of him back in the neighborhood. Not that you ever had the guts to tell him to his face."

"Don't you ever shut up and stop asking questions? They say people change, but you're still a nosy asshole and a wise guy, Kronchek. You'd be better off worrying about yourself at the moment."

"Why should I worry, Billy? Can't a guy come to visit an old friend without being threatened? How's Debbie doing? That was an awful quick move right after Paulie's death, even for a weasel like you."

I never cared much for Billy one way or the other, but as Rich's lapdog, he disgusted me, so I couldn't resist provoking him. Billy started to reach inside his jacket as he flushed with a mélange of embarrassment and anger.

"I'm going to shut you up, Kronchek. I've wanted to crack your head since we were six."

All my systems were primed, the revenge factor well tuned, and the moral outrage set on high. I turned on Billy with a quickness that surprised him, pinning his arm inside his jacket and him against the wall. I had been kicked around a lot in the last week, and there was some unrequited rage to release on Billy's face. He had been a good friend of Paulie's, but I wondered if he knew that he was in bed with Paulie's possible killer. Just as I cocked my fist back the door opened, and I figured the two goons were about save Billy's ass and crush mine.

"Boys, boys, come on, break it up. We're not in eighth grade anymore. Matt, let him go, and Billy, take your hand out of your jacket. Play nice. Billy, go out front and lock up. Wait for me in the poolroom. Matt and I need to talk."

Rich Donato had entered the room without a sound, his sunglasses hiding any trace of intention or emotion, except for the total command that he had over Billy. Rich had grown since I'd seen him last, but he was at least four inches shorter than me, slim, but solidly built. He wore an expensive leather jacket, tailored black pants, and Italian shoes. His dark black hair was slicked back, missing the right side part that he had as a kid. Rich had always been a good looking guy, except for a large nose, but now he was all smoothness and slick, with gold chains and a matching Rolex watch. Not a wrinkle in his clothes or a hair out of place, with everything well oiled, including his mind, I'm sure. His movements reminded me of a snake, gliding, sliding, more than walking. The cologne was a bit overpowering for my taste, but even the expensive fragrance couldn't mask the fact that he had never kicked the cigarette habit.

Billy and I disengaged, and although he bumped me in passing, I let it go. My true purpose had arrived and Billy no longer held my interest.

"I'm going to mess you up next time, if there is a next time for you, shit head."

He exposed the blackjack under his coat, making certain that I understood his intentions. He was laughable as a gangster.

"You're making a lot threats, Billy boy. I can't wait. You are a classy one, though, I must say. Now I know what you were doing over Debbie's the other night. A little spy job for Rich and a loss of virginity for you. If you go any lower, Billy, you'll have to dig a hole. You ought to eat something. You look like that skeleton costume you wore in fifth grade. "

He started back toward me with the blackjack firmly in his hand, but Rich turned him aside. Billy flipped me the finger, slamming the door on the way out. Rich and I stood facing each other alone, save for the ghosts of Bellington past, Vietnam present, and the uncertain future.

Chapter 30

Rich threw his arm around my shoulder, giving me what only could be described as an affectionate, manly-type hug. He was laughing his ass off and seemed genuinely pleased to see me.

"Shit, Kronchek! You have a God-given talent for pissing people off. It seems that everyone I've come in contact with in the last two weeks is ripped at you or wants you dead. You are a 'fly in the ointment' as my mom used to say. My God how everything comes around full circle!"

"That's kind of the reason I'm here, Rich, because besides purposely irritating pieces of crud like Billy, I haven't been trying to piss anyone off, but it just seems to happen. Like you said, it's a talent and I can't get out of my own way. Let's put an end to all this shit right now."

"Now there's a good idea, Matt, but maybe you know too much and it can't be ended so easily. You seemed to have started something rolling that won't stop. Tell me what you think you know, and maybe we can work something out. You'll have to be willing to play ball, but that has never been your forte. Tell the truth, Matt, because you always were a crappy liar."

Rich opened a couple of beers, handing one to me before he sat down. Removing his sunglasses, he sat in a higher chair. From his dominant position, he gave me his full attention, boring into my face with unblinking eyes as I spoke.

"As I'm sure you already know, Tommy told me at Paulie's funeral that

Paulie was killed by Americans because of drugs, and that he was afraid for his own life. Wanted me to do something about it to pay back a debt that he owed Paulie, but I really didn't have much interest or anything to go on, not to mention the fact that he had been unreliable his whole life.

"That night he turns up dead, and I know he didn't do it to himself because I was the one who found him. I don't how the cops missed it, but there were no indications of prior heroin use that I could see. The story began to ring a bit truer with his death. By pure accident, I connect Ronald Williams with Paulie and Tommy, and he ties me to everyone else because of a date with his sister."

"Yea, I saw the headlines of the brave rescue of your girlfriend from Simon Rebrone at the hospital. Pretty cool work, Matt. Rebrone was a total nut job. Stupid bastard almost got us killed in Nam more than once. We'd be out on patrol and the acid head would start screaming from hallucinations. He drew heavy enemy fire on us one night, and only half of us came back alive. I gave that prick so much acid that it bought him a ticket straight home to the loony bin, courtesy of a fried brain. I had no intention of coming home from that fucked-up war in a box, or with part of me missing because of some juiced-up lunatic. Continue, but start telling me something that I don't already know."

"It added up eventually that someone was watching me, and the same face with sunglasses kept popping up everywhere. At the funerals, in the unit picture, and a name that Debbie remembered Tommy's uncle saying when you left the funeral. I finally recognized you and it wasn't hard to guess that you were the one in charge. And that's all I know for sure."

"What's all you know, Matt? Sum it up. Knowing you, you must have an opinion, and certainly a moral judgment. What do you think is going on?"

I continued my analysis, leaving out the contents of the letter. It made more sense to let Rich start asking the questions. That way, he might implicate himself.

"Well, Rich, I figure you must be a drug dealer, and until recently I had no basic moral judgment concerning that particular occupation, except now I see the misery it eventually causes. It's eating up the poor people in the cities, bringing in crime and violence, and adding more burdens to their already difficult lives, but those issues are beyond me right now.

"I came for personal reasons. Your past petty thefts and now your new business is basically beneath my contempt, but murder, especially the murder of a friend is something else. There's no turning of the head if you killed Paulie or Tommy. I'm going to ask you once, and I'm telling you not to lie because I watched you con and swindle for years. You're good, but I studied you and learned that everybody gives it away in some manner, even you. Did you have anything to do with them getting killed?"

"Great speech, Kronchek, but you wasted it on me because I have no reason to lie. I also don't give one small shit for those junkies in the city. You came to me for a deal because you're worried. You're close about the drugs. It would be was a drug dealer, at least the heroin part. We're still moving the soft stuff like weed, LSD, and little speed. We can get all the grass we need from Latin America. I don't need Vietnam any more, except for the burnt-out customers it provides us when the soldiers return, not to mention you rebellious turn on, tune out, college students. Business is booming in these trying times, my friend. I'm only giving people want they want, and what the law won't let them have. The high risk makes it a good profit item. When I see an addict's desperate and grateful face as he gets his fix, I feel sort of like the druggies' Robin Hood, with profit for me, of course.

"As far as Paulie goes, I didn't make the final decision, but Ronald made the right business move. Paulie didn't give him a choice. Vietnam changed Paulie. The little chicken shit turned into a man. At first he did what we told him, but I guess he got a case of Kronchek-like moral outrage over our methods, and was ready to turn us in. Ronald decided that he needed to be eliminated and I had already gone home. Check the dates. I tried to talk him out of squealing before I left, but he wouldn't listen to my requests or threats. Me and a lot of other people would have been put in a military prison for twenty years or life. That wasn't happening. He made the choice, Kronchek. I could have saved him from Ronald. Part of trying to be a moral hero involves the risk of death. You probably never told him that, did you?"

The years had changed me also. After reading the letter, I had come to the pool hall with the intention of killing Rich. I should have pulled the knife and finished him right there, but it wasn't in me to kill with such premeditated, calculated purpose, and a knife is an up close and personal weapon. It would have to be reactionary, and a part of me hoped that he would make a move, but I needed to hear Rich's version of Paulie's last days. A rash act would not take me where I wanted to go. I had guessed who was responsible, and the letter confirmed it, but the why of it was important to me because I needed to understand what was going on in a war that I had turned my head from. I shook and flushed from the strain of trying to control my reactions.

"You want to kill me, don't you, Kronchek. It's bubbling out of you like lava from a volcano. You have always been one angry son of a bitch, especially after Nellie took a dive off the bridge. It's kind of ironic, isn't it? Everybody just about fought everyone else back in the neighborhood, except you and I never went at it. We came close several times, especially if I said something nasty about your precious Nellie, but it never happened. Why do you suppose that is, Kronchek?"

I had never thought about that before, but found it interesting that he had. I rewound my memory back through the years, reliving the feelings and situations before coming to a conclusion.

"I think that on some deep level it was too serious between us. I was always on one line, you were on another, and neither of us was able or willing to stand in the middle. It's no different right now. If we go at each other, one of us will die because we stand so firmly apart in the way we view the world. We each look out at life and see totally different things, and we must have recognized that fact on some level of our consciousnesses."

"My, my, you've always been a philosopher, Kronchek, and I think you've discovered the essence of our relationship, but unfortunately, Paulie finally saw it your way. Who would ever want to read between the lines; there's nothing there. There's chumps on one side and me on the other."

"No, Rich, everything is there. All the shit that people are afraid to say, what the government doesn't want you to know, and the latent traits of a friend that I never recognized or allowed to surface because I had pigeonholed him his whole life. Humor me a little, and tell me what made Paulie stop being Paulie, and why you had to kill him."

"Get it through your fucking thick skull, Kronchek. I didn't kill him, Ronald did. You already got your revenge on Ronald, but you just have to know everything, don't you? Well, I hope you can handle the truth, but remember that I didn't kill him. He knew the consequences, and made his own decision.

"Paulie hooked up with a Vietnamese girlfriend, wife of a dead Viet Cong, or so we figured. She lived in one of the villages where we picked up our drugs. Her father was the leader of the village and our middleman. She had two little kids, and Paulie gave them clothes, food, and medicine, whatever they needed. He became their de-facto father and her provider, and get ready, her lover. That's the prime reason he helped us in the beginning. He wanted the money to take care of them."

"Wait a minute. You're trying to tell me that Paulie, totally controlled Paulie, was cheating on Debbie. That he basically had a family in Vietnam."

"I'm not sure why you need to hear this, Kronchek, and I can't figure why you always want to understand everything about life. It just mystifies me. Well, understand this about Vietnam. You weren't there, and you'd better hope that you never have to go. It wasn't like cheating; it was like living in an alternate universe. You have no conception what it was like. Some guys had to build a separate life that had some meaning or they would go out of their mind. For Paulie, it had to be something noble, for me, whores and money did just fine. Everyday some poor sap would get a 'Dear John' letter from his girlfriend that would shatter his reality, and then we would see the news of the protests back home and the names we were being called. The soldiers constructed a new life in self-defense against returning home to rejection, and as a relief from the loneliness and fear."

Everything was starting to add up as Rich gave me new insight into the experience of Vietnam, but I wanted to hear it all.

"So what happened to this woman after Paulie was killed?"

"You're getting ahead of yourself. The village leader was a known Cong sympathizer, but we didn't give a shit. It wasn't about the war with us; it was all business. Vietnam was just a sewer to exploit. The headman loved money, but in the end, he turned out to be a patriot. He set us up for the Cong one night while we were making a pickup. They nailed two of our guys, but we held them off until an air strike pulverized the village, sending the gooks back into the brush.

"Ronald went into a rage, and not even I could stop him. Their leader was nowhere to be found, and Paulie's girlfriend started running, so Ronald gunned her and the baby down right in front of Paulie. Paulie screamed and cried at Ronald, but Ronald just laughed and pushed him down into the mud. Paulie flipped and tried to hit Ronald, but Ronald was too strong. Another unit came along ending the whole fight.

"On the way back Paulie told me that he was going to stop our drug operation and intended to give all the information to a Captain from Military Intelligence who had been nosing around our base. I tried to talk him out of it and make him understand what we had at stake, explaining the consequences, but he was devastated, and nothing was going to change his mind. The Vietnamese woman was carrying his baby, Kronchek, so I don't think that Paulie wanted to live. That was my last night in Nam. I shipped out the next morning, knowing what Paulie's fate would be when Ronald caught up with him. I didn't kill him, and he would be alive today if he didn't flip out over that battle. Paulie was supposed to be one of us, and they tried to ambush our unit. What were we supposed to do?"

Rich's version differed from Paulie's, and it appeared that each contained some lies—direct by Rich, and by omission from Paulie. By combining the two, the truth was slowly being exposed, but I needed to hear more.

"Why didn't you order Ronald not to do it, Rich. He would've listened to you. How could anything like drugs be worth someone's life? For Christ's sake, you grew up with the kid. Is money that important to you, precious enough to kill a friend, or was it more than that?"

"It was business, Kronchek, simple business and the threat of prison time, so Ronald didn't have a choice. It's not just about money. It's about keeping people under control, about being independent of all the nine-to-fives in the world. My dad worked his ass off, staying away for months at a time and never being around for us. Don't mistake my calm tone for any sort of sympathy. Squealers die, but just so you know, I would have had done it cleanly and quietly, maybe poisoned him if he didn't listen to reason."

"What's the difference? You killing him with poison or Ronald blowing him up? He's still dead and a little kid was killed in the bargain. You're fucking animals."

"I'll ignore the insult for now because I want to settle this and make you understand what you've gotten into. Ronald was an angry man, very much like you, but with a different mode of expression. Paulie embarrassed him; undermining his authority and making him look vulnerable, so Ronald had to make an example of him. He took the surviving child of Paulie's girlfriend, gave him a jacket of explosives and told him to go hug Paulie. You know the rest. The kid thought he was getting a new jacket, and Paulie was thrilled that the kid was still alive. It was incredibly cruel, but they never felt a thing. Nobody thought about turning evidence after that sick scene. It was very effective."

I remained composed, although I felt like puking. The intense anger was held in check from the revelations hidden in Rich's lies. He had no compunction about admitting that he was a drug dealer that would kill if necessary, but he lied about what had happened in the village.

Ronald had been worried about the drug business, but Rich was bent on hiding any facts about the massacre. Was he ashamed and guilty or was he just worried about being arrested? What was the FBI's role in all this, and did they even have an inkling of what had gone on? I needed to keep him talking, plus I wanted to know who killed Tommy.

"Did you kill Tommy, Rich? I know it wasn't an accident, but I guess I already told you that. Why did you have to do that? He wouldn't have told anyone else. The guy was terrified, and he had never trusted the authorities."

"I didn't do it, but you and my guy had a close call at Tommy's. Ten more seconds and we would have had this conversation at Tommy's house, but why do you care? He was a piece of shit his whole life, and all you did is fight with him. He made all of us miserable."

"He risked or gave up his life to pay back a debt to Paulie. He showed me a part of him that I never would have believed existed. Where was the business angle in killing him?"

"He needed to understand that he had to keep his mouth shut, so I sent Billy over to give him a scare. Tommy had already blabbed to you and look where we are now. Killing anyone is risky, Kronchek, and despite what you think of me, it's a last resort. It's the fix for a screw-up, and I screwed up by sending Billy to Tommy's house to threaten him. Billy was supposed to put the fear of Ronald in Tommy, but Tommy ridiculed him and reminded him of the time that he beat Billy up in third grade and ripped his shirt. Tommy laughed in his face, telling Billy to cry and piss his pants. That was too much to take even for Billy. Billy pushed him and Tommy hit his head on the side of the bowl. Billy assumed that Tommy was dead, so he shot him up with some high-grade smack to cover the accident. Don't get me wrong. I don't care that Tommy's dead, but it was a stupid move by a fuck-up."

"So why tell me all this, Rich? I didn't know any of it for sure, and there was nothing I could do about it, so why the uncharacteristic candor? You were right before. I wanted to kill you if you were responsible for Paulie's death, but I decided a few minutes ago that I don't want to be like you. This fucking war has everyone wrapped up so tight and turned around that we'll never get over it, except for you. You already have. See ya around, Rich, and thanks for reminding me what kind of person I want to be. I gotta go."

"Unfortunately, Matt, I can't allow that just now. You got what you came here for, but I didn't. Where are Paulie's letters from Vietnam?"

Now we were getting to the point.

"I don't need your permission to leave, and I don't know what letters you're talking about. Paulie hadn't written to me in months, and besides, his letters are my private property. Get out of my way before I change my mind about violence."

"Billy, Joe, get in here!"

The door unlocked quickly, with Billy and the giant thug blocking the door. It seemed to be the only way out. I had boxed myself into a corner, and this new development had taken me completely by surprise. Joe pushed me into the chair, frisked me, and found the knife. He jabbed it lightly into my hand, producing a sharp pain and a trickle of blood. The three of them stared down at me as time froze in the room. I didn't have a plan or a reaction for this situation, but I still had the letter. Nothing would happen until Rich was able to put it in his hands.

Chapter 31

Remaining outwardly calm as Rich took the knife from Joe, I decided to let events determine my reactions. Rich told him to wait in the front, which evened the odds a bit. After he left, the lock snapped shut and the refrigerator door near the bar squeaked open. Apparently Joe was settling in for a long wait with a cold brew. Rich put the knife on the table just out of my reach, but close enough to tempt me. He was toying with me, daring me to make a move.

"Billy, get my briefcase and then go out with Joe to make sure all the doors are locked. We wouldn't want Kronchek to take off on us."

Rich flipped him a set of keys, and Billy went into a wide closet, pushing aside some boxes and unlocking a heavy-duty metal cabinet where he removed a black leather briefcase. The doors were left carelessly open, and I could see bags of grass and white powder. As Billy attempted to open the briefcase, Rich exploded with a verbal barrage.

"Don't you listen! I told you to bring me the briefcase, not to unlock it. Close those doors. He's seen everything. That stuff was supposed to be in my van by now. You're such an idiot. Give me the case and go."

"Jeez, Rich, don't put me down like that in front of Kronchek. I'm the one on that's on your side."

"Well, Billy, Rich is right, but he didn't expound on your deficiencies to the proper degree. You're an idiot, a lackey, and a weasel. Get out bitch!"

Before Rich could intervene, Billy threw a wide hay-maker at my head, but he was painfully slow. Being athletic was something Billy could never be accused of. I was still seated, so my punches would have no leverage. I blocked his blow with my left arm, lifting my leg into his groin as he came forward. My ankle caught him square in the balls, with my foot halfway up his ass. It was a pure reaction to a threat, and all my frustration began to emerge in the form of violence. My vow of passivity, sworn to a few minutes before, was vetoed by my anger. As Billy staggered back gasping in testicular pain, I leapt from the chair and caught him with a straight right to the bridge of his nose. He now couldn't breathe or see and I would have continued to beat him if I didn't hear the click of a gun in harmony with Rich's voice.

"Stop, Kronchek, or I'll blow out your knee. Sit back down in the chair. Joe! Get in here and haul Billy out. Lock the door and have him wash that blood off his face."

Billy's voice returned, but it was hoarse and sputtering between desperate gasps for air.

"You're not going to let him get away with what he did to me are you? Shoot him. He knows too much already."

"Shut up, Billy! You know too much, and you're half as smart as he is. Should I shoot you, because I really want to right now? You just created chaos, and I don't like chaos. You gave him an opportunity where there was none before. I wanted this situation under control, and you almost fucked it up. I met him here to get something, something you can't get from a dead man."

Rich moved the gun's aim from my legs to Billy's head.

"No, no! Please don't, Rich! I'm sorry, but I need a fix, and he really makes me angry. Look, I'm shaking and cold. Please!"

Rich pulled out a small paper packet, throwing it to Billy near the door.

"It's okay, Billy. Maybe I'll give you a shot at him when we're done. Wash your face and put some ice on it. Then do a few lines to chill out, and make sure to share a little with Joe. I know Kronchek wouldn't want to make him nervous right now."

They left the room and I relaxed my defensive posture, although Rich still had the gun in his hand. I glanced at the knife and it didn't escape Rich's notice.

"You can try for it if you want, but I wouldn't suggest it. I'm pretty good with this thing, thanks to the Army, so you can answer my question with a bullet in your arm, or we can relax and talk it out. You should be a little easier on Billy. He's got a pretty bad heroin problem. Billy snorts it so his mom won't see the tracks, but he's gonna need the needle soon to keep his rush at the level he needs. That's what keeps him bound to me. I'm done playing with you, and I want some answers. Where are the last two letters that Paulie sent you."

"They're in my room at school, but I told you that it was at least two months since I got one. He was pretty pissed off at me because I kept criticizing the war, and then suddenly he stopped writing. I figured Paulie was done talking to me, and at the time I didn't want to listen to him anyway. There were no other letters."

Rich unlocked the briefcase, pulling out a small stack of envelopes held together by an elastic band. He took the top one out and threw it on my lap. It was addressed to Debbie with Paulie's return address.

"Read it, Kronchek, and then tell me your story again. This is his final letter to his girlfriend. Billy snagged these the other night when he was over there. He wasn't supposed to screw her, just get the letters, but Billy hasn't had much luck with the ladies, so he got excited."

The letter was dated Aug 8, 1969, one day before Paulie was killed.

Dear Debbie,

Hope everything is going well at home. I love you and miss you horribly. I dream about my mother's cooking, the movies with you, and everything about Bellington. When I come home, I never want to leave again, not even for a vacation. I can't imagine any place in America as bad as Vietnam, and everyday gets worse. Fresh troops arrive daily, with more kids dying. I'm afraid that I'll be killed and never see you again, and lately I've been more frightened than I was when I first arrived here.

I can't live with this war anymore. Seeing guys younger than me killed is hard to accept. Vietnamese villagers are sometimes caught in the crossfire, especially when it's hard to distinguish the enemy from our allies. I've seen some horrible things. I haven't written because I was away from the base for three weeks, and have been constantly busy with the wounded.

Matt was right. This is not our country or our war, and it frightens me to see what it's doing to the Americans over here and at home. I wonder if the scars, and I mean the psychological ones, will ever heal. I've changed and I hope it doesn't scare you when I come home. You begin to lose a sense of what is right and wrong when you're trying to stay alive to make it home. I want to leave now, and I'm going to talk to someone about it. I'm writing to Matt and asking him what I should do. I know that at least he'll have an opinion or a plan of action.

Debbie, I love you, and I hope that I'll be with you soon.

Love,
Paulie

Short, sweet and very touching, but not too surprising from what I knew. If I saw this letter last week, I would have had a lot of questions. She never mentioned that he was going to write to me.

"I don't see your point, Rich. He only said that he intended to write to me, but apparently he hadn't, because like I said, I didn't get any more letters. My last letter from Paulie was more than a month before this one; maybe two."

"I might be convinced to believe that, except for the fact that one of our guys in Nam saw him writing to you when he returned to the base."

"Maybe he wrote it, and didn't send it because I never got it! Ronald did kill him, remember? Is it too hard for you to understand or do I have to bring Billy in here to explain it to you? I can't see what the big deal over a letter is since you've already admitted to complicity in two murders."

"Cut the shit, Kronchek! I didn't murder anyone. The letter was mailed. My guy followed him, but couldn't stop it. There were too many people around. By writing to you, he sealed his death warrant. They tried everything to get the letter before it went out, but his timing was perfect. He popped it in the mailbags as they were leaving the base.

"Paulie knew that he was done, so he turned to the most self-righteous, persistent bastard that he knew. You! And the big deal is that it's in writing. It can corroborate the information that you already have.

I'm not going to jail. One more time and then I start breaking your fingers, and if torturing you doesn't work, we can start on your girlfriend or your roommate. Think about it, smart guy. If you and the letter exist, one of you has to go, and if I can't destroy the letter, then guess what happens to all of you. Where is it?"

I should have brought the letter back to Leo for safekeeping, but I had been so desperate to confront Rich with revenge on my mind that I had plowed ahead. Paulie's letter and Rich's lies now explained why people were dying over this business. I didn't want to put Karen in danger, but I also didn't want to give up our ticket out of this jam. The letter gave me leverage with the Feds and with Rich. I decided to play it out for a while more.

"Suppose I do have this letter, Rich. If I give it to you, why would you let me go? I know everything about your operation. If Paulie laid it all out in writing, then I must say that what Americans are willing to do to other Americans for a few bucks makes me sick. American kids are already dying in rice paddies for no reason, but a person like you will taint them all if this shit goes public. It's the War that's supposed to suck, Rich, not the people who are forced to fight it. You're a disgusting person, and you've been lying to me because you're afraid."

"What lies, Kronchek? I told you about the drugs and Tommy. What do I have to be afraid of? Billy will get Tommy's death pinned on him, not me. You're the one who should be afraid because I'm going start hurting you, and then I'll send Joe for your girlfriend."

"You are a major disappointment to me, Rich. I'm always telling everybody how smart you are, but I just realized that you're pretty dumb. You make Billy look like frigging Einstein."

I was on a cocky roll, acting cute, intending to expound further on his dumbness when he smacked the gun handle just above my left eye. The fleshy, blood-rich tissue opened immediately into a wide gash. The blow knocked me to the floor, as blood flooded my eye and streamed down my cheek. It didn't hurt much, but I had stupidly underestimated his temper. My headache returned with a vengeance. I was dealing with a desperate man, someone who had lacked a moral anchor his entire life. He hadn't really changed; the stakes were just higher. Not even a cynic like me would have expected Rich to drop to such a low point. He pulled me back to the chair as I tried to check the flow of blood from the wound using the end of my shirt.

"Now who looks stupid, asshole? Don't ever try to play me the way you do with Billy. That eye was just a warm up, and if you don't give me that letter or tell me where it is, I'll really start to hurt you. Now who's afraid?"

"Not me, Rich, not me. You think that you're the toughest thing I've ever faced? I don't want to die, but I won't be ashamed of my life when I do. I didn't help massacre a whole village of mostly women and children or ship heroin in body bags. Wouldn't the Army and even your fellow soldiers be interested in those examples of your essence as a sub-human?"

He went to whack me again, but I put my arm out as I blurted out the only words that interested him.

"I've got the letter!"

Rich relaxed his arm. "Now we're starting to reach an understanding. Tell me where it is, and I'll send Billy to get it. No stalling."

I needed more time. "What happens to me once you have the letter?"

"I haven't decided yet, but I give you my word that no one else will be hurt. If you don't give to me, then I'll mess up your girlfriend's pretty face, and let Billy and Joe have a go at your roommate."

"Your word, Rich? Your word? After what you did to that village in Vietnam, you think that you have any character or credibility left at all. You're ashamed, aren't you, but you won't admit it?"

As I spoke that last sentence, Rich's face contorted into a collage of rage, embarrassment, and self-pity. He slammed the butt of the gun onto the fingers of my right hand, producing excruciating pain, tearing up the nerves that ran the length of my arm. I doubled over, falling off the chair again as I clutched my hand in agony, with each second of searing pain feeling like an hour. Rich stuck the gun in my ear.

"Your mouth was always a problem, Kronchek, but this time it's going to get you killed. You mention that village again, and neither one of us will have to worry about the letter."

Chapter 32

Karen had heard a lifetime of stories about Mike, but they certainly didn't match the fit, broad-shouldered, clean-cut soldier in front of her. She had always imagined Mike as more like a cross between Leo and Matt. Leo knew Mike from parties in Bellington and visits to New Haven, but hadn't seen him in two years. There was a link named Matt Kronchek that connected the three of them into a solid chain. Mike had gotten Matt into several scrapes and trouble back in Bellington, and Matt had used that experience to pull Leo out of a boatload of jams in New Haven.

Mike was all business and professionalism as they went quietly out the side door to the back yard where two men in suits stood waiting in the shadows. It was late for Bellington, with all of the neighbor's lights extinguished; the distant glow of the streetlights providing a small measure of visibility in the cloudy night. They moved to the edge of the woods where they wouldn't be seen or heard.

As they drew closer, Leo froze for an instant, then raised his fists and moved aggressively toward the men. Karen began to run in reaction to Leo's behavior, but Mike gently held her back.

"What's the big idea, Mike? These are the two Feds who lied to me and then conned me into to spying on Matt. They made me their donkey, and I'm going to give them a beating."

Mike stood between them, motioning with his hands for Leo to calm down.

"Leo, stop. Karen, this is Agent Francis and Agent Lloyd. They're here to help Matt."

"I know who they are. Help crap! They're lying sacks of shit. They hit him in the ribs today. That was a big help considering the shape he was in."

Totally confused, Karen's reflexes were jumping as they reacted out of instinct to Leo's emotions, but she wanted to hear Mike out if there was a chance of helping Matt.

"Leo, shut up! Please tell me what this is all about. I'm sick of this. We're standing around arguing, and stupid Matt is alone with that killer. What the hell is going on?"

Mike gave Leo a quick pat on the shoulder and the fists went down, but didn't unclench. Mike had seen Leo in action, and if it got out of hand, the whole neighborhood would be up.

"I can't tell you everything, but—"

"Now there's a surprise—"

"Leo, shut up!" said Karen and Mike in harmony.

Mike had to crack a smile even though Leo was starting to piss everyone off. Mike put his arm around Leo's shoulder.

"Christ, Leo, did Kronchek infect you with his cynicism? I feel like he's right next to me. Give me a break. I don't have much time.

"As I said, I can't tell you everything, but I'm in Military Intelligence. Matt thought I went to Korea from Germany, and so did everyone else, including my family. In reality, I was reassigned to Washington working on issues coming out of Vietnam, mostly small time drug cases. The military has been very concerned about the level of drug abuse in Vietnam and whether it will follow the men home.

Word began leaking out of Vietnam concerning some major drug smuggling that was totally different than we had seen before. We've intercepted hundreds of packages that contained dope, but this was a new level. The other thing that made this case unusual was that we received a special request from J. Edgar himself to look into it on the Vietnam end, and he insisted that it be given the highest level of secrecy. Working with the Bureau is not something that we usually do, but their access in a foreign country is limited."

Agent Francis cut Mike off. "Sergeant Rotillo, I think you're breaking that level of security with these people. We don't owe them an explanation. They need to give us some answers, or Kronchek will be tomorrow's news."

Leo and Karen watched Mike's face tighten as he attempted to control his anger. He reminded them a little of Matt, except that by now Matt would have been in the middle of a screaming fit. They both thought that it must be a neighborhood trait, but Mike had obviously acquired discipline during his time in the service.

"Agent Francis, I have no intention of giving up any classified information. I know my job and I know it well, so let me do it. We do owe them an explanation; actually we owe the American public an explanation, but that will never happen, and if I know Matt Kronchek, Leo has been told to give you two nothing, so I need to convince him that we're on his side."

"He's right, G-Men. Matt told me never to talk to you guys again unless I lie. You better let Mike continue or else we're gone, plus we already know everything that he just said and then some."

Lloyd stepped into the conversation. "Finish, Rotillo, but if you screw up it's all our asses, and keep the little ape quiet."

"Thank you, but if you continue insulting him, the last thing we'll have is quiet. I've seen this 'little ape' tear up a room with ten people in it."

Mike continued. "The assignment came as a surprise considering that I was new to the job, but the word was that something bigger than the drug problem was going down, and everyone else would be occupied with damage control. Hoover's request didn't mean shit to them. The first alarm bell was the total stonewall job from the CIA when I made some inquires on the Vietnam end. Instinct told me to back away quickly, and if I hadn't, my investigation would have been over before it had started. They didn't want me anywhere near this issue, which the FBI already knew, but hadn't informed our office. Most Americans would be pretty surprised to learn that the intelligence agencies don't communicate with each other very well, which has turned out to be the crux of this whole case.

"Luckily an officer that had gone through training with me was on assignment in Vietnam. He was investigating drug dealing and other rackets in the Saigon area and had heard the same rumors-someone was in the process of shipping large quantities home. He told me that he had narrowed the activity down to a couple of units, and was a day away from getting some specific information from one of the soldiers. I asked him to send me what he had and to call me if the guy talked. The next day, he became violently ill and needed to be shipped home for treatment, but not before he sent out the info. I received all his reports and the rosters of the suspected units."

Karen stopped him. "Wait a minute. You mean to tell me that you've been investigating the same crap that Matt has gotten tangled up in? That's just too much of a coincidence."

Leo was totally perplexed. "What are you talking about Karen? He hasn't said anything about Paulie or Tommy or Don—Oh, now I get it."

"I guess I'm not giving away any secrets since you two seem to know almost as much as me by your tone. Anyway, as you figured, one unit's names jumped out at me instantly. It was like a role call of my eighth grade graduation. I became very excited considering that I had grown up with these guys. The problem was that by the time I received the records, Paulie Kovak was dead, Rich Donato had been shipped home, and Tommy was already collecting disability from a leg wound."

Leo cut in. "Matt said that Tommy shot himself in the leg to get a pass home. He was afraid of the guys in his unit."

"See, you do know more than me, but before I could question Tommy, he OD's and now I've only got Rich. You call it a weird coincidence, Karen, but I think that's a bit mild considering what pops up next. As I tried to locate Donato, one of my guys was checking the other names. He goes to the V.A. hospital to question Simon Rebrone and finds out that he's been sent to a maximum-security psychiatric unit, and is in no condition to provide information. When he brought back the report concerning Rebrone's attack on you, I felt like I was dreaming when Matt's name leaps out as the hero."

"He did save my life, but the Rebrone connection wasn't necessarily a coincidence. Tommy told Matt to look in New Haven for the answers and something about cobras. Rebrone had a cobra tattoo on his arm and his ranting gave a name to Paulie's killer's. Things really got out of control."

Leo cut in again. "Yea, that bastard Williams almost killed us both, and now these assholes are trying to pin a murder on us."

Mike was losing his patience. "Leo, give it a break. We're all basically on the same side. I finally connected up with these two a couple of hours ago when I found out that they were in Bellington watching, to my total surprise, Matt Kronchek. We both knew about Paulie being ready to talk before he died, and I gave them what I had about Donato, which is all they wanted Matt for. They filled me in about Williams' death, and we all agreed that Matt had become the common denominator. I still can't believe it. The cobra thing; however, was just a joke of Tommy's. Three of them got drunk one night and went to a tattoo parlor. There was no gang called the Cobra's, but a lot of guys in Nam started to believe it."

Karen grabbed Mike by the shirt. "Matt had nothing to do with any of this, except what was forced on him. He's trying to put an end to it tonight, but the dumb ass is trying to do it by himself, mainly because your FBI buddies demanded a name or he goes to jail."

"Hey, no one's a better friend of mine than Matt, and I'm thrilled that the intense bastard finally got a woman to put up with him, but Matt's impulsive nature has had an effect on both of you. We all know now that he didn't do anything wrong, except maybe for Agent Lloyd. He doesn't like Matt, but Matt has that effect on certain people.'

Agent Francis said, "Rotillo, I've had enough with the trips down memory lane. A lost minute could cost us the case and maybe your friend's life."

Francis turned to Leo and Karen. "Where did he go to meet Donato? I don't know how he got by our guys, but he's obviously gone. Tell us now so we can end it and put you all back in school where you belong."

Leo took a threatening step forward, but Mike stepped in the gap.

"Tell him, Leo. We might not have much time. Matt and Donato together have always been like a match and dynamite."

"He went to meet him at a —"

Putting her hand over Leo's mouth Karen said, "Wait. We'll tell you, but we want to go with you. Right now I don't trust anyone and I want to be there if anything happens. He was there for me at the hospital."

Mike said, "Man, you are the perfect match for Kronchek. He has truly found someone who understands his paranoia. You know that he was never really the same after Nellie died. I mean, he appeared to be okay on the outside, but I could always see it. I'm glad he found you. You two can come with me. Now please, where is he?"

Lloyd put his arm out. "They're not coming, Rotillo. This is our case and you can back off now. We'll let you know how it turns out. Sorry, Army boy, but we have to follow procedure. You wouldn't want me to call your commanding officer, would you?"

Mike felt trapped until Agent Francis took control. "Lloyd, how did you ever get to be a Federal Agent? Did you cheat or have the standards been reduced to nothing? I could overrule you on this, but I don't have to. I took the time to check and found out that Donato hasn't been officially discharged from the Army. He's Rotillo's man, not ours. We'll handle anything that may constitute a federal offense, but he has to bring Donato in under Army rules. Let's do this together for a change."

Leo checked Karen's eyes before he spoke, and they said *go ahead because we have no choice.*

"He went to meet Donato at a pool hall on South Main. He left over an hour ago."

Mike grabbed Karen by the arm, motioning for Leo to follow. The Agents jumped in their own car and they squealed away from Matt's house leaving a trail of rubber smoke and sulfur smell behind. The neighborhood lit up like a Christmas tree while Mrs. Kronchek snored on in somnolent peace.

Chapter 33

Physically beaten, with Rich's last two blows adding to the damage of the previous week, my body curled into the fetal position in an attempt to ease the reawakened headache and the throbbing of my crushed fingers.

The gun dropped on the table with a thud, bouncing slightly and coming to rest on the edge of my knife—a sharp, metallic clink signaling the meeting of weapons. Rich lifted me on to the couch, sitting down beside me, pulling my head sharply to face his. There appeared to be moisture in his eyes, and I remembered thinking that I had never seen Rich Donato cry.

"Listen to me, Kronchek. Listen, and don't talk because every time you open your mouth, you make me flip. I don't want to hurt you. As a matter of fact, the blood is making me sick, but I have to destroy that letter. All my life, I took advantage of people's trust and greed. I robbed and cheated them, sold them booze and drugs, and I don't have a single regret about any of it, not even robbing the corner store. I just provided what people wanted and gave trusting chumps what they deserved. It was my risk, so it's my profit."

Rich's command of my attention produced a disconcerting feeling. Maybe a priest felt this way before a confession. Tension filled the silence, while I waited for a lifetime of transgressions to be revealed. I cracked first and spoke.

"Mr. Figaro's store went out of business a couple of years ago. Did you know that, Rich? He was losing too much money and had to close the place. He went to work for that big new supermarket, but he only lasted a month before he had a heart attack. He was a great guy, and I have a lot of guilt about not turning you in. The code of the neighborhood was total bullshit! I was only protecting a future criminal."

"I did him a favor, Kronchek. You can't trust people the way he did and survive, and besides, his days were numbered. The neighborhood stores are all going away. Figaro makes my point. Chumps don't make it, and if you don't take care of yourself, who will?"

"How about friends? Don't friends help each other and watch each other's back? Didn't I pull Tommy off you once in seventh grade when he was whaling the shit out of you? Nobody can go it alone, Rich. Do you have any friends? Is Billy your only friend, because if he is, you've got real problems?"

"Yea, you did pull Tommy off me, but do you remember what happened to you? He beat your ass good that day, and I went home with his wallet when he dropped it during the fight. Did you learn anything, Kronchek? No you didn't because you continually stick your nose where it doesn't belong, and you always end up in trouble."

"Okay, Donato, now that we're done analyzing each other, is there something you want to tell me because I need some stitches, and I think you broke some of my fingers."

Rich's damp and distant eyes looked right past me, and as I attempted to penetrate the mist, all the conflicting, cloudy feelings of the past two weeks were starting to clear a bit. Not like the sunshine after a thunderstorm, but more like the gradual brightening of the atmosphere after days of gloomy weather. I was almost there; I could taste the revelation, the new level of awareness, but something was missing. I needed to talk it out a little more.

"This might seem a little hollow coming from a guy in my shape, but you aren't going to hurt me any more. Since Paulie's funeral, I've been slapped, kicked, punched, and almost crushed to death. I've had enough. You're going to hear me out and answer my questions before you raise your hand to me again. If you even twitch, I'll do anything to stop you from hurting me, even if I have to bite your face off. You'll never get that letter if I'm dead, and I'm guessing that you'll never sleep right again if you think that it's out there somewhere waiting to be found."

Rich had never taken well to threats, but I could tell from his eyes that he understood my commitment to fight back. Fear wouldn't seal his decision, but he would choose the best path to get him what he wanted.

"I'm not afraid of you, Kronchek, and—"

"I'm not asking you to be afraid, Rich, and I'm not predicting how it's going to turn out. I just wanted to make it clear as to my actions."

"Just say what you have to say and let's finish this!"

"This is only between you and me. You have my word, and you know that it's good. You can't deny that. I need you to answer one question for me, and then you can have the letter. I need the truth, and it will never leave this room."

"You're going to give the letter to me, one way or the other, but I'll play your game."

"What happened at the village—"

"I told you never to mention that again! I warned you, Kronchek! Goddamn you!"

Rich completely lost his cool, something I don't think I had ever seen him do. His dark skin flushed with blood, the mixture forming a blackened crimson as he moved to reach for the gun. I had always taken reasonable chances, but I was never much for long shots, and Rich did exactly as I thought he would. My foot was already out as he left the couch, and it sent him flying face first into the edge of the table. The hard oak opened his forehead like a ripe melon, with the blood turning his face into a red mask. I was on him quickly, with my knee in his back and his greasy hair firmly in my grasp. The boys outside heard the noise.

"Rich, is everything okay in there? Do you need our help because Billy's itching to lay a beating on that punk?"

I leaned over to Rich's ear while keeping a tight fist in his hair.

"Tell them to go away or you'll force me to grab that gun. I'm not taking any more punishment, especially from that big ape."

"The gun's not loaded, Kronchek, but I'll tell them to leave. They'll have their time with you soon enough. Everything's fine, Joe. Kronchek just took a little spill. Ha, ha."

Joe and Billy laughed hard, apparently enjoying the mental image of me on the ground. The refrigerator opened once again for an obligatory drink in celebration of Kronchek's pain. If only they could see the reality beyond the door.

Rich's speech began to slur, indicating to me that he had come close to being knocked cold.

"You always have to be so difficult, Kronchek. I don't even remember not knowing you, but you always did things the hard way, and that fact stands clearest in my memory of you. Even when a situation was hopeless, like now, you just kept coming back for more. Remember when Tommy and his five nut ball cousins had us cornered on the way to Figaro's store?"

"Yea, how could I forget that beating. They took our money and threw us in the thorn bushes. I got the worst of it because I tried to fight back."

"Right, and if you think a little harder, we could have avoided the whole thing if you had just given up your dollar, but not you. You had to stand on the principle of it all, and where did it get you? Where are you going with this? You're not getting out of here, so why not make it easy."

"Nice parable there, Rich, but this time you're the one that's making it difficult. You only have to answer one question, and you can have the letter. I don't give a shit about it. I need to understand something, and you could be smart by taking your own advice. I'm in control right now, and if I'm not leaving, neither are you. We don't have much time to settle this, so why make it difficult."

"Now you're in a rush? Where you going?"

"Nowhere. In about ten or twenty minutes Leo's going to come flying in here and neither one of us will get what we want."

"You're bluffing, Kronchek, and if you're not, Joe will rip the little bastard to pieces."

"There's no bluff. I told him to stay with Karen and my mother, but I knew he wouldn't listen. As a matter of fact, I depended on it because he's a loyal friend. I wasn't stupid enough to come here without backup. I know Leo, and he'll be here soon, probably with the FBI on his tail, if Joe's lucky."

"Have you totally lost it, Kronchek? Ask me your question and then give me the letter. What's this bullshit about the FBI?"

"You can believe it or not, but they've been to see me twice. They don't know your name and I don't think they even know what you've done with the body bags, but their superiors do, and according to the agents, Hoover himself wants it kept quiet. You're in deep shit, and if they follow Leo, which shouldn't be too difficult, then I'll never be able to give you the letter. Your name won't even be in the paper. They'll make you disappear into an isolation cell at a federal prison. They threatened me with jail if I didn't turn over your name by Monday, but it's all going to happen tonight. I'll be lucky if I'm not in a cell next to you."

"If you're telling the truth, then wouldn't it have been easier to turn me in. I can't believe that even you would risk everything just to ask me a question."

"Well, I did come originally for revenge, but now it's not so simple. I've been afraid of Vietnam, but only in a selfish way. All war is wrong, but that War is foolish, unnecessary, and immoral. Kids that we went to grammar school with are dying for bullshit geopolitical strategy. I won't go there even if it means jail or Canada, but a big chunk of our generation have been forced by circumstance to fight, and I need to understand what they experienced. I need to know what drives a person to do what you did in that village; what a human being can be reduced to."

Rich lurched, struggling against my grasp at the mention of the atrocity, but I pulled his head back sharply as I levered my knee in his back.

"What do you care? Are you some sick fuck who likes to hear the details? Does everyone have to be the perfect Matt Kronchek who always does the right thing?"

"It bothers me because I think that I would have done the same thing when the first shots went off. What's the right thing when your life is on the line? I'm afraid that nothing really matters and everything is out of our control. Maybe I would have just tried to survive like everyone else."

"So you're a lot more like me than you think, and that thought disturbs you, huh, Kronchek?"

"No, no. It's not as simple as that. I think everyone is more alike in certain situations than they would like to believe, but it's what came after that's so disturbing. That's where I can see the difference between us. Why didn't you stop Ronald from killing the survivors? You had leverage with him and he would have listened."

"Yea, he would have on any other day but that one. Ronald was in a psychotic rage, detached from reality. Our drug pickup was lost, and that was all that mattered to him. There was a whole side of me that wanted to walk out of the village with those people still alive, but I was afraid of what those survivors could mean to my life. Look where I am now. I'm the only one left from that day, except for crazy Rebrone, but Paulie's letter tells it all, I'm sure. You're right. It doesn't really matter. They're dead and I'm alive, and nothing I do will change that fact. Is that what you want to know, because if it is, give me the letter now."

"I want to know if it bothers you, Rich, if you're sorry, and if you would give back all the drug business if they could be alive today. We never stood on the same line, but we grew up together, and I'd like to think that you're sorry for what happened."

"That village is something I never want to think about again or have anyone ever know about. It's the only thing I've ever done that I'm ashamed of. The nightmares never stop unless I drug myself to sleep. I lied before. There was no attack. They were just innocent villagers: women, children and old men. Not a single shot was fired at us. I panicked and blew the top of an old woman's head clean off. Her mouth was still moving and I could see her brain. I closed my eyes and pumped twenty more rounds into her to put her out of her misery. That letter has to be destroyed. I can't answer your question because everything I did before that day is who I am, who I've always been. I would like to think that I would do the right thing so they could be alive, but I'm not sure. Figure out your answer from that. I am sorry, but you can't take a life back. There's no do-overs, so why even think about it."

I let Rich up carefully, positioning my body between him and the weapons. He was right. There are no take-backs or do-overs like the games we played as kids, but I could see by the tear-diluted blood that he wasn't a heartless monster. A criminal yes, a killer by choice-no. I think all human beings are capable of killing when they are threatened.

"The letter is under the trash can in front of the building. It's yours. I want the public to know about the massacre, but I don't want to allow the government to put your name or any other soldier's name on it, especially Paulie's. It's their responsibility for sending us there, but letter or no letter, no one will listen to me anyway; unless you talk, and I don't see that happening."

"So you're going to just let me off the hook. After I destroy the letter, you're the only one besides me who knows what happened that day. How do you know I'll let you go?"

"I didn't let you off of anything, Rich. Only you could have done that, and you've decided not to, so the nightmares will continue. Trust me on that one because I've had a lot of experience in that department. You're screwed anyway, and I guess I'll end up wondering for the rest of my life whether or not you would have let me go. I hope that I'll convince myself that you would have."

"What do you mean, I would have—"

Before he could finish, the sound of shattering glass and splintering wood echoed from the front room, along with the feral cry of a natural warrior. Leo was in the house. Rich gave me a nod and a slight smile of respect as he went to the closet and grabbed a large suitcase from the metal cabinet. He glanced back one more time before heading down the backstairs; appearing conflicted, but still aware of he what had to do. It truly came natural to him.

He was only gone a second when I heard a brief scuffle, with footsteps coming back up the stairs. Agent Francis backed Rich into the room at gun point just as the door to the pool room caved in with Leo on top of it. Through the opening I thought I saw a familiar face in a military uniform, but it was out of place. He stood over the motionless bodies of Billy and Joe as Karen ran into the room, walking right over Leo and jumping into my arms. The soldier turned and looked up, and there was Mike Rotillo laughing his old mocking laugh and shaking his well-groomed head. The sight of Mike stunned me, but the circle had been completed and my breath came out easy for the first time in weeks.

Chapter 34

I passed out. Whether it was from the loss of blood, the concussion, or the shock of seeing Mike, I'll never know. I don't care to. The blackness came as a welcome relief from the existential tension of the past few weeks. By the time I came to, Karen was trying to close the cut over my eye with gauze and tape, and my vision cleared to Billy, Joe and Rich in cuffs. Mike and the FBI agents were in a heated discussion, while Leo sucked on a beer as he described his fight moves, even though no one was listening. According to Karen, Leo had rushed up the stairs ahead of everyone, kicked the door in, dispatched poor Billy with one shot, and was on big Joe before he knew what hit him. By the time Mike and Karen made it up the stairs, the fight was over, and Leo was already crashing through the back door of the poolroom.

Apparently, there were some complicated jurisdictional issues involved. Mike claimed Donato under military law and insisted that the FBI call the locals on Billy and Joe. Agent Lloyd and Mike appeared as if they were about to come to blows over Donato, when Agent Francis stepped between them, pulling Mike aside for a private conversation.

"Rotillo, Donato has been discharged from the Army for a month. It's not like me to disregard the rules, but a part of me respects Kronchek so I wanted to give his friends a break. Legally, he's all ours. We'll call you if we find out anything pertinent to the military side of things. As far as those two go, we'll turn them over to the local police once we determine if they know anything."

I had heard enough of this shit. I jumped up from the couch, joining the circle of negotiators without an invitation.

"Mike, I need to talk to you alone."

"Matt, not now. You're not a part of this any more. Take your friends and go. Forget it ever happened."

Pulling Mike to the far side of the room, I said, "If I take my friends, then you'd have to go also. Right? If we're still friends."

"Knock it off, Matt. This isn't a simple matter of the code of the neighborhood. We're not kids anymore, and these two are serious. Lloyd wants to haul all your asses in. They're worried about what information you might have, and what you might say to the wrong people, especially you, Matt."

"Well, Mike, it sounds like you want to call the locals in for Billy and Joe. If you do that, then they're going to give the cops our names even if we split, and what choice do I have but to talk my way out of it when the Bellington Police come knocking at my door. My name will be in the paper, along with yours and the drug story. I don't think your superiors will appreciate that, not to mention our mothers."

"Matt, I have a job to do. I'm a soldier and you're a college student, so why don't we just go back to doing what we know and let these guys finish it. We'll always be friends, but this is out of your league."

"It might be, but you and your FBI friends don't even know what you're looking for. I do. You'll have to believe me on this, please. Let the FBI take all of them. I hate whom you work for, but you've always been and will be one of my best friends, and I'm telling you to let it go."

"I can't do that, Matt. I've got to find the truth—"

"The truth? Screw the truth, Mike! Screw it because nobody wants to know it. Nobody! And even if they did, they wouldn't recognize it if it were standing right in front of them, which it usually is. Let them take these guys, and I'll show you what everybody wants to know. I'll let you decide what to do with it, but don't tell these agents that I know anything or I'm fucked forever. They're going to get nothing from Donato, except a drug conviction, and maybe less than that on the other two. Billy's a jerk, but he's an addict, and he needs help, not jail."

I glanced across the room, having sensed that all eyes were on Mike and I. Karen and Leo could see and feel my agitation, while the agents were clearly losing their patience. Donato eyed me suspiciously, wondering if I had broken my word about the letter. I could see that the Army's discipline had conditioned Mike to think along a path of orders and commands, but he had only trained under their way for the past two years. He knew; he had to know from all the time we had spent together, that I had something, and the old Mike couldn't resist the temptation to find out what it was.

"Agent Francis, take them away. The Army has no interest in this matter any longer nor is it in our jurisdiction. Is Matt free to go with a guarantee of no further contact from your people?"

The agents talked it over in hushed tones. Lloyd obviously didn't want to accept the deal, but in the end, Francis won out.

"Okay, Rotillo, you've got a deal, but it's dependent on a gag order and any new evidence of his involvement that I might get out of these guys. If I hear about Kronchek or his friends talking to anyone about these matters, I'll find a way to bust him. Come on, Lloyd, let's get these guys to New Haven."

Lloyd hooked their cuffs together, leading them down the back stairs like a chain gang. Francis stayed behind.

"Rotillo, I want to talk to Kronchek for a minute alone. Do you mind taking the others into the front room?"

Mike led Karen out, but Leo didn't budge.

"I'm not going anywhere without Matt. You guys slapped him around before and it ain't happening again."

"Leo, go with Mike and Karen. I'll be fine. Agent Francis never hit me. It was the other one. Please go so we can get out of here, and grab the rest of the beer."

Leo left reluctantly, but happily loaded a case of cold beer into a couple of bags before he went out of the room.

Francis gave me a long look before he spoke. "You are a mess, Kronchek. Did you get what you came here for?"

"Well, I got some deformed fingers and a split eyebrow, but besides that, I can't say that I'm sure. I came for the truth or an understanding of reality, but that's never cut and dry, so I guess my answer is probably yes and no."

"How can you think the truth is vague? Isn't it an absolute concept? It's either true or it isn't?"

"Come on, Agent Francis. You've been in a war, and you deal with all kinds of freaky people in your job. You know that the truth is dependent on where you're standing or who's in charge. The winners get to write the history books. Sometimes it makes it hard to tell what's real. Maybe everyone has their own particular reality, and perhaps that's why we feel alone a lot or wake up in the middle of the night terrified."

"Wait a minute. You think that there no absolute truths? No right and wrong? Come on, Kronchek, if we don't believe in something, then all hell breaks loose."

"Exactly. Hasn't it already? Every few years, we open up Pandora's box and let the bad stuff out, and Vietnam is the latest plague. Look how many people believe we belong there, and look how many people think we should leave. The honorable, heroic, patriotic deaths of 1969, will be the wasted lives after we have to leave Vietnam, and we will leave with that war not settled. That much I'll guarantee. Who's right, and who's wrong, Agent Francis? I feel so bad for everyone in that war, I just want to cry."

"So then you think the war is wrong?"

"From my point of view, absolutely, but does my opinion matter?"

"Of course it does, but having an opinion doesn't make you right. You seem beaten, Kronchek, and it doesn't fit you well. I think I liked it better when you were a cocky, sarcastic punk. What happened here tonight?"

"The very thing that you and Lloyd are looking for is just what your boss doesn't want you or the rest of the country to find out. Everything's over, Agent Francis, so just let it lie. The smartest thing would be to run Donato up on a Federal drug rap, and when he gets out in five years or so, the War will be over; hopefully. Then none of it will matter to anyone."

"Didn't you come here to find something? We figured, including your friends, that you came for revenge."

"I don't know about all that any more, and I don't want revenge on anyone. I've had enough of that in my life. I just know that like Korea, we have another shitty war with thousands of lives lost and ten times that number ruined. For what? For nothing, Agent Francis, and that's the only reality I see right now. If we really wanted to do something noble, we would help those poor bastards when they come home, instead of trying to find out what they did wrong. Nobody wins this war. There won't be any heroes or cowards, just victims. That's the only truth I see, the only one I want revealed. I'm going to protest the war with everything I've got, even if I have to drop out of school."

"It's worth a shot, but I think it will end only when the big boys want it to end."

"We'll see. I do have a deal for you if it's off the record."

"Okay, it's off the record. You have my word. And what would the deal be?"

"I want you to give a direct message to J. Edgar from me in exchange for a tip."

"That might not be easy, but I'll see what I can do. What's your tip?"

"I'm sure that you'll soon realize that Donato is a small time dealer. The question you should really ask yourself is why so much heroin is getting in from Southeast Asia. Tell Hoover to dump my file because I don't like to be spied on. Think about six letters, all uppercase, three and three: M-O-B and C-I-A."

"Interesting, and it might explain quite a few things. Did someone tell you this or are you just guessing?

I put my hand out and Francis shook it with a firm grip.

"I'm not the one who has to guess or know. You do. Take it easy and keep your kids out of wars. Oh, and tell Lloyd that I love him. We're all God's children, even him."

Francis laughed softly, shaking his head.

"I'll tell him, but I'll wait until we're well on the road to New Haven. I never thought I'd say this, but I'm glad you got your personality back. You take it easy, Kronchek, and stay out of trouble."

"If life were only that simple, Agent Francis, I would."

Chapter 35

After I left Agent Francis, Mike turned out the lights and propped up the broken doors. Let someone else find the place empty tomorrow and try to figure out what happened. The letter was where I had left it. While everyone was locking up and getting in the car, I grabbed the envelope and stuffed it in my coat. We all piled into Mike's car, with Leo in the front, and Karen and I leaning against the back door in total exhaustion.

"So where to, Matt? I should bring you guys home in case your mother wakes up."

"Not yet, Mike. Go by the bridge. I want to get out for a minute."

"Why would you want to do that? You haven't been on that street in eight years. You have to let that go, Matt. It wasn't your fault."

"I am trying to let it go. That's why I want you to go there. I need to put it behind me. I have to talk to Karen alone."

"If that's what you want pal, you've got it."

Mike pulled a sharp right off of a completely deserted Main Street; then he hung a hard left by an abandoned factory were his dad had worked. It was booming with all three shifts working the night that Nellie died, and I still remember the factory workers among the crowd on the bridge. They were on their coffee break and had been drawn to the accident by the lights and sirens.

We drove slowly by the neglected parking lot, still lit by sporadic overhead lights. The tar had wide cracks, with grass and weeds firmly established in the seams. Overgrown brush and small trees encroached upon the edges of the fence, giving a sense that nature was trying to reclaim some territory. Mike's car climbed the long hill to the bridge and pulled to a stop at the peak.

"I'll just be a minute. Karen, come with me."

"No, Matt. I'm freaked out. This place is creepy."

It had always been an eerie place in the dark, and the years had not changed that fact. The town still hadn't put up a fence or barrier to prevent anyone from trying a stupid stunt, although I don't recall anyone trying to jump the bridge since Nellie's death.

"Karen, please come with me. I need you to see this. I can't do it alone."

As I said before, Karen was the ultimate caregiver, and if I needed her, then she would be there despite her fears. She took my hand, gripping it hard as she walked determinedly, but with reluctance, to the edge of the low cement wall, her free arm around my waist for support.

"Why are we doing this, Matt? I'm afraid to look down, especially after what you told me."

"Almost every night for eight years, I've had a nightmare over what happened to Nellie. The worst part was not when I found Nellie on the tracks, but when I looked back down later and saw the body bag. From up here, you see it from her eyes, and you have a small understanding of the pain she lived with. To be able to jump from this height face-first is terrifying. Imagine what you're trying to escape. Only when I look down from this spot do I truly realize what had been done to her, and what has and is still being done to children."

Sobbing, Karen walked to the edge, peering silently into the void, with the deadly rails that had snuffed out Nellie's life slightly illuminated by the glow from the distant train yard.

"She must have been a very sad girl, but she was lucky to have at least you to care about her. You were too young to see it coming. Do you think anyone your age back then would have guessed?"

"I don't think it was just my age, Karen, but lack of exposure and experience. I thought I had caught up, but the events of the last few weeks have made me feel as if I'm always two steps behind. I've been running since the night that I found her, thinking that if I kept moving, then I would be okay. I've been wrong. I need to engage in life again; to be more aware of what might be around the corner."

"Nobody can predict the future, Matt, but I think you're on the right path. Tonight the wall around you has started to come down, and I feel that I know you for the first time. I like what I see, although you need a lot of work."

"I am a work in progress, and always will be. You have to understand that about me, and be willing to accept what goes with the deal before we take the next step."

Karen answered the challenge by throwing her arms around me, pulling my head down to meet her kiss. The kiss was long and full of commitment, but it was my hug back that told me I was getting better. The past seemed more distant, and the burden of my guilt had lost some of its weight, but there was still unfinished business in the present. I half carried Karen back to the car, glancing back one time to say goodbye to Nellie.

"Here's the deal, guys. I owe Mike an explanation, but we need to cover with my mother, if we're not too late. Leo, we're going to bring you and Karen back to my house. If my mother's up, tell her that we went to a party and that I had to drive someone home. She'll go back to bed, and I'll sneak in later and hit the sack."

Leo shook his head. "That won't work, Matt. She'll see your smashed-up face in the morning when you get up."

"No. She goes to work for eight and I don't intend on getting up until she leaves. We'll split and I won't come home again until the cut heals. I've got a dozen scars over my eyes from basketball, so one more won't be noticed. I'll be home in an hour or so. Leo, leave some beer."

It was amazing that Leo didn't give me an argument, but when I looked over the front seat, he was dead asleep. Karen woke him up, basically dragging him to the door and leaning him against the house while she ran back to kiss me goodbye.

"Hurry back, Matt. No more secret agent stuff, okay?"

"No more James Bond, just an explanation to someone who deserves one. See you in the morning."

Mike drove off and said, "Where to?"

"How about the park? It'll be just like old times, except we never had the beer back then, so in the future, tonight will be the good old days."

Mike left his car in an empty lot, deciding to walk the last block to the park. We cut through a familiar yard or two and climbed the fence, my smashed fingers aching with the effort. The picnic tables were still on a small knoll on the edge of the woods twelve feet above the basketball court. We popped open a couple of beers, taking several swigs before I reached into my pocket and handed Mike the letter and my flashlight. He read it through without a word between us, the silence broken only by the gurgling of beer and the turning of pages.

Mike rubbed his eyes and face several times before he spoke.

"So everything and more that those Feds and I were looking for is right here in Paulie's letter. How long have you had this?"

"Just since tonight, only a couple of hours. I found it by accident in my cellar, about to be thrown out with the newspapers. I know it's hard to believe, but the whole thing just fell into place. Donato knows I have it, and I broke my word by letting you read it. He's the only one that participated in the massacre that's not insane or dead."

"I thought you were bullshitting when you said that we didn't want to find what we were looking for, but I don't get one thing."

"What?"

"I know you as well as anyone, and I understand how you feel about the war, so why aren't you running to the newspapers with this? You've got a big story here, a story that will help the protests. I can't say that this is a good thing for the military, and if you weren't my friend, I wouldn't give it back."

"It should be simple, shouldn't it, Mike? Donato has led a twisted life, and I can't even fathom what was done to those people in the village, but who's really to blame? Do you really think that the government or the military is going to take responsibility for the atrocities? Donato has screwed a lot of people over the years, but he's no killer, and how about Paulie? If this letter goes public, and the military can't cover it up, what do you think will happen? Do you think that they'll stop the war or blame it on government policy?"

Mike shook his head. "No. They'll look for or create a scapegoat, and they have a perfect one in Donato considering his criminal record and this arrest tonight. But, Matt, why do you care what happens to that asshole? Look at what he's done with drugs and the body bag shipments, not to mention Paulie and Tommy. Isn't it perfect justice?"

"No, no it's not. There would be no justice in screwing Donato. He found a conscience, and that will keep him occupied for a long time, maybe the rest of his life. Nailing him just gives a free pass to the government, and what about Paulie? It's his letter, and he admits to shooting at the villagers, so his name will be associated with the massacre along with Donato's. Maybe only his. A dead man who can't defend himself is the perfect fall guy."

"But it's what happened, Matt. Do you actually want to cover this up, because you certainly are making my job a lot easier?"

"No, I don't want to cover it up. I want you to investigate the massacre without putting a name on it. I have to step away or those FBI boys will nail my ass. Mike, I thought about it lot while Donato and I were going at it tonight, and believe it or not, I probably would have done the same thing if the shooting started. I know you don't agree with me, but those guys shouldn't have been in that situation. We don't belong there and these tragedies happen because those kids in Vietnam are scared and they're just trying to survive. Besides, the four who killed the wounded are all dead. Expose the truth of the situation, but don't let the Army put Paulie's or Donato's name on it. Put the atrocity on the front page, but leave the government with no specific person to blame, except themselves."

"Okay, I'll try do that for Paulie, but what do you want me to do with the letter. If I take this back to my superiors, they'll confiscate it. Without it, though, I won't have much of a case."

"It has to be destroyed. Debbie and even Paulie's asshole parents don't ever need to find out what's in that letter. Screw your superiors. You said that you had connections in Vietnam. Have them check out that village for you, and if they find something, you can leak it to the media, anonymously of course. Trust me, they'll know what to do with it. Got a match?"

"Yea, but are you sure this is what you want to do? Your plan probably won't work."

I can't say that I didn't have second thoughts as I lit the pages. Was it guilt over my previous lack of understanding concerning Paulie's plight in Vietnam? Was I sacrificing the greater cause for my friend's good name? Yea, maybe, but I had learned to separate the conflict from the victims who were forced to fight it, and no one was going to put Paulie's name on this war. The blame belonged to all of us: the government and the people who promoted it; and those of us that had tried to ignore it.

Mike and I drank and talked, but only of the past. As the eastern sky began to lighten, I felt like a semi-drunk Cinderella who had stayed too long. I needed to get home before my mother woke up. We climbed the fence, deciding it would be better if I ran home rather than risk my mother hearing the car. Mike and I shook hands, speaking no further of our deal. I knew he would do his best.

When I saw him again, our conversation was brief and neither of us referred to that night. The War had ended, and it had changed both of us, as it had done to every male of our generation. It impacted many women who had lost boyfriends, husbands and sons, but thirty years later I still find that the divisive passion is strongest among men. There's a lot of anger, guilt, and confusion that we still need to come to terms with, but the most important fact is whether we learned anything. I can't answer that. Maybe I'm afraid that we haven't.

Chapter 36

Leo and I returned to classes, and Karen went back to the hospital to finish her training as our everyday lives returned to normal. I never revealed the existence of the letter to Leo or Karen because the knowledge contained within those pages could only bring danger and questions that I didn't care to answer. If they were ever challenged, they could honestly avow that they didn't know anything.

I bought three papers every day, checking for any news of the massacre or Donato's arrest. As the weeks went by, the whole experience seemed like a dream until mid-November when a freelance reporter named Seymour Hersch and several news magazines broke the story of a massacre at My Lai, Vietnam. This was not Paulie's atrocity, but a much more horrific one that had occurred in March of 1968 and was covered up by the Army until November of 1969.

The United States Army killed over 500 civilians, including women and children, on March 16, 1968. The details are beyond gruesome and well documented, so I don't need to expound on the carnage. The cover-up appeared to have involved the highest level of military command. Only one man was convicted from a group of one hundred and fifty one that entered the village that day-Lieutenant William Calley. His name and My Lai will be linked forever.

Calley's name is the only one that I remember from the tragedy, and the parallels did not escape me. When the government screws up, it looks for a fall guy, one sacrificial lamb to blame for its mistakes. They would have done the same thing to Paulie if I had disclosed his letter, and Mike would have gotten nowhere with a more detailed investigation.

The brave exposure of My Lai by an ex-GI named Ridenhour and the excellent coverage by Hersch, changed public opinion about the war. The number of people who believed that the Vietnam War was a mistake went over fifty per cent for the first time. Our country was beginning to come back together because of the courage of these men. I had lacked that courage in my desire to protect Paulie's name.

Many Vietnamese and some American soldiers claimed that there were several My Lai's throughout the war, and from what I knew, it was probably accurate, but who was responsible? A debate raged in America, with some claiming Calley as a hero, some as a monster, and others believing he was a young man put in a impossible position by a government that taught and encouraged brutal methods of dealing with the Viet Cong.

If I had never read Paulie's letter or spoken to Rich, I would have wanted Calley's entire unit sentenced to life in prison, but I now had a better understanding of what they had faced over there. Those men are not off the hook because they have to live with the images of horror for the rest of their lives. Make no mistake—they are culpable, just like Donato, but the ultimate blame has to be on a government that conducts an immoral foreign policy.

My generation will never escape Vietnam. Certain soldiers view themselves as war heroes, while some of us protesters remember ourselves as heroes for peace. Did the protests prolong the war or did they help end it? I guess it depends on which side of the line you're standing. I used to get involved in that debate, but I only see it one way now. I see us all as victims, and it doesn't matter who was right or wrong. I believe that most of us truly felt we were doing the right thing, but the dead are dead, and that will never change. We are at peace with the Vietnamese now, but it is still a communist country. So what was it all about? Nothing that would have benefited the citizens of Vietnam or America, and at the time of this writing, we're at it in again in Iraq.

Paulie and I couldn't relate to each other for awhile while he was in

Vietnam, but his death brought us together again in spirit, and the experience helped me to exorcize some of my own demons. Paulie was ready to take responsibility for his part in the village, but he wasn't alive to make that decision. He wanted me to show the letter to the authorities and expose the war for what it was.

In the end, I couldn't do it. I couldn't let him or even Donato, take all the blame for the atrocities in Vietnam. If My Lai had never been discovered, they would have been the poster boys for a few bad Americans. Most people know killing is wrong, but when it's condoned by a government that has control over your life, the decision to kill or go to prison pulls some people apart. After all, self-survival is the strongest instinct. Paulie and I were conflicted in different ways, but the basics of our decisions were the same. Maybe I was wrong in burning the letter, but I would do it again.

I protested hard the second semester of my senior year, boycotting classes, attending marches, and attempting to advance the principles of peace, but the war raged on. Karen accepted a full time job and we made plans to get married in August of 1970, but my future was uncertain and I had some difficult decisions ahead of me.

And I almost had to make one. To equalize the economic inequities of the draft, the government instituted a lottery based on your birth date. My number was drawn at 172, almost right in the middle, and they drafted me in December of 1970. I filed for Conscientious Objector status, and was given a hearing by the Bellington Draft Board. It was a memorable day. The board consisted of men and women that had helped me grow up in Bellington, keeping me safe, educating me and teaching me to think on my own. I told them that I believed killing was wrong, and even though I was not religious, the Ten Commandments made that crystal clear.

They gave me about ten minutes of their time. Two weeks later, I received a notice informing me of the rejection of my Conscientious Objector status. It was unanimous-eight to zero. The nice people of Bellington had sent me a message. Move on son; get out of here and fight. The betrayal that I had felt eight years before was now complete. I was to report for boot camp in June of 1971, so Karen and I made plans to move to Canada after graduate school. Fortunately, it never came to that point.

I failed a medical exam from one of the military doctors because of an old football injury to my shoulder. I guess my coach gave us good advice when he told us to play hurt.

I had been ready to leave my family, friends and country for what I believed in. I can't apologize for not wanting to kill or be killed for something I saw as wrong. When all is said and done, you are a pawn on the chessboard of life, nothing more, unless you make a stand.

On May 4, 1970 the Vietnam War came home to the entire country at Kent State University in Ohio. Students were protesting the bombing of Cambodia when National Guard troops opened fire with live ammunition, killing four students and wounding several others. Americans were now killing Americans at home over the Vietnam War. College students had been killed for expressing their opinion in a raucous, but peaceful demonstration. They were in the process of leaving the grounds when the troops opened fire.

Alison Krause, Jeffrey Miller, Sandra Schewer and William Schroeder gave their lives for the hope of peace. America was stunned, angry, and hurt deeply. The incident dug deep into everyone's gut. If I had been disillusioned with my government before, Kent State kicked my fury up a hundred notches. Combined with previous experiences, my cynicism became so ingrained that to this day, I question anything that comes out of the mouth of a politician.

The Paris Peace Agreement was signed January 27, 1973, and the American Army presence in Vietnam ended in March of that year. Predictably, two years later the North Vietnamese Army overran the South, uniting Vietnam into one country. We had given up 50,000 American lives, millions of Vietnamese lives, and the end result was the same as if we had not fought the war.

A bit of optimism remained. I hoped that America had learned from its mistakes in Vietnam. Sadly enough, President George Bush ended my small vestige of confidence in elected officials when he ordered the invasion of Iraq in March of 2003. We are again in a country where we are doing the dying and fighting among a populace that views us as invaders. The death toll of Americans is 2100 and counting, and I feel now that we will never learn. We seem determined to shove our way of life down other people's throats—even if we have to kill them to get it done.

Donato spent the next seven years in a federal prison for drug trafficking. I never saw or spoke to him again, although I heard that he's doing quite well as a legitimate businessman, finally using his brains for something positive. For awhile, I worried a little that he might come looking for me, but he didn't want any reminders of that day in the village. I'd like to believe that his experiences on that sad day ended up making him a better person, and for my own peace of mind I'm going to continue to believe it.

Mike did some intervention and got Billy placed in a drug treatment program instead of prison. He had a few early relapses, but now he's doing well as an insurance salesman in Bellington. Bill got married and divorced twice with no children. We got together once at a reunion, making our peace and moving on.

I knew I didn't have to worry about Debbie. She stayed in Florida with her grandmother, spending a few years in college where she met and eventually married a local politician who later became the Governor. I read the guy's victory speech, and he stated that he couldn't have done it without her help. Only I knew that it was the dead-ass truth. She invited me to the wedding, but I declined, preferring to let the ghosts lie still in our minds. Her memories of Paulie had hopefully been put to rest, so who was I to interfere with that.

My nightmares concerning Nellie decreased in frequency, but never left completely as I built my relationship with Karen. I wondered about those vivid dreams of the graveyard. They had been so real and prophetic, except for the last empty grave. No one else had died like Rich had said they would in the dream.

One night, after a long exhausting protest on campus, I found myself in humanity's graveyard soon after I closed my eyes. My dad stood in front of the gravestone, urging me closer, speaking to me as I walked.

"You must have inherited a talent for cheating death from your mother, Matt. No one has ever been here three times without a permanent placement."

"So, whose grave is that, Dad, if it wasn't mine or Rich's?"

My dad stepped away from the stone.

"It's yours. Rich was right, but it's not time yet. There's a place for everyone here, Matt. You have to learn to accept that. No one gets a free pass, not even you. Ever since you were three, you've been afraid of dying, but you need to live your life without looking over your shoulder for the Grim Reaper. It's hard to live if you worry about dying all the time."

My name and date of birth were carved in the stone, along with the word died. There was no other date.

"So when will it be?"

"Even if I knew, I wouldn't tell you. It's that singular mystery that drives our ambition, focuses our energy, and helps keep us honest. Go live, Matt. Leave the past behind where it belongs, and take the future as a sweet surprise, good or bad."

I threw my arms around my dad, and it felt so real, but a millisecond later I awoke in my bed, the feel of the hug still fresh in my senses. I will never believe that it didn't happen, and it served as a strong balm in healing my battered brain. I would try to move on, one moment at a time.

I've decided to skip the future of Karen, Leo and I. There are many more stories to tell, so there's no real ending when it comes to us, but there was one piece of unfinished business in this chain of events.

About two weeks after Donato's arrest, Agent Francis called and gave me the results of Ronald's autopsy to ease my mind. I guess the Fed and I had connected on some level. The coroner found a large amount of heroin in Ronald's system, but the heroin hadn't done him in. The main cause of death was an embolism from an air bubble that had entered his bloodstream and brain. They believed that someone entered his hospital room and shot him up with the intent to kill him.

Francis said that Leo and I were off the hook. The receptionist testified that only two people had asked for his room number. The cop on duty, after a lot of questioning, admitted taking a couple of breaks later in the afternoon. Donato was identified by the receptionist as being at the hospital around the time of the cop's break. The other person was a woman.

Donato was their main suspect, but they had no evidence to pin the crime on him. Donato admitted to visiting Ronald, but swore that Ronald was dead when he arrived at the room. Agent Francis asked if I had any idea of the woman's identity or if Donato had given me any indication that he had killed Ronald.

I told one lie and one truth. Donato hadn't said a thing to me, but I didn't believe that he had it in him. That was the truth. I said I didn't have any clue as to the woman, but I did, and that was the lie. Agent Francis thanked me and told me to take life a little easier.

She had held two jobs since the beginning of college, but now with her mother's illness, it wasn't enough. She worked at a women's clinic in New Haven at night and part time in the college library during the afternoon. Her brother was clean, but had dropped out of school to get a job.

Wanda was at work in the reference section when I quietly came up behind her. It was raining like hell outside, with the thick clouds causing the back corner of the library to be very dim. She hadn't seen me since the day we pulled her brother out of the gutter, and I knew now why she had been avoiding me.

"Wanda."

"Christ sakes, Kronchek! Your honky ass scared the hell out of me! What are you doing sneaking 'round the library like a burglar?"

"I'm not the one that's been hiding out, Wanda. Karen asked me the other day how you were doing, and I thought it was strange that you never checked to see how we made out, but I received a call today that cleared it all up. This is the second time in two weeks that I need to know a basic question of human nature."

"You gonna talk in riddles or are gonna say what you came here to say?"

"Okay, Wanda. Would you have let Leo and I go down for Ronald, or would you have stepped forward and admitted to killing him?"

"Killing Ronald? Whatcha talking about? You're the one that smashed his face in. I was nowhere near the bar that day."

"Your indignant tone is almost believable, but it had to be you. It wasn't the heroin that killed him, Wanda; it was the air bubble that you left in the needle. I know why you did it. I do understand how afraid you were for your brother, but I'm freaked out that you might have let Leo and I take the fall."

Wanda strained heavily to hold back the choking sobs that forced their way through her lips. The effort at control made her dizzy, and I caught her before she hit the bookshelves. Once in my grip, the tears flowed in torments, with my shirt and chest cutting off the noise and soaking up the liquid guilt.

"I'm a horrible person. I killed him and I would have let you two take the blame for it. Two guys who did more for me than anyone except my Mamma, but I couldn't take the chance that he would come after my brother again. I used to love him, but he became a totally different person. I'm so sorry, Kronchek. I know that I'm going to jail, so I'll tell the police the truth."

"Nobody's going to jail, Wanda. You did what you thought you had to do to protect your brother, and it's not like Ronald was a Boy Scout. The police don't have a clue and Leo and I are not suspects. You know; in the end I didn't even hate Ronald. He was just what he was, but he had to be stopped. It has been one fucked up year, and I think things are going to get worse before they get better.

"We can't change what's happened and we won't even be able stop the stuff that's coming, but we can't give up. You keep fighting for all that important stuff. We can't afford to lose somebody like you, and neither can your family."

"But, Kronchek—"

"No, Wanda. Let it go. I think you'll be harder on yourself than any court. After the War ends and the racial shit calms down, we'll have a lot wounds to heal. All of us, including Ronald to some degree, have been victims of our circumstances, but the clouds are starting to clear. The things people do to each other, its just—"

Wanda stopped me in mid sentence, placing her tiny hand over my mouth.

"Enough. You aren't half-bad for a white boy. Bye, Matt."

I turned away without another word, bouncing down the library steps as if I had no weight. The storm had broken, with the sun piercing the clouds like sharp rays of optimism. A metaphorical weather pattern had defined the day. Leo stood outside the library dribbling a basketball, Karen was waiting for me in the car, and Wanda had finally called me Matt. That was enough to keep me going for now.

Printed in the United States
61092LVS00002B/229

9 781424 128372